Praise for Lisa T

'*Her Mother's Lies* is a heart-rending and authentically drawn story about that most complex of family relationships: mothers and daughters. I loved it.'
Kate Riordan

'Lisa Timoney's debut has all the elements of a fabulous family drama . . . it kept me turning the pages from beginning to end!'
Kerry Fisher

'Heartbreaking and life affirming.'
Emma Robinson

'A warm-hearted, page-turning read.'
Ali Mercer

'A thoughtful family drama about a tangle of past secrets.'
Jill Childs

'A gripping story of family secrets, love and past tragedy that kept me hooked from beginning to end. A seriously impressive debut.'
Annie Lyons

'An assured debut about family, loyalty and secrets.'
Laura Pearson

'A moving, compelling family drama which keeps you turning the pages.'
Linda Green

HIS SECRET WIFE

Lisa started her career teaching English and Drama, and when she had her family, combined all three to write novels about family drama. Originally from Yorkshire, she now lives in a London suburb with her husband and two teenage daughters, so expects there's plenty more drama to come. This is Lisa's third book.

By the same author:

Her Daughter's Secret
Her Mother's Lies

His Secret Wife

LISA TIMONEY

avon.

Published by AVON
A division of HarperCollins*Publishers*
1 London Bridge Street
London SE1 9GF

www.harpercollins.co.uk

HarperCollins*Publishers*
Macken House, 39/40 Mayor Street Upper,
Dublin 1, D01 C9W8
Ireland

A Paperback Original 2023

1

First published in Great Britain by HarperCollins*Publishers* 2023

A catalogue copy of this book is available from the British Library.

ISBN: 978-0-00-855321-0

Typeset in Sabon by Palimpsest Book Production Ltd, Falkirk, Stirlingshire
Printed and bound in the UK using 100% renewable electricity
at CPI Group (UK) Ltd

For
Eva and Isla,
my extraordinary, much cherished girls.
It's never dull.

Prologue

I hadn't planned to propose. Maybe it was the pregnancy hormones, or the buzz of first-night nerves, but when he came backstage with that soppy, proud look on his face, I was overwhelmed with love and out it came: 'Marry me?'

I remember the actors hushing each other in the dressing room, turning from their mirrors to gape at us, make-up-smeared wet wipes still in their fingers. He and I stood, gazing at each other for what felt like seconds too long. I couldn't read his changing expression and my heartbeat thumped in my ears. In that moment, I was sure he was going to say no.

I opened my mouth to say something about it being a joke – after all, everyone knew I wasn't the marrying kind – when he lunged forwards and lifted me off my feet.

'Alright,' he whispered into my hair. He raised his head until our eyes were level. 'Why not?'

I cried, he cried and the whole cast enveloped us in a huge, grease-painty hug.

Even then *Why not?* struck me as an odd thing to say. But I was caught up in the moment. I should have thought about it before accepting his plan for a tiny wedding ceremony in Venice. We were no spring chickens, he argued, and since we already had a baby on the way, the white wedding ship had sailed. I should have questioned it when he said his dad was the only family he had, and he was an invalid living in Scotland. I thought it was uncharacteristically romantic when he told me he didn't need anyone else to witness our commitment. It was about him and me. And the baby growing inside of me.

I should have asked a million questions. But I didn't because my stupid, love-swollen heart convinced me I knew everything about this charismatic, beautiful man.

Who says *why not?* when someone proposes marriage?

Someone with reasons why not . . . that's who.

Chapter One

Elle

Rob packed his suitcase like someone on daytime TV demonstrating the most efficient way to fit everything in a bag. I admired this skill once upon a time. If I'm honest, I admired everything about him once, but recently this systematic rolling of shirts made me either want to cry or pluck his pants out and throw them at his head. I resented that he didn't have a problem with leaving us for a few nights every week. Actually, it was more than a few.

I missed admiring him. I was good at being an appreciative wife, it had been the one thing I excelled at. Surely he missed my gratitude too?

'Can't you stay one more day?' I wheedled to no avail. I tried a brighter tone. 'Harry would love to tell you about his first day at junior school.'

Lately, Harry was struggling with Rob working away so much. And much as I didn't want to antagonise Rob, if Harry had a problem, I did too.

'You know I can't.' He shook out a pair of expensive

jeans, folded them and lay them flat. He turned in the arms of a linen shirt, then rolled it from the collar into a narrow cylindrical shape. He lay it next to the others in his case; a row of black, white and grey shirt-sausages. I glanced at the clothes still hanging on his side of our wardrobe and the muted colours matched my mood.

Can't stay, or won't? I was tempted to ask. I wondered how he'd react if I did. The compliant wife, coming out of her box. It was happening more and more, that urge to push open the cardboard flaps. I counted to five before saying, 'Just this once?'

He turned and put his hands on my shoulders, wrinkling his eyes and making his mouth turn down. It always made me feel like he was looking right inside me. If he was, would he see how much Harry and I needed him today? Or would he just see his nagging wife, who was never happy with her lot? I must've been biting the inside of my cheek because he gave my shoulder the little tap he always did to make me stop. 'You think I don't want to be here when Harry gets back?'

He'd played his trump card early today. I leaned in and felt his arms drop down my back as I held him tightly. 'Sorry. I know you do. Sorry.'

'Roooar!'

We both turned to see Harry swiping his long hair out of his eyes as he brandished a plastic triceratops at us from the doorway.

'Can I take this with me today?'

'Not the triceratops.' I let go of Rob and walked towards our son. 'Those horns could do someone a mischief.' I tickled Harry under the arm and he pulled his elbows in as he giggled.

'Diplodocus?'

I astonished myself by being able to bring a diplodocus immediately to mind. I'd learned a lot since Harry became obsessed with dinosaurs. He loved this set, which he'd got for his seventh birthday last week. 'Alright, but you'll need to keep it in your bag until playtime.' I let him go, kissing the top of his blonde head.

'And don't lose it,' added Rob.

We raised knowing eyebrows at each other. Harry lost just about everything he touched. I joked that he'd make a terrible burglar because of the trail he always left behind him. It was like living with a snail, only the slime was made up of sweet wrappers, coloured pencils and now, plastic bloody dinosaurs.

Rob wasn't much better, but he seemed to think he was tidy and efficient. One day I'd point out that we could all be tidy and efficient if we had someone always following behind, clearing up our mess. But not today.

When Harry's footsteps bounced away down the stairs Rob asked, 'Seriously, should he be taking anything into school? We'll never see it again and he'll be upset when he hasn't got the full set anymore. Juniors isn't like infants, is it? They're not going to be doing show and tell?'

'He's nervous,' I said. 'Having a dinosaur in his bag might make him feel more confident.'

Rob whipped the zip around to close the case. 'A haircut wouldn't do him any harm, either. He's going to get bullied for looking like a girl.'

'I did my best. He point blank refused. Sorry.' I didn't want to admit that I liked his white-blonde hair long because it made him look younger. I wasn't quite ready for my little boy to be in big school. 'Anyway, I think it suits him. He's got a lifetime of boring short back and sides ahead of him, don't you think?'

Rob didn't look convinced, but he didn't argue. I felt my heart drop, like it always did, as his case clonked against the banisters when he followed me downstairs.

* * *

Harry hid his face in my tummy when we got to the gates of Panthom Junior School. I watched leagues of children kiss their parents goodbye and skip towards their friends. I nodded at the other mums as they passed, hoping the cold wind whipping the freshly fallen leaves around the playground would keep the colour out of my cheeks. None of the other kids in Harry's year clung on to their mothers.

A pretty woman, who I presumed to be the parent of an older child, let her gaze rest on Rob. She half smiled. Watching him out of the corner of my eye, I was relieved to see he hardly seemed to register her. His apparent obliviousness to other women never failed to amaze me. I was glad. I needed the reassurance. I had a husband who women found attractive, and he worked away half the week. If he was the kind of man who gave other women the eye, I don't think we'd have survived the last ten years. I wouldn't have, anyway.

'Come on, Harry,' Rob cajoled. 'I've got to get to work.'

'You don't want to be the last one in, do you?' I said. I felt Harry's head rise towards my ribs and hated myself for using his nerves against him. I knew he'd struggle if everyone looked up to see him coming into the classroom late.

'Will you be here when I come out?' He looked at Rob with those huge blue eyes. I had to turn away.

'I can't, mate.' Rob crouched so he was face to face with our beautiful boy. 'But I'll be back in a few days. You can tell me all about it then.' He pulled a piece of folded paper from his pocket and handed it to Harry. 'That's you today.'

Harry opened the paper and smiled at the line drawing of him, with bulging muscles, riding a tyrannosaurus into school. 'Thanks Daddy.'

Rob knocked his knuckles against Harry's then gave him a nudge on the back. Harry sloped off in the direction of the double doors.

'Let's get off.' Rob took a step towards the gate.

'Just a sec, sorry, he'll want to wave before he goes in.' I kept my eye on my son, knowing he'd turn before he went inside. When he looked back and waved limply, I waved, my heart aching to see him disappear. 'Now we can.' I hoped Rob might take my hand like he used to, but he took long strides and I had to half-run to catch up.

When we reached his car, I felt like I had to try again, for Harry's sake. 'He's finding it hard, now he's older – you being away so much. It wasn't meant to be forever, was it? Just until . . .'

Rob sighed. 'Until everything was secure, yes.' He pulled his car keys from his pocket. 'After what happened, I don't think I'll ever feel completely secure again. Will you?' He looked me up and down and I became aware of my expensive trainers, my top-of-the-range gym kit. I knew what was coming and the guilt hit before the words.

'Oh, lovely Elle.' He kissed me on the forehead. 'Do you think I want to be away from you? From our boy? I do what I have to do to keep our family going. You know most of our revenue comes from the London office; if I gave that up, we'd sink.'

'I could go back to work—'

'This again?' He took a step away from me. 'We've talked about this. There's no way you'd be able to earn enough to even make a dent in our outgoings. You'd need to get qualified, and you know what that takes? Money.'

'I know. Sorry.' I dropped my eyes to the pavement. I could kick myself for bringing it up again before he left. When I was younger, I'd worked my way up from the make-up counter to window-dresser at the department store, but I was only able to do that because my mum used to go out with the owner, and I was probably cheaper than a qualified designer. The store had closed when I was on maternity leave with Harry, and Rob was right, I'd have to train properly to get the same job somewhere else. I was a shop girl with aspirations, and my aspirations didn't earn above minimum wage.

'To be honest, it feels a bit like emotional blackmail when you talk like this.' He turned the car key over in his fingers.

'I'm not—'

'What do you want me to do?' He looked at me, as if searching my face for a solution.

He was right. It wasn't fair. I had nothing to complain about. My mum's words rang in my ears '*Hold on to that golden ticket, my girl.*' 'I'm sorry. It's hard without you, that's all.'

He pulled me towards him. My muscles weakened as his hand cupped the back of my head. 'I'm just doing what I need to. For all of us. And you want to be around for Harry after school and in the holidays, don't you? I think he needs that stability. We're fortunate we can give him that.'

That sealed it. I would never let Harry have the same upbringing as me: dropped off with one pretend aunty after another, while Mum looked in all the wrong places for a golden ticket of her own. 'I just miss you.'

I waited for him to say the same to me. He squeezed me a little tighter and kissed the top of my head. 'I know, beautiful, I know.'

I watched him drive away, trying to hold back the tears,

determined to stop myself next time I got the urge to whine. As my mum had reminded me from the minute I met Rob to the day she died, I was lucky to have a husband like him. He was a good man trying to do the best for his family. My life was nearer to perfect than most people I knew. I had a husband who provided for us, a gorgeous boy, a beautiful home. What did I have to complain about?

I repeated it all the way home like a mantra: *my life is perfect, my life is perfect, my life is perfect.*

Chapter Two

Elle

I'd been running for five minutes when Nicky stepped onto the treadmill next to mine. She was the only school mum I knew well because her daughter, Grace, and Harry had been through infants together. I glanced over and smiled, pressing the down arrow on the control pad to slow my pace. 'Hi.'

'Wotcha. Freedom at last.' She pumped her arms in the air. 'Did you cry at drop-off this morning?'

I laughed nervously, hoping she hadn't seen Harry clinging to me. 'Did you?'

'Are you kidding me? I was counting down the days to September. I did a victory parade around the playground this morning. Six weeks is too damned long for my kids to be out of school.' Her feet thumped on the running deck, picking up pace. 'Anyway, I meant did you cry when you were saying goodbye to that gorgeous husband of yours.' She smirked and waved her index finger at me, 'I saw you canoodling by the car.'

I laughed again, privately pleased with her interpretation of events. 'We were not canoodling.'

'Whatevs.' She ran steadily, her breathing even.

I envied Nicky's fitness. I envied her shape too, every muscle defined and strong. I looked down at my flat stomach and toned thighs. Not bad for thirty-two, I supposed. I allowed myself a second to imagine my tummy rounding and my belly button popping out like it had when I was expecting Harry. I pushed the thought away. We'd been trying for four years, and Rob was right: what's meant to be will be. No point obsessing over it.

'What did you get up to over the holidays?' I asked.

'What didn't we do?' Nicky rolled her eyes. 'Pottery painting, nature trails, endless bloody play dates. The little sods need entertaining every minute of every day, don't they? It's exhausting.'

I thought about Harry sitting on the carpet in front of the sofa, lining up his dinosaurs according to which period they existed, then researching exactly what food they ate and how they moved. He only remembered to eat because I put a plate in front of him. 'Yeah. Nightmare.'

'Thank goodness for our place in Tuscany. The villa's on a complex with a shared pool, so at least there's other kids for my two to play with. I actually got to read a book this year. A whole book. Imagine! I can't remember when that last happened on holiday.'

I nodded in feigned recognition. I'd read a whole series of Angela Marsons novels in August while Harry drew pictures of dinosaurs or read about the Jurassic period on my laptop. I should be glad he wasn't a demanding child. And he was an only one, so it was natural that he was better at entertaining himself.

The thudding of our feet synchronised. 'Do your two ever get obsessed with things?' I kept my tone neutral, so she didn't know I was worried about Harry. I'd hate for anyone to suspect I thought there was anything wrong. Not that there was anything wrong.

'What do you mean?'

'Like, so into something you can't tear them away?'

Nicky pushed the keypad, upping her pace. 'They'd be on the iPad all day if I let them. Is that what you mean?'

I didn't know what I was trying to say to be honest, so I said, 'Yep.' Then I pushed myself to match Nicky's pace even though it made my lungs burn.

* * *

At pick-up time, I stood beside Nicky in the middle of a group of mums she seemed to know well. They were all in gym kit or designer jeans and chatted effortlessly as we waited for the Year Three kids to emerge from school. I glanced around, glad I'd put my best jeans on. I looked like I fitted in, even if I didn't feel like it. I wondered if they could all smell the desperation coming off me. I felt like my pores were secreting *please like me* vibes. Why was I so pathetic? I scanned the other mums' faces, trying to work out if any of them felt nervous about being in this unfamiliar playground with people they hardly knew. If they did, they were masking it well.

'I hope they've all had a good day,' I said, smiling. Nobody seemed to hear me. Nothing new there. I let my smile drop, ready to pick it up again if anyone looked my way.

Nicky had already collected her youngest, Teddie, from infants. He wound himself around her legs as his big sister,

Grace, came tumbling towards us, school bag flying behind her. She was a chaotic jumble of words and facial expressions. I could see why Nicky was exhausted.

'There's Harry,' Grace said, pointing at the double doors at the end of the playground. She jumped up and down, waving.

When I looked from her to my lovely boy, it seemed like they were a different species. He walked slowly towards us, his face blank.

'See you tomorrow,' I said to Nicky's brood, my heart rate quickening as I broke from the group and strode towards Harry, now hoping I remained as invisible as I'd been before. When I reached him, I took his face in my hands. I looked into his eyes. 'Okay?'

He nodded.

'Really? Only you look . . .' He looked like a ghost of a boy.

He pulled his head away and looked into the space behind me. 'Is Daddy here?'

'Not today,' I said lightly. 'Tell me all about your day.'

'I'm tired,' he said. 'Juniors is hard. It's all new. I want to see Daddy.'

'You can talk to him later.' I took his hand, smiling brightly as we passed the other mums on our way out of the grounds. He gave monosyllabic answers to my questions on the walk home. By the time we got to our house, I was drained from keeping up the false energy. I opened his school bag as soon as I closed the door behind us. 'Let's find your diplodocus, shall we?'

Harry sat on the bottom stair with his arms wrapped around his legs. I rummaged through the bag, but the dinosaur wasn't in there.

'I lost him,' he whimpered. 'I didn't know where to look

for him because juniors is too big, and I don't know where I'm supposed to go.'

I heard a sob and dropped the bag on the hall floor. Kneeling in front of Harry, I lifted the hair that dropped over his eyes. His eyelids were closed, and tears poured down his face.

Chapter Three

Jen

When would actors realise their head shots needed to be more recent than their Tinder profile pictures? Today's auditions had been torturous. I usually loved casting; it was one of my favourite parts of the job. And I thought casting Cleopatra would be a joy. I mean, how often do you get such a magnificent female lead? But no one who came through the studio today looked anything like I expected them to.

I had a vision for this play. I knew what I wanted, which was why I called in the people I did. It was so frustrating that agents didn't keep portfolios up to date. Actors were generally a thick-skinned lot, but surely they must feel some shame when they came for their call and found me looking from their photo to them in confusion?

'What about her?' Mel, the producer, asked, pointing to a Polaroid of a short blonde with a pixie cut.

'She's about twelve! One of the extraordinary things about this play is that a man falls for a woman who is not still going through fucking puberty.'

Casting Antony had been easy. There were no end of men who could carry off a sexy, belligerent hero. It wasn't a stretch for most actors, playing a two-timing, self-assured man, and Ed was ideal because he also had a very slight Italian accent. And biceps that belonged on a warrior. That helped.

My phone alarm beeped. 'Bollocks.' I threw the rest of the Polaroids on the table. 'I'm going to be late to pick Cora up if I don't leave now.'

I'm sure I saw Mel's eyes roll. I didn't blame her. I'd be irritated if my boss always had to rush off during an important meeting to pick their kid up from school. Before I had Cora, I had no idea of the guilt involved in being a mum. Guilt because you always felt like you were letting your colleagues down. Guilt because your kid was in after-school club every day. Guilt because finding the perfect Cleopatra seemed more important and a lot more stimulating than watching *Finding Nemo* with a seven-year-old. For the first time in my life, I felt like I was doing badly at everything.

It wasn't that I resented any of it. I loved being Cora's mum. But I couldn't help thinking having a kid at forty was poor planning; not that Bill and I did any planning on that front. Even that thought gave me a shiver of pleasure. By the time Cora arrived my life was already established, and I liked it. I was happy. Not that I'd change it now. It's just that, for the last seven years, everything had felt like a compromise.

* * *

'I did a picture of us at after-school club. Do you think Daddy will like it?' Cora thrust a piece of paper between the car head rests and waved it in front of my eyes.

'I'm driving. You'll get us both killed.' I pushed the paper away. 'Show me when we get home.'

'I drew a dog as well and Maisie said I couldn't draw a dog because we don't have a dog, but I said I could because I want a dog and anyway, it's my picture and I can draw what I like.'

My shoulders were still tight from the afternoon, and I could feel a headache radiating up from the base of my skull. 'You can draw whatever you want. Don't let anyone crush your dreams, baby girl.'

'Can we get a dog then?'

'What? No.'

I heard Cora bounce in her car seat and looked through the rear-view mirror to see her pout. 'You said I shouldn't let anyone crush my dreams. My dream is to get a dog, so—'

'Please don't.' I couldn't have this argument again. Not now.

'Maisie's got a dog called Bertie but he poos on the carpet. When I get a dog, I'm going to train it not to poo at all because I don't want to have to pick it up in one of those bags because it would be all warm and gooey . . .'

I tuned out. I did that a lot when Cora was chatting. What she said was often entertaining, she was a funny kid, but there was just so much of it. And the flow seemed to get even more rapid when she was tired. Bill and I often laughed about the fact we knew it was bedtime when Cora stopped breathing between sentences.

* * *

Cora was still in the middle of telling me about what her new teacher in the junior school, Mrs Daniels, said about her drawing when I heard Bill's key in the lock.

'Thank god.'

'Mummy, you interrupted. You said it's rude to interrupt.'

I stuck my tongue out at her on my way into the hall.

'Hello gorgeous man.' Bill grinned at me before kicking the door closed behind him and taking me in his arms. Much as I loved the time I had to myself when he worked away, having him back where I could touch him was better. We kissed, our bodies pressed together.

'You two are very revolting,' said Cora, snaking between us and pushing us apart.

'Hello pumpkin. I missed you. How is big school?' Bill lifted Cora and plonked a loud kiss on her cheek.

'Good. I like it. My teacher's called Mrs Daniels, and she has grey hair and nice shoes. I think her favourite colour is purple because she looks like a purple person. I'm a yellow person because that's what colour I feel like.' She paused briefly. 'What colour do you feel like, Daddy?'

'Erm, orange?'

'Yes, you can be orange. I think Mummy is red, or maybe she's purple like Mrs Daniels, only a brighter purple. Anyway, Mrs Daniels said I was clever for knowing how to spell *yesterday*. Do you want to see my drawing?'

Bill ignored my groan. 'I really, really do,' he said. 'Let me get my coat off and I'll be right with you.'

As ever, I marvelled at his ability to be enthusiastic about every word coming out of Cora's mouth. I watched him shake off his leather jacket and hang it on the hook nearest the door. I supposed it was easier to be tolerant when he wasn't here all of the time. 'Let your dad get in the house,' I said. 'He can look at your picture over dinner.'

'What is for dinner?' Cora's voice was quiet.

Her fussy eating was driving me mad. 'Salmon.'

'Can I—'

'It's salmon.' I tried to be less brusque, but it was exhausting, trying to make sure she ate nutritious food when her likes and dislikes were unpredictable to say the least.

'But it's slimy. It makes my tummy feel googly.'

I walked into the kitchen, hearing their footsteps follow mine on the tiles.

'Can I have pasta?'

I wanted to scream.

'How about you have pasta with your salmon?' Bill said, coming over to where I was leaning against the sink looking out onto my square patch of garden. He lay his hands on my shoulders and squeezed. 'You do ours and I'll do some pasta and pesto to go with Cora's. Okay?'

I felt thin arms circle my waist. 'I'm sorry, Mummy. Please don't be cross.'

I crouched down and hugged my little girl. 'I'm not cross. I just get tired when I think about what to feed you. That's all.'

She stroked my face. 'I'm sorry,' she said again, making it impossible to be anything but charmed. She was a magician, this pixie-faced child of mine.

* * *

Later, I lay on the couch with the gin and tonic Bill poured for me, watching the two of them on the carpet with a pad of plain paper and coloured pencils in front of them.

'I'll draw the head, then you draw the body,' said Cora. Bill crawled towards her and peered over her shoulder. 'No, Daddy!' she giggled and pushed him, 'No peeking.' He pretended to fall over and lay on his back, holding his arm as though mortally wounded.

I caught his eye and he stilled. We gazed at each other. Warmth flooded me. When I'd recovered from the heartache of being dumped by my first love on the day we graduated, which, admittedly, took a couple of years, I'd got used to the fact I was meant to be alone forever. It was safer. Nobody would ever hurt me again. I was content with the fact that I didn't need anyone, and nobody needed me. I was free. But then I'd met this man who made me feel safe, not vulnerable, and I decided to change the habit of twenty-odd years and go with it instead of protecting myself from potential heartbreak. And it was the best decision I'd ever made.

The scene in front of me felt like a fairytale. Cute little girl, adoring husband and father and, on top of all that, I fancied the pants off him. I sipped my drink and sighed at the perfection of it all.

At that exact moment, the alarm on his phone sounded. He snapped his gaze away from mine and sat upright, taking the phone from his pocket. Cora looked up, a mix of disappointment and acceptance in her eyes.

None of us said a word as he stood and went out to the garden to make his seven o'clock phone call.

Chapter Four

Jen

As soon as Femi strode into the studio, I knew she was my Cleopatra. She exuded confidence, her shoulders back, chin high. Strands of grey threaded through her tight braids, confirming what I'd read in her bio; she was almost the same age as me. But unlike me, she had flawless skin and stunning high cheekbones. When she stood centre stage to begin her audition piece, Cleopatra's monologue in Act Five, everyone in the room fell silent.

She extended her toned arm slowly, following it with her feline eyes, drawling, 'Give me my robe, put on my crown; I have immortal longings in me.'

I was mesmerised by her speech. It took an effort to tear my eyes away and scrutinise Ed, who was sitting to my right. That's when I knew for sure there would be chemistry. The man was practically dribbling.

'Welcome to the company,' I said to Femi, after a brief conversation with Mel, who was as blown away by Femi's performance as I was. I held out my hand. Femi took it in both hers and grinned broadly, showing white teeth with a small gap between the front two. 'That was impressive.'

'Thanks.' She grinned wider. 'I was properly nervous. I haven't done any Shakespeare before. I haven't done much for years to be honest.'

I glanced down at her bio. 'Yeah, I saw there's a few years' gap.'

She shrugged. 'Marriage. Kids. You know.'

'Yep.' I smiled. I did know. 'You're ready to commit now?' It was probably an unfair question, but I could feel in my gut that she would make the most incredible Cleopatra and I didn't want to start something with such potential only to have it snatched away when she realised she'd taken on too much. 'It's a big role.'

'That's why I really want it,' she said, her face serious. 'My youngest is fifteen. I'm divorced. It's time to put me first again. I'm committed. Don't you worry about that.'

A flash of envy took me by surprise. I swallowed it down, hating myself for betraying Cora like that.

'My queen.' Ed appeared by my side and gave a deep bow. When he raised his head, his cheeks were ruddy. It could have been the blood flowing to his face, but I suspected he was blushing.

Femi laughed. She raised her eyebrows, then, playing along, regally offered her hand for him to kiss. I watched as he took it and looked into her eyes as he held his lips to her skin.

* * *

'They are absolutely perfect together. I can't believe we've found our Cleopatra after all those endless auditions. Honestly, you should have seen Ed. I think he's fallen in lust,' I told Bill in our kitchen when I got home that evening.

'We only blocked two scenes, but they had such authenticity in both of them.'

'Result,' said Bill. 'There's nothing like chemistry to light up a stage.' He passed me a glass of Malbec.

'There's nothing like chemistry, full stop,' I said, tugging him towards me and kissing him deeply. He kissed me back, only breaking away when we heard a creaking sound on the floor above. We stood, frozen, waiting for the sound of small feet on the stairs, but none came.

I followed him through to our small sitting room and we arranged ourselves on the sofa as we always did, him laying his legs across my thighs so I could run my nails up and down his calves. If someone had told me eight years ago that I'd trust a man enough to let him move into my house six weeks after meeting him, I'd have said they were mad. If they'd told me I'd let him take off his socks and hitch up his trouser legs and I'd actually enjoy scratching his skin as we talked and sipped the wine we discovered on our honeymoon, I'd probably have laughed myself hoarse.

Yet there we were, with a child asleep upstairs, and me, stroking him as though he were an enormous cat. Funny old world.

'I hope they keep all those sexy chemical shenanigans on stage,' I said. 'It's all very well having the perfect acting partner, but if they start shagging IRL, things can get very messy very quickly.'

Rob tugged his jeans to above his knees and shifted so I had access to his left leg. 'Worked for Brad and Angelina.'

I gave him a firm stare. 'Not sure Jennifer Aniston would agree with your take on that. And they're divorced now, anyway.'

'They had a good run and about twelve million children first, though.'

I glared at him. 'Is that how you measure a successful marriage? A good run? Sprogs?'

He shrugged. 'You never know what's going on behind the scenes. I think people tend to do the best they can. Better not to judge.'

'I don't want anything going on behind my scenes, thank you very much. Ed is married. I've met his wife. Femi's a free agent, but he isn't single, so he shouldn't even be flirting with another woman.'

'Unless he's acting.'

'Yes. Unless he's acting. I don't know why people behave as if a theatre company is different to any other professional working environment. Everyone has to get *close*.' I dug my nails into the soft muscle of his calf. 'They're lucky I stay professional, otherwise it would become one great big love-in, and then where would we be?'

'Where would you be?'

'Captain-less. Rudderless. All at sea.'

'Is that right?' Bill sounded sceptical.

'Yes. I'm always right. We know this. Anyway, I'm glad you're not an actor. I wouldn't cope with you kissing another woman.' I felt the familiar tug of fear, the undercurrent that told me I was a fool for investing so completely in anyone but myself. I pushed it down. Just because I'd been hurt by one man, didn't mean Bill was made of the same shoddy material as him. Aaron had been little more than a kid when he made all those promises to me. Bill was twice his age and twice the man.

He lifted his legs and moved towards me. He took the glass from where it rested in my hand on the sofa arm and put it on the floor. My heart fluttered in anticipation as he leaned in, and the fear was washed away. He paused, his face tantalisingly close to mine. I could smell the wine on his breath and a tingling dappled between my legs.

'Like this?' he whispered, softly dabbing his lips on mine. 'Or this?' He flicked his tongue into my mouth then pulled back.

I cupped the back of his head with my hand and drew him towards me, pushing my lips onto his, feeling his hot mouth kissing me more urgently.

'Mummy.'

I pulled away and dropped my head on the back of the sofa, closing my eyes.

'That's gross,' said Cora.

I opened my eyes and looked at my watch. It was nine-thirty. I tried to keep the irritation out of my voice, 'What are you doing up at this time, Mrs?'

Before she could answer Bill scooped her onto his knee. 'Still can't sleep?'

Cora shook her head. Her blue eyes looked dolefully up at her daddy, and I couldn't help feeling like we were being played.

'She was up and down a lot before you got back from rehearsals,' he said to me. 'Poor little lamb.'

'You're not going to get to sleep if you're not in bed, are you?' I tweaked her nose and she smiled briefly then her lips turned down at the edges.

'I can't make my thinking stop,' she said. 'I don't want to be thinkful all the time because I keep thinking bad things.'

'What bad things?' asked Bill. I lay my head back so neither of them could see me rolling my eyes.

'About when I won't be able to live with you and Mummy anymore.' Her voice sounded tearful.

I lifted my head. 'We won't chuck you out until you're eighteen. Don't worry.' I tickled her under the chin, hoping to deffuse the situation. Bedtime was no time to be discussing deepest fears. I knew a procrastination technique when I saw it. But instead of giggling, a fat tear sprung from the corner of her eye and dripped down the side of her nose. I instantly felt bad. 'Oh, sweetheart. I was only joking. You can live here forever. Forever and ever and ever . . . as long as you learn to tidy your bedroom before you're twenty-five, and maybe flush the loo three times out of five.'

My jokes didn't work either. More tears bubbled up and fell. 'But one day you and Daddy might be dead people and I'll be all on my own.'

That hit hard. When I found out I was pregnant soon after my fortieth birthday, it had occurred to me I wouldn't be around to protect that child as long as someone younger would. 'Ah,' I said, narrowing my eyes and smiling. 'Although I plan to live until I'm a hundred and twelve, I also did another very sensible thing to make sure you are never alone. Do you know what that is?'

She shook her head. The wonder in her eyes made my heart contract. 'I married a toy boy.'

Bill gasped. 'A toy boy?'

Cora's eyes searched our faces, trying to work out why we were laughing. 'What's a toy boy?'

'A man who is younger than a woman. A plaything,' said Bill, looking at me with an eyebrow raised.

'Oscar next door is younger than me. Is he a toy boy?'

Over Bill's guffawing, I asked, 'Do you want Oscar to be your boyfriend?'

Cora stuck out her bottom lip and crossed her arms. 'No! I don't ever want a boyfriend. Boys are stinky and the boys in my class don't even know how to line up after break.'

'Well then, he's not your toy boy. Daddy's only my toy boy because we got married. He's only forty-two, you see, so he's my insurance that you'll still have somebody to look after you whatever happens.' I'd dug myself into a hole and didn't know how to get out. I couldn't promise Bill would always be around. Look at his dad, stuck in that care home with early-onset dementia. What were you supposed to say to a child when they're scared you're going to die? *Yep, two things are inevitable, kid: death and taxes*?

Cora picked up a strand of my hair and twirled it around her finger. 'But you're going to live until you're a hundred and twelve?'

'I'm going to do my very best.' I snuggled into them both. My family.

Bill lifted Cora in his arms. 'Let's get you back to bed, pumpkin. Give Mummy a kiss goodnight.'

I kissed her on the end of her tiny nose and watched her wrap her arms around Bill's neck as he carried her from the room. He was such a brilliant dad. He was a brilliant husband. I'd been right to drop my guard for him. He would never let either of us down.

Chapter Five

Elle

I felt bad about getting a babysitter, partly because it seemed like an indulgence, but also because Harry hated it when I went out without him.

His bottom lip wobbled when he came into my bedroom and saw me in a shiny top and my best skinny jeans. 'I don't want you to go out,' he said. 'I want you to stay with me.'

'I'm only going for a couple of hours,' I said, stroking the hair out of his face. 'And you'll be asleep, so I'll be back before you notice I'm gone.'

'Why can't Daddy look after me?'

It was a question I was asking myself more and more these days. 'He has to work.'

Work. That word held so much power. I imagined what it must be like to have a career that made you feel like somebody important outside your own home. I allowed myself to fantasise about walking into a meeting where people actually wanted to hear what I had to say. It must feel empowering.

I sighed, letting the vision slip from my mind. I was never going to be somebody people listened to. I wasn't even heard in this house. I felt a surge of jealousy for the other mums who had husbands reliably at home to help with bath time on a Friday night. At least Sally, whose husband left her out of the blue last year, had the benefit of having every other weekend off from the children. And she got to date other men.

It wasn't that I wanted to date anyone else. In fact, the thought of sitting across from a stranger, trying to make small talk while they marked me out of ten, made my stomach churn. It was more that I'd like to date my husband.

It would be nice to have someone's attention trained on me from across a table in a restaurant for once. 'It's been almost eight years now,' I muttered to myself as I dragged the straighteners through my hair. I hadn't had time to dry it properly because Harry wanted to show me a website about dinosaur remains in Dorset, so it sizzled, and steam rose from the iron. I smelled burned hair and scowled at my reflection in the mirror.

My lips twisted to the side, teeth searching out any roughness in the smooth skin inside my cheek. I really should stop biting my cheeks. Rob had pointed out the lines it was making around my mouth. I'd look like I smoked twenty a day like my mum if I wasn't careful. An image of her in the hospice, cheekbones protruding from her emaciated face, licking her pale tongue over cracked lips, made me pause. The damp hair crackled and I dragged the straighteners away.

I made myself push down the image of Mum and directed my thoughts back to Rob. Once, I'd been brave enough to point out that he had bad habits too. He bit his cuticles until they were bloody, but he said it was work stress making him do it. I couldn't argue with that, could I? I didn't bring it up again, even when the sound of him biting and plucking away at his cuticles made concentrating on the TV impossible.

I switched off the straighteners and grabbed my make-up bag. I had five minutes to do my face before the babysitter arrived. If I didn't want Harry to kick off, I had to make sure he was ready for bed, then spend at least fifteen minutes reading to him. I paused in front of the mirror, mascara wand hovering above my top lashes, suddenly drained of energy. Was it worth the effort?

I swiped the brush up and down, then poked at a claggy black mass that had collected on the end lashes. I was only thirty-two. Of course it was worth the effort. I sometimes felt like, if Rob and Harry had their way, none of us would ever see anyone else. They were both happy to spend all weekend indoors, Rob doing whatever he did on his phone and laptop. He once told Harry off for spending too long on my iPad while he held his phone in one hand, had his laptop open on his knees and the TV on in the background. I'd pointed out the hypocrisy, but he didn't seem to hear me.

'Why do you have to go out?' Harry said.

'Because Sandy invited me, and it would be rude to say no.'

Sandy was like the head girl of the school social scene, and I'd been flattered to be included. It felt like, after only two weeks at the new school, I was on the cusp of being invited to join a private members' club where the benefits were never having to stand on your own in the playground, pretending to read emails so people thought you were too busy for friends.

'Go and do your teeth.' I dabbed on some pink lip gloss and shoved my make-up back in the bag. That would have to do. There was a knock at the door, so I rushed downstairs to answer it.

'Meghan, hi.' I waited for her to kick off her trainers

then ushered her into the front room. 'Harry's nearly ready for bed. Sorry. I'll read his story and get off.'

Meghan dropped her bag by the side of the sofa. 'I'll do his story if you like?'

I hesitated. 'I'm not sure . . . He might . . .'

'I know he's a bit shy. Why don't you check if he'll be okay with that?'

Shy didn't seem like exactly the right word. Rob thought Harry's reluctance to speak to people he didn't know well was perfectly normal. When I lay awake at night worrying about my little boy, I had my doubts.

'I'll check.'

I felt peculiarly nervous when I pushed open the door of Harry's bedroom. I was already jittery about my night out, so I needed him to be calm. He was sitting on the end of his bed, swooping his pterodactyl from side to side. I ignored the mess on the floor I'd asked him to clear up earlier in the day. I'd learned to pick my battles with Harry.

'All ready for bed?'

He nodded, thrusting the toy from side to side.

'I'm running a bit late.' I sat next to him. 'Is it alright if Meghan comes up and reads your story tonight?'

Harry moved the pterodactyl quickly in front of us, shaking his head. His hair fell over his face. When I tried to sweep it out of his eyes he dipped out of reach, then stood, flying the dinosaur around the room. I watched him move in front of the backdrop of the planets we'd had painted as a feature wall when he was obsessed with stars and planets. Little did we know that obsession would soon be overtaken by dinosaurs.

'Come on, Harry. You're seven now. You're a big boy. Why don't you try being brave and let Meghan read your story? You like Meghan.'

He shook his head again.

'Yes you do. She's lovely. Talk to me, sweetheart. Tell me why you don't want Meghan to read to you.'

His arm stilled. He held the toy to his chest, walked past me to the bed and climbed under the duvet, turning his head towards the wall.

'Oh Harry. Don't be like that.' I felt for his foot under the quilt and tickled his sole. 'At least give me a kiss goodnight.'

He pulled his foot away from my hand. My heart dropped. I couldn't work out whether he was being manipulative or was genuinely upset.

'Harry?' He didn't move. The blue duvet cover printed with dinosaurs rose and fell with his breathing. 'Please, sweetheart, give me a kiss before I go out.'

The duvet shifted and he turned. My stomach balled when I saw tears on his beautiful face. He sat up, leaning forwards to wrap his arms around me. I felt the wetness of his cheek next to mine and his ribs pulse with quiet sobbing.

'It's alright, I'll read your story. Okay? It's alright, darling.' I ran my hand over his back, feeling his spine under my fingers. How could I have thought he was trying to manipulate me? His heart beat fast against my chest. He felt tiny and fragile. 'Lie down.' I released him and he lay his head on the pillow, wiping the wetness away with the sleeve of his pyjamas. 'Shall we read *Dinosaur Dinopedia*?' I resisted the urge to say *again*.

He nodded. I willed him to speak to me, but knew he wouldn't. When he was upset, it was like a shutter came down. He turned back to the wall. I started to read and didn't stop until his breathing was steady and I knew he was fast asleep.

***

'What time do you call this?' yelled Nicky over the music in the busy bar. The handsome young bartender ignored people trying to get his attention and made a beeline for Nicky. People did that for the kind of women I was meeting tonight. They were polished to a high gloss – the kind of finish you can only get with money and confidence.

The low-ceilinged room pulsed with a subdued bass. Self-consciously trendy bars like this always made me anxious, with their burnished walls, modern art and blue lights in the toilets to hinder the coke users.

'Sorry!' I shouted back. I was about to explain I'd had to read to Harry until he fell asleep, but stopped myself on imagining Nicky's response. I bet her two read to each other and soothed themselves to sleep. She didn't need to know how badly I'd done at establishing Harry's routines. 'Time got away from me. You know what it's like.'

She handed me a bottle of Prosecco and pointed to a raised area, cordoned off by a red rope. 'Take that up there. I'll bring you a glass.'

Sandy and two other mums I was on nodding terms with were sitting on curved velvet banquettes. My sparkly top looked dull in comparison to the shimmer coming off these three women. Their cheekbones and brows shone with highlighter, competing with the sheen of their tiny clothes. They all smiled with straight, whitened teeth when I unhooked the rope with one hand and raised the bottle with the other.

'Elle.' Sandy stood and air kissed my cheeks. 'So glad you could come. You know Cecily and Lexie, don't you?'

They remained seated and I got the ridiculous urge to curtsy. How did some women make me feel so inferior? 'So sorry I'm late. Good to meet you . . . properly, I mean.' My cheeks burned. 'Without the children.'

Nicky joined us and passed the flute to Sandy as though she were the only person qualified to dole out drinks.

'I can't believe this is the first time you've been out with us,' said Sandy. She tipped a flute and expertly poured a glass of Prosecco, handing it to me. 'Here's to many more.' We all leaned in and clinked the top of our glasses together. I willed my brain to think of something clever or interesting to say, desperate to become a true part of this group. I imagined myself back in my school days, with braces and dark-blonde hair, watching the popular girls with designer rucksacks and glowing skin, wondering how you joined their elite tribe.

Turned out, if you stretch to five feet nine, get a good hair colourist, a big house and handsome husband, you eventually get a chance to be included. Deep down, I knew this was shallow, but I was still grateful to be here, at my initiation ceremony.

'We were talking about little Morton Shaw,' said Sandy conspiratorially. 'Do you know the boy I mean? In our class. Dark hair and glasses. Always looks confused?'

I did know the boy she meant. My heart went out to him whenever I saw him stumble over his too long trousers. He seemed to always be lost, somehow, his brow furrowed as he peered through the thick lenses of his glasses. I nodded. 'He's incredibly bright, according to Harry. Always comes top in tests.'

'Exactly!' said Sandy, as though I'd confirmed something she'd said. '*Rain Man*, am I right?'

The others laughed. I joined in, trying to gauge whether she meant it cruelly.

'Is it any surprise he's a little weirdo, though?' said Cecily, one perfectly shaped eyebrow arched. 'With a mother like that. Have you seen the state of her?'

'Sorry? Weirdo?' I said, unable to stop myself.

Cecily straightened her back. 'Strange, then.' She looked at me with a challenge in her eyes. 'Don't you think they're both a bit odd?'

He's a seven-year-old boy, I should have said. *He's putting our kids to shame academically.* I should have told her to leave him alone and stop being such a bitch. But I didn't. I smiled. I nodded. I sipped my overpriced drink and I tried to fit in.

Because I had the uneasy feeling my son didn't exactly fit in. Not in the *poor, with braces, mousy hair and an embarrassing mum* way, but in a less tangible, more worrying way. And I had to protect him from a world that might call him a little weirdo too. I would do the fitting in for both of us.

***

When I got home, I checked on Harry while Meghan put her trainers on. He looked so peaceful as he slept. The four glasses of bubbles I'd drunk must've made me sentimental because looking at his rosebud lips, slightly parted, and his hair fanning across the pillow, I felt the urge to cry.

I sensed Meghan hovering at the bottom of the stairs, waiting for her fee. I tiptoed down and took the money from my purse and gave it to her. She smiled and thanked me.

'Did he come down at all?' I asked. I knew he wouldn't have, but thought it polite to check.

'No,' she said. 'He's definitely the best behaved seven-year-old boy I've ever sat for.' She smiled, tipping her head to one side. 'You know, it's funny, now I come to think of it.' Her eyes flicked to the left as though trying to remember something. 'I don't think I've ever heard him speak.'

Chapter Six

Elle

A week later, Harry didn't appear through the doors to the school when the rest of his class skipped out at the end of the day. I was keen to get home and lie down with a hot water bottle on my throbbing stomach. I was sure the heavy ache I got for the first few days of my period was a recent thing. Maybe I should get it checked out. There had to be some reason I wasn't getting pregnant, and it couldn't be Rob, because he'd been tested and got the all clear.

I wished I'd put my jacket over my running kit. The heavy clouds were growing darker and cold spits of rain fell on my face. I avoided the pitying looks I knew were thrown my way as the last of the mums took the hands of their offspring and led them out of the playground.

Steeling myself, I approached the glass door. Before I could press the buzzer for the school secretary to let me in, I saw Harry standing in reception, head bowed. His teacher, Mrs Wheeler, was crouched on her haunches, her skirt tucked under her bottom as she tried to look into Harry's face under his hair.

I pressed the buzzer urgently. Nobody came. I pressed it again, overriding the concern that people would think I was pushy for not waiting. It was all I could do to stop myself banging on the glass. When I pushed down hard a third time, Mrs Wheeler looked up and I saw relief on her face as she stood and hurried to let me in.

'Mrs Clarke,' she said, standing aside for me to come in. 'I was just about to come and find you.'

Harry rushed to me and pushed his face against my ribcage.

'Sorry. What's wrong? What's happened?' I looked from Harry to Mrs Wheeler.

'Harry . . .' Mrs Wheeler dipped to Harry's level again.

His hands reached around me and gripped the back of my T-shirt.

'Harry,' she tried again. 'Will you sit in the office for a minute while I talk to your mum?'

Harry shook his head. I was mortified. I would never have defied a teacher like that when I was his age. 'Harry,' I tried to make my voice firm. 'Please go and sit where you are asked while I talk to Mrs Wheeler.' I half-heartedly tugged at his arms, but he held on to me more tightly.

Heat rushed to my face. I gripped his arms firmly, trying to ignore how thin and fragile they felt. 'Come on. Please let go.' I pulled him free and saw a damp patch from his tears on the front of my T-shirt. 'What's going on?' I looked up at Mrs Wheeler's concerned face. 'What's happened?'

She shook her head. 'Nothing much, or at least nothing specific,' she said. 'I just wanted to flag some concerns. It certainly doesn't warrant this kind of upset. Harry,' she said in a more sing-song tone. 'You're not in trouble. You haven't done anything wrong. I just want to chat to your mum. Can I do that? Just for a few minutes?'

A tear dropped from Harry's chin to the floor as he nodded. He didn't look up at me as he allowed Mrs Wheeler to lead him through a door to the right. The urge to follow was almost irresistible. Instead, I stood, biting the inside of my cheek, until she emerged with an artificially bright smile. She led me to the nearest empty classroom.

'Sorry, he's not usually . . . What's happened?' I asked.

She looked like she was searching for the right words. 'I don't want to get this out of proportion. I mean, I don't want either of you to think there's a big problem,' she said. 'It's more that there's a few small issues, which, when added up, are giving me cause for concern.'

'Sorry, issues?' My heart thumped in my throat.

'He's a very well-behaved boy.'

I nodded.

'But it can be difficult to engage him, in activities, I mean.'

'Okay. Sorry . . . I'm not sure what . . . Can you give me an example?' I was desperate for her to get to the point. I needed to get back to my crying child.

'Over the last few weeks, he's become . . . how can I put it?' She seemed to look for the right phrase among the children's bright pictures on the wall behind me. 'Withdrawn. That's it. He's withdrawn. It's as though he's with us in body but not in mind.'

'I'm sorry. I still don't know exactly what you mean.'

She scrunched her nose. 'He seems like he's daydreaming a lot of the time. He often forgets to take the right book or equipment to the different classrooms we have for science.'

'Okay.' That didn't sound too bad. 'But juniors is different to infants, isn't it?' Harry had told me he didn't like moving from one classroom to another. Having different teachers for some subjects seemed to have unnerved him too. 'Aren't a lot of the children finding the changes hard? I expect it's a bit disorientating at first, when you're only seven.'

Mrs Wheeler leaned against a desk, then stood again when it scraped noisily across the floor under her weight. 'Yes, but it's not just that. I'm finding him a bit of an enigma. He's so compliant, in most ways he's an ideal student. His written work is good, and he seems to understand what I explain in lessons.' She paused. 'But he refuses to answer questions. He point blank refuses.'

'Refuses?' This didn't sound like Harry at all. 'What does he say?'

'That's the thing; he doesn't say anything. He just stares at the table.'

'He's ignoring you?' Shame prickled my skin. 'When you speak to him directly?'

'Yes.'

'He's pretty shy.' There was that word again, coming out of my mouth this time. 'Perhaps he doesn't want the whole class watching him. He doesn't like talking in front of an audience.'

'Well . . . the thing is . . . his response seems . . .' She paused. 'It's different, somehow. It seems more like he won't speak. There's something in his expression. He looks like something's worrying him . . . sorry to ask this, but is everything alright at home?'

Sweat dampened my top lip. 'Yes. Perfectly alright.' I wished I hadn't used the word *perfectly*; it sounded as if I was trying to cover something up. 'I mean, it's fine. Harry doesn't like his dad working away as much as he does, but . . .' But what? 'I'm so sorry about him refusing to talk. I'll speak to him.' I needed to get out of that room. 'I'll make sure it never happens again.'

'Mrs Clarke, that's not—'

I didn't want to hear any more. I was mortified my child was being defiant. I could almost hear what the other mums would say about my poor parenting. 'Thank you for drawing it to my attention,' I said, moving towards the door. 'Harry's father and I will speak to him, and we'll make sure he behaves better in future.'

'Can I—' Mrs Wheeler walked briskly in front of me. 'Just a second. I think it might help if Harry saw the school counsellor, Claire.'

'Sorry, a counsellor?'

'Claire Dixon. She's very nice. I think, perhaps, it would be good for Harry to have a session with her. It's funded by the school, the first one at least. I can arrange a meeting.'

I nodded, biting back my humiliation. How could my child need counselling for defiant behaviour? 'The first one's funded by the school? Sorry, what does that mean?'

'We have a peripatetic counsellor who visits us regularly, but . . . how can I put this?' She shifted her weight onto her other foot. 'Since Harry isn't struggling academically, isn't disruptive and isn't falling significantly behind, I'm not sure the school would be able to justify the budget for more than one session.'

'There's not much point to just one, is there?' I was relieved I had an excuse to say no.

'If Claire thinks Harry would benefit, she does have a private practice after school. She's a qualified child psychologist, working as a school counsellor to fit in with her family commitments. She's very good. It might be worth a try.'

I couldn't see Rob agreeing to pay for a counsellor for what he was convinced was just shyness. 'I don't know—'

'Can I set up the first session? It might put our minds at rest.'

I bit my cheek, mulling it over. 'Okay. Thanks.' I didn't know what else I could say without seeming difficult. Then Mrs Wheeler might think it ran in the family. I left the room and hurried down the corridor, the rubber soles of my trainers squeaking on the shiny floor. The secretary must've seen me coming because Harry emerged through the door. I took his hand and pulled him out into the playground. I knew I was walking too quickly. He was almost running to keep up.

'Well, that was embarrassing.'

'What did she say?' The tremble in his voice made me slow down.

'She said you won't answer questions. That you refuse.'

'I don't know the answers.'

'That's not true, is it?'

He started to snivel, but I was too shaken to console him. I wasn't even sure I wanted to. I strode on in silence. His hand became slippery in mine. Ordinarily I would wipe the sweat from my hand on my leggings, but somehow, I couldn't let go while he was quietly crying. I was angry with him. Ashamed, even. I couldn't believe Mrs Wheeler thought he needed to see a counsellor. And why had she asked if everything was alright at home? What did she think was going on? Oh, god; what if the other mums heard about it?

I strode quicker, my stomach churning, but, despite my spiralling thoughts, letting Harry's little hand out of mine would feel like a rejection. However fraught I was, I wanted him to know I would always be there to hold his hand in mine.

Chapter Seven

Elle

Rob parked in the drive and turned the car engine off just after seven. I watched him through the window, sitting in the car as the late September rain spattered on the windscreen, face animated as though he were talking to the invisible man. He was smiling and gesticulating. He looked happy. I wondered who he was talking to. Who made him throw his head back and laugh like that?

I willed him to come inside. He'd been away for five days, and I knew how much Harry wanted a hug from his daddy. When Rob reached a finger towards the dashboard and pressed a button, I stepped back from the window. Sure enough, I heard his key in the lock a minute later and the sound of his case dropping to the floor.

'I thought I heard the car,' I said, finding him in the hall. 'But I wasn't sure because you didn't come in.'

'I was listening to the end of a podcast,' he said, pecking me on the cheek as he walked past. 'You smell nice.'

'Was it good?'

'Bit dull, actually,' he said, rolling his shoulders as he walked to the kitchen.

'Really? What's it called? I need a new—'

'Where's the little man?'

It was as if I hadn't spoken. 'In the bath. I'm glad, actually, because I wanted to talk to you about something.'

Rob opened the fridge. 'Course, but can it wait? I'm tired and hungry.'

I reached past him into the fridge and took out a bowl of stir-fry covered in cling film. I'd eaten my portion with Harry. 'Sorry. If you ever told me what time you're planning to be back, I could have something ready.'

He sat at the kitchen table and scrolled through his phone as though I hadn't said a word. I heated up his food. Over the sound of the microwave I said, 'Harry's teacher called me in to talk about some concerns she's got.'

He heard that. He put his phone face down on the table. 'Concerns?'

'She says he won't answer questions in class.'

He pulled a face. 'Maybe he doesn't know the answers.'

'He said that, but she thinks he does.' I opened the microwave and stirred the food. 'She thinks it's defiance.'

Rob laughed. 'If it is, it's the first defiant thing he's ever done. I'm proud of him.'

I shoved the dish back in and reset the timer. 'Rob, seriously, she says he's disorganised and forgetful too. She wants him to see the school's counsellor.'

'Counsellor?' He gave a derisive snort. 'For god's sake, talk about overreacting. He's just gone seven. Of course he's disorganised and forgetful. I'm in my forties and I'm disorganised and forgetful sometimes.'

He wasn't wrong there. 'Sometimes?'

He raised an amused eyebrow at me and carried on

speaking, 'I'm not kidding, I'm relieved he's showing a bit of backbone. I was worried he was going to be a pushover. I'm glad he's got it in him to put up a fight.'

'Yeah,' I said, over the ping of the microwave timer, 'I know what you mean, but I think we need to take it seriously because his teacher seems genuinely concerned.' I didn't add that I was getting quite worried too. Not that that would have made any difference. I grabbed a tea towel and lifted the hot bowl, carrying it carefully to the table. I took a spoon and a fork and handed them to Rob, who gave me a tired smile of thanks.

'You should have been there,' I said. 'It was mortifying. I felt like a terrible parent.' His face grew wearier and I realised what I'd said. 'Sorry. I don't mean you should have been there . . . not in the physical sense.'

'I wish I could have been there. But I was at *work*.' He emphasised the last word.

My stomach shrivelled into a tight ball. 'I know, I—'

'Do you mind if I eat this in peace,' he said, digging his fork into a lump of chicken. 'It's been a long week. I'm tired. Maybe we could do the checklist of all the things I'm doing wrong after dinner?'

'Don't be like . . .' I trailed off. There was no point trying to justify myself. I'd never managed to make him see my point of view in all the time I'd known him. I hovered in the doorway considering whether I should tell him my period had started. I needed a hug, some consolation. He shovelled food into his mouth, eyes on his phone screen.

I left him to eat and went upstairs. Harry was sitting on my bed drying himself in a huge white towel. 'Alright, Mr?'

He nodded. I sat next to him and swaddled him with the towel, pulling him onto my knee. He let me cradle him. It was impossible to stay upset with him for long, especially since, when I looked down, he could so easily have been that little baby I used to hold in my arms and sing to after his bath. I leaned over and dropped kisses on his damp cheeks. He giggled. Breathing in the scent of washing powder and soap, holding him close to my body like this, I could convince myself he was still my gorgeous, tiny baby boy.

We sat like that for a while, our breathing falling in time with one another. I wondered what was going on in his head. Did other little boys let their mothers wrap them up and hold them like this? I suspected not. Briefly, I was glad my period had come. In this moment it felt like I was only meant to have this one, perfect child. Like he needed me as much as I needed him. I didn't want anything to exist that might break this precious bond.

Then he farted.

'Harry!'

He sniggered and wriggled away from me.

'You absolute monster!' I flapped my hand in front of my nose and chased him into his bedroom. 'That's shocking behaviour.' I tried to sound serious, but the laughter hiccupped through my words. I opened a drawer and took out a clean pair of pyjamas. 'Put these on and come down and say goodnight to Daddy.'

'Daddy's here?' He grabbed the pyjamas and dragged them on. 'I didn't hear him come in.' I heard some reproach in his voice and wondered if he would have allowed me to cuddle him in the towel if he'd known his dad was downstairs. In truth, I knew the answer.

He galloped downstairs and by the time I'd hung his wet towel on the radiator and followed him down, Harry was sitting next to Rob at the table, telling him all about a new dinosaur fossil that had been found on a dig in the midlands. I sat gingerly, reluctant to interrupt.

But what he needed was a father who took his teacher's concerns seriously. And I needed a husband who actually listened to what I said once in a while.

'I told your dad about what Mrs Wheeler said.' Harry's gaze dropped to the table. 'We're not cross with you, but we do need you to stop ignoring Mrs Wheeler when she speaks to you. Isn't that right, Robin?' I hoped Rob realised that me using his full name was an indication I needed him to be a grown-up about this.

'It's good manners to answer when someone speaks to you,' said Rob. I felt my shoulders relax.

'I can't,' said Harry quietly.

'Oh, come on,' I said, exasperated. 'When I came down here you were talking about archaeology. I'm pretty sure some of the children in your class don't even know what an archeologist is.'

'It's not the same,' said Harry. His chin puckered. 'I want to talk, but I can't.'

That didn't make any sense. I didn't want to upset him, but this was a rare opportunity to have Rob back me up in something important. 'We want you to show Mrs Wheeler how clever you really are. She can't see it if you don't answer her when she speaks to you. She might think you're a rude boy, and you're not, are you? You don't want anyone to think you have bad manners.' I knew I certainly didn't want anyone to think he had bad manners. That would be a direct reflection on my parenting.

He shook his head. Tears brimmed in his eyes. I looked at Rob imploringly, but he was gazing at Harry. 'No need to be upset, fella,' he said.

'Sorry, but it's not hard to answer a few questions, is it?' I knew I sounded terse, but really, he was a bright boy. How hard was it?

'Will you try?' said Rob.

Harry nodded. 'I'm tired,' he said and for the first time I noticed there were dark circles under his eyes. He wiped his face with the sleeve of his pyjama top. 'Will you read my story, Daddy?'

'Of course I will.' Rob stood, waited for Harry to climb down from his chair, then took his hand and they both left the room.

Harry didn't even say goodnight to me. Rob was clearly pissed off with me too. How was I getting it so wrong? I was trying to be a good mum. I really was. So why did it feel like the perfect little family I'd tried so hard to stitch together was coming apart at the seams?

Chapter Eight

Elle

I was called into school to see the counsellor after Harry's first session. My stomach churned as I carefully applied my make-up, wondering what she'd discovered about my boy and my family. On the drive there, I tried imagining how we looked from the outside. We appeared normal. In the family portrait hanging on the wall in my hallway, the three of us looked like a set of catalogue models. Maybe this was my comeuppance for being proud of that. It's all very well being perfect on the outside, I thought, pulling up in the school car park, but if your insides don't match, the rot will work itself to the surface in the end.

Claire Dixon wasn't what I'd expected. When I envisaged a counsellor, I saw a matronly, older woman in tie-dyed clothes who smelled of patchouli oil. Instead, I was greeted by a slim woman in her late thirties wearing a smart blue suit. Her dark hair was pulled back in a sleek ponytail and she smelled of Jo Malone Pomegranate Noir perfume.

'Thank you for coming in, Mrs Clarke.'

'Hi,' I said, smiling nervously. 'Thanks for seeing me. Sorry my husband couldn't make it.' Rob didn't even know I was coming today. I wondered if she could tell I was lying. 'How did Harry get on yesterday?' I sat opposite her in the narrow office, holding my bag on my lap.

She looked up to the left then back at me. 'Well . . .' She tapped her Biro on her front teeth. 'Harry didn't seem able to speak when he came in yesterday.'

My toes curled inside my boots. 'I don't know why he's doing this. He's not a naughty—'

Claire put her hand out to stop me. 'I'm not for one second suggesting he was being defiant. In fact, he looked quite upset.'

My brain conjured a painful image of Harry sitting in the chair I was in now, tears pooling in his eyes. 'Then why doesn't he speak? Then there wouldn't be anything to be upset about.'

Claire nodded. 'I think that's what we need to get to the bottom of.' She narrowed her eyes. 'Would you say Harry is an anxious child?'

'Anxious?' I shifted in my seat. 'I don't know. You don't think of seven-year-olds as anxious, do you? I mean, he's quiet and can be a bit of a scaredy-cat. But it's not that he can't talk. He's a very bright boy. He's articulate, at home, I mean, he's got an excellent vocabulary.' I felt like I was babbling so I stopped abruptly.

'Okay,' Claire said thoughtfully. 'So, he doesn't seem overly worried when he's at home?'

'No.' I paused. 'It's my fault, isn't it, him not speaking?' I said, talking fast again. 'I've got used to answering for him. When we're out, at the shops or something, and somebody talks to him, he looks up at me like he's pleading with me to answer for him, so that's what I end up doing.

That's a mistake, isn't it? I've mollycoddled him so much he's forgotten how to speak for himself, haven't I?' Rob had almost said as much, and he was right. I'd spent so much time making sure Harry was comfortable, I'd stripped his confidence.

'Please, don't blame yourself. There can be all kinds of reasons why people behave the way they do. I think our first step is to work out what's stopping Harry from communicating verbally.'

'It's not like he can't talk. He talks normally at home.'

She looked at some notes on the desk by her side. 'Did he find the transition to junior school difficult?'

I was back on sturdy ground with this one. I sat straighter. 'Yes. He's struggled since he started juniors, especially with organisation. He forgets everything and he's terrified of getting told off for having the wrong equipment and things like that. He loses everything. Mind like a sieve.'

Claire smiled. 'That must make him quite anxious.'

'Maybe.' I hooked the strap of my handbag over my fingers and twisted it around. 'Do you think this silence is something to do with him being a bit anxious, then, or . . .' Or what?

She smiled at me, 'As soon as I know more, I'll share it with you, okay?' She looked at her watch. 'Sorry, this has been such a short meeting. I haven't got much to feed back yet and I've got another appointment in a minute. I've got a couple of ideas for how we can help Harry.'

'I need to stop talking for him, don't I? Make him stand on his own two feet.' I was ashamed of myself for not seeing it before. What a terrible mother I was.

'I'm not sure that's a good idea,' she said. 'If Harry clams up because he's anxious, then forcing him into situations where he has to speak might make things worse.'

'Sorry,' I said. God, I was awful. I had no idea how to parent my son. 'What do you suggest?' I focused on her face, desperate to learn.

'If it's okay with you, I'd like to start by screening him to see if he has any neurodiverse conditions that might be causing the executive function issues, because anxiety can be caused by that, or run side by side.'

Dread settled in my stomach.

'But in the meantime, I think it's important we don't make Harry any more anxious. I'll speak to Mrs Wheeler about strategies and keep you up to date.'

'Okay.' This all seemed to have escalated quickly. I thought I'd come in to talk about Harry being quiet and now it was all about anxiety and strategies. I swallowed and blinked, trying to stop myself from looking weak and pathetic as well as a useless mother.

Claire lifted a colourful leaflet from a pile on her desk and handed it to me. 'This is information about a support group I run for the parents of children who have ADHD, that's Attention Deficit Hyperactivity Disorder.'

'Oh, Harry definitely doesn't have ADHD,' I said, feeling confident of that at least. 'He's the opposite of hyperactive. He can sit quietly for hours.'

'You'd be surprised how often I hear that,' said Claire. 'ADHD isn't exactly what you think it is. There's an inattentive subtype of the condition which often goes undiagnosed. Does anyone in your family have ADHD, do you know?'

I thought of my mum but didn't think being man-hungry and unreliable counted. I was sure neither Rob nor I had ADHD. We'd have noticed. 'Not that I know of, why?'

'It's generally a genetic condition. It's often the case that parents only get diagnosed when they realise their children have it.'

I shook my head. 'I can't think of anyone, sorry.' Was I sorry, or relieved?

'Okay, well, if it's alright with you, I'd like to do the screening, just in case.'

I nodded.

'I know this is all new and a bit scary, and even if Harry doesn't have any neurodiversity, perhaps it would help to meet other parents who are going through the counselling and diagnosis process.'

I took the paper from her and shoved it in my bag. 'Okay, right, thanks.'

'I'll let you know what Mrs Wheeler and I plan to do to help Harry, and get back to you as soon as I can. In the meantime, I'll send through the screening questionnaires for you to fill out at home. Okay?'

I nodded, despite feeling like my head was filled with cotton wool. Had she told me what I needed to do to help Harry? He relied on me, and I was getting it wrong. I wanted somebody to tell me how to keep my little boy safe. I clearly wasn't up to the job on my own.

Chapter Nine

Jen

I could hear Cora's crying as soon as I opened the door. Her sobs were always a full-body experience: great big shuddering wails at a noise level that could pierce brickwork. And they were exhaustingly regular. I felt myself droop.

When she was tiny, every little cry had me running to check she was alright. These days the sound of the first sniffle had my eyes rolling to the back of my head. I knew that made me an awful mother, but I couldn't help thinking about the boy who cried wolf when she set off on another ear-splitting trauma-fest.

'What is it this time?' I shouted from the hallway, easing my feet out of my Doc boots. I heard murmured voices then a slightly quieter sob. I knew Bill would be soothing Cora, trying to calm her down with soft words and cuddles. It was irritating. I'd tried telling him not to indulge her, partly because it made things harder for me when he wasn't here, and she wanted the same level of attention from me. On top of that, I knew how often she cried at school and was afraid she was one good sniff away from being labelled a cry-baby forever.

I went through to the front room and there they were, Cora snuggled in Bill's lap. 'It's ten o'clock. You should have been asleep three hours ago. What's going on?'

Bill stroked Cora's hair. 'She can't sleep. Apparently Mrs Daniels told her off for forgetting her pencil case.'

I sighed. 'There's an easy solution to that, isn't there? Don't forget your pencil case again.' I couldn't keep the frustration out of my voice. 'There's no need to kick off every time someone looks at you the wrong way. For god's sake, Cora, you've got to toughen up. Resilience, that's the word for it, isn't it? Where's your resilience?' I'd always been proud of my resilience. I could take the knock and get back up on my own. Admittedly, it had taken me longer after Aaron fucked off, but I'd got there, eventually. What doesn't kill you, and all that.

I watched a tear roll down Cora's cheek and the word *weak* occurred to me. I felt immediately guilty and replaced it with *sensitive*. But she didn't get this sensitivity from me.

Cora snivelled. 'I try to be a rememberer, but I think about something else and then all the remembering goes away, even when I try really hard to catch it in my head. Mrs Daniels tells me off all the time. And she says I talk too much.'

You do talk too much. 'I thought you liked Mrs Daniels?'

'I do,' Cora said through her tears. 'But she doesn't like me anymore. She thinks I'm naughty.' She buried her head in Bill's chest.

He wrapped his arms around her, making shushing noises. I lifted my hands in exasperation, but he shrugged in reply and stroked Cora's dark hair.

'I'm sure she doesn't think you're naughty,' said Bill.

'She does.' Cora tipped her head up to look at him and the sight of her wet, blue eyes softened my irritation.

'You're the least naughty girl I've ever met,' I said, more calmly. 'Okay is your favourite word. Weirdo,' I added, in the hope it would make her smile.

She almost did. 'Mrs Daniels says I'm a daydreamer and I ask too many questions instead of using my listening ears.'

'She said that?' Bill looked at me with narrowed eyes. 'That's not exactly encouraging, is it?'

I sat straighter. 'Does she tell the other children off a lot too?'

'Only the ones who are naughty.'

This didn't make any sense. Cora was about as far away from naughty as it was possible to get. In fact, she was such a people pleaser I worried she would be taken advantage of when she was older. She was sweet, kind and empathetic, the sort of kid who cries when someone else falls over. *Sensitive.* 'Do you want me to speak to Mrs Daniels?'

Cora's eyes widened. 'No! Please don't, Mummy. Please, no.'

'But—' Bill started.

'No, Daddy. You can't. She'll think I'm a tell-tale. I just need to do better remembering. I'll try really, especially hard and I won't ever talk, and I'll always use my listening ears.' She was gulping and sobbing. Her head spun to look at me then back at Bill. 'Please don't tell Mrs Daniels I said anything.'

'Okay, sweetheart, okay,' Bill soothed. 'You've got nothing to worry about. It's all alright, lovely girl.'

We eventually managed to stop her crying and got her up to bed. Back downstairs, Bill said, 'We are going to speak to this Mrs Daniels, right?'

'Hundred percent,' I said. Cora might be sensitive, but I wasn't. This needed nipping in the bud. 'I'll make an appointment to see her first thing in the morning. We don't want this carrying on after half-term. Let's see if she's ready to pick on someone her own size.'

'Oh, poor woman,' said Bill, pulling a scared face.

'Yep. Send her your hopes and prayers, my man. Hopes and prayers.'

* * *

I was hoping and praying that Cora hadn't seen me sneak into reception at the end of school two days later. She was at after-school club in the gym, but I was still worried about the fallout if she spotted me making my way to her classroom. I could do without the drama, but Mrs Daniels needed to see what she was up against. Cora was tiny and tearful. I was not.

Mrs Daniels stood when I opened the door. The two adult-sized chairs facing each other in front of the wooden desk looked like seats for giants among the room filled with miniature chairs and tables. She gestured for me to sit. 'Thank you for coming in, Mrs . . .' She tucked one side of her neat, grey bob behind her ear and glanced down at a piece of paper with a few lines of handwriting on. 'Glasson. I'm sorry I couldn't see you yesterday. I was on a course.'

I didn't correct her with a curt '*It's Ms, actually*' but it did irritate me that she used a title indicating my irrelevant romantic attachment to a man. Why any self-respecting woman changed her name or title when she got married was beyond me. 'No problem. I—'

She lifted her hand. 'Before you say anything, I think I owe you, or, more accurately, Cora, an apology.'

I blinked. 'An apology?'

'The course I was on yesterday was very interesting. Enlightening, in fact. It's made me reassess a lot of what I do in the classroom for children with additional needs.'

I wasn't following. She couldn't mean Cora, because, if anything, she was an over-achiever. She certainly didn't have any additional needs. I hoped she hadn't got the children mixed up. Annoyance bubbled in my stomach. I was missing the end of a rehearsal for this.

I opened my mouth to speak but Mrs Daniels said, 'I don't think I've been fair on Cora.'

She had the right kid, then. I closed my mouth. This wasn't how I thought this would go.

'She's a lovely little girl,' she said.

'Thank you.' That sounded more like my daughter. I took a breath. 'Can I ask why, in that case, she feels like you pick on her?' Mrs Daniels' face fell. 'Not that she actually used those words. What she actually said was you think she's naughty and you don't like her.'

Mrs Daniels shook her head. 'Right. I'm sorry. I probably have been overly firm with her. She's very chatty, she asks a lot of questions when, if she listened, she'd already know the answers, and she's always forgetting—'

'She's an August baby, so she's only just gone seven. She's one of the youngest in the year, so I think—'

'Absolutely.' Mrs Daniels was nodding. Her hair escaped from behind her ear. She tucked it back.

Why did she keep agreeing with me? I thought we were on different sides. The adrenaline I'd felt before this meeting was swilling around my system with nowhere to go. 'She's been very upset.'

'Yes, the crying. That's another thing that led me to think about Cora's . . .' She paused, biting her bottom lip.

'Cora's what?'

She moved her bottom further back in the chair and leaned forwards. 'Can I list some of what I believe to be Cora's traits and see if you agree?'

Traits? I nodded, defensively clenching my teeth. My adrenaline surged again, ready and willing to fight for Cora.

'Empathetic.'

I nodded. Maybe this wasn't going to be all bad. This was the most confusing meeting I'd ever had.

'She has big emotions she can't always control.'

'Yes, but, as I said, she's seven. And she feels things deeply. That's not a bad thing, is it? At least she's not a psychopath.' I stopped. By the stunned look on Mrs Daniels' face, I surmised other mothers didn't say things like that about kids in Year Three.

'Right, right, definitely no psychopathic traits, but she cries very easily, doesn't she?'

I couldn't deny that. 'Go on.'

'She's a clever girl, but she does drift off. Her attention, I mean. She's very easily distracted.'

'Yep.'

'Forgetful?'

'Yes. Annoyingly so.'

'Is she untidy at home?'

That seemed like a peculiar question for a teacher to ask. I half felt like telling her to mind her own business but my defensiveness was turning to curiosity and I wanted to know where this was going. 'Her bedroom is like a bomb site, but I expect that's the same for most kids her age.'

Her head bobbed with tiny nods as though everything I said was adding a piece to a jigsaw only she could see. 'Does she find it easy to turn off her thoughts? For example, can she get to sleep easily at night?'

'God, no. She overthinks everything. She's often still awake when we go to bed.'

'Does she talk more than usual when she's tired?'

That question brought me up short. It was a running joke between me, Bill and Cora that she was like a wind-up toy when she was over-tired. She kept running off at the mouth until exhaustion forced her to sleep. 'How do you know that?'

'I didn't, but I suspected it might be the case. I only learned yesterday that that's how mild—' She stopped abruptly.

'What?'

'Erm.' She scratched the side of her nose. 'I can't say for sure. I'm not really meant to . . .'

I spoke firmly, looking her directly in the eye. 'Please tell me why you're asking all these questions?'

'Maybe you should speak to our school counsellor, Claire—'

I wasn't about to be fobbed off. 'You were leading up to something. What was it?'

'I'm sorry, I'm really not allowed to even suggest a diagnosis. It's completely unprofessional—'

I leaned forwards. 'Diagnosis? For what?'

She closed her eyes and breathed in. 'I really shouldn't be telling you this, but since you're so insistent . . . and, as I said, I can't say for certain that Cora has . . . The course I was on yesterday was about recognising attention deficit hyperactivity disorder, especially the inattentive subtype, which often goes undiagnosed.'

'ADHD?'

'Yes.' She opened her eyes and nodded, as if her jigsaw was finished. She put her head on one side. 'So I think making an appointment for Cora to see our counsellor would be the best next step.'

The phrase *a little knowledge is a dangerous thing* popped into my mind. This woman had been on a course and thought she could apply what she'd learned to my perfectly normal little girl to justify all the times she'd treated her unfairly. I wasn't going to allow Cora to be her guinea pig. She could try out her newly learned strategies for children with, what did she call it, *additional needs*?

Maybe I should have said all of that, but I was too cross to put the correct words in the correct order, so instead I said, 'What a load of bollocks,' stood up and marched from the room.

Chapter Ten

Elle

'Harry still isn't speaking in class,' Mrs Wheeler said, when she called after school the week before October half-term. 'I saw Grace talking to him at playtime, but I couldn't see if he talked back.'

'Was he playing with the others?' I asked, crossing my fingers on the hand not holding the phone. There was a pause.

'He tends to spend most breaks on his own. I'm sorry, Mrs Clarke, I know that's not what you want to hear.' Her voice brightened, 'At least nobody seems to be bothering him. It's not like he's a target, or anything like that. It's more . . . well, he's kind of overlooked.'

I imagined my gorgeous boy wandering around the playground on his own and felt the weight of sadness in my gut.

'He's still seeing Claire after school once a week, isn't he?' Mrs Wheeler said.

'Yes. She's emailed some screening things, some forms

for us to fill in.' I felt like I should say *us*, even though Rob had refused to have anything to do with them.

'Good. Good. Yes, I think we need to get to the bottom of why Harry doesn't feel comfortable talking. Claire said something about anxiety. She's researching it and she's going to share what she finds out, so hopefully we'll know more soon. Bye, Mrs Clarke. Have a pleasant evening.'

'Okay, thanks for calling. Bye.' I clicked off the call feeling even more wretched than I had before.

* * *

It was warm for October, and I watched as the pink sunset was swallowed by dusk before pushing the door to the garden open when Rob rang at seven o'clock. The outside light sprang on, illuminating the neat borders and too-long grass.

I didn't want Harry to overhear our conversation. I'd agreed for him to carry on seeing Claire after the first session, transferring the money for six appointments from our joint account, but I hadn't mentioned that to Rob yet.

I'd filled the forms in, ticking boxes about whether my little boy found socialising hard and if he got easily distracted. How could I answer yes and no at the same time? If he was meant to collect something from upstairs, he would invariably get distracted by a toy and completely forget the thing he went up for. But if he was reading up on how a meteor wiped out the dinosaurs, he could concentrate for a full day without stopping to eat.

In the end, it didn't matter that Rob wasn't involved in the form filling. He wouldn't have been able to answer most of the questions accurately anyway. He wasn't here enough to be anything other than *fun dad*. All the real parenting was down to me. And I was clearly getting it horribly wrong.

'How many times do I have to tell you, there is nothing

wrong with the boy?' Rob said, after I recounted the phone call with Mrs Wheeler. 'That teacher is a jobsworth who's egging you on to see issues where there aren't any.' Rob's voice was tinny through the phone speaker. 'Honestly, Elle, you know the boy. He's shy, that's all.'

'But what if that's not all?' I wondered if he could hear the tears in my voice. Or if he'd care if he did. 'Harry is having a tough time. I can't ignore what his teacher's saying.' I cradled the phone between my chin and neck, tugging the dead head of a rose from the stem.

'There's nothing wrong with him!' His voice had risen an octave. 'Jesus, I was exactly like that at his age, and I'm doing alright, aren't I? I didn't need a counsellor or some mumbo jumbo form-filling exercise to build a successful advertising agency, did I?'

'If it's that successful, you can afford to spend more time with your son.' *And me*. I didn't add that. It was the first time I'd issued a direct challenge and it made my innards curl up tight. While I waited for him to explode, I peeled the velvety soft petals from the rose and sprinkled them in the flowerbed. I smelled my fingers, the scent taking me back to when I used to make rose petal perfume with my best friend when I was little. The thought that Harry had never had a close friendship made my throat tighten.

'Oh, for fuck's sake. I can't do this, Elle. I'm meant to be pitching to a new client in an attempt to keep the roof over our heads.' He paused and I heard what sounded like a child's voice in the background.

'Who's that?'

'Eh?'

'I thought I heard a child talking.'

'Yes, Elle. That's exactly what you heard.' He tutted. 'You heard my other child from my other family. The one I choose to be with just to make Harry's and your life miserable.' Sarcasm dripped from his words.

'There's no need to be cruel, Rob.'

'Sorry, but it feels like that's what you must think, that I've got somewhere I'd rather be. Otherwise, you wouldn't keep making me feel bad for not being with the two people who mean the most to me.' There was a pause and a muffled sound as though he had his hand over the speaker. 'I need to get off. I've got to prepare this pitch.'

'Alright.' I was relieved he'd said *the two people*.

'Bye. Give Harry a kiss from me.'

I wiped the mascara from under my eyes before I came in from the garden. The phone was still warm in my hand. I clicked the camera to selfie mode to check my eyes weren't too red rimmed.

I swooped the patio doors closed and clicked down the lock, pulling it hard to make sure it was secure. The outside light extinguished, turning the garden an eerie grey. Recently, when Rob was away, I'd started to check all the locks at least twice before I went to bed.

I walked through the kitchen and a brightly coloured leaflet caught my eye. It was the one Claire had given to me last week, for the support group she ran in a neighbouring town. 'ADHD is not what you think,' I remembered her saying.

I picked it up and read the details. There was a meeting the day Harry went back to school after half-term. Something moved outside the patio door, and I spun in time to catch a shadow disappear around the side of the house. Goosebumps rose on my arms. It was probably a fox – the light sensor would have been tripped by anything bigger – but my nerves still jangled. I was feeling like this more and more these days. I wished I had somebody to talk to about it, but I couldn't afford to show my hand to Nicky or the other school mums. I could imagine them talking behind my back, calling Harry a *weirdo* this time. I looked again at the leaflet, reading the word 'support'. That's exactly what I needed right now, a bit of support.

Chapter Eleven

Elle

When I walked into the lobby of the church hall the first day after Harry's half-term, I was already stressed. I'd got stuck in the full car park and had to do a four-hundred-point turn to get out. Then I tried every side street before giving up and parking a ten-minute walk away. I'd marched through the drizzle, and by the time I followed the signs to where the support group was held, the session was halfway through.

I rolled up to the balls of my feet and back down again, trying to muster the courage to push the hall door open. Through the glass panel, I could see groups of women, holding cups in their hands and chatting. I watched for a moment, the urge to turn around and go home rising. I heard a door behind me bang shut and a large woman in a baggy T-shirt and leggings hurried towards me.

'Alright,' she said. 'You new?' Her smile was welcoming, despite the gaps between her upper teeth.

I nodded.

'Come on then.'

She pushed the door and held it open for me to pass through. The voices of about forty women burbled. I hadn't expected to see so many people there. I had to lean forwards to hear what the woman was saying. 'Sorry, I didn't catch that.'

'I said, is your little shit giving you hell as well?' She nodded as if I'd already agreed. 'Bet you're glad they're back at school today. I know I am. Boy or girl?'

An image of Harry choosing to play quietly with his dinosaurs for most of the week sprang into my head. 'Boy. Seven.'

The woman flung her head back. 'Gahhh, I feel for you! Monsters at that age, they are. Three quarters testosterone. Either got their hands around some other kid's neck or down their own pants. Am I right?'

I was freed from answering by a tap on my arm. I turned to see Claire Dixon.

'Hello. Glad you could make it.'

'Hi.' I tried to cover how overwhelmed I felt with a smile.

'Don't worry,' she said. Clearly my smile was unconvincing. 'It's not always as loud as this. We're just having a coffee and a chat before the speaker comes on.'

She led me towards a trestle table set with a huge metal urn and cups. I shook my head. 'The last thing I need right now is caffeine. I'm a bit nervous. Sorry.'

'I get it. You've had a lot to take in recently.'

We both looked around the hall at the animated faces. I didn't see anyone who I'd feel comfortable approaching. I felt like I was in the wrong room. 'You said there's a speaker?'

'Yes,' said Claire. 'Every few weeks I get a specialist along to talk about one aspect of ADHD or ASD – that's autism spectrum disorder, and then people can ask questions and get some feedback without having to wait for a referral or an email reply. You know what it can be like, trying to get answers to questions from specialists. They're so overloaded with cases. Waiting lists are getting longer by the day.'

I didn't know what it was like, but I feared I was about to find out.

The woman with the missing teeth appeared at Claire's shoulder. She yelled, 'I was just sympathising with her. She's got a seven-year-old boy, poor cow!' She threw her head back and laughed.

'You should get a seat at the front, Lizzie,' said Claire, gesturing to where rows of chairs were set out at the far end of the hall facing a lectern. 'I think you'll find this week's talk interesting. It's on oppositional defiance.'

'Fuck, yeah,' said Lizzie. 'I need to know how to stop my lot battering everyone.' She laughed again and tottered away towards the chairs.

'She's a character,' said Claire, watching as Lizzie bashed people on the back in greeting as she moved through the room. 'You remember what I said about ADHD being genetic? She's a case in point. A gem of a woman, full of life, but her whole family are on the extreme end of the hyperactive subtype. Four kids with opposition defiance and impulse control issues, and she's still smiling, bless her.'

She must have seen the look of horror on my face. 'We're very open here. I'm not betraying any confidences. The point of the group is to be as honest as you feel comfortable being, because then you'll see you're not alone. Remember, everyone is different, so not everything you'll hear will apply to your family.'

A tall man in a brown suit walked towards the lectern. He looked around the room, stopping and waving when he saw Claire. 'Excuse me,' she said. 'Time for the talk. Find a seat. I'll introduce you to some of the others afterwards. Okay?'

I nodded mutely, walking to the back row of seats and

perching on a chair. Claire, now standing next to the man at the front, gave an ear-splitting whistle. All the women in the room turned and followed her instruction to take a seat. Where were the dads? I gave my head a shake. Where was Rob? I watched the women move to the chairs, trying to pick out one who looked approachable, but I couldn't see a single person who I thought I'd have anything in common with.

I knew, deep down, I was the strange one in this room, with my expensive white jumper and highlighted choppy bob. The women on the estate where I grew up all had scraped back ponytails and wore this uniform of jeans or leggings with oversized T-shirts and hoodies. They didn't go to the dental hygienist every six months like I did now because they couldn't afford to. If it was a choice between your kid's school shoes and stained teeth, the teeth came a poor second. However worried about money Rob said he was, the balance on our joint account was always healthy. I reminded myself to be more grateful to Rob for that, at least.

The estate had been full of Lizzies: unabashed, life-embracing women with big personalities. But my mum wasn't one of them. She was always searching for a man to make her life complete. It was the other women who looked out for me when I was left to fend for myself.

Rob had lifted me from that life. When he was rebranding the department store where I was the window dresser, he would take me out to nice restaurants and seemed to presume I was used to that kind of thing. I didn't tell him about my past until six months in to our relationship. That's when he opened up to me about how young his parents were when they had him, about his alcoholic father and how he was mainly brought up by his grandparents. Our disjointed upbringings were part of our connection. That's why we decided to raise Harry differently, to always put him first. Although, since all this business at school with Harry, I couldn't help thinking I was the only one keeping my side of the bargain.

The man in the suit began to speak, but his voice was too quiet to hear.

'Can you speak up, please?' called someone in the middle.

'Yeah. We can't hear at the back,' said someone else.

The man flicked a nervous look at Claire, who was sitting to his right, then cleared his throat and started again. 'Sorry about that. I usually have a microphone.' He coughed. 'Good afternoon, everyone,' he said. 'I'm Professor Ian Thirsk and I've been invited here by Claire,' – he gestured limply towards Claire, who smiled encouragingly – 'to talk to you about oppositional defiant disorder. This condition is often comorbid, that is to say, runs alongside, other disorders like ADHD, which is why I'm here at your support group, today.'

I wriggled on the hard seat, unsure I wanted to hear what this man had to say. Despite its size, the room felt overwhelmingly stuffy. The windows were steaming up from the bottom, misting the clouds which were dissolving to allow for patches of pale blue autumn sky.

'Oppositional defiant disorder, which I'll refer to as ODD for the rest of this talk, is a condition in which a child displays an ongoing pattern of behaviours which could be described as angry or irritable. Someone with ODD might be argumentative, vindictive even, to people they perceive as having authority over them.' He looked up and smiled with tight lips. 'I can see many of you are nodding already' He shuffled his cue cards and continued, 'ODD can easily be mistaken for rebellion or attention seeking, but unlike regular acting up, the conflict caused by a child with this disorder, can complicate family life, friendships and academic achievement.'

He looked around his audience. 'Can I ask, by a show

of hands, how many of you recognise these attributes in the young people you care for?'

I came to this support group because these women might have children like Harry, my sweet, shy boy. Surely none of them were experiencing anything like what this man was talking about. Panic tightened my throat as I saw one hand after another raised in the air until about a third of the room had their hands up. *Oh god*, I thought, *is this what's going to happen to Harry?* Was his silence and ignoring his teacher the start of something far more extreme? I breathed in but couldn't get the air to the bottom of my lungs. I tried again, but my head felt lighter with every inhalation.

The room was too hot. The high neck of my jumper felt like it was strangling me. I breathed in again but couldn't grab hold of the air. I heard the man continue his speech, but it sounded far away. He was talking about children with ODD throwing tantrums and hurting people. I heard the words, '*lying, stealing, truancy*' and I couldn't bear to listen anymore.

I stood, trying to ignore the faces turning at the scraping back of the chair legs. I wanted to cover my ears to stop those terrifying words from adding to my fears for my little boy. It turned out, my boy who I'd always thought was perfect, probably wasn't perfect at all. He might have some kind of condition. Claire seemed to think he might have ADHD, which could come along with all manner of horrifying things. What did the future have in store for my poor, poor child?

Outside, I leaned against the solid stone of the church. I bent over to try to steady my spinning head and as the wind whipped my hair around my face, I cried for the perfect child I used to have, but now feared I'd lost.

Chapter Twelve

Jen

Sod's law that Bill would be visiting his dad in his care home in Scotland when I needed to talk to him face to face. I understood why he couldn't move his father closer, though. Early-onset dementia is hard enough to deal with without being shunted to unfamiliar surroundings. It was another reason Bill was a kinder and more thoughtful person than me, always putting someone else's needs first.

The phone rang at 7pm. I left Cora in bed, telling her she could read one more story while I talked to Daddy.

I ran through everything Mrs Daniels had said with Bill, finishing with, 'I had to drag it out of her, but in the end she said she thinks Cora might have some kind of ADHD subtype.'

'You are kidding me?' He practically roared. I was surprised by the vehemence of his reaction. I'd been annoyed, but he seemed to be hitting the roof.

'She went on a course—'

'For fuck's sake!' The consonants came out hard.

I took the phone away from my ear and scowled. I put it back to my ear. 'Alright Captain Shouty, wind your neck in. I'm telling you what happened. Don't yell at me. God, it's not as if anyone's saying there's something wrong with you, is it?'

The line went quiet. 'Sorry. It's just that . . . a little knowledge is a dangerous thing.'

I laughed. That was more like the Bill I knew and loved. We thought the same way. 'That's exactly what I was thinking when I was listening to her spouting on about how forgetful Cora is. She gets that from you, by the way.'

He snorted. 'Yeah, sorry about that.'

There was the sound of footsteps upstairs. I sighed inwardly, hoping we weren't going to have one of those nights where Cora was up and down with various excuses every hour.

Bill sighed. 'One course and she's diagnosing everyone. It's ridiculous. The world's gone mad.'

'If you start quoting Piers Morgan, you're never getting laid again.'

'As if you could resist me.'

He had a point. 'You keep telling yourself that, pal.'

'Whatever.' I could tell he was smiling. His voice became serious again. 'Did you tell Mrs Daniels Cora was top of the class all the way through infants?'

'I didn't need to. She knows she's bright. She's not denying that. She even apologised for telling her off.'

'That's something.'

'Yeah.' I waited half a second, heard the toilet flush upstairs and footsteps patter along the landing. Then I said what had been niggling me since the meeting with Mrs Daniels. 'Don't bite my head off, but . . . do you think she might be on to something; I mean Cora does—'

'Don't, Jen.' There was a mettle in his voice I rarely heard. 'There is nothing wrong with Cora. She's a perfectly normal, brilliantly creative little girl who has big feelings. At least she's not a psychopath.'

'That's what I said to Mrs Daniels! Exactly that.' We both laughed.

'I've got to go,' said Bill softly. 'Promise me you won't worry about this. Neither of us want Cora to be caught up in a system that labels other people just so they don't have to hold up a mirror to their own wrongdoings, do we?'

He was right. I went in to challenge Mrs Daniels, and she'd managed to turn all the blame on Cora. A clever strategy if it worked. 'Okay. Love you. See you at the end of the week.'

'Remember, there's nothing wrong with her. It's other people who are the problem. Promise me, you won't give it another thought. I miss you,' said Bill. 'I love you.'

'I love you too. Bye, then. Bye.' I had the same warm glow I always got when I put the phone down after talking to him. I'd thought I was happy on my own, but the feeling I got from knowing there was one other person who always had my back, who'd chosen me over all the other humans on this planet, was grounding in a way I didn't know I'd missed. He was mine. I was his. Cora was ours. Mrs Daniels and her stupid course could sod off. All was good in the world.

* * *

The feeling of wellbeing had completely gone by the second time I was woken with a tap, tap tap on my arm. I rolled over and picked up my phone to see the time. 3.34am. Cora's elfin face was illuminated by the light on the screen.

Her doleful eyes blinked slowly. 'I'm sorry, Mummy. I didn't want to wake you up—'

'You clearly did,' I said, lying back on my pillow. 'Otherwise, you wouldn't be here poking my arm.'

'I'm scared,' she said.

If Bill was here, he'd roll out of bed and take her back to her own room, soothe whatever mad dream or crazy idea she'd had and return to our bed before I'd fully woken up. I missed my husband. 'Scared of what?'

'I don't know,' she said, a sad V-shape forming between her eyebrows. 'It's just a swirly feeling in my tummy. I don't know why it's there.'

I pushed my head back into the pillow in frustration. 'If you don't know why you're scared, I can't help you, can I? What do you want me to do?'

'I don't know.' She tugged at the hem of her pyjama top and looked so sweet and tiny that all of my defences crumbled. 'Can I sleep with you?'

Bill and I had never allowed Cora to sleep in our bed. We'd been forced to skip the traditional courtship thing because I got pregnant so soon after we met, but the chemistry between us had never waned in the way I feared it would after having a baby. Our bed wasn't just for sleeping in, so having a small child in there with us would simply not work. Anyway, it was important for children to sleep independently. We both agreed on that.

But I was so, so tired, and I had a crucial rehearsal the following day.

'Get in.' I rolled over. 'But don't wriggle about.'

Three long hours later, neither of us had had a wink of sleep. Cora was like a heat-seeking missile, constantly shuffling to my side of the bed, but completely incapable of staying still. Even when she was wedged close to my back, I could feel her curling her toes and picking at the edge of my pillowcase with her fingers.

'We might as well get up,' I said, looking at the shadow under the curtains which had turned a lighter shade of grey. I turned when I felt Cora's body shuddering next to me. 'What's the matter?'

'I'm tired.'

'Me too.' I lay back down and snaked one arm under her to pull her into a hug. I smelled the top of her head as she tucked herself into me, and all my annoyance was lost in her warm-body scent and the thin limbs winding around me. We lay there, breathing together and it was the first time she was still. We must've fallen asleep because the next thing I knew the Red Hot Chili Peppers' 'Give it Away' played through the speaker of my phone.

'Your alarm is weird,' Cora said, untangling herself from me. I turned to stop the music, wiggling my fingers to try to get the blood flowing back into the arm that had gone numb under Cora's weight.

'Up and at 'em,' I said, feeling anything but capable of being up and at 'em. 'Come on. You don't want to be late for school.' I lowered my voice to a comic bass. 'Mrs Daniels will say it's poor organisation.' My legs felt too heavy when I dropped them onto the floor. Every movement was an effort. This was going to be a long day.

'Can I stay with you today? Please, Mummy. I'm too sleepy to go to school and if I'm tired and I don't do everything Mrs Daniels tells me to, she's going to be cross with me.'

'I've got to go to work, sweetheart.'

She jumped onto her knees and steepled her fingers together. 'Please can I come with you, Mummy? Please.' She drew out the last please and when I looked at her pleading face with the dark circles under her big blue eyes, I couldn't resist.

'You'll have to be very quiet.' She jumped up and down on her knees. 'And it's only this once. We're not going to make a habit of it, okay?'

'I pinky promise,' she said, thrusting her fist towards me with her little finger extended. We hooked fingers and shook up and down.

'You'll be as quiet as a mouse?' I said, already wondering what on earth I was thinking of. She nodded, bounced down from the bed and scampered across the landing to her own room. I wished I had her energy after so few hours' sleep, especially since we were blocking Cleopatra's death scene today.

Chapter Thirteen

Jen

Mel's eyes followed Cora and me as we walked across the studio floor to the small kitchen. I'd regretted saying Cora could come from the minute I'd agreed, and the look on Mel's face confirmed it was a stupid idea. I could have kicked myself for breaking my own rule of not mixing professional and personal lives. If I blurred the lines, then I couldn't criticise anyone else for doing the same. I was an idiot.

I sat Cora down on one of the tatty armchairs in the far corner of the kitchen and gave her my phone to play with.

Back in the studio, I held my hand up in apology. 'I know, I know.'

'It's not like you to bring Cora in.' I was sure I heard disapproval in Mel's voice.

I resented her tone. I wasn't the kind of mum who jumped through hoops to keep their little princess happy. 'Bad night. This is a one-off. I won't let her interfere; I promise.' I took my job as artistic director of the small suburban theatre seriously and I'd never let them down, so she could damned well back off. 'Is the scene set?'

'All ready,' she said. 'We've only got Femi in this morning, right?'

'Yep. I really want to nail this scene. If you can read in for the other characters until they get here after lunch, that will free me up to work with her.'

Mel nodded. We'd worked together since before Cora was born, but we'd never become anything more than colleagues. In the early days, she'd invited me to her house for dinner and to the pub a couple of times, but I always declined. It made sense to me to keep people I worked with at arm's length. When you became friends, it complicated the dynamic, especially with the cast. It's hard to direct someone and push them to give their very best performance if you know all about their personal lives. You'd have to start making allowances and I certainly didn't want anyone making allowances for me.

I suspected Mel had hoped I might not come back after my short maternity leave, so she could take over my position, but I couldn't wait to get back to work. I got the feeling she disapproved of me somehow, but I chose not to dwell on it.

Femi arrived a couple of minutes later, a bluster of energy and colour. It was the first time I'd seen her without her hair tightly braided. A blood red scarf was tied around her afro, seeming to pull her cheekbones even higher towards her cat-like eyes.

'Ooof,' I said. 'You look bloody gorgeous.'

'Why, thank you.' She patted her hair. 'You like it?'

A small voice came from behind Femi, 'You look pretty.'

Femi spun around to find Cora looking up at her, her face full of awe. She crouched down. 'Thank you. I think you're very pretty too.' She took Cora's hand and shook it. 'What's your name?'

'I'm Cora. That's my mummy.' She pointed to me, and I felt a peculiar mix of pride in my gorgeous daughter and shame that I'd brought my home life into work.

'Well, it's lovely to meet you, Cora. I look forward to getting your notes on my performance later.'

'What's notes? Is it like when I copy something off the whiteboard?'

I strode towards Cora, pushing her back into the kitchen. 'Nothing for you to worry about. She's not really here, are you Cora?'

Cora shook her head and mimed zipping up her mouth before disappearing through to the kitchen.

I turned back to Femi. 'Sorry about that. Bad night's sleep. Didn't really have a choice.' I grimaced, noticing she was looking at me quizzically.

'I didn't know you had a daughter.'

'Busted. But let's forget about the fruit of my womb.' I gave a tight smile. 'And start where the clown brings the snake in.'

She gave her head a quick shake then shrugged off her jacket. 'Hast thou the pretty worm of Nilus there, that kills and pains not?'

'Exactly.' She followed me to centre stage. Mel flicked off the house lights and I waited for my eyes to adjust to the stage lights trained on the performance area. 'The clown will put the basket down on this mark.' I pointed at the cross of masking tape on the wooden floor. 'Then I want you to slowly circle the basket as the clown speaks. Keep your eyes on it the whole time, make small steps, then stop suddenly, facing the audience, when you say "Get thee hence, farewell."'

Femi was a dream to direct. She trod around the invisible basket in slow, balletic steps, never faltering with a line. When I stopped her for a note on pitch or tone, she repeated the line back exactly as I directed, and remembered it for the next run-through. The tremble in her voice when she clasped an invisible snake to her chest and said, 'Dost thou not see my baby at my breast, that sucks the nurse asleep?' made tears clog my throat.

'Bravo!' Mel and I clapped as Femi grinned and did a comic curtsy. 'You've earned your lunch today.'

I opened the kitchen door but was brought up short by the sight of Cora curled up in the armchair, fast asleep. The other two backed out. I followed, then turned back. 'I'll wake her up,' I said, reaching for the door handle again. I'd promised Cora wouldn't interfere and here she was, stopping us from eating lunch. Heat rose up my neck. Why couldn't she have slept last night instead of disrupting today?

'Don't,' said Femi. 'You both had a rough night, right?'

I nodded, 'But you can't not eat because my kid is having a kip in the kitchen.' My cheeks burned. I knew I'd be furious if anyone else in the company made a mistake like this.

'I'll pop to the corner shop and get us some sandwiches. Let her sleep,' said Mel. She held her finger in the air. 'No arguments.'

I don't know if it was the exhaustion or the kindness that made my bottom lip wobble when Mel marched out of the studio.

'Hey,' said Femi, pulling me into her arms. 'You okay?'

I'd never let an actor see me cry before, never mind give me a cuddle. Hardly anyone saw me cry. This was humiliating. 'Sorry,' I pulled back, but she took my hand and looked deep into my eyes.

'You look like someone who's got a lot going on.'

'Not really,' I said, sniffing. I pulled my hands from hers, mortified that she was seeing me in this state. 'I'm so sorry. This is so unprofessional.'

'Pufft,' she exhaled. 'We have trust, don't we? I trust you to direct me, you trust me to give my best. That makes us friends. A circle of trust, right?'

I wasn't friends with the cast. That was one of my rules. I tried to swallow down the emotions, but I was so tired they threatened to overwhelm me.

'What is it?' The softness of her voice was soothing.

'I'm worried about Cora,' I said and relief at allowing what was festering in my brain to take shape flooded through me. 'Her teacher thinks she has some kind of special needs.'

'Special needs?'

'ADHD.'

'Ah,' said Femi. 'It's amazing that they can recognise the signs early these days. So much better for everyone.'

I shifted to look at her face. 'What do you mean?'

'Well, my niece, Layla, she didn't get diagnosed until she was at uni, and she had it tough. I mean really tough.' She smiled reassuringly, 'But when she got her diagnosis, she could make sense of why she sometimes felt different and did the things she did.' She laughed. 'Or didn't do. The rest of the family could too. And she could let go of the shame she'd built up, you know?'

I didn't know. 'What shame?'

'She was always so emotional, and her friends couldn't always handle it. Struggling with emotional regulation is really common, apparently. And we all thought she was lazy because she couldn't ever finish anything, just didn't have the motivation. She's mega bright but got worse grades than she should because she didn't do enough revision, then we'd have a go at her and she'd hate on herself. She hated herself for the state of her room, for getting distracted and spending hours watching TikToks instead of doing all the stuff she meant to do.'

'Did she talk a lot?'

Femi laughed. 'A lot! She still does, though. The meds they gave her haven't changed her personality at all, thank god, but they help her focus and get stuff done, and she knows a lot of the stuff she blamed herself for wasn't her fault. Her brain's wired differently, it doesn't . . . what did she say . . .?' Her slanted eyes narrowed, 'It doesn't provide the same rewards for starting and finishing tasks as other people get, chemically, I mean. Something to do with the way happy chemicals are released. Science shizzle, anyway.' She shrugged. 'I don't know the ins and outs, but getting diagnosed was the best thing she ever did, for her and for us. We understand her better. We're a close family, you know?'

I jumped at the sound of Mel coming back into the room. She paused briefly in the doorway when she saw us huddled together. 'Alright?'

I leaned back from Femi. 'Yep. I'm getting emotional in my old age. Hormones.' Femi tipped her head to one side, but I avoided looking at her. I'd let my guard down and that was unprofessional. I couldn't let it happen again.

My exhausted brain was spinning. I'd felt a peculiar shift when she talked about her niece. I'd been so adamant there was nothing going on with Cora. But what if I was wrong? What if our refusal to listen to her teacher meant we were forcing her into a life filled with self-loathing and shame?

While Mel and Femi ate their sandwiches, I sneaked into the kitchen and stood over my sleeping child, watching her chest rise and fall. Her thick lashes lay on her soft, pale cheeks and I was flooded with love for her. I couldn't bear to think of her experiencing anything but joy. She let out a quiet moan and curled smaller. It looked as though the tired old chair was cradling her. That's what I wanted to do – hold her to me so the world couldn't hurt her.

I decided to call Mrs Daniels the next day. What harm could it do to work out if this beautiful girl needed a little help to love herself as much as she deserved to be loved? I would keep Bill out of it. He'd made his view clear. No need to worry him unnecessarily, not when he already had his dad to think about. I'd had years of sorting things out on my own. And this might be the most important one yet.

Chapter Fourteen

Elle

Rob had been distant since he came home. I did my usual trick of being everyone's Disney princess, trying to make them all happy, but he rarely even glanced up from his phone to look at me. At least he was paying attention to Harry. They were drawing together at the kitchen table, and it was the most animated I'd seen Harry in ages.

'Clear away those pens and paper,' I said, when dinner was ready, a spicy chili for Rob and me, and spaghetti Bolognese for Harry.

'I hope it's hot enough,' I said, placing a dish of steaming food on the table in front of Rob. 'If not, there's some jalapeños in the fridge.'

'Yeah, jalapenos would be good,' he said, not moving.

I sighed and handed Harry his plate before going to the fridge and getting the peppers. Rob was already tucking in when I sat down, but Harry waited, watching for me to pick up my fork before he did the same. I gave him a grateful smile.

'How was school?' Rob said to Harry. My stomach clenched. I should have told him not to bring school up until Harry had eaten. It seemed to quash his appetite if we talked about his day at the table.

'Okay,' said Harry, his eyes on the spaghetti twirling around his fork.

'Good,' said Rob, grinning as if the matter was now settled. 'That's good.'

I waited for him to look at me with an *I told you so* stare, but he turned back to his food.

'Can we go swimming on Saturday, Daddy?' Harry looked at Rob and the hope on his face made me stop chewing. 'Please,' Harry added, when Rob didn't answer straight away.

'Not sure I'm going to be here, pal.' Rob rubbed the top of Harry's head, seemingly oblivious to the disappointment on his son's face. 'Work, you know?'

'Oh, Rob. Please. You've only just got back.' I couldn't stop myself. 'You're away more than half the week now. Sorry, but we need—' I was interrupted by an insistent knocking on the door, followed by the ringing of the doorbell.

'What the . . .?' With a puzzled expression, Rob stood and went into the hall.

I followed. When he opened the door, Michael staggered into the hall.

'Dad.' Rob sounded confused. His father leaned against the wall, knocking our framed family portrait askew.

'Pay that man, will you?' Michael flailed his arm towards an angry-looking man in a car at the end of the drive. 'Taxi,' he said, 'Miserable bugger. Kept telling me not to throw up.' He blinked slowly. 'I never throw up in cars.' He stood taller, as if not vomiting in a cab was something he should be commended for.

'Why is Grandad here?' said Harry, watching Rob walk down the path in his socks and his grandfather trying to stay upright against the wall. 'What's wrong with him?'

'Sorry, but why are you here, Michael?' There were few people I would be so blunt with, but Michael was drunk, and drunk Michael was intolerable. This was the first time he'd turned up in this state since Harry was born, and I could see from my son's furrowed brow it was unsettling him. The last thing he needed now was more instability in his life.

'Pissed,' said Michael.

'I can see that.' He wobbled, knocking the photograph of the three of us onto the floor. The glass cracked down the middle, splitting the picture in two – me and Harry on one side, Rob on the other.

'Oh, Michael.' I picked up the frame then pushed Michael past Harry into the kitchen. I put the picture in a drawer to sort out later. 'Sit down.' He sat in my chair. I watched in astonishment as he picked up my fork and dug it into my food. 'That's—' Before I said anything more, he'd already shovelled chili into his mouth, nodding as if it was exactly what he needed right now.

'S'nice,' he said. 'That jalapeño?'

I snatched the jar away from him. 'Michael, you can't just . . .' I saw Harry's anxious face in my peripheral vision and calmed my voice. 'Sorry, but I think it might be best if you go upstairs and have a lie-down.'

'I'll be alright when I've eaten this.' He lowered his head towards the dish and thrust a forkful into his mouth.

The front door slammed, and Rob came into the kitchen, cheeks flushed. 'That cost forty quid.' He moved my plate out of Michael's reach, leaving him with a fork dangling from his hand. 'What's going on?'

Michael chewed, blinking up at his son. 'Little relapse,' he drawled. 'Nothing to worry about. I'll get back on the wagon tomorrow.'

Harry's hand slipped into mine. He shuffled close to my side. Although I'd seen Rob's father in this state many times in the early days of our relationship, Michael had been sober for the last seven years, so this was new to Harry. The memory of the way he used to turn up, shouting in the street, banging on the door and windows until we let him in made me shudder. I could still smell the vodka-laced vomit I'd often find spattered on the floor around the toilet bowl.

'Can you get him upstairs?' I whispered to Rob. 'Harry doesn't need to see this.'

'Come on, Dad,' said Rob, putting his arm under Michael's armpit and hoisting him to a standing position.

'Let's have a little drink, shall we?' said Michael, bits of dark meat dropping from his mouth onto the floor tiles. He turned to me. 'Get us some vodka, there's a good girl.' He rummaged in the inside pocket of his suit and pulled out a packet of cigarettes and a lighter.

'You know you can't smoke in here,' I said.

Rob took the cigarettes from Michael's hand. 'Don't be an idiot, Dad. Come on.'

'Mummy,' Harry's voice was quiet, 'Why does Grandad sound like that?'

I pulled him closer to me, wrapping my arm tight around his shoulders. 'He's had too much wine,' I said. 'He's going upstairs to sleep it off, then he'll be back to normal. Okay?' I felt him nod as we both watched Rob half carry Michael towards the stairs. There was some grunting and thudding, then heavy footsteps along the landing above our heads.

'Finish your dinner, then it's bath time.' I made my voice bright and airy as if there was absolutely nothing to worry about. Inside I was exasperated. Rob had only been home once in almost a week. Harry needed to spend some time with him. He'd been asking when Rob was coming home more and more, and now here he was. But Michael was back to his old ways, taking up the time Rob owed to his son.

* * *

When Rob came down half an hour later, I didn't seem to be able to drop the artificially bright voice. 'Daddy will do your bath and story,' I said to Harry, 'won't you, Daddy?'

Rob's brow furrowed. He pulled out the second phone, which he only used for work, and shook it. 'I'd love to, but I've got to call the freelancers about the London jobs. You know I always have a debrief at seven.'

'I'm sure that can wait for half an hour, just this once. After all, we haven't seen you for a while and your dad caused a bit of a drama earlier. A bit unsettling for all of us. I'm sure you'd like to spend a bit of time with Harry after that, wouldn't you?' I was getting braver, and I could see Rob didn't like it.

He frowned at me over Harry's head. 'Course. Come on, pal.'

After his bath, Harry came down to say goodnight. I hugged him, enjoying the smell of shampoo and clean laundry. 'Where's Daddy?' I asked.

'The alarm went off on his phone. He said he had to make his work call before he read my story.'

I swore in my head. I thought of my mum and what she would have done in this situation. She'd probably think I was one of life's winners – two handsome men under my roof. She'd be oblivious to the fact one of them appeared to find me practically invisible and the other was a freshly lapsed alcoholic.

'But look at your lovely big house,' she'd say. 'Isn't that worth putting up with a bit of crap for? I'd do anything for a life like yours.' Her voice echoed in my head. Holding Harry on my lap, I viewed my kitchen as she might: the glossy units, the real oak table my family ate at, rather than eating on trays in front of the television like Mum and I used to. She'd never had anything remotely like this. A pang of grief made me inhale sharply. She hadn't been perfect, but she had loved me, in her own way.

My eyes trailed through the patio doors into the darkening garden. I refocused, seeing the reflection of me and my boy in the glass. I wanted him to always know he was loved, that he was my number one priority. My head rested on his shoulder, his almost white hair and my highlighted bob mingled together making us one.

That image was what being Harry's mum felt like to me. I was him and he was me. Every emotion he felt was amplified as it travelled through me. I kissed the top of his head, wrapping my arms more tightly around him. 'I love you, my sweet, sweet boy.'

He twisted in my lap, turning to throw his arms around my neck. He kissed my cheek and lay his head on my shoulder. We stayed like this, me watching our melded reflection as the light outside faded to black.

* * *

Rob came downstairs after taking Harry to bed. He looked flustered. 'I need to get off first thing tomorrow morning. Can you tell Harry when he gets up?'

'You've only just got here,' I whispered, aware that Harry might still be awake and hear harsh words. 'And why didn't you tell him yourself?'

'I didn't want to upset him before he went to sleep.'

So I had to upset him in the morning? 'Can't you stay a few more nights? Harry needs you. He's really struggling—'

Rob bit the cuticle at the side of his thumb. 'He's fine. He's a normal, happy little boy.'

'When you're here, yes. But not when he's outside this house.'

He dropped his hands to his sides, his palms slapping against his jeans. 'I'm sorry, Elle. He seems fine to me, and I can't be in two places at once. I can't keep having the same discussion. I need some sleep.' He walked away, shaking his head, as though I was a lunatic who couldn't see reason.

I heard a noise in the hall a couple of hours later and turned, expecting to see Rob. Before, when we had a disagreement, I would follow him and try to make things right. I'd inevitably end up apologising and he'd magnanimously forgive me and fall into the sleep of the blameless, oblivious to the tears soaking into my pillow.

Now I was standing my ground, I hoped tonight he'd realised how unreasonable he was being and come down to apologise. How foolish of me. Instead, Michael's head appeared sheepishly around the sitting room door.

'Sorry,' he mouthed.

Swallowing my disappointment, I put the phone I'd been scrolling through on the arm of the sofa. I looked at him and could tell he'd sobered up a little. 'What's brought that on after all these years?'

He shuffled into the room patting down his grey-blonde waves. He was still a good-looking man at sixty-two, despite his bloodshot eyes and the pillow-crease across his cheek. He tugged up the knees of his crumpled suit trousers and sat gingerly on a chair. 'Bad day at the office.'

I raised an eyebrow.

'The office I no longer lease. For the company I no longer own.' His voice was still slurred.

'Oh.' I didn't say any more because this wasn't the first time Michael had lost a business; I could think of at least three companies he'd started and then thrown in over the last ten years.

He lay his head back on the chair. 'I'm too old for all this.'

I wondered what he meant by *all this*: the business, his girlfriend who was a similar age to Rob, or the booze?

'Sorry Michael, but you can't turn up in that state again. Harry was really unnerved.'

'I said sorry.' His voice had a note of petulance. That was Michael all over. He seemed to think he was allowed to do whatever he wanted as long as he offered one insincere apology.

'I mean it, Michael.'

He sat straight and fixed me with cold eyes. 'I'm sure you do.' He leaned forwards. 'Because it's important to make everything look perfect, isn't it, Elle? Crucial Harry doesn't see any of life's ugly realities. And we mustn't embarrass ourselves in front of the neighbours, must we? Wouldn't want anything to interfere with the image of the perfect family.'

I could smell the stale alcohol on his breath from across the room. 'You're still drunk.'

He sneered. 'What was it Winston Churchill said? "I may be drunk, Miss, but in the morning, I will be sober and you will still be . . ."' He paused. 'But you're not ugly, are you?' He slumped against the cushions. 'What will you be in the morning?' He tapped his lip in mock consideration.

'Michael—'

'Scared. No, that's not right. Pretending not to be scared. That's it.' He fixed his gaze on me, the blue of his irises vivid against the bloodshot pink. 'That's what I've always felt coming off you, Elle, fear. What is it you're so frightened of, eh? Him leaving you?' He gestured towards the ceiling. 'I wouldn't worry about that. He already has. He's never really been fully committed, has he? He was like that as a boy, always looking over your shoulder to see the next good thing coming along.'

'How would you know?' Tears threatened at the back of my eyes. 'Where were you when he was growing up?'

Michael closed his eyes and my fury burned hotter. His voice sounded blurry as if he were falling asleep. 'I was there as much as I could be. Anyway, you try having a kid at twenty, see how long you stick around.' He opened one eye and looked at me. 'You wouldn't though, would you? Little Miss Perfect. I bet you kept your knickers on until you met a man who could afford to give you the life you thought you deserved.'

'Fuck you, Michael.' The tears came then, hot and fast. I swiped them away, not wanting to give him the satisfaction. But I needn't have bothered because he was already asleep, mouth hanging open, oblivious to the pain his words had caused.

Chapter Fifteen

Elle

When my morning alarm sounded, two days later, I turned it off and whimpered. For the last few nights, every time I drifted into sleep, a new scenario of Harry being in danger paraded behind my eyes. I sat up, a dark feeling squatting behind my clavicle. I'd been crying in my sleep again. As I wiped tears from my cheeks, my mind presented me with the last horrifying dream where I was trying to phone Rob because I couldn't find Harry. I'd frantically searched the house, becoming more desperate with every second, then I'd picked up my phone to get help.

I think I'd started to sob when I couldn't navigate the phone's menu. Every icon I pressed led me to a cartoon instead of the call screen. When the alarm woke me, I remember thinking it was the phone ringing in my hand to tell me it was too late to save my boy.

I got out of bed and walked across the hall to Harry's room, the residual fear from the dream making my breath shallow. I pushed his door and was able to drag in a lungful of air when I saw the mound of his body under his duvet.

'Morning Harry!' I said brightly. 'It's another beautiful day.'

* * *

When I opened the front door to Michael later that morning, I hoped for an apology at the very least. I should have known better.

'I think I left my phone here.' As he walked past me into the hall, I smelled the unmistakable stench of another bender.

I should have slammed the door in his face. Instead, I said, 'Coffee?' He probably didn't even remember what he'd said to me. Even if he did, I doubted he'd care.

'Thanks.'

I made the coffee, listening to footsteps upstairs, then the sound of drawers slamming shut. He came into the kitchen, a defeated expression on his face.

'No phone?'

He shook his head and slumped into a chair.

'Where could you have left it?'

He looked up through his eyelashes. 'Your guess is as good as mine.'

I kept my mouth shut but inside my head I was railing at him. He'd done so well. Seven years of recovery down the toilet. I put two spoons of sugar in his coffee and handed it to him.

I noticed he was wearing the same crumpled suit as two days ago. 'Have you been home?' He lifted the coffee to his lips. His hands were shaking, and I felt a moment of sympathy. 'Are things okay with Lucy?'

'I think she's realised I'm not the sugar daddy she thought I was,' he said bitterly. 'She's not exactly being supportive about the business going up in smoke.'

Once again, I bit my lip. This was typical Michael, blaming someone else for what was going wrong in his life. Even though Lucy was nearly twenty years younger than Michael, she didn't seem like a gold-digger to me. I wondered how much his drinking had to do with their troubles. More than the business collapse, I bet.

'Can I have a shower?'

'Course.'

'I'll borrow some of Robin's clothes, then I suppose I'd better go on bended knee to the luminous Lucy.' He said it with a derision in his voice I felt sure she didn't deserve.

'When did you last go back to hers?' Michael had moved in with Lucy weeks after meeting her. He'd sold his flat and invested all the sale proceeds in his new venture. The venture that had now gone to pot.

'Three, maybe four days ago.'

'And you haven't been in touch since?'

He shook his head. 'Not since the night I came here. I was hoping I'd left my phone by the bed.'

'She must be going out of her mind!' I was back in last night's nightmare, trying desperately to call Rob while the screen played cartoons. Poor Lucy must be worried sick.

Michael's bottom lip jutted out in a childish way I recognised from living with Rob and Harry. 'If she was that worried, she'd have called here.'

I imagined how I'd feel if I didn't know where Rob was for days on end. 'Sorry, Michael, but it's not up to her to track you down,' I said. 'You should have let her know you're not dead in a gutter somewhere.' He was an irresponsible man-child. 'You've got to see this isn't fair on her?'

'I'm not having the time of my life, either,' he muttered, then, to my surprise, he started to cry.

In the decade I'd known Rob's dad, I'd never seen him

cry. I didn't know he was capable of it. I tentatively put my arm across his shoulders, unsure of whether it was the right thing to do. He seemed suddenly pathetic. Broken, somehow.

Eventually the weeping slowed to gasped breaths. Finally, he stood and tore off a piece of kitchen paper from the roll on the worktop. He blew his nose then turned to me, with an embarrassed smile. Tears glistened on his eyelashes making his blue eyes sparkle. There it was – the charisma he'd always relied on and that he'd passed down to Rob. If his stories were to be believed, it had got Michael into a lot of tricky situations. It had got him out of more.

I thought I was immune to Michael's charms, but there was something in those glistening eyes that made me want to help him. 'What happens now?' I said.

He sat, letting out a long sigh. 'Now I go back to AA meetings.'

'I think that's a good idea.'

He snorted a short laugh. 'You know, I used to think I was different to all those other helpless souls in AA. I'd leave one group because there was nobody like me there. I'd get messed up, then when I couldn't live with myself anymore, I'd go to a new meeting in a new place, thinking I'd meet people like me, you know, in the posher areas?'

He looked at me and I nodded, even though I had no idea what he meant.

'There'd be people who looked like they hadn't slept in days. Some of them smelled. Then there were the people you'd never think were alcoholics. Mums, you know, like middle-aged women with sensible shoes.' He blew his nose again. 'Anyway, I thought I was different to them. All of them. They were losers and I was a successful businessman. I was still functioning, making the wheels turn, you know?'

He rubbed a hand over his face, the stubble making a scratching sound against his palm. 'And you know what?' He looked at me with eyes like lasers. 'I couldn't have been more wrong. The old fellas that smelled of wee, the grandmas with slack faces, the smart young men in sharp suits . . . they were all like me. They were me. They were struggling with exactly the same demons, the relentless pull of the booze that won't leave your head until you pour it down your throat. They were looking for someone, anyone, to help them, or at least to say, I understand. I'm like you and I understand.' He buried his face in his hands. His shoulders shook and I felt, suddenly, like I understood every word he said.

An image of Lizzie from the support group, with her missing teeth, sprang into my mind. Blood rushed to my face as I realised I'd gone to that meeting thinking I was different to her and the other mums there. I'd left because I was scared of admitting my family might be like theirs. I felt dizzy at the realisation that I'd been stupid enough to walk away from the only help I was likely to get. It wasn't as though I could talk to Nicky or the other school mums about what we were going through. I couldn't even rely on my own husband for help. I needed to talk to people who would truly understand.

'Is there an AA meeting you could go to today?'

'Can I look at your phone? There'll be a list.'

We found one in a church hall half an hour's drive away. Michael went upstairs to shower and change and all the time he was getting ready, then during the drive to the meeting and as I waited in the car while he was inside, I thought about what a fool I'd been to walk out of that support group. The following week, I resolved to go again.

Chapter Sixteen

Jen

Mrs Daniels had sounded pleased when I called to apologise for swearing and marching out. I didn't mind apologising. I classed it as one of my strengths, although Bill had roared with laughter when I told him that. He was shit at apologising, but he promised he'd work on it.

'I think it would be useful for Cora to see our peripatetic school counsellor to start the screening process,' Mrs Daniels said over the phone. 'She's called Claire Dixon. Her background is child psychology and she's very good. Is it okay with you if I set up an appointment?'

I'd agreed and the three of us exchanged emails, arranging for Cora to have some screening. In one email, Claire sent through a leaflet for a support group she ran and, since I'd decided to keep an open mind and it was at a time I didn't have rehearsals scheduled, I thought I'd give it a go.

***

I was early and managed to nab a car parking space in front of the church. I followed the signs for the hall around the back and when I went inside, there was only one woman in the brightly lit room. She stopped setting out chairs in a circle when she saw me and walked briskly over.

'Hello. I'm Claire.' She shook my hand.

'Claire Dixon?'

She nodded, smiling. 'That's me.'

She reminded me of that psychologist woman in *Billions*, dressed smartly in tailored trousers and a fitted top. 'I'm Jen Glasson, you're due to meet my daughter, Cora, next week at Kirkfile Juniors.'

'Ah, yes. It's good to put a face to the email address.' She laughed.

I looked at the circle of chairs. 'What goes on here, then? What am I letting myself in for?'

'Nothing too scary, hopefully. We've got a few new mums.' She leaned in. 'It's always the mums.' The conspiratorial way she said it made me nod. It *was* always the mums. Carrying the burden of care for a family's wellbeing always seemed to come down to the mother. The load felt heavy today.

Despite that, it felt strange that I was doing this behind Bill's back. I didn't need to worry him, especially since I'd agreed with him that Mrs Daniels was talking rubbish at first. Now, I was less sure. I knew he wouldn't condone me coming today. But I was doing it for Cora, and that was what mattered. I would sort this out for her and present him with any results. Then he wouldn't be able to argue.

'And we don't have a speaker booked in today,' Claire continued, 'so I thought it would be good to get to know each other a bit.' She glanced up as a few other women entered the hall behind me. 'Don't feel obliged to speak if you're not comfortable with it. Lots of people prefer to listen. That's fine too.'

'Oh, don't worry about me on that front. I'm in the theatre, daaaaarling.' I gave her a pantomime wink. 'It's shutting me up that's the problem.'

'Excellent,' said Claire. 'I love the theatre,' she said. 'Are you an actor, or—' She waved at someone behind me, and I turned to see a woman gesturing her over to the other side of the room. 'Ah, sorry. Looks like we'll have to talk later. Get yourself a coffee.' She pointed at a trestle table with an urn and some cups. 'And I'll see you in a bit.'

I was relieved the chat was cut short. I was used to seeing disappointment on people's faces when they discovered I was only the director, as if that was a less impressive job than acting. I usually resisted the temptation to tell them everything, from the choice of play to how the actor said their lines was down to me. I just thought it loudly.

I took a coffee over to the circle of chairs and watched the women arrive. They were a jumbled group, most of them younger than me. A woman with a bobbled jumper seemed to know everyone by name. She greeted all of them as they came through the door. When she threw her head back and laughed, I saw that some of her top teeth were missing. I made a conscious note in my head of the way she constantly moved as she talked. She flung her arms around as though she was trying to expel some excess energy flowing through her. She'd make a great character. I wracked my brains to think of a play where there was a woman who might suit these mannerisms. I couldn't think of one. Perhaps I'd write one. She looked like she deserved a leading role.

'Hi,' said a quiet voice to my left.

I tore my eyes away from the lively woman and turned to the one who'd spoken. She'd sat down two chairs away, leaving a gap in the middle as though she thought I was contagious.

'Hello. You new too?' I decided she must be because she looked terrified. With one more glance around the room, I could see why someone with a less robust disposition than mine might be intimidated. The noise was growing as more women joined the circle. 'Mind if I . . .?' I gestured to the chair between us. She shook her head, making her golden chin-length hair float around her face like a halo.

'My first time too,' I said, sliding into the vacant chair.

'Sorry, I er . . . I have been once before,' she said.

'Right. Maybe you could show me the ropes?'

Her face seemed to twitch. 'I wasn't here long last time, sorry.'

'No worries. We can work it out together.' This place was full of characters. I would write this woman, with her pretty, perfectly symmetrical face and apology-Tourette's as a heroine who starts off terrified of her own shadow and ends up ruling the world. 'I'm Jen, good to meet you.'

'Elle,' she said. 'Nice to meet you too.'

Claire stood in front of a chair and gave the loudest whistle I've heard outside of a standing ovation. Elle seemed to jump out of her skin. I laughed at her reaction. She looked embarrassed, but then laughed too, which was a relief because she was sweet, and I felt strangely motherly towards her. Motherhood had made me weird. Before I had Cora I would never have felt protective of a grown woman. I'd have been more likely to dismiss her as lacking backbone. I was getting soft in my old age.

'Thank you all for coming today,' said Claire. 'Good to see so many familiar faces. We've got a few new people with us too, so I thought it would be a good idea to get to know each other as a group. Please don't feel any obligation to speak, it's important you do what feels comfortable. I'm going to start by introducing myself; I'm Claire Dixon, and I'm a psychologist with a special interest in neurodiversity. Most of you know me as a peripatetic school counsellor, which I've been doing since I had my own children. School hours and all that.' There was a murmuring of solidarity around the circle. 'I'm the first port of call if you or your child's teachers have any concerns.'

I glanced at the rapt faces. It was clear all these women rated this Claire.

'Lizzie's very kindly agreed to start us off. If you could tell us a bit about yourself and your family?' Claire said.

The woman with the missing teeth cleared her throat. Her expression was serious for the first time. 'I'm Lizzie Calder, and I have four kids with combined type ADHD, which is no surprise, because I'm a freaking nightmare!' She let out a roar and laughter bellowed from around the circle.

Lizzie ran her hand over her face, as if to flatten out the smile. 'Seriously, though. Finding out I had ADHD was a bloody godsend, because I could forgive myself, you know, for being a bit, you know, all over the place, like.'

A few of the women nodded.

'Could you give us an example of how the ADHD affects family life?' said Claire.

'For me or the kids?'

'Either? Both?'

Lizzie grimaced. 'We've got the lot between us, plus the shit that comes along with it. ODD, anxiety, dyslexia, impulse control issues.' She shifted in her chair. 'My eldest had an eating disorder, but that's calmed down a bit now. They're all completely hyper and I'm always up the school for something or other.' She held out her hand. 'Don't mean to scare anybody, you know. You new ones. It's different for everyone, like. I mean, I've got four kids and all of them have something different going on.'

'Thanks Lizzie. That's a really good point,' said Claire.

I was beginning to think maybe I was in the wrong group. None of that applied to Cora at all. I glanced at Claire and saw she was looking directly at me.

'Jen. You said you might be happy to speak?'

I nodded, although I felt my face redden.

'Would you be okay to tell us a bit about why you're here?'

Adrenaline flushed through me. Despite my job, I still had an attack of the jitters before addressing a group. Even when I was pulled on stage on the final night, my heart would pound, and my hands would grow slippery with sweat.

I breathed in through my nose. 'Okay, yes.' I screwed my face up then relaxed it. 'But to be honest, I'm not absolutely sure I am here for the same kind of thing as Lizzie. That doesn't sound like my daughter. I don't see how it can be the same condition.'

I felt Elle turn towards me.

Claire nodded, 'Lizzie was right when she said everyone is different. It's a complex, often misunderstood disorder, with various subtypes.'

'I did say that,' said Lizzie, nodding then guffawing.

Claire waited for the laughter to subside. 'Could you tell us something about what's going on with your daughter?'

'Okay, but don't hate me,' I said. 'My daughter is the most compliant child I've ever met. Her favourite word is "okay".'

'Can we hate you a little bit?' said a woman across the circle.

I nodded and pinched my thumb and forefinger together. 'A little bit. Especially because she's academically bright too, top of the class.' I paused. 'At least, she used to be.'

'What's changed?' asked Claire.

'I think going into juniors has unsettled her. She's getting in trouble for being disorganised and forgetful. Her teacher says she's always daydreaming.' I saw a few heads nod. 'And she's not sleeping well. She says she can't switch her thoughts off. And, my god, does that girl talk!'

'More when she's tired?' asked a woman with pink hair to my right.

'Yep. And she cries at everything. I mean everything. If she gets told off, if she bangs her knee, at films, if someone else falls over. I mean, I used to think she was just wonderfully empathetic, but now she's tired a lot of the time, it's like she's constantly on the verge of tears.'

I saw recognition on more faces. Perhaps I wasn't in the wrong place after all.

'Thanks, Jen.' Claire turned her attention to the rest of the room. 'I'm in no position to give a diagnosis, but to me, those traits could indicate what we used to call ADD, which is now ADHD, inattentive subtype. Anyone else recognise those traits in their children?'

About half the hands in the room went up, including Elle's. Her eyes were moist.

Another two women spoke about their experiences. By the end I was counting my lucky stars Cora seemed to come under the inattentive banner. Some people's households sounded like battlefields.

'That was intense,' I said to Elle, when it was time to leave.

'You were brave,' she said. 'I'd rather die than speak to a group of people I didn't know.'

I put my handbag over my shoulder, an uncomfortable feeling creeping over me. 'I feel like I've been disloyal, exposing Cora like that.' Now the adrenaline had left my system, I felt suddenly drained. 'It's not really fair, is it, telling all these people what might be wrong with her?'

'That's not how it came across,' Elle said. 'And I don't know . . . It's not easy, is it? Any of this? I mean, don't we deserve a bit of support? That's what this group's for, isn't it? So we've got people to talk to. I don't know about you, but I sometimes feel like I'm only alive to look after everyone else. There's no one looking out for me.' She looked down, as if she thought she'd said too much.

I thought of Bill and his refusal to accept Cora was anything but *normal*. 'You're absolutely right. Put your own oxygen mask on first?'

She smiled shyly and nodded.

I was used to doing everything on my own, but since all this business with Cora had started, I'd felt like there were shifting plates under my feet. The ground I walked on wasn't solid anymore. Elle was biting the inside of her mouth. She looked like a puppy recently parted from its mother, trembling in a box, unsure of its new home.

'Want to swap numbers?' I said, surprising myself. I wasn't the kind of person who initiated friendships and I wished I hadn't when I saw the shock on her face. It wasn't as if I was on the lookout for new friends. I didn't know what had come over me. 'Don't feel you have to—' I shrugged, feeling foolish.

She seemed to recover herself, scrabbling in her bag and pulling out her phone. 'Sorry, yes. That would be great.' She looked into my face and set her shoulders back. 'Fancy going for coffee now? Sorry, you probably don't have time, I—'

'I have time,' I said, relieved to feel like I was back in charge. It would be a kindness to help out this terrified-looking young woman. It wasn't like we were suddenly going to be best friends or anything. 'Let's get coffee.'

'Great,' she said and smiled her nervous smile before walking alongside me from the room.

Chapter Seventeen

Elle

We left our cars and walked along pavements made slippery by fallen leaves to a small parade of shops that I'd noticed when I first came to the group and had to park miles away. I scrabbled around in my brain for things to say to this stranger, but she seemed happy to chat about the weather. I looked up at the low-hanging clouds and agreed it looked like rain was on its way. Soon we found a coffee shop called Rooted halfway down the parade, with a rustic sign outside advertising a list of fancy coffees.

Inside it was all reclaimed wood and brushed steel. A chalked menu hung from a thick rope on the wall behind the counter. Rich-looking cakes and pastries sat under glass domes.

'What do you fancy?' said Jen when we stood at the counter. 'Artisanal macchiato oat milk double-shot with a side of sourdough starter?'

I was about to stutter a reply when she laughed and said, 'I'm having a flat white.'

'Flat white sounds good. Thanks.' I needed caffeine. Bad dreams and broken sleep seemed to be my norm these days. I was drained.

I sat at a table near the window and watched Jen order. She had clever brown eyes, a large nose and pronounced cheekbones. She wasn't traditionally pretty but something about her was very attractive. It was her confidence, I decided. She oozed it. Even the streaks of grey running through her thick dark hair said, *I'm ageing, get over it*, rather than, *I haven't had time to get to the hairdressers.*

'Thanks so much, I really appreciate it. My turn next time,' I said when she placed an enormous coffee in front of me and sat down. Then I felt presumptuous for suggesting she'd want to hang out again. My mind whirred. Should I apologise? I decided to plough on. 'How old is your daughter? Cora, did you say her name was?'

'Just gone seven.' She looked at me, a corner of her mouth twitching up. 'I know, I'm ancient to have a seven-year-old, aren't I? I started late.'

'Sorry.' I could have kicked myself for not controlling my expression. I must have looked surprised. 'No, I—'

'Don't worry, you didn't look as shocked as the people who think I'm her grandma.'

'They don't?'

'Oh, they do. And they're very vocal about it too.' She sipped her coffee. 'In fairness, forty is pretty old to have a baby.'

I did the maths. She must be forty-seven, fifteen years older than me. 'My son's seven too.'

'Ah, what's his name?'

'Harry.' Even saying his name made my insides melt.

'Has he had a diagnosis? Do you mind me asking? I'm new to all this. I don't know what the protocol is.'

I shook my head, then looked up as a big man wearing an apron approached the table with a plate.

'Thanks,' said Jen, grinning up at the man.

'Warm apple strudel,' he said, placing the pastry in the middle of the table.

'Great,' said Jen. 'Smells divine. Could we get two side plates and two forks please?' She turned to me. 'I thought we deserved a treat.'

'No probs,' said the man and wandered back to the counter.

'I bloody love apple strudel,' said Jen, leaning over and breathing in the cinnamon and pastry scent wafting up from the plate.

I tried to imagine myself ordering a random item to share with a stranger. I couldn't. I'd end up agonising over whether they would like a chocolate muffin or pineapple upside down cake. I'd either buy nothing or everything on the menu so I didn't get it wrong. It occurred to me that Jen might have asked whether I liked strudel, but I suppose I could order something for myself if I didn't. I wondered what it was like to be so comfortable in your own skin.

I took a bite. The apple filling was as hot as lava. I wafted my hand in front of my face in panic as it burned holes in my tongue.

'Spit it out,' said Jen, thrusting her napkin under my chin. 'Go on, spit.'

I did, then grabbed the napkin from her and folded it tightly, mortified I'd just spat into her hand. 'I'm so sorry.'

She laughed. 'Don't apologise. I know exactly what that feels like. If you hadn't spat it out, you'd be peeling dead skin from the roof of your mouth for days.'

I ran my scorched tongue around my mouth, painfully conscious of the moisture seeping through the napkin next to my plate. I was tempted to put it in my bag out of sight, but that would probably make me look even more strange.

'You were telling me about Harry,' she said, as though I hadn't made a monumental fool of myself. She opened up her pastry with her fork, watching the steam rise from the pale-yellow mush.

'Yeah, erm . . .' I wondered how much to disclose to this woman I'd only just met. But then, I'd deposited the contents of my mouth into her hand, so maybe the time for being coy had passed. 'I probably shouldn't say it about my own child, but he's a lovely little boy. Very sweet, very loving. He's incredibly well behaved.' Was I protesting too much? 'But there are three things I'm worried about, well, most worried about, anyway.'

'And they are?'

'Well, since he went up to junior school, he can't seem to stay on task. He's always forgetting things, so easily distracted. But the odd thing is, if he's interested in something, you can't tear him away, like literally, he'll forget to eat he's so focused.'

'I know somebody like that,' said Jen. 'What kind of things does he focus on?'

'It used to be planets.' I thought back to when we would lie on canvas loungers in the garden, staring up at the stars while he told me everything he knew about the solar system. Back then, we'd thought he was a genius. A part of me still did. 'Then it was dinosaurs and anything Jurassic.'

'He sounds like a fascinating little chap. I bet his teachers love him.'

'Not recently,' I said. 'They haven't . . . I mean . . . The problem is, he doesn't speak to anyone outside our house. He used to.' I thought of the most recent conversation with Mrs Wheeler where she'd told me Harry still wasn't speaking to anyone at school. 'He's always been reserved, but he never seemed to have a problem talking at infants. Now he doesn't speak to anyone he doesn't know really well.'

'He doesn't talk to anyone at school? Not even his friends?'

I poked at the strudel and decided to tell the painful truth about my lovely boy. 'That's the third thing. He doesn't really have friends. I used to think he was just shy. My husband thinks it's still that. He got on okay with other kids in nursery and infants, but if I'm honest, he was probably playing alongside them, not really with them, not what the teachers call *interacting*. His teacher described it as being "overlooked" by other kids.'

Jen's mouth turned down at the corners. 'Bless him. Must be a real worry for you?'

'I wish I knew what's going on in his head. Claire's been brilliant. We've been seeing her privately; it's costing a fortune.' I thought about the next transfer I'd have to make and winced. 'Last time I spoke to her she mentioned something about an anxiety condition she's researching, but that's not massively reassuring. I started to look up stuff on the internet, but it was all too scary.' I didn't add that the last time I'd done an internet search on children's mental health, I'd spent the following night wide awake, envisioning a horrifying future for Harry filled with zombifying medication and probing psychiatrists. I shrugged, feigning nonchalance. 'We all have our things, don't we?'

'Amen to that, sister. I've got the opposite problem; I literally cannot shut Cora up. If you shook our two kids up in a bag, you might end up with one normal one.' She slapped her hand over her mouth. 'God, sorry. I didn't mean your boy's not normal. That came out wrong.'

I curled my lip, hoping it looked comical, not insane. 'I think you might have a point.'

The man in the apron came towards us. 'Everything alright, ladies?'

'Good, thanks,' said Jen. 'This strudel's delicious. So good we won't even sue for the first-degree burns to her mouth.' She pointed at me.

'Hot, was it?' he said. 'That's the thing with fruit, you see. Gets hot.' He shook his head as though hot fruit was a grave matter. 'Anyway.' His face brightened, 'I just wanted to tell you lovely ladies about my new room downstairs.'

'Oh yeah?' Jen narrowed her eyes and pouted. 'Do we look like women who should know about what you do in your cellar?'

He laughed nervously. He looked at me and cocked his head at Jen, 'Feisty one, your friend, isn't she?'

Jen was twitching her lips suggestively, making me giggle.

The man addressed me again. 'You might be interested, anyway. I've converted the downstairs into a children's play area, you know, for when the mums want to have a coffee and that, but they want somewhere the children can play so they're not interrupted.'

'Oh.' I flushed because he was directing this at me, after Jen had already said people would never expect us to have children the same age. I flapped my hand back and forwards across the table. 'We both have seven-year-olds.'

He looked between us and did a head wobble, as though he was re-evaluating the situation. 'I've got stuff down there for them an' all. Games. Snakes and ladders, a massive Connect Four. Have a look before you go. See what you think.'

'We will, thanks,' I said.

'Another coffee?' He pointed at our empty cups.

Jen looked at her watch. 'Gah, I'd better get off. I've got to plan tomorrow's rehearsal.'

'Rehearsal?' Elle said.

'Yeah. I'm the artistic director at Kirkfile Theatre. We're putting on *Antony and Cleopatra* after pantomime season.' She tutted. 'You know that's one thing I hate about being a mum.' She paused. 'I probably shouldn't say I hate it, should I? But I don't like the fact we've been talking for forty minutes about our kids, and we haven't said anything about ourselves. It's like you become an empty vessel when you're a mother, just there to carry around the triumphs and failures of your child. I sometimes wish I could be Jen again, not just Cora's mum.'

I made myself busy tidying my fork and napkin onto my plate because I couldn't think of a suitable reply. Having Harry was the greatest achievement of my life and I had been happy with that. The only thing I yearned for was another baby. Admittedly, I would have liked to have retrained after Harry started school and I failed to get pregnant, especially if it meant I could ease the burden on Rob. But he was so against it and I suppose he was right that Harry needed me to be at home. I looked at the confident woman in the grey linen dress and biker boots and felt a prick of envy. She seemed to have it all worked out. I wondered what it was like to have a career like hers, to be something more than someone's mum, or wife: to be a person in your own right.

We followed the cafe owner's directions down the stairs at the back of the room to the cellar.

'Wow,' said Jen, casting her eyes over the ball pit in the far corner and the Jenga blocks on low tables. She pointed at the red and blue Connect Four which was waist-height at least. 'Cora would love it here.'

'Harry would too,' I said, with less conviction. Surely he would?

Jen turned to me. 'Whereabouts do you live?'

'Panthom. It's a village about half an hour away.'

'I'm about half an hour in the opposite direction.' She looked around the room again. 'Does Harry finish school at three?'

I nodded, not daring to hope she was going to suggest we all meet up.

'So, we could all get here for, say, three forty-five? I mean, if you fancied getting the kids together? They might be good for each other. It's worth giving it a try, see if Cora can bring Harry out of himself?'

It felt a bit like an act of charity, but I didn't care if it meant Harry might make a friend. I didn't let my excitement show in case it scared her off. 'We could do that.'

'I don't usually have rehearsals on Mondays and Tuesdays. Cora goes to after-school club most days, but I think she'd be delighted to come and play here instead.'

I bit my inside cheek. 'She wouldn't be that delighted if Harry doesn't speak to her.'

Jen laughed. 'I'd be surprised if she even noticed. Honestly. Bill and I have always said she'll be a perfect radio DJ when she's older because she's happy to talk to herself. She used to talk to Siri on my iPad when she was younger. It's not like she'd let Harry get a word in even if he wanted to.'

'Okay. Great, if you're sure?'

She turned and marched up the stairs. 'Let's give it a go. If it doesn't work, it doesn't work. Next Tuesday good for you?'

'Yes, next Tuesday's fine.' I was glad I was following behind because I couldn't keep the delighted grin off my face. Even if Harry didn't talk, I suspected he would play the games with Cora, especially if she was chattering away and taking the pressure off him.

And I so wanted to spend time with Jen. I might have only just met her, but somehow I felt in my core that I could trust her with my fears and with my precious boy.

Chapter Eighteen

Elle

I got home from picking Harry up from school to find Rob and Michael sitting at the kitchen table. I could smell smoke. I saw a small plate with grey ash and the stub of a cigarette squashed into it.

'Hello fella,' Michael said to Harry, offering his fist for him to bump.

Harry was hesitant and I wondered if Michael knew how much he'd shaken his trust last time he saw him. I watched Harry's eyes assess his grandad and I knew he was working out if he was safe. He looked up at me, as if asking for my confirmation. I smiled. He returned the bump then climbed onto Rob's lap.

Michael rose and kissed my cheek. 'How was your day?'

I narrowed my eyes. I knew Michael was grateful to me for taking him to the meeting, but this gentlemanly performance felt like just that, a performance.

'Good, thanks.' I picked up the plate and tipped the contents in the bin. 'Sorry, Michael, but I would really appreciate it if you could you go into the garden to smoke?' I made it sound like a question and smiled tightly, feeling like, somehow, I was the one overstepping the mark.

'Yes, sorry,' Michael slapped the back of his hand. 'Won't do it again.'

I looked at Rob, ignoring the inference that I was the grown-up telling off a child. 'You're home early. Not that I'm complaining.' I opened the fridge. 'You staying for dinner, Michael?' I hoped the answer was no because I wasn't sure the chicken I was planning to cook would spin out to four.

'If that's alright?'

Rob said, 'Dad called me at work.'

'You found your phone?' I asked Michael.

'Yeah, someone handed it in at the pub.' He patted his pocket.

'Anyway,' said Rob as if he was annoyed at a prepared speech being interrupted, 'Dad had something to run by me. That's why I'm home early.'

'Oh yeah?' I assessed the content of the fridge, trying to work out what I could add to the tray bake to plump it up. I turned back to them. 'Everything alright?'

Michael grimaced. 'That depends . . .' He rocked awkwardly with his hands in his pockets.

'What's going on?'

Michael shuffled his feet. 'Why don't you and me go upstairs,' he said to Harry. 'Let your mummy and daddy talk. You can teach me the names of those dinosaurs again. I've completely forgotten them all.'

Rob tipped his legs so Harry was standing on the tiles. 'Go on, son. Make sure he learns them properly this time.' Michael held his hand out for Harry and Harry took it.

I listened for their footsteps to reach the top of the stairs before fixing my eyes on Rob. 'What is going on?'

'Sit down.' He smiled and drew back the chair next to him.

I sat. He lay his hand over mine. My instinct was to pull my hand away, not because it didn't feel good – it did. Usually, I was desperate for Rob to touch me with affection, but I knew this wasn't as simple as that. He was buttering me up and, maybe some of Jen's confidence from the other day had rubbed off on me, because I wasn't in the mood to be manipulated. 'So?'

Rob took his hand back. 'Dad's in a bit of a situation.'

'Situation? Does this situation involve Lucy getting sick of his drinking and chucking him out?'

'It's a bit more complex than that.'

I'd never understood Rob's unerring loyalty to Michael. He wasn't blind to his erratic behaviour. He got annoyed with him in the same way I did, but he always forgave more quickly and forgot the bad times. Having a father who was only twenty years older than him must have blurred the parent-child dynamic. Michael probably seemed glamorous and enigmatic, with his endless excitement about some new venture that promised to make him a millionaire, and a parade of beautiful women on his arm.

And he was absent for much of the time when Rob was growing up, and we always want the people who don't want us, don't we?

'He needs somewhere to stay, just until he gets back on his feet.'

'You're not suggesting he moves in here?' He couldn't be serious. Not after the way Michael had behaved in front of Harry.

'Not moves in—'

'Please tell me you're joking? After the state he was in last time?'

'He's sober again now.'

I threw my arms in the air. 'How long for?'

Rob shook his head. 'I thought you were more charitable than this, Elle. Kinder.'

That stopped me in my tracks. 'What about Harry?'

'What about Harry? It would do him good to have someone else around. You're always complaining about him not speaking to anyone. He talks to Dad, doesn't he? They get on really well. Dad's a big kid, really. He loves playing and it would be good for Harry to have him here.'

I couldn't argue with that. Michael seemed to bring out Harry's playful side. But it wasn't the only point. 'I'm sorry, Rob, but it's not as if you're ever here yourself. Surely you can see it's a bit much to invite your dad to move in with us when you're only here one or two days a week? I'm really sorry, but I don't want to end up living with your dad instead of you.'

'He hasn't got anywhere else to go.'

I had an idea. It was a good one. 'What about the flat in London?'

'Eh?' His face creased up as though it was the most preposterous suggestion I'd ever made.

'The flat. Surely that's the best solution?'

'It's not big enough.' He sat back, crossing his arms across his chest. 'You know it's only one pokey bedroom.'

I only knew that because that's what he told me. Whenever I'd suggested Harry and I visited him at the flat in the school holidays, he'd say he was working late into the night so there was no point. He told me the flat was tiny and in a rough neighbourhood and he wouldn't feel safe having Harry and me there.

'Well, I think it's better than him moving in here, don't you, if you really think about it? I'm sorry but I don't feel comfortable about your dad being here all the time. It's not like he'll be going out to work.' I envisioned myself ending up cooking and cleaning for a man who wasn't my husband. 'It would be different if you were here more, but . . .'

Rob looked defeated. He tapped the table with his forefinger and sighed. 'What if I was?'

'What?'

'What if I was here, say, five nights a week? Would that make it viable?'

'But you said you couldn't—'

He leaned forwards, resting his forearms on the table. The was resignation in his voice. 'I'm not saying it would be easy. I'd have to do a hell of a lot of juggling.' He intertwined his fingers and we both watched his knuckles turn red then white. 'But if I have to make sacrifices to make sure you're happy and Dad has somewhere to live, then that's what I'll have to do.'

I opened my mouth to say I didn't want him to make sacrifices. But I closed it, because that wasn't true. I didn't want him to view spending more time with me and Harry as a sacrifice. I raised my chin. 'That could work.'

He lifted his arms from the table and gave a small, bitter laugh. 'Right,' he said, 'you win.'

He stood and headed towards the stairs, leaving me with the feeling that I'd ruined his life. If I'd won, the victory felt very hollow indeed.

Chapter Nineteen

Jen

My mouth went dry when I first poked about in the sore patch in my left breast and found, not a lump exactly, but certainly a mass of some kind. It felt like a ridge, but it could just be a rib. I went to the bathroom and stripped off my shirt and bra. Standing in front of the cabinet mirror I examined my boobs to see if there were any changes. My heart beat more quickly when I saw puckered skin. I turned and examined the other breast in the same place. The skin wasn't exactly smooth, but it didn't have the same orange peel look the other one did.

It's cellulite, I told myself, turning from one side to the other, hoping to see something different. I'd put a few pounds on recently. I put it down to the peri menopause. The HRT gel the doctor prescribed had worked miracles on my moods. I no longer woke up feeling like I was on fire in the middle of the night, and I was less tired and edgy, but it hadn't made it any easier to shift the weight creeping on around my middle. I lifted my breast and let it fall. The puckering was still there. I ran my finger across the sore area, then pushed it deeper into the flesh until I was sure I could feel something. Was it a lump? Re-clasping my bra and doing up the buttons on my oversized shirt, I couldn't be sure.

I listened to a tinny version of Vivaldi's 'Four Seasons' for forty torturous minutes before I got through to the GP's receptionist. 'Could I make an appointment? For as soon as possible, please.'

'I'll see what I've got,' said the disinterested voice on the other end of the line. 'I've got one on the twenty-ninth of November. Twelve o'clock?'

I looked at the calendar on my phone. That was nearly three weeks away. 'Have you got anything before that?'

'It's the first available, I'm afraid. Unless it's an emergency. Is it an emergency?'

I pressed at my chest, feeling the sore patch, but couldn't locate the ridged part through my clothes. Maybe I was overreacting, it was probably nothing. 'Not . . . Okay. The twenty-ninth at twelve.'

* * *

I woke at 3am and couldn't force my thoughts to behave. Most of the time I enjoyed sleeping on my own, but now I wished Bill was next to me in the big bed. I kept imagining a future where Cora had to watch me go through treatment that made me weak and my hair fall out in handfuls. I wanted a hug. I needed Bill to tell me everything was going to be alright.

First thing in the morning I called him, but he didn't pick up. I held the phone next to my ear, working out whether I should leave a message or not. I didn't usually because he could see my name in his list of missed calls, so would know

I wanted to speak to him. He had me in his contacts as Frank Walters, not Jen. It was a running joke about a band called Frank and Walters who we'd danced to on an early date. He'd called me Frank for a while, but it hadn't stuck the way Bill had for him. I couldn't imagine calling him anything but Bill now. Even Cora had been surprised when she found out it wasn't actually his first name.

I clicked off the call feeling unusually sorry for myself. I briefly wondered what it would be like to be the kind of person who had close female friends to confide in. I dismissed the thought. If I was only thinking about girly bonding when I needed to get something off my chest and Bill wasn't around, I would make a crappy friend.

'Good morning, I love you,' Cora said when I pushed open her bedroom door and turned on the light. I closed my eyes for a second, hating myself for ever thinking negative thoughts about this wonderful child.

'Good morning, I love you too.'

She jumped out of bed and did a pantomime stretch, long, skinny arms reaching for the ceiling. 'What day is it?'

'Wednesday.' It blew my mind that neither Cora nor Bill ever seemed to know what day of the week it was. It was like time didn't exist as a tangible thing for either of them, which was all very well until I had to be the one reminding them of everything on the calendar. The only thing Bill ever did regularly was call the care home at seven, and he needed his phone alarm to remind him to do that. 'Yesterday was Tuesday. That's how I work it out.'

'Monday, Tuesday, Wednesday, Thursday, Friday, Saturday, Sunday,' she trilled. 'See, I do know.'

'It's taken you long enough. Now do the months.'

'Mummy,' she said, 'I'm not at school yet.' The smile dropped from her face. 'I don't want to go to school.'

'What? You love school.' This wasn't strictly true. She used to love school when she was in infants. In fact, after her first half-term, she'd called me a meanie for not allowing her to go in during the school holidays. But recently, she'd been making up excuses so she could stay at home.

She sat on her bed. 'No, I don't. Mrs Daniels doesn't like me, and my friends think I'm annoying because I cry all the time.'

'You don't cry all the time.' I was so tired, I wanted to cry myself.

'They say I'm too cryish. And Kieran is always mean to me, so I have to cry.'

I sat next to her on the colourful duvet cover. 'What does he do?'

She twisted and untwisted her fingers. 'He's behind me in the line after break and lunch and he calls me a cry-baby and gets everyone else to join in until all the crying bubbles up inside me and I can't stop it coming out and then he's right and he laughs.'

Fury burned in my chest. The little shit. 'That's bullying. We have to tell your teacher.'

'No, Mummy. You can't. He picks on everyone, not just me.' The pleading in her voice was the same as when she'd begged us not to speak to Mrs Daniels before. I couldn't bear to hear about the things causing her pain and not do anything. I needed to fix it.

'Then it's even more important we tell. If we make him stop then everyone will be happier, won't they?' I put my arm around her and squeezed her in, wincing as her shoulder dug into the sore place in my breast.

She pulled herself away from me and stood, her fists tight by her sides. 'No. I don't want you to, and you have to listen to me because you always do what you think is right like what I think doesn't matter and that's not fair because you should listen to me because . . .' She seemed to run out of steam. Fat tears plopped onto the carpet.

'Okay, sweetheart.' I took one of her balled fists in my hand and unfurled the fingers. I ran my nail around her palm like I used to when we played round and round the garden like a teddy bear. She must've recognised the tickling feeling because her lips rose at the edges.

'You won't say anything, will you?'

'Not if you think you can handle it on your own.'

She nodded.

'And do you remember what to do if you feel like you're going to cry?'

'Breathe in through my nose and count to seven, then out through my mouth and think about my happy place.'

'And that is . . .'

'Lying on a Lilo in a swimming pool in the sunshine.'

I thought back to when we'd tried to manage Cora's heightened emotions before there was any talk of ADHD. We'd asked her to visualise a place where she knew she'd be happy, and Bill foolishly suggested the beach. Cora was horrified. Even when she was a baby, she refused to touch sand. She'd stay on the blanket and cry if any grains got onto her skin. She was terrified of the sea too. She said it was a dark, scary place with creatures waiting to nibble her toes. Typical of Bill not to remember that; he could only ever tear himself away from his beloved work for a few days at a time, even for family holidays. I put a spike in that thought, aware that when I was tired and out of sorts, I'd started to feel ripples of resentment towards Bill.

'Good. Now come on, let's get you ready for school.'

'But Mrs Daniels—'

I gritted my teeth. 'Mrs Daniels does like you. She told me herself.'

'She just wants to—'

'Enough,' I snapped. 'Be downstairs in five minutes for breakfast.' I left the room, steeling myself against the sound of sobbing from my daughter's bedroom.

Chapter Twenty

Jen

I arrived at the studio to find Mel, Femi and Ed picking up sweet wrappers and discarded plastic bottles from the floor.

'Youth theatre,' said Mel, waving an empty can of Red Bull at me. 'Messy little shits.'

'Right,' I said, flinging my bag on a chair. 'That's it. They've left the place like this once too often. I'm not having it.' I searched my bag for my phone. 'I'm going to ring Simon now and tell him to disband the company. They can't leave the studio in this state when we've got work to do. It's not acceptable.' I scrolled through my contacts for the group leader, Simon's, number.

'You can't shut down youth theatre because of a few crisp packets,' said Mel, frowning.

'Watch me.' I pressed the call icon and held it to my ear. Mel marched over and snatched the phone from my hand, pulling my hair with it. 'Ow. That hurt.'

'Stop acting like a fucking dictator, then.' Mel clicked off the call. The ghost of the dial tone stopped, leaving the room in silence.

They were all staring at me. I felt hot. 'I am not a dictator, I'm just sick of being taken for a mug.' I gestured to the remaining mess. 'Are you happy to do this every week?'

'No.' Mel slipped my phone back in my bag. 'But I think a strongly worded email would be better than blowing apart a group that's achieving a lot. Those kids work hard and some of them haven't got much positive stuff going on in their lives. They need this. I know you like to have your voice heard, Jen, but there are ways and means. Right? A bit of diplomacy wouldn't go amiss now and again.'

She was right. Of course she was. I threw my hands up. 'Oh, ignore me. I'm just tired. Sorry for overreacting.' I tried to smile. I looked over to where Femi and Ed stood close together. 'Thanks for coming in early and helping clear up. When the others get here, we'll run Act One.' I went to the kitchen to try to get my head in the game and make a strong cup of coffee.

Half an hour later the lighting was set and I sat front and centre of the performance area with my notebook on my lap, jumpy from two hits of caffeine. When Femi walked onto stage, I was mesmerised. I lay my pen on the paper and watched every detail of her expression, listened to the cadence of her voice as she looked up into Ed's eyes and said, 'If it be love indeed, tell me how much.'

He returned her gaze and the space between them seemed to thicken and throb with desire.

'There's beggary in the love that can be reckoned.' Ed's voice had exactly the right combination of lust and playfulness. I lost myself for a few blissful minutes as they parried, their voices rising and falling as they mirrored each other's actions exactly as I'd directed.

When Ed said, 'Fie, wrangling queen! Whom every thing becomes, to chide, to laugh, to weep,' I had a memory of being in bed with Bill soon after we met. He was on top of me, kissing my neck and I felt passive somehow, so I twisted away and climbed on top. I held his wrists above his head, pinning him to the mattress as I moved with him inside me. I chose our rhythm, I made sure my pleasure was the focus for both of us and afterwards, as we lay sticky and sated, Bill had told me I was the most challenging and captivating woman he had ever met.

A minute later, when Mel called scene, I realised I'd missed the last few lines. 'Bravo,' I said. 'You two have the best chemistry in this play since Dench and Hopkins.' I clapped my hands together. 'That's what I'm going to put on the posters.'

Everyone in the studio laughed and murmured agreement as Ed and Femi grinned and high fived each other.

'Take ten,' I said, taking my phone from my bag. I was certain there would be a missed call from Bill, or a message at least. The screen was blank. I clicked open the calls list and there was nothing new. It was hours since I'd rung him. Surely, he could work out that if I called it was because I wanted him to ring me back. It wasn't as though I was the kind of wife who needed to hear his voice every five minutes. Needy, I was not.

Even when he was away for days, we only usually spoke once in the evening, so what did he think a missed call meant? It wasn't as if I ever rang to ask him to pick up a bloody loaf of bread on the way home. Not that the fucker would remember it if I did. Had he any idea how low maintenance I was? I didn't think most wives would be as flexible as me about him coming and going according to what work he had on. I think most wives would like to be the priority once in a blue frigging moon.

I threw the phone back in my bag. I couldn't face the small talk with the others in the kitchen, so I locked myself in a toilet cubicle and pressed down on the area deep in my breast that felt like a bruise. It was still there. I dabbed at my tears of frustration with toilet roll, furious I was ruining my mascara. I cursed my weakness for needing Bill more than I ever thought I would. I cursed him for not being there.

* * *

He didn't call me until the usual time. I'd made dinner, stayed with Cora while she bathed and got ready for bed, all the time listening to the torrent of dreadful things that had happened in her day. I felt like an oversaturated sponge, full of all her cares and overflowing with my own.

'About time,' I said, answering after the first ring.

'Oh,' he sounded surprised. 'I called as soon as I could.'

I took the phone away from my ear and gave it a firm stare. *You're that important, are you, big man?* I put it back to my ear.

'You alright?' he asked.

'I'm fine.'

'You don't sound fine.'

I sighed, even though I knew he'd hear. 'I'm tired, that's all. I think you forget that I'm a working single mum most of the time. It's fucking exhausting.'

The line was quiet. We didn't often have a cross word, but the fact he wasn't there when I really wanted him to be, made me feel defensive.

'Sorry.'

I smiled despite myself. 'You're learning.'

He laughed. 'I've got a good teacher.' His voice had the lascivious tone that generally gave me goosebumps, but my body wasn't responding as usual today.

'When are you back?' I would put off telling him about the lump until I saw him face to face.

I heard him exhale. 'I've got more on than usual at the moment. It's all good, because the client wants a ton of work punting out, but the problem is, he wants it quick.'

That wasn't what I wanted to hear. 'I'm pretty knackered, so I could do with—'

He carried on as though he hadn't heard me, which made my blood boil, 'I'll have to let you know. I mean there's no point coming back just in time to go to bed and then leaving before Cora gets up, is there?'

Yes, I wanted to say, *yes there fucking is*. 'Suit yourself.'

He paused, as if he was considering his next move. 'Has something happened? Is Cora alright?'

A blockage swelled in my throat. What about me? Why didn't he ask if I was alright too? Wasn't that what husbands were supposed to do? I swallowed hard. 'Fine. Look, I've got to get off. Speak to you tomorrow. Love you.'

I ended the call without waiting for him to say he loved me back. It was the first time I'd ever felt like Bill was letting both Cora and me down. He hadn't listened to what I was saying. I knew I hadn't been explicit, but he should know me well enough to know I'm not feeling great. I was hot with anger at myself for wanting to cry. I wasn't that person. I didn't need a man to coddle me when I was feeling fragile, but I did need him to hear me out.

The phone call I'd had that afternoon from Claire Dixon had capped off what was already a shitty day. She'd met with Cora and thought it was well worth carrying on with the screening process for the inattentive subtype of ADHD. I knew it was coming. I'd read a few articles about it and so much of what I read I could recognise in Cora. Now I felt overwhelmed by that, on top of everything else.

I could have done with a bit of support from my husband, but, apparently, he was too busy for us.

Fuck him, I thought. I didn't need him. I would prove to myself I wasn't a fragile little woman with no voice. I would sort everything out on my own.

Chapter Twenty-One

Elle

I didn't tell Harry we were going to meet with Jen and Cora until I picked him up from school. I didn't want him worrying all day about meeting new people.

'Here we are,' I said, pulling the car up to the kerb in a side street near Rooted. 'Out you get.' I heard Harry unclick his seatbelt and took a deep breath before stepping from the car and opening his door. 'Would you like a hot chocolate when we get there? It's freezing, isn't it?'

Harry nodded. That wasn't a great sign. If he wasn't talking to me, then he was unlikely to speak to Jen or Cora. I wanted to beg him to talk to them. I so wanted to make this work.

He slipped his hand into mine as we walked along the pavement. The brown and red leaves had gone from the tarmac, replaced by a glittering frost. I gave his hand a squeeze, smiling down at him with a brightness I didn't feel. Rooted's windows were too steamed up to see whether Jen and Cora were already inside. When I pushed open the door the heat from the cafe after the cold outside made my nose run.

I was blowing my nose when I heard a child's voice say, 'Are you Harry?'

We both turned to see a tiny, dark-haired girl with vivid blue eyes staring at Harry with her head on one side.

'My mummy said I was going to play with somebody called Harry today and I think you look like a Harry. Are you a Harry?'

Jen appeared at the top of the stairs at the back of the cafe. 'Ah, there you are. Hello. Cora heard the bell above the door and scooted straight up here.' She looked down at Harry. 'She's been very excited to meet you, Harry. I have too.'

'Hello,' I said. Harry took my hand again and I had to quickly swap the tissue to the other hand then into my pocket. He looked up at me, lips pursed, and his concerned eyes seemed to beg me to speak for him. I crouched down so we were face to face. I gestured to the little girl in the gingham school dress and blue cardigan. 'That's Cora. She's here to play with you. Why don't you let her show you the games in the room down those stairs?' I pointed to where Jen had emerged from. 'And we'll come down with a hot chocolate in a minute.'

He gripped my hand more tightly. I could have wailed. I bit my inside cheek, trying to think of a bribe that might work. I knew this would happen. I should never have got my hopes up. 'Harry, pl—'

'Come on Harry.' Cora marched over to us and took hold of Harry's other hand. She looked him directly in the eye. 'You've got blue eyes like me and my daddy. That means you're in our gang.'

Harry looked at me questioningly, and I nodded. 'It's true.'

'Come on,' said Cora, pulling Harry's hand, and to my astonishment, he released his grip on me and followed her to the top of the stairs. Jen shifted out of the way. I waited for him to turn and run back, but to my surprise he followed Cora, who was still chattering away, without a backwards glance.

I stood, slack jawed, as Jen looked from me to the stairs and back again.

'I take it you weren't expecting that?' she said, grinning.

'I was not.' I was scared to move in case I broke the spell and Harry would reappear and hide himself behind me. 'Drinks are on me.'

We queued behind a pair of teenagers with rolled up school skirts and smudged eyeliner. When we got to the front, the man in the apron smiled. 'Good to see you two back again. I knew that room would be a hit with the mums.'

We were interrupted by the clatter of shoes rushing up the stairs. My heart stalled when I saw Cora run to her mum's side. 'Harry says please can he have marshmallows on his hot chocolate like me because he likes them like I do.' She turned her striking eyes to me. 'Is he allowed? I'm allowed, but not all the time but Mummy said today was a special day because I'm making a new friend, so I'm allowed marshmallows on mine. Is Harry allowed?'

'Please,' Jen said to Cora.

'Please,' Cora said to me.

'Harry said that?'

Cora's eyebrows knitted. 'I'm not lying. Kieran in my class lies because he said he didn't push Toby in the playground, but he did. But I don't tell lies like Kieran does.'

I gave my head a shake, 'Sorry, I didn't mean I didn't believe you. I just wondered if he said the words out loud or if he nodded when you asked him if he wanted marshmallows?'

'Oh,' she said. 'Not out loud.'

My heart sank.

'Out quiet.'

'Sorry?'

'He said it out quiet. He wasn't loud, he sort of whispered it.'

'He spoke to you?'

Cora looked up at Jen with her nose wrinkled as if to ask why I was asking such weird questions.

'Did he say actual words?' said Jen.

'How would I know what he'd said if he didn't say words?' She looked at me again. 'It sounded like English words, not like Valdemar in the other class who's from somewhere that's not in England and he talks in words I don't know. Harry says English words, doesn't he? I know he does,' she said, her brow still furrowed, 'because he knows marshmallows and that's a hard word.' She turned to Jen, 'Isn't it, Mummy?'

Jen ran her hand over Cora's hair, then kissed the top of her head. 'It is a hard word and you can tell Harry he can have marshmallows.'

'Thank you.' Cora skipped off down the stairs.

'Two hot chocolates with extra marshmallows, then?' asked the man behind the counter, who'd been following the exchange with interest.

'Sorry, I said Harry could have them without asking you. That's breaking the mum code, isn't it?' said Jen, grimacing.

'If he's talking, he can have as many marshmallows as he likes.' I still didn't believe it, but hope had ignited inside me, and it felt good. I turned to the man, 'Can I have a decaf flat white, please.' I'd switched to decaf in the hope I might get more than a few fitful hours' sleep. 'Jen?'

'Same, thanks.'

While the coffee machine squealed and hissed, I tried to manage my rising hope. It would be a miracle if Harry spoke to a girl he'd only just met. He hadn't spoken to anyone at school for weeks now.

The man put two hot chocolates with pink and white balls on the counter. The coffees seemed to take an age to make, and the marshmallows began to disappear into swirls of squirty cream. How could this be taking so long?

'Take those and I'll bring the coffees down in a minute,' said the man, as though he'd felt my impatience.

We thanked him and as I walked down the stairs, I had to remind myself to breathe. The two children were standing either side of the huge Connect Four. Cora was facing me, animated as she talked, holding a red circular counter in her hand. Harry had his back to me, so I couldn't tell if he was speaking.

He held up a blue counter and I watched as Cora's mouth closed and she stared intently at his face. I listened, willing my ears to pick up his voice, but I could only hear the spit and gurgle of the coffee machine upstairs.

Suddenly Cora burst out laughing, then Harry threw his head back and I heard it, his gorgeous little-boy laughter. I couldn't believe what was happening. Not only had Harry said something, however quietly, to make Cora laugh, he was laughing himself, loud enough for Jen and me to hear.

'She's a miracle worker,' I whispered to Jen, unable to keep the crack out of my voice. 'A bloody wonder.'

'Ah, she's alright,' said Jen, her face glowing with pride. 'I suppose she'll do.'

Chapter Twenty-Two

Jen

It was good to feel proud of Cora again. It was a welcome change after all the business with Mrs Daniels and the counsellor. When she was in infants, we'd got used to her being exceptional and I suppose hubris got the better of me. I got complacent, always leaving parents' evenings swollen with pride after hearing how well Cora was doing academically and socially. 'She has an excellent vocabulary,' her teacher would say. 'She's so thoughtful and considerate.'

I'd foolishly thought I must be acing this parenting lark, since my child was turning out so well. What magnificent genes Bill and I had passed on. What phenomenal values we were instilling in our perfect child.

Now that excellent vocabulary was spilling out unmanaged and her thoughtfulness had turned to sleepless nights of overthinking, I was less pleased with myself, and, to my shame, less pleased with her.

So it was gratifying to hear her being called a miracle worker by another mother, especially one I liked as much as this young woman sitting across from me now. I'd persuaded myself that I was trying to do a good deed, introducing the children to each other, but I must be getting soft, because I'd been really looking forward to seeing Elle again. The good deed seemed to be working out too because, watching Cora, I could see her quick eyes assessing the small boy, working out the best way to make him happy. She had a sixth sense for other people's feelings.

I hadn't told many people about what happened the day my uncle died because the looks of incredulity on the faces of those I did, stopped me. I was downstairs when I got the call telling me my mother's brother had died suddenly from a heart attack. Cora was playing in her bedroom upstairs. Seconds after I ended the call, Cora came down and wrapped her arms around me. 'Are you alright?' she asked. 'I could feel your sadness from upstairs.' It didn't matter if anyone else believed me. That's what happened.

Other than a brief laugh, I hadn't heard Harry's voice yet, but they did seem to be communicating. Elle's son had his back to us, but from what I'd seen of him, he was a beautiful-looking child with a round face and shaggy white-blonde hair. Cora looked like a different species with her sharp pixie chin and shiny dark brown hair, but somehow, they seemed to make a pair.

I was expecting some awkwardness while Cora danced around and cajoled Harry, eventually giving in and playing on her own. Instead, they appeared to be playing together like old friends.

I turned to see Elle looking at the two of them, misty-eyed. 'I can't believe it,' she said. 'I just can't believe it.'

'Best stop watching them,' I said. 'Or they'll get self-conscious and stop acting naturally.'

'Good point.' Elle turned to me, but her eyes kept flitting towards the children.

'Here we go,' said the man, appearing at the bottom of the stairs. 'Two decaf flat whites.'

'Thank you,' I said. 'Sorry, I don't know your name. I've been calling you Mr Rooted in my head.'

The man laughed. 'I quite like that, but it's Gary.'

'Gary. Thanks. I'm Jen and this is Elle.' I took a mug from him and Elle did the same.

'You two enjoying yourselves?' Gary yelled towards the children. Elle stiffened.

'Yes, thank you. We like this game, don't we, Harry?' said Cora. Harry didn't turn around, but he nodded and Elle's face relaxed.

'Righto,' said Gary. 'You know where I am if you want anything else.'

'A small Caribbean island and private jet for me,' I said. 'Just the one. I'm not greedy.'

Gary wrinkled his nose. 'Eh?'

'You did say *anything*.'

Gary looked at me and pointed, laughing nervously. 'You're a one,' he said. He shook his head and laughed.

'You scare him,' said Elle, smiling, when he disappeared back upstairs.

'I shouldn't be so mean,' I said. 'I see the look of surprise on men's faces when I backchat and sometimes feel sorry for them. They don't expect it, do they?'

'I think it's impressive.' Elle stirred her coffee. 'I don't think I've ever scared anyone in my life.'

There was a moment's silence where I enjoyed being thought of as impressive. I sipped the froth from the top of the coffee, swallowing the creamy foam. The moment stretched and I shifted uncomfortably in my seat. It was a long time since I'd needed to make small talk. It wasn't my forte. I put my cup down. 'How's your week been so far?' I asked, knowing it was a weak opener.

'Oh, fine. Nothing to report. Sorry, I lead a pretty dull life.' Elle's lips scrunched and moved to the side as she nibbled the inside of her cheek. 'How about you? Anything interesting happening?'

My mind immediately went to examining my left breast in the bathroom mirror. 'Work's going okay,' I said. 'The last rehearsal was very promising, actually.'

Elle seemed to perk up. 'Ah, yes, you work at the theatre, don't you? That sounds glamorous. What is it you do, day to day, I mean?'

That was something I could get my teeth into. I began by explaining the audition process, the muscles in my shoulders loosening as I spoke. When I was halfway through explaining how I block a scene, using masking tape on the floor as markers for the cast, Cora and Harry climbed onto the chairs next to us. Harry watched Cora as she used a spoon to fish the misshapen marshmallow pieces from the deflated cream. He picked up his spoon and did the same.

'This is nice,' said Cora, 'isn't it, Harry?'

Harry nodded.

'The cream is the best bit, isn't it, Harry?'

He nodded again.

'Have you had one with marshmallows before? I have, haven't I, Mummy?' She turned to me briefly for confirmation. I nodded and she carried on. 'But not all the time because I'm not allowed because it's got too much sugar and it makes me bounce around the room like this.' She jumped up from her chair and leapt from one leg to the other. 'Boing, boing, boing.'

'And because you won't eat anything nutritious,' I shouted

over her. I turned to Elle. 'Honestly, I have done everything you can think of to stop her being a fussy eater, but has any of it worked?'

Harry watched Cora and giggled.

'Come on Harry. Boing, boing.' Cora jumped and twisted.

Harry stood up and jumped about, copying Cora, laughing audibly. Elle started laughing too and soon Harry joined in with Cora's chant, 'Boing, boing.' They bounced back to the Connect Four.

Elle seemed to be holding her breath. Her eyes shone and my heart went out to her. I couldn't imagine being so thrilled to see my child bouncing and shouting. Cora did it all the damned time. I was more likely to be telling her to be quiet than holding my breath in the hope she might make a noise.

I realised there was so much about being Cora's mum I took for granted. Bill was always pointing out how unusual she was, exclaiming about the quirky phrases she made up, roaring with laughter when she mimicked voices she heard on the TV, agog when she made an astute observation. I should be more like him, more grateful.

Then I remembered how he'd let me down, and felt it pierce me again.

Elle must've seen a change in my expression. 'You okay?' she asked.

I don't know what it was that made me confide in her. Maybe the way she looked at her son with eyes that held nothing but love made me feel she was someone I could trust.

'I found a lump,' I said. 'In my breast. Well, not a lump exactly, I'm not even sure there's anything there, it could just be a rib I'm feeling, but it's sore and the skin is puckered, so . . .' I stopped and stared into my cup, unsure of why I'd blurted that out. I wasn't a blurter. I'd never overshared in my life. Why was I starting now?

'Oh, that must be worrying,' she said. 'Have you seen a doctor?'

'I made an appointment. It's in a couple of weeks.'

'Weeks?' I heard shock in her voice but couldn't force myself to raise my eyes to her face.

'I'm sure it's nothing . . .' In fact, when I'd felt for it that morning, I couldn't pinpoint where the pain or the ridged section was. I'd felt giddy with relief, but now, as I pressed my arm against my breast, it hurt again. Was it normal for something like that to come and go?

'Yeah,' she said. 'Best to make sure though, you know, have it confirmed. That's a long time to have that hanging over you.' She sipped her coffee. 'What did your husband say? Have you shown him?'

And that's when it slipped out, the whole sorry tale of him working away and me not feeling like I could rely on him for the first time in our entire relationship. Saying it out loud made it all real and I felt even more let down. Why didn't he call me back straight away? Was that a normal way for a husband to behave?

She took a deep breath. 'Are you sure you don't want to tell him? From what you've said, he sounds like . . . I mean, he might act differently if you tell him how you feel. And . . . you might need him.'

'That's the thing,' I said, embarrassed to hear my voice cracking. 'I don't want to need him. I can manage perfectly well on my own. I have, all my adult life.' I rubbed my forehead, where a headache was beginning to thump. 'I know I'm cutting my nose off to spite my face, I know I am. But I'm so pissed off with him, I don't want him involved. Pride before a fall and all that, but it's just how I feel right now.'

'I hear you. Honestly, I do. My husband works away a

lot too,' said Elle. 'I know what you mean about having to handle stuff on your own. Mine won't even accept there's anything to worry about with Harry.'

'Oh my god!' I jolted upright, 'Bill's the same about Cora.' I examined the face of the woman sitting opposite me, counting the ways we were living parallel lives. 'So, we both have kids who might have ADHD and anxiety stuff, our husbands both work away and refuse to believe there's anything wrong with their little darlings!'

'We're married to the same man!' Elle laughed.

'You can have him, I'm better off on my own,' I said, sarcastically.

'I sometimes think that,' said Elle. 'But Harry loves his dad. I grew up without a dad and it's not what I want for Harry.' She looked at me earnestly. 'Are you really not going to tell Bill about your lump?'

I shook my head. 'I'm a stubborn old bat and I'll probably regret it, but I want to prove to myself I can still handle shit on my own.'

'Okay, but . . .' She bit her cheek. 'Can I help? Maybe you could tell me what's going on, if you're worried and you want to talk, now I know anyway. I mean, you probably have loads of friends you can talk to.' She shrugged, 'But I'm here if you need one more.' She looked over at the children who were now stacking Jenga blocks on a low table. 'To be honest, I'm really hoping we can meet up again, so Harry can keep benefiting from Cora's magical powers.'

I looked at her hopeful face, glad she presumed I had a myriad of friends to turn to. In fact, after opening up to her, I was questioning why I'd always kept people at arm's length. Then I remembered Aaron professing his undying love, then promptly dumping me for the new love of his life. Everyone lets you down in the end. There's no point investing time and energy in people who will inevitably drop away when whatever brought you together is last week's chip paper. I'd let my guard down and trusted Bill completely, and where was he now?

'You're very kind, but I'll be fine. I'm sure it's nothing. Honestly.'

Her eyes flicked over my face and I'm sure I saw disappointment there. I bit my tongue. I didn't want to push her away entirely, I just didn't want to rely on anyone else.

'Okay, if you're sure.'

I painted on a smile. 'I'm probably making a fuss about nothing.' I hoped, with all my heart, that was the case.

Chapter Twenty-Three

Elle

Rob was sighing when he came into the kitchen on Wednesday. I tensed, waiting for bad news, but he lay his hand on my shoulder and looked into the pan at the sizzling bacon. I realised I did that a lot, anticipated his feelings before I could relax. I was always listening for signs of discontentment. I tried to imagine Rob listening out for me. It wouldn't happen. He didn't even hear me when I spoke.

'Smells good.' He lifted his hand, and I missed the warmth of it. 'You look after us, don't you?'

I smiled at him over my shoulder, the unexpected compliment boosting my mood. 'I do my best. I can't believe how much your dad eats,' I whispered over the spitting fat. 'I swear I'm buying twice as much as I do for the three of us.'

'You know what he's like,' said Rob. 'This happened last time he got sober; do you remember? He compensated for not drinking by eating crap.'

I cast my mind back to when I was pregnant with Harry.

We'd joked that Michael's body was coming out in sympathy because his stomach seemed to be growing at the same rate as mine.

'Yeah, but he didn't live with us then, did he?'

'I know. It won't be forever, I promise.'

I didn't know whether he meant the eating or the living with us. 'I think we should try to get him some help,' I whispered. 'To make sure he can keep up the recovery.'

'He's going to AA,' said Rob. 'He's doing fine. It was just a blip. He'll be on to the next thing before we know it.'

I remembered how quickly Michael's snacking turned to an obsession with the gym after he started to date a woman who was a health freak. He lost his belly more quickly than I did after I gave birth to Harry. Michael wasn't a man who did things by halves. That's another thing he'd passed on to his son.

Harry came into the kitchen holding a pad in the air. 'Draw-off?' he said to Rob. I smiled at my little family, feeling more optimistic than I had in a while. We'd met with Jen and Cora three times and Harry had talked to Cora on each occasion. He'd spoken in front of Jen every time we'd met too. Despite feeling hopeful, I hadn't mentioned any of it to Rob. I didn't want to tell him I'd gone behind his back by engaging with the counsellor and the support group. He must have noticed I was more relaxed though, despite Michael still hanging around.

'Choose your weapon,' said Rob, scrabbling in Harry's dinosaur pencil case for a coloured pencil.

I watched Rob and Harry choose their colours and set the timer on Rob's phone for two minutes. They started drawing, heads close to the paper, arms shielding their work. My mind wandered to Jen. Jen was keeping things to herself because she wanted to prove she was self-sufficient. I didn't get it. But then, was my secrecy cowardly? I didn't want to rock the boat, but did that make it any more justifiable?

I would tell Rob soon, I decided. It was so good having him home most of the time over the last few weeks. I'd even had a couple of nights' decent sleep. We hadn't had any time to ourselves since Michael always seemed to be in the room with us, but I was sure there was more colour in Harry's cheeks now he could rely on his daddy being around.

'Time's up!' shouted Harry when the alarm trilled. 'Mummy. You're the judge. Whose is best?'

'No chance,' I said, buttering one side of the bread for the sandwiches and squirting ketchup on the other. 'You can't ask me to choose between my two favourite boys.' I dropped bacon on the ketchup and squished the buttered slice on top. 'Michael, breakfast!' I shouted.

He ambled into the room, scratching his messy hair. He wore the same shirt as yesterday and the buttons were askew. 'Bacon. Perfect.'

When he took the plate from me, I breathed in to see if I could smell alcohol, but all I could smell was bacon. I assessed his bloodshot eyes. He didn't look great.

'Which is best, Dad?' said Rob. 'Harry's piddling little pterodactyl, or my fabulous albertosaurus?'

'Stop leading the judge,' I said, bringing the other plates to the table.

'Well, I've never heard of yours,' said Michael, taking a bite of his sandwich. Ketchup dropped onto his shirt. He looked down and rubbed it in with his thumb. 'You've made it up.'

'I have not!' said Rob. 'Tell him, Harry.'

Harry shook his head. He eyed Michael warily, as though he knew something was awry.

'Use your words. Go on, you know exactly what this is.'

Rob glared at Harry, and I wanted to lift him onto my lap and wrap him up.

Harry looked at me imploringly. I hesitated, willing him to speak. Instead, he waved his hand for me to come closer. 'It's a large theropod,' he whispered close to my ear, 'from Canada.'

Rob's face turned dark. 'Tell your grandad what it is.'

Harry looked down at his paper.

'He said it's a large theropod and it was found in Canada,' I said, with a challenge in my voice I hoped would make Rob drop it.

'You say it, Harry.' Rob's voice was stern.

'Eat up,' I said. 'Lots to do today.' Harry stared at me, his lips parted, as though he was about to say something, but no words came out of his mouth.

Rob was still eyeing Harry and I willed him not to make a fuss. How could he fail to see Harry was struggling and he wasn't helping? I could tell Michael was in a state, whatever Rob said. Harry could too, and it clearly unnerved him. Abruptly, Rob turned to me. 'Something's come up at work. I've got to go down for a couple of days.'

I tensed. He'd kept to his word for the last few weeks, and I'd been secretly hoping he'd got used to being around and we would slot into a new routine. 'Will you be back by Saturday?'

'I don't know yet. It depends on what needs doing.'

'Surely you won't have to work at the weekend. I thought—'

'Do you think I want to work at the weekend?' He dropped the crust of his sandwich on the plate. 'Don't you think I'd rather be here with my family?'

I remembered the planned meal out with Nicky and the others that evening. I had no idea why they'd booked to go out mid-week, but I was glad to be invited so I'd said yes. 'I'm going out. I need you to—'

'Dad will babysit, won't you Dad?' Rob said, taking his plate and leaving it on the surface above the dishwasher.

'No problem,' said Michael. 'We'll have a boys' night in, won't we, little man?' He ruffled Harry's hair. Harry carried on colouring in his pterodactyl.

I followed Rob when he went upstairs to our bedroom and closed the door behind us. 'I'm sorry, but I honestly can't understand why you would have to leave now. It's not fair on me or Harry.'

He started to roll his shirts. 'You still get to go out,' he said. 'I wish I was going to a fancy restaurant instead of driving to the office because some idiot's about to miss a deadline and I have to clear up their mess.'

'Sorry, but isn't it time they started to clean up their own mess? It's been eight years.'

He turned to me. 'Tell me about it! But they're freelancers, aren't they? They couldn't give a toss about delivering the project on time. It's my name on this. It's my reputation at stake.' He glanced at the new dress I'd bought for tonight hanging on the wardrobe door, the price label still attached. He walked over and held the label between his fingers. 'And there are perks to me being the boss, aren't there?'

'I told you I only got it because it was in the sale,' I said defensively, wishing I'd never spotted the geometric print dress in the window of the little boutique in town. 'And that's not fair, Rob. You're always telling me to treat myself, then you use it against me when I do.'

'I'm not using it against you. I just want a bit of support, that's all.' He must've been riled because he threw a shirt into the bag rather than rolling it. 'For god's sake, Elle. What do you think I'll be doing while you're drinking

Prosecco tonight? I'll be holed up in that scuzzy flat, listening to god knows who knocking on the drug dealer's door downstairs.'

'I'm not going tonight, if you're not here to look after Harry.'

'Seriously?' I started at the ferocity of his words. 'You're going to lay that on me? There's another adult in the house, but you're not going to go out because I've got to work? And you say you don't emotionally blackmail me?'

'I'm not . . .' I bit my cheek, trying to keep away the tears I felt rising. Surely he'd seen his dad rubbing ketchup into his shirt? When he was in his right mind, he prided himself on his looks. 'Did you see the state of your dad? I'm sure he's drinking again. I don't think he's in a fit state to look after Harry.'

Rob dropped onto the bed. He rubbed his hand over his face, letting out an exasperated sigh. 'Harry's not made of glass, you know? And Dad is doing his best. He's sober. Stop expecting the worst from him. Do you need him to have a level five diploma in childcare or something?'

'That's not . . .' I couldn't find the words. It was like Rob was intentionally misconstruing what I was trying to say.

'I'm wrong for going to work, Dad's not up to the job of caring for your precious boy. Jesus, we can't do anything right, can we?' He turned away from me and shook his head. 'Is it any surprise the kid won't speak up for himself when you treat him as if he's some kind of deity? Maybe it's time we looked at why he's turning out like he is.'

I felt like I'd been punched. 'Turning out like he is? What do you mean? He's being assessed for—'

'Look up Munchausen's by proxy,' Rob said.

'What?'

He stood and turned away from me to zip up his bag. 'It's when a parent makes out there's something wrong with the child, so they get some attention.'

'You can't be serious?' My head spun. Was I understanding him correctly? Surely he couldn't mean that?

'I used to think it was the school who wanted to tick their boxes, but now I'm not so sure.'

'For god's sake, Rob. You can't seriously think I'm capable of that?'

He strode towards the door. 'I'm not sure about anything anymore. Maybe it's not full-blown Munchausen's, but it's got out of hand. You're obsessed with something being wrong with that boy. All I know is nothing seems to satisfy you . . .' He shrugged and flung open the door.

I stood, feeling too heavy to move as I heard him yell goodbye to Harry and Michael from the hall. The front door slammed. I heard light footsteps running into the hallway and imagined Harry's face as he listened to the engine start and realised his daddy was driving away without even a kiss goodbye. He'd never done that before and I hated him for it.

But, if Rob was right, he was still a better parent than I was. He might be absent, but I was the one causing Harry actual harm.

Chapter Twenty-Four

Elle

I didn't want to go out that evening anymore. I tried on the black and white dress but instead of the confident, attractive woman I'd seen in the fitting room mirror, I felt exposed. The print was too bold, and the halter-neck left too much bare skin on my shoulders and back. I felt foolish for ever thinking I could get away with something like that. I changed into jeans and a black shirt.

I texted Nicky to say I'd be late, and they should order without me and put Harry to bed. Before I left, I tiptoed to his room and peeked through the gap in the door. His body was still, and I could hear his steady breath, so I carried on down the stairs. Michael was in the front room watching a documentary which kept cutting to sepia images of soldiers in trenches.

He looked up and smiled. His face seemed hazy, somehow. My stomach tightened. I glanced around the room looking for evidence he'd been drinking. 'I don't have to go tonight if you'd rather have some company.'

He picked up his phone. 'I've had orders from above. If you try to stay home, I'm supposed to shove you out of the door.'

'He said that?' I reached my hand out for his phone, but he lowered it and slipped it in his pocket.

'Words to that effect.'

I could imagine exactly what Rob had said in his attempt to ensure I didn't blame him for cancelling a night out. I was about to ask Michael if he thought I mollycoddled Harry, but, looking at him, lounging on my sofa as if he owned the place, I decided not to. Why did I need validation from a man who'd left his own child for his parents to bring up for swathes of his childhood?

Michael behaved more like an unpredictable best friend than a father. Harry didn't have a decent role model between us. No wonder he was floundering with us lot responsible for him.

'Off you go then,' said Michael. 'Enjoy yourself. Let your hair down for once.'

I narrowed my eyes. Was he calling me uptight? 'Call me if Harry needs me,' I said. 'I won't be late.'

He waved dismissively, his eyes on the television where a convoy of tanks were rolling past a group of dead-eyed people.

'Bye,' I said, pausing at the bottom of the stairs and listening for any sound before getting in my Mini and driving to town.

* * *

There was already an empty bottle on the table when I got to the Royal Indian. Nicky was waving a slender arm to get the attention of a waiter when she spotted me and waved more frantically. I weaved through the tables covered in white tablecloths, dipping out of the way of silver wine coolers balanced on stands and waiting staff holding steaming platters at shoulder height.

'So sorry I'm late,' I said, air-kissing everyone in turn.

'I'm beginning to think that's your thing,' said Sandy, 'Making everyone wait for you.'

'God, no,' I said, mortified she would think I had contrived a *thing*. Who did that? 'I'm just disorganised.'

'Where's the dress?' asked Nicky. 'I was telling this lot how gorgeous you look in it.'

Glancing around the table now, I could see I was woefully under-dressed. Lexie's bustier pushed up her orb-shaped breasts in a way that would have made my halter-neck look demure.

'Attack of the nerves,' I said, grimacing. 'Silly really.'

'I know a cure for that!' Sandy pointed to the waiter who'd arrived carrying a bottle aloft.

I hovered my hand over the glass in front of me. 'Not for me, thanks. I'm driving.'

'You are kidding,' said Nicky. 'Why did you bring the car?'

'I was already running late, so . . .' I let the sentence drift, watching the bubbles rise in Cecily's glass as the waiter poured. Suddenly I desperately wanted a drink. I could already feel the bubbles on my tongue and my muscles relaxing as the alcohol eased the tension from my body.

'Leave the car,' said Sandy. 'Pick it up in the morning.'

The waiter stood behind me, his head slightly cocked to the side.

'Oh, go on then,' I said. Hadn't Rob insisted I come out? Hadn't Michael instructed me to let my hair down?

An hour later, everything was hilarious. Lexie was telling a story about her ex-mother-in-law being conned out of thousands of pounds by a cat-fisher. Although I knew I should be appalled, the way she described her ex-husband's domineering mother falling in love with a 'millionaire' with momentary cash-flow problems, made us all roar with laughter.

'And it turned out she'd been having online kinky sex-chats with a nineteen-year-old!' said Lexie, wiping away tears of mirth.

'Did she get her money back?' I said, trying to capture my breath.

'No!' Lexie shrieked. 'After we found out the handsome man called Raif was actually a pimply boy called Kyle she was too embarrassed to go to the police.' She picked up her glass and swigged. 'She could afford to lose the money. Her dignity, though? She's never getting that back.'

Sandy ordered another bottle to go with our main courses. I'd only picked at my prawn puri starter. The bubbles from the Prosecco seemed to fill my stomach and when the chicken jalfrezi appeared in front of me, I barely touched it.

'Oh, I know what I meant to ask you,' said Nicky, filling all our glasses up again. 'Grace said something odd the other day about Harry.'

I swallowed; my tongue stuck to the top of my mouth. I dislodged it and tried to smile. 'Oh?'

'Yeah. She said he doesn't talk. Like, at all. Never says a word.'

She looked at me, her elbow resting on the table, her finger tracing the lip of the flute. Sweat dampened my armpits. 'They go through phases, kids, don't they?' I took a drink. The bubbles stalled at the back of my throat and stung my nose.

The other three were now leaning on their elbows, cupping their curious faces. 'He doesn't speak?' said Lexie. 'To anyone?'

'Well, obviously he speaks to me and Rob,' I said, 'And Rob's dad.'

'But, like, he won't speak to his friends?' Sandy's frozen face wrinkled as much as her Botox allowed, making sharp creases at the side of her nose. 'That's weird.'

There it was, the word I'd been waiting for. Suddenly, all the humour from before dissolved and I saw the evening for what it had been: a mean and judgemental series of stories, all mocking people who these women considered beneath them. All of their eyes were trained on me, the sockets seeming to grow bigger, and I imagined their incisors sharpening inside their mouths, ready to tear me and my little boy to pieces.

My phone rang, bringing me back to the room full of posers in expensive clothes, eating overpriced curry and drinking so much they forgot to hide their ugly insides.

I pulled my phone from my bag and saw Michael's face flash up on the screen. I turned away from the table and swiped to answer the call. I dug my finger in my other ear, trying to hear above the din of the restaurant.

And then, in chilling clarity, I heard my son wail.

Chapter Twenty-Five

Jen

By early afternoon, Act Two Scene Five was going well. Femi bared her teeth, snarling, as Cleopatra fell into a jealous rage when she discovered Antony had married Octavia in Rome. She'd just finished saying, 'Report the feature of Octavia; her years, her inclination, let him not leave out the colour of her hair,' when I noticed her come out of character and look over my head to the back of the room.

I followed her gaze through the shadows. When my eyes adjusted, I saw Bill leaning on the wall by the door. My heart leaped, then I remembered I was pissed off with him. He had hardly been around the last few weeks, and I missed him more than I expected. I still hadn't told him about my doctor's appointment, or the Tuesdays Cora and I now regularly spent with Elle and Harry. I was feeling guarded for the first time in our relationship and, if he wasn't around, he couldn't expect me to share everything with him, could he?

I turned to the stage. 'Good work, everyone. Take five.'

I made my feet slow to a saunter as I approached him.

'You managed to tear yourself away from your scintillating work then? I'm honoured.'

'Whoa, whoa, whoa, that's not the reception I was hoping for.' He reached his arms towards me but I held back.

'You should have told me you were coming.' I nodded towards the performance area. 'You're not the only one with important work to do, you know.'

Irritation passed across his face. 'I thought it would be a nice surprise. Sorry.' He paused. 'Have I done something to upset you?'

I glanced back at the bright circle. All the actors had gone to the kitchen. I had a decision to make: either belly-ache about the time he wasn't around or make the most of the time he was. I smelled his sandalwood scent, looked at his gorgeous face and the decision was out of my hands. I took a step towards him and lowered my voice, 'I just missed you, that's all.'

He grasped my elbows and pulled me towards him, 'How much?'

I checked behind me. The room was still empty. I held the back of his head as I kissed him deeply and our hips automatically met, pushing together. He was already hard. 'This much.' I rubbed my groin against his, enjoying his gasp of pleasure.

I heard the kitchen door open and pulled away. He bit his bottom lip and looked at me through his top lashes with a pained smile. 'When can you get home?' he said, his voice thick with desire.

'Leave it with me,' I said. 'I'll be as quick as I can.'

I joined the others in the kitchen. Ed was sitting in one of the armchairs with Femi perched on the arm. 'Was that your old man?' she said.

'Yes, that was Bill.'

'He's fit.' She put a lot of energy into the last word, and I laughed.

'Oi,' said Ed.

'You're gorgeous too,' she said, tweaking his chin.

I looked from one to the other. I'd presumed he was protesting on my behalf, but it appeared it was on his own.

'He is, as you so elegantly put it, fit. And I suspect he's not home for long, so is it okay if we wrap things up as soon as we can?'

'Far be it from us to interfere with your afternoon delight.' Femi winked. I wasn't sure how I felt about this level of familiarity, but the thought was lost when she stood and I was sure I saw Ed's hand glide across her bottom.

'I'll lock up, if you want to get off. The scene's blocked, we'll run it a couple of times and call it a day,' said Mel.

I hesitated. Was I being unprofessional again? 'Actually, don't worry –'

'Go on,' she said. 'It's fine.'

'Okay, thanks,' I said, grabbing my coat and bag and making for the door before I could think any more about how I'd feel if Mel did the same.

* * *

Bill and I didn't speak when I got home. We went straight to our bedroom and tore off our clothes. He smelled right, he tasted right and when he was inside me, I was full, sated, like his body was meant to fit exactly inside mine.

'I needed that,' I said, lying back on the pillow after we both came.

'I'd never have known,' he said, and I batted him limply on the arm.

'Would you rather I was a prim and ladylike wife, all

perfectly put together on the outside, but uptight in the bedroom?'

He was quiet. I raised myself on my elbow to look at him but managed to poke the sore patch in my breast. I winced.

His head turned. 'You alright?'

'Yeah,' I said. I didn't want to ruin the moment. It was rare to have the house to ourselves and we didn't have to pick Cora up for another hour. I'd tell him about the doctor's appointment tomorrow. I opened the top drawer of my bedside cabinet and took out the tiny vibrator I kept in there. 'I think I could go again. You?'

* * *

When the front door opened at ten past five, I listened for Cora's incessant chatter, but all was quiet. I went through to the hall to find Bill helping Cora take off her coat. Her eyes were red rimmed. When she saw me, she ran over and buried her head in my stomach.

'Hey, hey, what's going on?' I stroked her hair, looking at Bill for an explanation.

'There was an incident at school,' he said. 'Mrs Daniels called me in for a chat when I picked Cora up.'

I felt Cora's head shift and looked down at her tearful upturned face. 'I was bad, Mummy. I did a horrible thing.' She continued through gasping sobs, 'and I'm not even sorry, not really, because I didn't mean to do it, only I did and then I wasn't really sad that I did do it, so I'm a terrible person and everybody will hate me.'

'Slow down, slow down, 'I said. 'What happened?'

Bill picked Cora up and carried her through to the front room. 'Nobody hates you.'

'What happened?' I stood in front of the sofa, exasperated.

'Cora hit Kieran on the hand with a stone.'

I couldn't grasp what he was saying. Cora cried when I squashed a wasp, how on earth had she gone from that to actual bodily harm? 'Tell me more.'

Over Cora's sobs, Bill said, 'They were in line, waiting to go inside after lunchtime play and Kieran was doing his usual trick of trying to make her cry. Apparently, she hit him with a stone and broke the skin on the back of his hand.'

'Wow.'

'I know.'

I made sure Cora's head was still buried in Bill's shoulder when I pumped my fist. He opened his eyes wide and gave an almost imperceptible nod.

'And what did Mrs Daniels say?' I hoped she'd acknowledge Cora had been provoked.

'She had to talk to us because, well . . . because Kieran was bleeding.'

Cora let out a new wail.

Bill stroked her head. 'And, obviously, Kieran's parents aren't thrilled.'

'They shouldn't have raised such a little shit then, should they?' Cora glanced around, her sobs quietening. I winked at her. 'I wouldn't necessarily say that to Mrs Daniels, though.'

Bill grimaced. 'That's kind of what I did say to Mrs Daniels.'

'Oh.' I wanted to high-five him, but that might be a step too far. 'What did she say?'

'Obviously she couldn't openly agree, but I got the impression she wanted to.'

'I'm a very bad girl,' said Cora. 'I don't even remember picking up the stone.'

'You were provoked,' I said. 'You hit a bully. That's not the same as hitting someone else.'

Bill frowned at me. 'You shouldn't hit anyone. But we do understand why you lashed out at Kieran. Mrs Daniels understands too.'

'Do Kieran's mummy and daddy understand?' Cora asked, eyes wide and hopeful.

'Well, probably not,' said Bill. Fresh tears dripped from her eyes. 'We have to imagine they love Kieran as much as we love you.'

'God knows why,' I said, ignoring Bill's chastising look.

'And you must never, ever hit anyone ever again. Do you understand?'

Cora nodded. Her tears splashed from her chin onto the pale hairs on Bill's forearm and I didn't think I could love either of them more.

* * *

It took hours to get Cora to close her eyes. I sat with her, stroking her hair back from her clammy forehead, but every time I thought she'd calmed down, her ribs would judder under my hand again and new tears would wet her pillow. By the time she'd dropped off, and I'd climbed into bed with Bill, I was ready for the sleep of the dead. I was in the fantastical state between wakefulness and sleep when I heard a ringing tone I didn't recognise somewhere in the room. I rolled over, hoping it was in my dream. The noise stopped, then started again seconds later.

I prised my eyes open and looked for our phones. Both mine and Bill's were plugged into chargers on our bedside tables, so the noise didn't make any sense. I shook his arm. 'What's that noise?'

The trilling stopped.

'What?' he said, gruffly, turning onto his back.

'There was a—' The sound started again.

'Shit,' Bill said, leaping from the bed.

'What is it?'

He grabbed the jacket he'd thrown off yesterday when we came home from the studio and rifled through the inside pockets. 'My work phone.'

I sat up. 'Since when have you had a work phone?'

'Hello,' he said into the phone.

'Bill?' He ignored me. 'It's nearly midnight. Who the hell is calling a work phone in the middle of the fucking night?'

He held his hand out, but I wasn't going to be told to shut up in my own bedroom.

'What's going on?'

He held the phone tightly to his chest. 'It's my dad. He's had a fall. Can you give me a minute to talk to the carer, please?'

He unhooked his bathrobe and left the room with the phone still pinned to his chest. I turned on my bedside lamp. That didn't make any sense. Why would the carer call his work phone rather than the phone that was plugged in by the bed?

A minute later he came back into the room. 'I've got to go.'

'What?'

'My dad's in a state after his fall and his carer can't cope with him on her own. It's a night shift and they're short-staffed.'

'I don't understand.' I looked at the device next to the bed.

He must've seen me shift towards it because he lunged for it and quickly glanced at the screen. 'Five missed calls. It was on silent.'

'Oh.' I was sure I'd caught a glimpse of a clear screen.

'That's why they must've rung the work phone.'

'Why haven't I got the number of the work phone? I didn't even know you had one.'

His lip curled in an expression I'd never seen him use before. 'It's for work.'

I didn't like the look on his face. 'Not a burner, then?' I set my jaw and tipped my head to the side.

He blinked and shook his head as though my question didn't merit a reply.

'I drew a picture for Cora to cheer her up. It's in the kitchen. Give it to her before school, will you?'

'Where are you going? Surely you're not going up to Scotland now?' I watched him get dressed, the huge shadow on the wall behind him mirroring his movements.

'What do you suggest I do? He's my dad.'

'But the carers . . . Surely they'll take him to hospital? Wouldn't it be better to drive up after you've had some sleep?'

He threw his arms out to the side, the dark giant behind him doing the same. 'I'm trying my best here, Jen. I know you want me to be here, and Cora needs me.' He let his arms drop. 'Work never lets up and my dad needs me too. It's like everybody wants more of me and I can't ever give enough. I'm being stretched too thin. Sometimes I think I'm going to break.'

I'd never heard him say anything like that before. I thought about how much more I'd needed him recently, and all the issues with Cora and now his dad. It must be a burden, having to look after everyone else. I climbed from the bed and wrapped him up in my arms. 'Sorry, of course you've got to go to your dad. Of course you have. Don't worry about me and Cora. We're made of stern stuff. I think Cora's proved that being violent as heck.'

'Violent as heck?' He laughed into my hair.

He lifted his head and looked at me through the thin light. 'You're amazing. If I had the choice, I'd spend every minute with you. You know that, don't you?'

I hugged him tightly, breathing in the scent of sweat and coconut shampoo, storing them away because I had the uneasy feeling I needed to remember how this moment felt: the sight of his blue eyes, full of regret at having to leave, the feel of his thick hair when I ran my fingers through it. The gentle touch of his lips on mine as he dropped the second phone in his pocket and kissed me goodbye.

Chapter Twenty-Six

Elle

The bottom of Rooted's window was covered in patchy fake snow and a laminated snowman waved at us from the door.

'Look Harry, he's saying hello,' I said and waved my gloved hand at the white figure in a bobble hat.

'Is Santa real?' said Harry, as we stepped inside. He stared at the chalked outline of Father Christmas on the board behind Gary's counter.

'That's a funny question,' I said, sweating under my puffer jacket. 'Have you got the picture Daddy drew of you on the back of Santa's sleigh to show Cora?' I hoped my deflection would be enough to distract him.

Harry patted his pocket. 'Yes. I think she'll like it because it's good, isn't it?' He looked up at me with Rob's eyes and I had to look away. Rob had been quiet since I made him rush home after Michael fell down the stairs. He didn't seem able to even look at me. I'd tried to play happy families, especially when we put up the Christmas tree, but Rob only seemed half with us. The connection we used to have was severed and I felt like he was floating away from me. Even thinking about Rob made my tummy churn. The combination of worrying about Harry, Michael's drinking and the state of my marriage made my brain fizz. I hoped an hour with Jen might help me feel calmer.

'I'm sure she will,' I said. I smiled at Gary. 'Hello. Love the decorations.'

'If you can't go mad at Christmas, when can you?' he said, grinning. 'And Easter, and Halloween and, well, whenever, really? Celebrate everything, that's what I say.'

'I think you've got the right idea,' I said, trying not to imagine Christmas dinner, Michael drunk at one end of the table, Rob, glowering, at the other. My cheeks felt tight with the effort of smiling. 'Are Jen and Cora here yet?'

'Not yet. Shall I bring your usual down?'

'Please.' I tapped my card on the reader and followed Harry downstairs. There was a tree in the far corner, its artificial limbs woven with red tinsel.

'It's like a grotto, this place.'

I turned when I heard Jen's voice. She looked impossibly stylish in a red beret and long black coat which nipped in at the waist and swished around her ankles. 'He loves a bit of tinsel, our Gary, doesn't he?' she said, trotting down the stairs, followed by Cora. When she got to me she gave me a warm hug, wrapping her arms right around me and squeezing. 'It's good to see you,' she said. I realised that simple affection and connection was precisely what I'd been lacking. I could still feel her warmth minutes later.

'I love Christmas, but Mummy says it isn't really Christmas yet, even though it's been December for a week, but I think the whole of December is Christmas because that's more fun, isn't it?' said Cora. 'I like the decorations and I like presents, but I don't like Brussels sprouts. Do you like Brussels sprouts, Harry?'

She marched over to him, as though she knew he wouldn't talk to her across the room. I watched as she sat close to him, and his lips started to move. They were soon chatting together, stacking Jenga blocks under the tree.

'How was your appointment?' I asked Jen, after we'd sat and taken off our coats and gloves.

'Oh, you know,' she said. 'Nothing definitive. The doctor had a good poke and prod but couldn't give me any answers. I knew she wouldn't really, but it would have been nice to have been told it wasn't worth worrying over.' She raised one eyebrow. 'It's the first time my tits have had this much attention in years, and it was from a woman who looked disturbingly like Gerard Depardieu. Really quite unnerving.'

Trust Jen to make me smile, even now. 'They're sending you for tests, then?'

She sighed, removed her beret and combed her fingers through her hair. 'Yeah. First a mammogram and ultrasound and then a biopsy if I need it.'

'Urgh. Sorry you've got to go through all that.' I really was sorry. It sometimes felt like Jen was the only person I could be truly myself with. I didn't tiptoe around her, wondering if I was saying the wrong thing like I did with Rob and Nicky and the other mums. Jen seemed to accept me just as I was. 'What did Bill say?'

Jen scrunched her face. 'Hmm. Didn't get chance to tell him.'

'He hasn't been home?' We had so much in common it was uncanny.

'He was, briefly, but his dad had a fall. He's in a care home in Scotland, so Bill had to rush off in the middle of the bloody night.'

'God! I had a nightmare with Rob's dad last week. What is it with middle-aged men and their fathers?'

'What happened?' said Jen, wrapping her hands around her coffee.

'Sorry, I didn't mean to switch the conversation to me.'

She flapped her hand dismissively. 'I've finished talking about me. Haven't told Bill. Gerard Depardieu felt me up. Going for tests. That's it. Tell me about Rob's dad. I could do with the distraction.'

I glanced over at the children. Harry was pulling an oblong block gingerly from a tower. His tongue stuck out of the side of his mouth like a caricature of a child concentrating. I lowered my voice. 'Rob's dad, Michael, is living with us at the moment.'

'Ooof. You're more tolerant than I am,' said Jen. 'I haven't even met Bill's dad. He had dementia before we knew each other, and Bill says he finds new people destabilising, poor sod. Funnily enough, he's called Mike.' She leaned in. 'I find it hard enough living with Bill half the time. I think I'd struggle to have anyone else in the house.'

'Yeah.' I paused, wondering whether to disclose the whole sorry mess. I took a breath. 'He's an alcoholic.'

'Shit.' Jen looked across at the kids. 'Not ideal when you've got a little one in the house, or at all, I imagine.'

'Exactly,' I said. 'But we thought he was doing well; he's been going to meetings and everything. Anyway, Rob persuaded me to go out last week and leave Michael to babysit.'

Jen hid her eyes with her hands. 'Oh no, don't tell me . . .'

I nodded. 'Yep. Poor Harry was woken up by his grandad falling down the stairs pissed.'

'Shit, shit, shit,' said Jen, peeking out from her hands. 'What happened then?'

'Harry found Michael's phone in his pocket, looked me up in the contact list and called me.'

'Legend!' said Jen, dropping her fingers onto the table and opening her mouth wide. 'He's such a star.' She looked over at Harry fondly. 'I don't think most kids his age would be bright enough to do that. I'm proud of the little man, so I can't imagine how you feel!'

'I know!' It felt good to have somebody appreciate how well my little boy had responded. Not that I'd told anyone else, but neither Michael nor Rob had paid much attention to how mature Harry had been. 'Michael had come round by the time I got a cab back and when Rob got home a couple of hours later, he seemed more pissed off with me for calling him than he did about his dad getting hammered and falling down the stairs when he was meant to be looking after our son.'

'Men can be dicks,' said Jen, shaking her head. 'How's grandad now?'

'He's doing a good job of acting contrite, but I'm not convinced. He's lost his business, his girlfriend and his home. He doesn't have a good enough reason not to drink, from what I can see. It's not that I'm not sympathetic . . . I mean, I know addiction isn't a choice, but I've got to put Harry first.'

'You have. What are you going to do?'

'I'm just waiting to get Christmas out of the way and then I'm putting my foot down. Rob needs to help him get straight. It's like he's in denial, just hoping Michael will suddenly get better. He seems to think I'm overreacting, but the man needs help and Rob can't expect me to let him stay indefinitely, not the way things are.'

'Has he managed to stop before?'

'Yeah. He stopped when I had Harry, but . . .'

'Perhaps you need to have another baby.'

I looked down at my hands and heard Jen take in a sharp breath.

'Sorry,' she said. 'That wasn't meant to be . . . I mean, did I hit a nerve?'

'Sorry, no, it's just that . . .' I glanced up and saw her concerned face. 'We've been trying for years. Nothing's happened. It took a year with Harry, but I thought, since we'd managed it once . . .'

'Tell me to sod off if you'd rather not say, but have you had tests? It could be something fixable.'

'Rob has. He went to a clinic in London and apparently everything's alright with him.'

'And you?'

'Rob says we have to let nature take its course. It's not like we've had much opportunity to, you know . . .' I felt heat in my cheeks. 'Because he's been away so much, and he doesn't seem like my greatest fan at the moment.'

Jen blew out air. 'His dad is staying with you. He works away while you keep everything going and he's pissed off with you? He's taking fucking liberties, if you don't mind me saying. If that was Bill, I'd be having a quiet word, possibly with an added knee to the groin.'

The heat spread across my whole face. It was alright for Jen. She clearly had a husband who listened when she talked, who saw her as an equal. She was the kind of woman who insisted on being heard. How would she understand what it was like to have been so blinded by admiration you didn't see how little you counted until the lines in your relationship had already been hacked into stone?

I looked over at the children to remind myself of why I stayed in a relationship where I was increasingly regarded as staff. Harry was smiling at something Cora had said. I watched as I tried to think of a response to Jen that didn't make me sound like the loser I was. Harry reached into his pocket and pulled out Rob's drawing. Cora walked around to take a better look so they both had their backs to us.

I sat up straight as Cora snatched the paper from Harry's fingers. Harry grabbed for it, but she shifted away. Harry lunged towards Cora, his hand reaching for the drawing, and they were shouting something at each other.

Jen jumped to her feet and rushed towards them, yelling, 'Cora, what on earth has got into you? Give that back to Harry.'

'But it's mine!' she yelled.

Harry grabbed for the paper again. Cora pushed him away and he toppled, face first, into the Christmas tree.

Chapter Twenty-Seven

Jen

I grabbed Cora by the wrist and pulled her back. She tried to jerk away. 'Stay here,' I snarled, as Elle lifted Harry from the tangled fronds of the fallen Christmas tree. He held his hand over his eyes. Elle pulled his fingers away. The colour drained from her face when she saw blood.

Cora screamed. 'What's wrong with Harry's eye, Mummy?' She tried to run towards him, but I gripped her wrist more tightly.

'It's okay, baby, it's alright,' said Elle. She seemed to sway, then right herself.

'Is it his eye, or . . .?' I tried to keep the panic from my voice.

She peered into his face. 'I don't know, I can't tell. Blink, Harry, can you?' She looked from Harry to me. 'I can't tell if it's his eye or the skin because of the blood. Should we call an ambulance?'

Harry started to whimper.

'It will be quicker if I drive us to A&E,' I said, ignoring Cora's increasingly loud sobbing.

'I'm sorry, I'm sorry, Harry. I'm sorry, Mummy,' she said. 'I didn't mean—'

'Get your coat on,' I snapped, unable to believe she'd hurt another child. She scurried to where her and Harry's coats were piled on a chair.

I joined Elle next to Harry, whose quiet moaning went directly to my heart. 'You're a very brave boy, Harry,' I said, resisting the urge to pull him into a hug. I presumed he must be in shock. Blood seeped from the corner of his left eye and down the side of his nose. My mind spun to all the terrible scenarios that could follow. What if he had to have an operation? What if he went blind? Elle's white face suggested she was thinking the same.

Cora handed Harry's coat to me. 'Come on Harry, let's pop this around your shoulders.' I shrouded him in his coat.

Elle blinked and tried to smile at Harry. I didn't know how she was keeping those tears at bay. I was struggling. 'What a brave boy you're being,' she said. 'Can you see okay, sweetheart?'

'I don't know,' Harry whispered.

My heart shrivelled in my chest.

'I'm sorry, Harry, I didn't mean to,' said Cora and it was the closest I'd ever come to slapping her.

I pulled my coat on and shoved my hat in my bag. Gary came rushing down the stairs. He looked at the collapsed tree and then at Harry's bleeding eye. 'What happened?'

'Harry fell into the tree.' I looked at Elle to see if she was going to expose Cora's part in it but she was examining Harry's eye with a stricken look on her face. 'We're going to take him to the hospital.'

Gary's forehead wrinkled. 'I should have known not to put a tree in a play area. I'm sorry, this is—'

'Could you grab Elle's things?' I said. 'Let's get everyone into my car and we can get Harry's eye looked at as quickly as possible.'

Gary rushed to the table and hauled everything into his arms then followed our sorry procession to the car. Heads turned as we left the cafe with Cora sobbing and Elle with her arms protectively around Harry's shoulder.

'It will be alright, sweetheart,' she repeated over and over, and I hoped, for all our sakes, that she was right.

* * *

Only Elle spoke on the way to the hospital, shushing and soothing Harry with soft words. I let the two of them out of the car at the entrance to the accident and emergency unit and watched, helpless, as she ushered Harry towards the sliding door.

'Will Harry be alright, Mummy?'

I turned to her, fury churning my insides. 'Why the hell did you push him?'

Her face crumpled. Tears cascaded down her cheeks. 'He said his daddy had done the picture, and he hadn't. It was my daddy.'

'What are you talking about?'

'The picture of Santa,' she said through hiccupping sobs.

I turned back to the windscreen, 'You have got to be kidding me.' I started the engine and waved an apology to a car indicating to pull in. 'Harry's in hospital because of a fight over a picture?'

'It was—'

'No, Cora, I don't want to hear it.' I cut her off. 'I'm too angry to discuss this now. This is the second time you've hurt someone. I can't believe this is happening. I'm beginning to think I don't know you at all.'

She howled and something about the pitch made me soften. I didn't want her to be distraught, but what was I supposed to do, turn a blind eye to her hurting other children just because she was upset afterwards? I toured the car park looking for a space, ignoring the sobbing from the back seat.

We found Elle and Harry in the children's waiting room. We walked past a woman with a pale face cradling a sleeping toddler in her arms, to where Elle sat on a blue plastic chair with her arm around Harry. She held a swab against his eye. The bright murals of cartoon characters on the walls clashed with the atmosphere of sadness and fear in the room.

Elle looked up and was about to say something when a nurse appeared from a door near reception and called, 'Harry Clarke?'

I glanced up at the familiar surname. It felt strange that I'd grown so close to Elle over the past few weeks, but I'd never asked her last name.

Elle led Harry past us and they disappeared through the door.

'Is Harry seeing the doctor now?' said Cora.

'He's probably being triaged; that means the nurse will work out who he needs to see.' She climbed onto my knee and wrapped her arms around my neck, burying her head in my hair. I felt her breath on my neck and automatically wound my arms around her.

'Will he be alright?' she whispered into my ear.

I rocked us both in the seat. 'I hope so.'

'Am I a bad person?' she said, pushing her head further into my hair. Her small body shuddered under my hands.

I didn't know how to answer. A week ago, I would have said the events of the last few days were impossible. I'd have bet my life that Cora was incapable of hurting anyone, but here we were, sitting in a hospital, because of what she'd done.

* * *

Ten minutes later, Elle and Harry reappeared. My heart pounded as I tried to read Elle's face, but it was concealed by her hair as she bowed to guide Harry back to the seats. Harry held the swab over his eye. He was shuffling, his school shoes scraping on the shiny lino floor. I had to force myself to stay seated. Cora lifted her head. I felt her take a breath to speak, so squeezed her around the middle as a warning. I felt her ribcage contract under my hands.

They sat next to us on the seats. If they weren't bolted to the wall, I wondered if Elle would shift hers away. 'What did the nurse say?'

Elle didn't look up. 'The cut's right at the corner, so she's not sure if there's any damage to his eye. He needs to see an optha . . .' she seemed to struggle to find the word.

'Ophthalmologist?'

'Yeah.' She stroked Harry's back. 'But you were very brave, weren't you, Harry?'

Harry didn't move.

'And if you could try to tell the eye doctor how it feels and what you can see, that will really help them work out what they need to do to make you better, won't it?'

Her voice was high and the hairs on my neck lifted as I realised what she meant. Harry wouldn't, or couldn't, speak to anyone at the hospital. I'd almost forgotten he didn't talk to anyone outside his home because he always spoke to Cora. I tried to remember if he'd ever spoken to me directly, or to Gary, but I couldn't recall a time he had. My heart contracted for the small, complicated little boy. I wanted to reach out and run my hand over his soft hair. The desire to comfort him was like an ache.

'God, this must be a nightmare for both of you,' I said. 'What can I do to help? Anything? Do you want something to eat? Can I call someone? Rob?'

Still looking at the top of Harry's bowed head, Elle said, 'I rang him when we were waiting. He'll be here in a bit.'

'Okay,' I said, imagining how Harry's dad would feel about Cora. 'Is there anything you need?'

'No,' said Elle. 'We just have to wait now.'

'Are you alright, Harry?' Cora leaned forwards, looking under Harry's hair.

He didn't respond.

'Harry?' she tried again.

Elle seemed to stiffen. 'Rob will be here soon, so why don't you two make a move? There's no point us all waiting.'

There was a sharpness to her voice that made me reach for my bag and lift Cora from my lap. 'Okay. If you're sure. I'll text you to see how he is, if that's alright.'

She nodded.

'I'm really sorry, Harry,' said Cora, crying as she stood in front of him as he hunched in the chair. 'I really didn't mean to.'

'Come on.' I took her hand. 'I hope you feel much better soon, Harry. Bye then.' It seemed like such a stupid thing to say. As though we were leaving a restaurant after a nice meal, not a hospital because my child might have damaged someone's sight.

I didn't look at Cora as I marched her from the children's waiting area through the main accident and emergency reception and out through the glass doors. I was aware of her eyes swivelling, taking in all the sorry souls waiting to be seen, and quickened my pace.

'Wait,' said Cora, tugging on my hand.

'Come on,' I pulled her along with me.

'I saw Daddy,' she said. Her head turned back to the entrance.

I was in no mood for messing about. 'Come on.'

'But Daddy has gone in there,' she said, trying to untangle her fingers from mine.

I stopped and tugged her to my side. Through clenched teeth I said, 'Daddy is in Scotland, and you, my lady, are in enough trouble as it is, so I suggest you stop messing about right now.'

'But Daddy . . .' She burst into sobs and at that moment I wished she was right. I wished Bill was only metres away and I could ask him what the fuck I was supposed to do about our increasingly unrecognisable child.

Chapter Twenty-Eight

Elle

When Rob found us in the waiting room, he kissed Harry on the head and tried to examine his eye, but he kept squirming away.

'Run me through what happened again,' he said. 'Someone pushed him into a Christmas tree?'

I tensed. 'She didn't push him into the tree, exactly. She pushed him and the tree was there.'

Rob shook his head. 'And where were you?'

I swallowed. 'At a cafe called Rooted.'

Harry's name was called, and we all stood abruptly and followed the nurse into the cubicle where a man in scrubs stood to greet us.

* * *

Luckily, it didn't look like the break in the skin had affected Harry's vision, although he needed to have more tests in the next few weeks to be certain. He wouldn't talk to the doctors, which was frustrating for all of us. I was shattered when we eventually got home and put Harry to bed. I forgot the awkward conversation about how and why this happened, so I was caught off guard when Rob asked again after we got home. 'So, it was a random kid who pushed him for no reason?'

'Not exactly.' I sighed. I lay my head back on the sofa cushion and decided I should tell Rob the truth. 'We met a mum and her daughter at a support group.'

'What?' His head tucked back into his neck. 'Support group for what?'

I closed my eyes, not wanting to see his reaction. 'Don't go mad. It was a group set up by the counsellor I told you about, ages ago, Claire Dixon. It's for parents of kids with ADHD.'

'For fuck's sake, Elle.' I heard him smack his hand against the cushion. 'I mean, what do you expect if you expose him to kids with all sorts of things going on?'

My eyes sprung open. 'You don't know what you're talking about.'

He pointed towards the ceiling. 'I know my son is up there after being hospitalised by a kid with some kind of hyperactive condition.'

'She's not like that.'

'The state of Harry's face suggests otherwise.' He shook his head as though he couldn't believe my naivety.

'She's a sweet kid and she's the only person outside this house Harry will talk to.'

Rob raised his eyes to the ceiling. 'Oh, well, that's alright then. He might be blind in one eye, but as long as they're having a nice chat, it's all good.'

'It was an accident.' I was sure it must've been an accident. I'd never seen Cora do anything violent before. I couldn't even imagine her having a mean thought. Was I kidding myself and only seeing what I wanted to?

'Yeah, but it was caused by a kid with issues.'

'If you met Cora, you wouldn't say that.'

His head twisted to face me. 'Cora?'

'That's her name. Her mum's called Jen and if you met them . . .' I stopped because all the blood seemed to have drained from Rob's face. 'You alright?'

He blinked and seemed to come back to life. 'I'm livid. I'm beyond furious that my little boy has been injured because of your irresponsible behaviour.'

'That's not fair.'

He stood, his face still deathly white. 'I don't want you to ever see those people again. I mean it, Elle.'

'But—'

'No. I am not joking. No more support group, no more cosy trips to the cafe. It stops now.'

'You can't tell me who I can and can't see.'

'I mean it, so you'd better listen carefully,' he said, his voice full of menace. 'You have a choice; stop seeing them, or—'

'Or what?' I couldn't believe he was issuing such a ridiculous ultimatum.

'Or something much worse could happen,' he said.

'Don't be so dramatic. You haven't even met them, and you've decided they're a lethal threat to our family. You're being ridiculous.'

'I'm being a father,' he snarled. 'I'm trying to protect my family. Maybe it's time you did the same.'

'Like your father does?' I shouted at his back as he stalked from the room. 'He's proved that he's a danger to Harry, but he's still here, isn't he?' I heard Rob's footsteps on the stairs. 'She's just a little girl,' I whispered to myself, ignoring the doubt tapping at the back of my mind. 'Just a normal little girl.'

Chapter Twenty-Nine

Jen

Cora hadn't stopped crying since we got home. I didn't know how to console her when I was so angry myself. I counted down the minutes to seven o'clock when Bill would call, and I could ask him what he thought I should do.

'Eat your pasta,' I said to Cora, who was snivelling at the table, a bowl of pasta mixed with green pesto in front of her. I didn't have the energy to make her eat vegetables tonight.

'I can't,' she said, between gasping breaths. 'My tummy feels like it's closed.'

I was completely torn. If the incident with Kieran hadn't happened, I was sure I'd take today's episode as unfortunate and out-of-character. But she'd already been in trouble for violence, and I'd seen her push Harry with my own eyes. I was sure she hadn't meant him to spear his eye with a Christmas tree branch, but actions have consequences. She needed to know that.

I wondered if I'd feel differently if I hadn't gone to the

support group. Now I knew Cora was being tested for ADHD, was I looking out for signs of impulsivity and oppositional defiance? Had I been blinkered to these characteristics in my own child before?

Another side of me was pierced by every whimper Cora made. She was utterly contrite. I'd never seen a sorrier person in my life. And she was inherently good, wasn't she?

I needed to speak to Bill. He'd put me right. I looked at the clock on my phone: 7.02pm. *Come on Bill*, I thought, *I need you*.

'What time is it?' Cora asked a few minutes later.

'Ten past seven.'

'Why hasn't Daddy called?'

'I don't know.' I pressed his number on my phone and held it to my ear. It went straight to voicemail. 'His phone must be turned off.'

'I want to talk to Daddy,' said Cora, sniffing.

'Me and you both, kid,' I said.

I tapped out a message to Elle, deleted it and tried again.

Any news? Really hope Harry's ok. Cora wants me to say sorry again. Jen x

I pressed send, then tried Bill's number again. Still no dial tone, just the sound of his voice. That was no good to me. I wished I'd demanded the number for his work phone.

My phone beeped in my hand. A message from Elle said:

Home now. H doing ok

There were no kisses at the end of the message. I scrolled up to our past messages and saw how all of Elle's previous texts were littered with smiley faced emojis and at least two kisses at the end of every message. I looked at my replies. There were no emojis. Just one terse kiss at the end of each one.

God, I was a stone-cold bitch. Would it have killed me

to put two kisses when everything Elle typed was full of energy and warmth? It wasn't like it didn't occur to me to put an extra x, it was just that I didn't like to be seen as effusive. I was withholding. I knew that and, in that moment, I hated myself for it.

If I hadn't kept everyone at arm's length, I might have someone to talk to now. I was kidding myself that I could handle everything on my own. And where was Bill? I'd needed him twice in the last few weeks and he was nowhere to be seen.

* * *

I thought all that crying might tire Cora out. No such luck. The following morning, we were both swollen-eyed and exhausted. I'd stopped attempting to call Bill at midnight. Acid swilled in my stomach at the thought something had happened to him. My morning coffee returned as bitter reflux as I tapped out a message to Elle.

Hope Harry's not too uncomfortable. Sending love from us both. Jen xx

I saw the grey dots jump in a speech bubble and closed my eyes, hoping when I opened them there would be a message saying Harry was absolutely fine. The phone dinged.

H sore, but doesn't seem like eyesight damaged. Booked in for more tests. Would help if he could speak to dr. X

Air left my lungs. Thank fuck for that.

'Cora,' I shouted upstairs. 'Looks like Harry will be alright.'

She appeared at the top of the stairs, looking tiny in her polka dot pyjamas. 'Can we see him?'

'Not today,' I said. 'I imagine he's pretty tired. I know I am.'

Cora's chin puckered. 'Can we send him a present?'

'That's a good idea.' I typed out a message asking for

Elle's address so we could send something for Harry. It wouldn't make amends, but it would be a start.

* * *

Mel sounded surprised when I called in sick. I couldn't remember a time when I'd been too ill to go into work, and I'd been proud of the fact. Once I'd given the whole cast a shocking cold which meant the understudy had to step in to play the Duchess of Malfi, but I'd told myself the lead was a prima donna and, if I could step up, she could too.

Looking back, I'd have saved everyone a lot of bother if I'd taken a couple of days off to get better – and less contagious. Ironic that now I'm sick and tired, rather than just sick, I can see my pride hasn't done me any favours over the years.

I told school Cora was ill because I knew she was too overwrought and emotional to cope. She'd been in tears most of the morning and kept asking why she couldn't talk to Daddy. I didn't know what to tell her. My stomach churned when I imagined all the situations that might cause this silence. I was trying to distract her as well as myself by walking along the high street to the old sweetshop to choose something to send to Harry. We found a big bar of chocolate with his name on the wrapper.

'Maybe a toy, as well?' I said, leading Cora towards the toyshop.

She came to an abrupt stop at the window. 'Wow,' she said, smiling for the first time since the incident.

The window was like a scene from *Jurassic Park*. On an uneven bed of artificial grass stood a terrifying selection of dinosaurs. I looked from the Lego versions to the blow-up plastic toys. 'Which one do you think he'd like?'

'That one.' Cora pointed at a huge threatening-looking

creature with long black claws and rows of pointy teeth in its open jaw.

'That might be a bit big,' I said.

'Can we look inside?' Cora cupped her face and peered into the glass, so her voice came out muffled. 'I think that's got a remote control. Harry would really, really love that.'

We went in and asked a stubby youth wearing a shirt with the shop's logo if he could show us the dinosaur from the window.

'It's a top-of-the-range velociraptor,' he said, walking us to a shelf filled with enormous boxes. 'Remote control. Roars, wags its waist and tail and can move forwards and backwards. Cool, right?' He tapped the top of a box which was almost as big as Cora. I peered at the picture on the side of a monstrous-looking dinosaur with a USB cable attached to its underbelly.

The youth followed my eyes. 'Yep, rechargeable. The remote control is fossil shaped. It's wicked.'

Cora turned to me and clasped her fingers together. 'Please, Mummy, please can we get it for Harry?'

'It's too big to post.'

'We can take it to his house now. Please, Mummy. Can we?'

I sighed and nodded. I wanted to cheer the poor boy up. Neither of us would rest until we saw Harry was okay, and the day was gaping, empty, in front of us. 'Alright then. I suppose we could go to Harry's house,' I said.

I mean, what harm could it do?

Chapter Thirty

Elle

I was checking if the pizza was done when I heard a knock at the front door. I slammed the oven shut and marched through to the hall. I had mixed feelings when I opened the door to see Jen standing in the doorstep carrying a huge box in her arms. Cora stood slightly behind her, holding on to Jen's coat.

'Hi,' I said, pulling the door closed behind me. However conflicted I felt, I knew Rob's stance.

'I'm sorry if this is a bad time,' said Jen, handing the box to me. 'But Cora wanted to give this to Harry to say how sorry she is about pushing him.'

Cora took a tentative step forwards and held out a chocolate bar with 'Harry' written on the purple wrapper. 'Please could you give this to Harry because I'm very sorry and I want him to know I won't ever be mean to him again.'

'Thank you,' I said. 'He will love that.' Whatever anger I'd felt after the accident melted away at the sight of her huge blue eyes ringed with dark circles. Of course she hadn't meant to hurt Harry. I'd known that all along, whatever Rob said.

'Is Harry here? Can I see him, please?' Cora asked.

I hesitated. I didn't want to risk Rob kicking off again.

'Please can I tell Harry I'm sorry and I want to be his friend. Do you think he will still be my friend if I tell him how sorry I am?'

That did it. She was the only friend Harry had. 'Come in,' I said, stepping aside to let them into the house. Sod Rob and his overreactions. His bloody dad was still living with us and I hadn't had a say in that. Why shouldn't I invite my friends in? It was my home too. In fact, since all the financial stuff happened, my name was the only one on the deeds.

Jen didn't move. 'We don't want to intrude,' she said.

'Come on. Harry's in the kitchen.' I looked down at Cora's nervous face. 'He looks like a pirate with an eye patch. Come and see.'

Cora nipped in front of Jen, who shrugged. 'Come through,' I said and led her to where Harry was drawing at the kitchen table. Cora was standing behind him, looking sheepish. The chocolate bar sat next to Harry's hand.

'Look what Cora and Jen have brought for you.' I put the box on the floor. Harry didn't look up. I didn't know if I should tell him off for being rude. They were standing right next to him, and I felt my shoulders tense as he resolutely stared at the paper. 'Maybe I'll give this remote-controlled velociraptor to Daddy, then,' I said, tapping my nail on the cardboard.

He glanced down at the box and the eye that wasn't covered in the white gauze widened. He climbed from the chair and kneeled beside the box.

'What do you say?' I chided.

Harry gazed up me, that familiar imploring look on his face.

'Harry.' I kept my voice light, hoping for a miracle.

'Don't worry,' said Jen. She bent to speak to Harry. 'I hope your eye's not too sore. Enjoy the dinosaur, Cora and I hope we'll see you soon.' She straightened up. 'Come on Cora, let's leave these two in peace.'

'Please can we stay, Mummy? I want to play with Harry.'

Colour bloomed on Jen's cheeks. 'Come on, Cora, we need—'

'Fancy a cuppa?' I said. I was nervous of Rob's reaction, but it wasn't as if Harry had any other friends who wanted to play with him, and they had been kind to bring what looked like an expensive gift.

Jen grimaced, looking from Cora to me. 'You sure?'

'Yeah.' I made the coffee while Jen helped Harry and Cora open the box and decipher the instructions. Harry didn't speak, but he seemed relaxed enough. Putting the capsules in the coffee machine, I thought how strange it was that I knew exactly how Jen liked her coffee. This woman, who I'd known a matter of weeks, was the person I felt most relaxed with in the whole world. Yesterday, I'd presumed our friendship was over, and I'd never see Jen and Cora again. Now I was intensely glad they were here.

When Jen and I went through to the sitting room, I saw her assess our white, artificial Christmas tree with its blue baubles and tried to read her face. I imagined she was the kind of person who had a real tree decorated in red and gold. I was distracted from my thoughts by the sound of Harry's voice giving quiet replies to Cora's babbling questions. It was incredible what that little girl could do.

I heard a creak on the floorboards upstairs. My heart flipped. Miraculously, Rob had taken the day off and he was upstairs now. Part of the reason I'd invited Jen to stay for coffee was so Rob could meet her. Then he'd see she wasn't an irresponsible mother and Cora wasn't the wild child he'd presumed she was. For once, I was standing my ground, making my point that he didn't get to dictate who I could and couldn't spend time with. It was exhilarating and terrifying in equal measure.

I tried to focus and answer Jen's questions about what the doctor had said about Harry's eye, but my nerves jangled when I heard Rob's footsteps on the stairs. I heard him walk through the hallway and waited for his reaction when he found two children in the kitchen instead of one.

There was an excited yelp which made Jen and me both turn our heads. Then we heard a voice shout, 'Daddy!'

But it wasn't Harry's voice I heard.

It was Cora's.

Chapter Thirty-One

Elle

Jen and I both rushed for the door. I stood back to let her pass because it seemed like the polite thing to do. My view was blocked by Jen, but I clearly heard her say, 'Bill?'

I stood on tiptoes to look over her shoulder and saw Rob, his face white, standing in our kitchen with Cora clinging to his waist. Harry was staring at them, his mouth hanging open.

'Rob, what's going on?' I couldn't work out how the scene in front of me could possibly make sense.

Jen spun around to face me. 'Rob is Robin?'

'I don't understand what's going on. Rob?'

Jen turned back towards the kitchen when Cora's frightened voice asked, 'Why are you at Harry's house, Daddy?'

'Yes, why are you at Harry's house, Robin?' Jen's voice rolled from somewhere deep inside her and I watched in confusion as Rob's eyes flitted between the faces of the children, a look of anguish in his eyes. His lips opened and closed but no sound came out.

Harry squeezed past Jen, who was still blocking the doorway, and grabbed hold of my waist. I put my hand on his back. He was trembling. A surge of adrenaline whooshed through my veins as I attempted to add up what was happening in my kitchen.

'Your husband's called Bill, isn't he?' I said to Jen.

'Bill's a nickname,' she growled, 'for Robin.'

My heart dropped down to my stomach. 'But he's my husband,' I managed to stutter. But he wasn't, was he? I looked past her to Rob, understanding growing like nausea inside me. 'God, Rob, is . . . is this why we had to get divorced?' I held the heel of my hand to my forehead as I put things together in my head. 'It wasn't about money, was it? It wasn't so the tax man didn't take the house. It was so you could marry her.' I pointed to Jen, who stood back, looking confused.

'I'm . . . god, I didn't mean this to . . .' Rob touched the back of Cora's head and dipped down, 'Can you go upstairs with Harry for a minute, sweetheart?'

'What the fucking hell is going on?' demanded Jen, marching into the kitchen and pulling Cora from Robin's side and into the hall as the little girl's eyes darted between the two.

Rob raised his arm, reaching for Cora, then shifted his gaze to Harry, quivering by my side, and dropped it. 'Please,' he said, 'Please don't make the children witness this.' His hand flew up to his mouth. 'I'm going to be sick.' He rushed to the sink and leaned over, lowering his head and closing his eyes.

I watched beads of sweat spring up on his forehead, aware of a whimpering sound coming from Cora. Then the front door opened behind me, and Michael barrelled in.

'What's going on?' he slurred.

Rob lifted his head from the sink. 'Not now, Dad. Go upstairs.'

'Dad?' Jen said. 'This is your dad?'

Rob took the tea towel and wiped it over his ashen face. He moved towards us, tears collecting in his eyes.

'Hello,' Michael said to Jen. A lascivious smile crept onto his face as he looked her up and down. 'Who do we have here?'

'You're Rob's dad?' Jen glared at Rob. 'You fucking liar.'

Michael screwed his face up. He turned to Rob, who slid past us and tried to manoeuvre Michael towards the stairs. 'Hold on.' He pulled his arm away from Rob. 'What is going on?' He looked at our stricken faces and down at Cora, who was now holding Jen's hand and snivelling. 'Explain to me who these people are and why that little girl is crying?' He waved a finger at Cora.

'Not now, Dad. You're drunk. Go to bed,' said Rob.

Jen pulled Cora in front of her and wrapped her arms around her shoulders. 'This is fresh news to all of us, but it looks like I'm your daughter-in-law, and this is your granddaughter.'

Her words felt like spears. I was such a mug. How had I not seen any of this? How had I allowed this to happen to Harry?

'What?' Michael's eyes flitted around the hall.

'Yep. Hard to believe, isn't it?' said Jen. 'I'm struggling to get my head around it too. From what I can gather, he,' she stabbed a finger at Rob, 'conned Elle into a divorce so he could marry me. And, get this . . .' She turned back to Michael who was gaping from her to Cora. 'Your arsehole son told me you had dementia and lived in a care home in Scotland. In fact, he got a call last week saying you'd had a fall, so he had to rush off in the middle of the night.'

'He did fall,' said Rob, weakly. He pointed at a green bruise on Michael's left cheek.

'Not in fucking Scotland!' roared Jen. Cora jumped. Her sobs became louder.

I felt Harry's face pushing into my waist and when I looked down my vision was blurred. I wiped the tears away, trying to put my thoughts in order when Michael sniffed loudly. 'What's that burning smell?'

I jumped, suddenly aware of the pizza I'd put in the oven before Jen arrived. Was that only twenty minutes ago? How could our lives have capsized in the time it takes to burn a pizza?

Rob rushed into the kitchen and opened the oven, wafting ineffectually at the smoke billowing out. 'For god's sake, Elle,' he said.

Something in me snapped. 'Really?' I screamed, 'Really? You've lied and cheated for at least eight fucking years, and you think you can have a go at me for burning a pizza? Christ, that's you all over, isn't it? You self-righteous prick.'

'You could have burned the house down.'

'You *have* burned the house down!' I shouted, my arms flung wide. 'You've burned our lives to the ground! Look at us, Rob.' He tipped the pizza into the bin, avoiding our eyes. I was glad to see his tears falling onto the shiny bin lid.

'Look at us,' said Jen, her voice low and menacing.

'Daddy?' said Cora.

Her little voice broke my heart. 'Get out, Rob,' I said. 'Get out now.'

He straightened, slashing tears off his cheeks with the back of his hand, 'You can't throw me out of my own house.'

I half coughed, half laughed. 'But it's not yours, is it? It's mine. And you're not my husband, so I *can* tell you to get out now. Who's going to stop me?' I said the last words slowly, watching his face as he realised he couldn't argue.

'Jen?' He turned to her. 'I . . .'

I followed his eyes and watched Jen's mouth open in disbelief. She shook her head. 'Come on, Cora.'

Cora resisted. 'Daddy?'

Rob moved towards her and bent to her level. Jen pulled Cora to her side. 'Don't you dare come near my child,' she snarled.

'She's my little girl too,' Rob's voice faltered. He sounded broken. Harry was still trembling, and water streamed down Cora's face. So much devastation. It was too much to bear.

'You need to leave, and you can take him with you,' I said, pointing at Michael and hating myself for the tears pouring down my cheeks. Jen wasn't crying. She stood like a magnificent figurehead, ploughing through the waves, indestructible.

But as soon as the thought occurred in my head, a sense of betrayal smashed into me. How could she appear so unmoved? Maybe because she was actually a bitch. How else could she take someone else's husband? She wasn't blameless in this. Rob was married to me when they met. Didn't she think to check if he was single? Maybe she did and didn't care. Me and my baby were probably irrelevant to her when she decided to get her claws into my husband.

'You can get out as well,' I said to Jen. 'Get out of my house, all of you.'

'Elle,' said Jen.

'Get out of my fucking house,' I was sobbing and shaking. I gripped on to Harry who was shivering so much I didn't know which tremors were his and which were mine. 'You two have done this to us,' I screamed. 'You deserve each other.'

'Elle, I didn't—' said Jen. She turned as Rob lay a hand on her arm. It looked like his touch burned her; she flung it away then pushed his chest. 'Don't you dare touch me,' she said. 'Ever again.' She led Cora to the door. When she opened it a whoosh of cold air slapped me in the face. The smoke filling the hallway cleared and I blinked at what was left behind.

Rob's slack face watched Jen settle Cora into the back seat of her car. His chest heaved, like a man dying of thirst watching an oasis disappear. He'd never looked at me with such longing. Bastard.

Michael wobbled. He put a hand on the banister, then leaned into it. 'Oh, son,' he said wearily, 'That poor little girl. A granddaughter. How could you . . . I thought you were better than that.'

'Why? Because you set me such a great example?' Rob snarled.

Michael looked suddenly old. 'I'm going to bed,' he said, and made his way slowly upstairs.

Michael clearly hadn't listened to what I'd said. I didn't have the energy to force him out when he was pissed, but I wasn't about to put up with Rob for another second. 'Get your stuff and get out,' I said, as he closed the front door. He didn't look at me, just wiped his eyes and nodded. He dropped his gaze to Harry, his chin puckering. He looked as though he might speak, but Harry turned his back. Rob swallowed, then followed his father upstairs.

I took Harry through to the front room. He sat with me on the sofa, tucked tight into my side. We listened to the footsteps moving around upstairs. 'You okay?' I said to him, not knowing what else to say. 'It will be alright,' I said when he didn't reply. I was lying. How could things ever be alright again?

We sat in silence until we heard Rob's footsteps on the stairs. He came half into the room. It seemed appropriate. He'd only ever been half with us. Now I understood why.

'I'm sorry,' he said. 'Honestly, Elle, I didn't want anyone to get hurt. I know you won't believe me, but I thought it was best for everyone . . .' His voice trailed off. 'Elle?'

I said nothing. I heard a stuttering breath, then he said, 'Love you, son.'

Harry didn't even look up.

The front door clicked closed. I felt a warm tear drop from Harry's chin onto my arm. Then another. And there was nothing I could say to comfort him, so we sat and cried together.

Chapter Thirty-Two

Jen

In the car on the way home Cora asked, 'Why is Daddy Harry's daddy too?' in between sobs.

I kept my eyes on the road. It occurred to me how easy it would be to veer off the dual carriageway and slam the car into a tree. I tightened my grip on the steering wheel. 'Because he was already married to Elle when I met him, but I didn't know. He lied to us,' I said.

'Why did he lie to us?' she said.

'Because it turns out he's not the person we thought he was.'

'Who is he, then?' Cora grizzled.

Damned good question, I thought, my knuckles whitening as I held on to the wheel. Who was my husband? Who was this man I'd shared my life, my home, my body and my child with for almost eight years? I thought I knew him.

Up until an hour ago, I would have told you I knew Bill inside and out. I corrected myself – I thought I knew Robin. A nickname felt too familiar. I would call him Robin from now onwards because he didn't deserve the intimacy of a name only he and I knew the background of. He'd tricked me into that intimacy, that trust.

This morning I'd believed I could predict every response, every action because he was my soul mate. He was a part of me. I'd thought he was the best part of me.

I'd thought I was a good judge of character. I kept most people at arm's length since Aaron had blown my trust apart twenty-five years ago. I'd learned from that and prided myself on being someone who could spot a dick on first sighting. Turns out I'd been taken for a fool by the biggest dick of all. What did that make me? Fool didn't seem to cover the fracturing of my self-belief. If I wasn't all of the things I thought I was, who was I?

'Is that why Harry had the same drawing as me?' Cora said.

I looked at her tear-stained face through the rear-view mirror. She was staring out of the window forlornly. 'What do you mean?'

'Yesterday,' she said. 'When I pushed Harry because he had my picture.'

I realised then, that after all the drama, the blood and the hospital, I hadn't listened to Cora when she tried to tell me why she'd pushed Harry into the tree. 'What do you mean he had your picture?' I indicated into our road, relieved to see my little house as I rounded the corner.

'You know the picture of me in Santa's sleigh that Daddy drew? You gave it to me after he'd gone to Scotland.'

'Yes.' I pictured the colourful drawing of a sleigh laden with presents and a caricature of Cora sitting on top of a sack, grinning and waving. Robin had asked me to give it to Cora as he rushed off, supposedly to help his father.

'Well, Harry had the same picture. I didn't see that it

was him on top of the sack in his one. I saw Santa and the sleigh, and I was cross because he said his daddy had drawn it and I knew my daddy had drawn it and Harry wouldn't give it back.'

I parked and pulled up the handbrake so forcefully it screeched. On top of everything else he had done, the fight that resulted in Harry getting injured was Robin's fault as well. He'd made my little girl injure another child. He'd made me question whether Cora was who I thought she was, and all the time, it was him, Robin fucking Clarke, who was the one I didn't know.

'I'm so sorry, Cora. I'm so sorry I didn't listen to you.'

'It's alright, Mummy. I sometimes forget to use my listening ears too.' She looked at me in the mirror and smiled so sadly I felt my heart split.

* * *

After a sleepless night huddled together in my bed, we spent the following day in our pyjamas eating strawberries dipped in Nutella in front of the television. Cora was quiet. That was worrying. Whenever I tried to get her to speak, she gave short answers, and I was too drained to try harder.

My mind kept drifting away from the saccharine American series Cora begged to watch, to mine and Robin's wedding. I hadn't had a single doubt on my wedding day. When we'd woken up in the huge bed in the Oriental Suite at Ca Maria Adele, I'd looked at my gorgeous husband-to-be and felt nothing but adoration and hope for our glorious future. A lump blocked my throat when I thought of the future we were meant to have. We were going to grow old together. When we had more time, we planned to tour the Amalfi coast in a vintage car. We said we'd go to the Edinburgh Fringe Festival and see brilliant new plays. We would die in each other's arms. I'd been certain of that. What an idiot I'd been.

What an idiot he'd taken me for.

After the sixth time Robin's number flashed up on my phone, the handset vibrating on the table, I blocked him. He sent email after email. I left them in my inbox. Whenever I was tempted to click one open, I made myself remember Cora's face, staring out of the car window on the way home from Elle's, and it was enough to make me close down the email app. I didn't turn my phone off in case Elle wanted to get in touch. She couldn't have meant the things she said when it all came out. Surely she'd come to her senses and realise Cora and I had been duped, just like her and Harry?

* * *

On Friday I really had to go to rehearsals. I forced myself to email Mrs Daniels, telling her Cora's father and I had separated, so Cora might be even more emotional than usual. Separated seemed like the wrong word to use now I knew we were never truly together in the first place. She replied, saying Claire was in school, so she'd arrange for Cora to see her. I was relieved. However humiliating I found the situation, I knew Cora might need to tell someone how she felt.

'Mrs Daniels has arranged for you to see Claire today,' I said, as she finished her toast. 'In case you want to get anything off your chest.'

She examined my face with her clever blue eyes. 'I don't know what to say,' she muttered. 'Is it a secret, what Daddy did? Should I pretend he isn't Harry's daddy and my daddy as well?'

Rage burned in my gut. She was seven. She shouldn't be asking if she should hide the truth to protect her parents.

'You say whatever you want,' I said, hugging her close. 'The main thing is that you feel better. If Claire can help you make sense of anything, then that's a good thing.'

'Okay,' she said, climbing down from the chair. She stopped in front of me and looked up. 'Will you be okay Mummy?'

I almost crumbled. I just about managed to keep it together to say, 'Don't worry about me. You don't ever have to worry about me. I'm a grown-up, remember, it's not your job to look after me. Now, come on, grab your bag, it's time to go.' When she left the room, I dug my nails into my palms, but the pain couldn't detract from the turmoil I felt. My poor, darling girl. I should have protected her from this.

The realisation that caring for Cora was down to me alone now took the air from my lungs. I'd always thought Robin was the better parent. Now he was gone, and Cora's entire welfare was down to me. I still had to have the mammogram and heaven knows what after that, and I was the only person who could care for my little girl. What if I died? What would happen to Cora? I might not even be around to make sure she was safe and loved. For the first time since I'd met Robin in that bar eight years ago, I felt terrified, helpless and alone.

Chapter Thirty-Three

Jen

When I walked into the studio, I was glad the lighting was already set so I could stay in darkness outside the performance area. I'd tried to conceal the purple circles under my eyes with make-up, but there was nothing I could do about them being bloodshot and puffy. Anyone looking closely would work out I'd been crying for most of the last twenty-four hours.

'You better?' asked Mel, narrowing her eyes as she peered at me through the gloom.

'Yep.' I was curt. I didn't want anyone prying, especially not someone who I needed to respect me. I raised my voice for the company to hear. 'First full run. Exciting! Let's make it a good one. Places please.'

We'd only get two days to run the play in the theatre after the pantomime run finished, so we needed to be tight before everyone broke for Christmas. I sat myself opposite centre stage with my notepad and pen ready.

The play ran smoothly. Not for the first time, I was glad

of the professionalism of this company. They followed my lead. They just got on with it. Ed looked tired, but he didn't miss a beat and he and Femi steamed when they were together on stage.

I felt tears of anger on my cheeks when in Act One Femi said, 'What, says the married woman you may go?' I swiped them away, only for more to come when she said, 'Why should I think you can be mine and true (though you in swearing shake the throned gods) Who have been false to Fulvia?'

Who would I be in this play? I wondered, as tears began to stream down my face. I was furious at myself for not being able to stop crying. I'd always admired Cleopatra for her strength and power. But I'd never considered the fact that Antony was married to Fulvia when they met. Then, after she died, he married Octavia and Cleopatra barely gave the other women another thought.

I watched as Antony protested his love for Cleopatra, the chemistry between Ed and Femi palpable as they stared into each other's eyes. Fury curdled in my stomach and seeped into my veins. When we reached the end of Act Two, I couldn't sit still for another second. 'Let's break,' I called. 'Good work, people. See you in fifteen.'

I pushed open the studio door. The bright winter sunshine hurt my eyes. I leaned on the brickwork, feeling the cold through my shirt. I was exhausted to my core. My breath fogged in the freezing air. I watched it swell into a cloud then disappear, revealing the morning frost still sparkling on the tarmac of the car park. I took a deep breath, feeling it sting when the cold air hit the back of my throat. I dug in my pocket for a tissue when I felt snot run onto my top lip and fresh tears pricked my eyes.

I banged the back of my head against the wall. It hurt,

so I did it again. Who was this woman, crying in a car park? This wasn't me. This wasn't who I wanted to be. I blew my nose and blinked until my eyes cleared. My fingers ached with the cold. I was about to go back in when I heard whispered voices around the corner of the building.

Curious, I pushed myself away from the wall and walked around the corner to find Femi and Ed in a clinch. White anger hurricaned through me. 'What the fuck do you think you are doing?' I shouted. They sprang apart. 'What is wrong with you people?' I reached them and dragged Ed backwards, even more outraged by the look of confusion on his face.

'I was—' started Femi.

'He's married, for fuck's sake. He's a married man. Doesn't that mean anything to anyone anymore?'

'I'm—'

I turned on Ed. 'Fucking weak. Weak and fucking selfish. What is wrong with you? You've got kids, for god's sake.'

I took a breath, then stopped. Ed was crying.

'Don't think you're going to get any sympathy like that,' I sneered.

'Stop it,' a voice behind me said.

I spun around to see Mel standing at the corner of the building. She clearly didn't understand what was going on. I gestured to Ed and Femi. 'I just caught—'

She marched to Ed and put her arm around his shoulder. She looked at me with contempt in her eyes. 'Ed's dad died yesterday.'

'But they were . . .' I was suddenly unsure of what I'd witnessed. 'Weren't you . . .?'

'I was consoling him. Somebody needed to take care of him,' said Femi, her voice flat. 'He's working so hard to stay in character, so he doesn't let *you* down.' I felt my lungs deflate.

'I'm sorry, I thought you two—'

'Give us some credit,' said Femi, rising to her full height. 'We're friends. Me and my kids were at Ed's house when he got the call from Sienna about his dad, because,' she spoke slowly, 'we are friends.'

'I'm sorry,' I said, aware of three sets of eyes boring into me. I looked at Ed. 'I'm so sorry. I didn't know.'

He shook his head, then ran his hands over his face. 'How would you know?' He sighed, his breath billowing white between us. 'We all try to keep to your professional standards.' He shrugged. 'No personal stuff, no home life, no friendships.' He looked me directly in the eye, 'No emotions off stage.'

I'm sure I wasn't the only one who saw the irony of his words when I said, 'I'm so sorry for your loss,' then collapsed into uncontrollable sobs.

* * *

I sat in a chair in the kitchen, my freezing fingers wrapped around the mug of coffee Mel handed to me. I felt raw and exposed for breaking down like that in front of Ed and Femi. That stung more than having been so wrong about them, and I knew that didn't cover me in glory. Why was I so bothered about appearing strong? Where had it got me?

I put the coffee on the table and started to lift myself from the chair.

'Where do you think you're going?' Mel's voice was harsh.

'Back in there.' I gestured towards the studio. 'There's a lot to get through.'

She crossed her arms over her chest. 'I've sent the cast home.'

'What?'

Mel shook her head, 'Jesus, do you learn nothing? You've just accused a grieving man of shagging his friend, then collapsed yourself and you think we can just carry on as if nothing has happened?'

'I didn't collapse.' I sat back in the chair, indignant. I ran through what had happened in my head, shame warming my cheeks. 'It's been a lot. That's all.'

'I know,' said Mel, her voice more gentle. 'There's no harm in asking for help, you know.'

I nearly said *who from?* but trapped the words behind my teeth. A few short weeks ago, the first person I would have turned to was Bill. More recently, it would have been Elle. Now, there was nobody.

'I don't need help,' I said. 'I need to get back to work.'

'No,' said Mel. I peered up at her face and saw her jaw was tight. The muscles in her cheeks jumped as though she was clenching and unclenching her back teeth.

'I'll be fine—'

'Even if that's true,' she cut me off. 'It's not about you, Jen. You're not the only one who's having a hard time and we don't think you're in the right state of mind—'

'We?'

'The trustees,' she said. 'I spoke to them after you nearly disbanded youth theatre for dropping a bit of litter—'

'You did fucking what?' I stood, a fierce heat radiating through me. 'You went to the trustees about me?'

'Oh, sit down,' said Mel, rolling her eyes. 'This is you all over: reactionary.'

Dumbstruck, I dropped back into the chair.

'We've been worried about you, that's all.' Mel rubbed her forehead and looked at me through pale lashes. 'Nobody's after your job, nobody wants to fill your shoes, if that's what you're thinking. We just want you to take a bit of time to sort out whatever's going on at home, then you can come back and give the company your full attention again.'

'The company has my full attention,' I said, the accusation stabbing at everything I believed about myself. I was strong, committed, capable. I wasn't someone who had emotional breakdowns at work and needed time off to deal with their personal life. That wasn't who I was.

'Oh, come on, Jen. Let the mask drop, for god's sake. Nobody's buying this whole *impressive and impenetrable* routine anymore. It's bollocks and it's starting to affect other people. Ed's in bits. He should never have had to pretend otherwise. And when you stop pretending, it will be better for all of us.' One side of her mouth rose in a wonky smile. 'Good job you're a director, not an actor,' she said. 'You'd be shit.'

'Thanks,' I said petulantly. But something in me had loosened while Mel was talking, and suddenly, it felt like a hard part of me dislodged and broke away. It was like I was unwinding, and with the tautness released, I could feel more tears threatening. 'How long?' I said, raising my chin.

'What?'

'How long have I been suspended for?'

Mel's shoulders dropped. 'Don't be like that. We just thought . . . it's nearly Christmas. The play's in great shape. We want you to take an early break and maybe a week or so after to get your personal life sorted. Let's talk in the New Year, if you're ready . . .'

'If I'm ready? If?' I stood. 'Right. That's me told. I'll go and sort my shit out, then, shall I?' I could feel Mel's eyes on me as I marched to the door. She said my name quietly, but I didn't turn back. I tried not to look around my beloved studio as I walked to the door. Mine and Mel's cars were the only ones left in the car park, but I still kept my head high and the tears at bay until the studio was out of sight in my rear-view mirror.

Then I pulled into a side street, lay my head against the steering wheel and sobbed as though my heart was breaking.

Chapter Thirty-Four

Elle

I was looking at my phone to see how long it was before I needed to pick Harry up from school when it burst into life in my hand, the vibrating and ringing making me jump. When Jen's name flashed up on the screen, I almost dropped it. I lifted a finger to press the red button to end the call but changed my mind and pressed the green one instead.

I put the phone to my ear and held my breath.

'Elle?'

The sound of her voice made my stomach lurch. 'What do you want?'

There was a muffled rustling sound, as though she was wiping her nose next to the speaker. I imagined her crying but dismissed the image. Jen didn't cry. She probably didn't know how.

'I don't know, if I'm honest.'

'Because I haven't got another husband, if that's what you're after.' I made my voice diamond hard. 'I've got a son though, but I'm not sure you'd want to add him to your collection. He's a little bit broken, you see, because his dad's just deserted him and pissed off with another woman.'

'For fuck's sake, Elle. You can't really—'

I hacked out a laugh, 'I'm so over being told what I can and can't do by you two.'

'You two?' she sounded angry, 'No, Elle. I'm not . . . Surely you don't—' Her voice cracked and I was glad.

'You've got what you wanted. Is that why you're calling, to gloat?'

'Wow, you don't know me at all, do you?' she said, then sighed. 'Look, I don't know why . . . It's just, it's hard. It's fucking hard. I suppose I thought you'd be the one person who understood. Clearly, I'm wrong.'

I groaned into the speaker. 'No, Jen, I don't understand, you see I've never stolen someone else's husband. I've never left a little boy without a father. I've never destroyed anyone's life, so forgive me if I don't sit quietly by and listen to how fucking hard this is for you.'

'I didn't—'

I took the phone from my ear and ended the call. How dare she? How fucking dare she ring me to complain about how hard she was finding things?

My pulse was still racing when Michael shuffled into the kitchen a minute later. 'I need you to leave,' I said. I was hot and angry after speaking to Jen and now was the right time to tackle the next person who was taking me for a mug. I didn't know what he was still doing here. He wasn't my problem. He was Rob's.

Michael sat on a chair and dropped his head into his hands. 'Have you heard from him?' he asked.

'No. And I don't want to.'

The silence buzzed between us. I thought about telling

him again that he had to move out, but the words stalled in my throat. He looked so pathetic. I knew his drinking was an illness and I pitied the shambolic man he'd become. But surely it was Rob's job to take care of him, not mine. Especially not now.

'It's my fault he's done this to you, ruined all your lives.'

I turned away. I didn't know what he wanted from me. I could agree. There was some truth in what he said. Rob had grown up thinking he was special, but it wasn't just Michael who'd made him feel like he was more than mortal on the rare occasions he'd dipped into his life when he was growing up. I know his grandma had treated him like a god, and I had, too. I'd been grateful to have him.

Maybe if I'd stood up to him more, he wouldn't have treated me as disposable. Maybe if I'd been more like Jen. That thought whooshed through me like a flame, bringing a fierce anger with it. 'It's Rob's fault he did what he did. He had a choice.'

Michael stood. He wobbled and held on to the back of the chair. 'I'll go this afternoon.' His voice was weak. When he lifted his head, his face was grey and gaunt.

'When did you last eat?'

He scrunched his face. 'Not sure.'

'Sit down.'

He did as he was told, picking at a bloodied hangnail on his thumb while I made a sandwich and a cup of tea. When I put the plate in front of him, he clutched my hand. 'I'm so sorry, Elle. You don't deserve any of this.'

I squeezed his fingers and pulled my hand away. 'Where will you go?'

'Honestly?' Tea sploshed over the side of the mug as he lifted it shakily to his dry lips. 'I don't know.'

Maybe it was because his dry, cracked lips reminded me

of Mum in her final days, ravaged by cancer, so withered and scared, but the hardness I'd built up against him melted away. I couldn't feel anything except pity. 'You can stay 'til after Christmas. That should give you time to get something organised. Okay?'

He didn't raise his head, just croaked, 'Thank you,' through his tears.

* * *

'Thank you for coming in,' said Claire, gesturing to a seat. There was barely enough room for two chairs in her narrow office. A fan heater plugged into the wall behind her whirred. The warm air penetrated my leggings, but the rest of me still felt cold from the short walk from the car park to the school.

I tried to meet her eyes, painfully aware of how I must look. I'd barely slept in the days since Rob left and I hadn't had the energy to put my face on before today's meeting. All my energy was going into making sure Harry was alright. And it wasn't working. He was sitting in the school office now and I couldn't imagine sending him into class. He'd been quiet with me and Michael since it all kicked off. I doubted he'd talk to anyone else.

'How's Harry's eye?' Claire asked.

'Not too bad,' I said. 'Now the swelling's gone down we can see his eye's not damaged. He's got a scab here,' I put my finger in the dip where my eye met my nose, 'that he keeps picking, but other than that, the doctor gave him the all clear.' The memory of the relief I'd felt when the doctor confirmed his sight wasn't damaged lifted me for a moment.

'Good stuff. Right, I've got back all the information from Harry's teachers and from you.' Claire tapped at a small keyboard on the desk and looked at the screen. 'What I haven't got is the full picture from Harry.'

'I don't know what you want me to do about that,' I said. I knew I sounded defensive, but, really, I could do without being told off right now.

Claire turned towards me and smiled sympathetically. 'Sorry, I didn't mean that to sound . . . What I meant was I can't give you a definitive diagnosis yet, but I do have a fairly good idea of what might be going on. I can't be certain at this early stage, but what I feel like I want to explore is a thing called selective mutism. It's an anxiety disorder. I'm not an expert in it, but I think that's what we might be looking at with Harry.'

'Selective mutism? You think he's choosing to be like this?'

She lifted her palms. 'It doesn't mean he's consciously choosing not to talk. Like so many conditions, it's got a title that doesn't really fit with the symptoms. From what I understand, the inability to speak in certain situations is the body's way of reacting to anxiety.

'To be honest, I'm still learning about selective mutism as I go along, which must be frustrating for you to hear. It's an uncommon disorder and I want to make sure I'm giving you best advice possible.'

I swallowed down the panicky feeling rising up my throat. A disorder. That sounded like it wasn't going to be resolved quickly. Maybe it was something that would affect his whole life. My poor, poor boy. On top of that, I'd been worrying about my finances now Rob had gone, almost as much as I worried about Harry. The joint account hadn't been topped up since Rob left and these sessions were already more than I could afford without asking him for more money. I didn't want to do that, and I wasn't sure he'd allow it, even if I did. I expected him to want to punish me for throwing him out.

'So, what's the next step?'

'I've been in touch with a specialist in London. She's the only specialist I can find in the UK, and she has pointed me in the direction of a method called either sliding in, or phasing in. It's kind of a desensitising programme.'

'Desensitising from what?'

'Well, the specialist described selective mutism as a kind of phobia. We have to presume Harry has a phobia of speaking to people he doesn't know very well.'

'Okay.' That made sense.

'So, putting him in a room full of people and asking him to talk is like putting someone who has a phobia of spiders in room filled with spiders.'

My stomach curled tight at the thought of my poor boy being put in that position every day. How did I not see how scared he was? 'Right. So, we can't carry on forcing Harry to come into school. Not when it's having this effect on him.'

Claire shook her head. 'We won't be forcing Harry to do anything. Our job is to help him.' She paused. 'But I've also been told avoidance isn't helpful. If he's allowed to stay away from school, then the problem isn't being dealt with, it's just being avoided.'

She offered me a tissue from the box on the desk which sat next to a wooden Christmas tree. I took it and was surprised to feel my cheeks were wet. I hadn't been aware I was crying.

'I suspect, from what I've heard from you and Harry's teachers, that he might have the inattentive subtype of ADHD, but I think we should aim to help him to use his voice first and then look at whatever other support he might need. That sound okay?'

I nodded, still mopping up my tears which were flowing

freely now. I was helpless to stop them, so didn't try. The front of my calves were starting to burn from the heater. I put my hand to the Lycra, and it felt scorching against my cold fingers.

Claire took a cardboard folder from her desk and handed it to me. 'I've printed off some information for you to have a look at.'

I tried and failed to stop my bottom lip trembling.

'I know it seems overwhelming, but you're not on your own. I promise.'

I was on my own. Entirely on my own.

'The fact Harry talks at home . . .' She looked at me for confirmation and I nodded. 'But not at school, gives us a starting point. If we can incrementally help him to relax, we can, hopefully, encourage him to speak. Ideally, we'll need you to come in early each day to start with. You'll be with Harry in his classroom, playing games and chatting exactly as you would at home, then, little by little, either me or Mrs Wheeler will come into the room. Will that be possible?'

I nodded. She passed another folder to me, along with another tissue. 'All the information on the process is in there. I know it's a lot to take in. The point of this meeting is to make sure you agree with what we think is going on with Harry, we'll go slowly, don't worry.'

Don't worry? That seemed like the most ridiculous phrase she could choose.

'We'll give Harry these cards.' She held up two pieces of cardboard the size of playing cards. The green one will tell his teacher he needs the toilet and the blue one means he needs help with his work.'

I looked at the cards knowing full well Harry would hate having to use them. They were just another reason for people to look at him. But surely it was better than him being unable to ask to go to the toilet?

'A buddy system can work well too,' Claire said. 'A bit further down the line, Harry could have one friend who he feels comfortable speaking to, and they could begin by relaying what he says. Is there anyone his age he speaks to?'

The image of Harry bouncing around Rooted shouting 'Boing, boing, boing,' with Cora burst into my head. 'Not anymore,' I spluttered. 'He did have a friend, not at school though.' I shook my head. 'Not a friend, exactly. A little girl called Cora.'

Claire rolled her bottom lip back over her teeth. 'Hm.' She seemed to notice how stifling the room had become and leaned down to switch off the heater. Without the fan, the room was uncomfortably silent.

I glanced up. Claire knew Cora. Of course she did. Jen and I met through her support group. 'You know, don't you?'

'All my meetings are confidential, but I do know Cora, yes.'

'And you know we've just discovered she's Harry's half-sister?'

Claire nodded. 'It must be a difficult time for all of you.'

I found myself laughing. To think that just a couple of months ago I'd been trying to portray the image of the perfect family and now, my dirty laundry was flying across two towns. 'Difficult, yes. That's one word for it.'

Claire passed a business card to me. 'Now my children are a bit older, I've started an evening practice. I'm working with adults as well as children, so if you feel like you want to talk . . .' She shrugged. 'My number's on there.'

I took the card. 'I don't suppose you work with alcoholics

as well, do you?' The image of the perfect family was so muddied, I may as well get the whole sorry mess into the open. 'My father-in-law . . . he's struggling.'

I kept my eyes on the card. I didn't want to see pity in her eyes.

Her voice was kind enough to show the pity anyway. 'It's not my area, but I can email you the details of some specialists.'

'Thank you,' I said, getting to my feet.

'Take care,' she said, as I left the room. I was too choked up to reply.

Chapter Thirty-Five

Jen

There was a knock at the door. I looked at my watch: 7pm. I shuddered. That was the time Robin called me when he was away, or he supposedly called his father when he was here. Now I knew he'd been calling Elle and Harry, not his father, and I was a fool for believing him.

I opened the door and gasped in disbelief when I saw Robin standing on the pavement. Elle's words rang in my ears. Since she'd made it clear she thought I was in on his lies, I was even more furious than before. To be deceived was hard enough. To be unjustly blamed made me burn with new fury. I used my anger to try to slam the door in Robin's face, but he shoved his shoulder against the wood and stuck his boot inside. 'Please,' he said, 'just give me a minute.'

'Fuck you.'

He heaved himself against the door. 'I just want to talk. I miss you. Both of you.'

'Fuck off, you egotistical, lying narcissist.'

I heard my neighbour's door open, and Paul's bald head appeared in the gap, hooded eyes narrowed. He flicked a stubby thumb towards Robin, who was huffing with the exertion of keeping the door from cracking the bones in his foot. 'You need a hand, Jen?'

'Fuck off, Paul,' said Robin.

Paul took another step forwards. 'Oh, yeah?'

I released the door and Robin tumbled into the hall. 'It's alright, Paul, thanks. He won't be staying long.'

Paul eyed Robin menacingly, then smiled at me. 'You knock on the wall if you need me, alright girl?'

'Will do. Thanks.' I pushed the door to.

Robin staggered to his feet. 'He's a dickhead.' He gestured at the closed door.

'Pot, kettle.'

'You told him what happened?' He sounded incredulous.

'I've told everyone who'll listen,' I said. And I had. Initially, I'd been ashamed I'd been taken in for so long. But shame loves secrecy. It burrows inside, and the silence feeds it and makes it swell, so I decided to expose Robin to everyone who knew him, so the shame was transferred to him. Had it worked? Not entirely. I still wanted to shrivel up and die when I thought of how gullible I'd been, but people's reactions had been affirming. I wasn't the villain, at least. He was. I just wished Elle had the fucking sense to see that.

I tried not to look at him standing, catching his breath in my hallway. I used to feel pure joy when he came through that door. And longing. The way my body responded to the sight of his strong forearms now, the blonde hairs thinning towards the back of his hands, was a betrayal. I couldn't look at his long fingers without wanting them to touch me. I turned away and marched past the Christmas tree into the kitchen. Cora was upstairs and I didn't want her to hear us. 'What do you want? I've given all your stuff to charity, so there's no point—'

'I want to explain.'

I rounded on him. 'It's all pretty clear, thanks, so you may as well turn around now and get the fuck out of my house.'

'It was you I wanted. It was always you.' His shoulders slumped. 'I know I messed things up, but you've got to believe me, it was always you.'

'Really?' I loaded mine and Cora's dinner dishes into the dishwasher, so I had something to do with my hands. I wanted him to see normal life went on, despite how much he'd hurt me. I still made dinner and loaded the dishwasher. He hadn't broken me.

'When you were with your beautiful, young, blonde, fit wife and your gorgeous son and heir?' I laughed bitterly, waving a wooden spoon around before chucking it in the machine. 'When you were in your big, detached house, you couldn't wait to get back to this little terrace.' I fluttered my hands around my narrow kitchen. 'And this peri-menopausal, dried-up old bag?'

'You're not . . .' he sighed. 'I only ever wanted to be with you. You're my soul mate, Jen. We were meant to be together, If I'd met you first, none of this would've happened.'

Something in me keened to reach out and touch his face. I forced myself to sneer. 'Bollocks. And it didn't just *happen*. You created this situation. This is all your doing.'

He took a step towards me. The smell of his sandalwood aftershave weakened my legs. I held on to the worktop while, in my mind, I could see the exact point on his chest where he sprayed it, below his clavicle, where the hairs were turning grey. 'I love you, Jen. I only love you. Nobody else matters.'

A new picture appeared in my mind: Elle, across the table at Rooted, asking me about how it went at the doctors, making sure I made an appointment to see a specialist, her gorgeous face filled with concern for me. 'What about Elle?'

It was the way he flapped his arm dismissively that made me snap. Despite the awful way she'd treated me, Elle had been my friend. She was once his wife, like me, and he thought he could wave her away as if she was an irrelevance. She should matter to him. Harry should matter. Whatever she thought of me, I knew they were hurting just like Cora and I were, and this fucking man thought he could come here and dismiss them, then wheedle his way back into my life.

'How dare you wave her away like an unpleasant smell. You've ruined her life, you arrogant prick. She thinks you and I cooked this up together, do you know that? She tore into me when I tried to tell her the truth, but I'm not surprised, when she's been lied to as much as I have. And poor Harry's—'

He shook his head, 'Harry's fine. That's part of Elle's problem, she's paranoid about Harry. If she just let him get on with it rather than fussing about him.'

'Harry *will* be fine,' I said, 'because, despite what she thinks of me, I can see she's a brilliant mother who is trying to get him the help he needs.'

'I'm not here to talk about Elle,' he said, a hint of irritation in his voice. 'I want to talk about us. I need you to understand that I want you, not her.'

'Is that right? Even though you let her think you were trying for a baby, you utter twat?'

His brow furrowed. 'What did she tell you?'

'You didn't even tell her you'd had a vasectomy, did you?'

He held his hands in front of him. 'She's tried to poison you against me—'

I couldn't believe how he was trying to spin this. 'She still doesn't know. Poor cow. Get out.' He put his hand on my arm. I ignored the warmth on my skin and shook him off. 'Get out now or I swear—'

He stood his ground. 'You didn't live with her. She's never happy. She nags and goes on and on.'

'Daddy?'

I looked over Robin's shoulder to see Cora standing, wide eyes staring up at him.

He spun around and grabbed her. 'Hello princess.' He kissed her cheek. 'You have no idea how much I've missed you.'

Cora looked from me to Robin, and I could see her trying to work out what was going on. 'Are you home now? Where's Harry? Is he at his house? Will you stay at our house now, or will you have to go and be Harry's daddy?' Her chin puckered.

I reached out and tried to take her from Robin, but he shifted away. He carried her through to the sitting room, talking in soothing tones. 'I'm back now, baby. I've come to stay with you and Mummy all the time. Is that okay?'

The fucking bastard. 'Cora, could you go upstairs please while me and Daddy have a talk?'

'I don't want to.' She clung on to Robin's neck.

'We can talk after Cora's gone to bed,' said Robin. He turned back to her. 'Tell me about school today. Who did you play with?'

I watched Cora's lips turn up in a smile and I despised him for putting me in this position. I spoke through clenched teeth. 'I need you to go. Now.'

'Please, Jen. Let's talk later.'

A flame of heat rushed through my body. I picked up

the glass bowl we'd bought in Venice on honeymoon, raised it high, then flung it to the ground. Cora screamed. Robin shielded her face and looked at me as though I'd lost my mind. 'Get out of my fucking house!' I screamed, picking up a glass paperweight with a silver stag inside and holding it above my head.

Robin put Cora in the chair nearest him, then stood, arms outstretched, 'Alright, alright, I'm going.'

'Mummy,' Cora wailed, curling her feet under her, making herself small in the chair.

What had I done? I lowered the paperweight and put it gently back on the mantelpiece. 'I'm sorry, sweetheart. It's alright, I'm so sorry. It's okay now,' I crooned, as I took her in my arms and rocked her backwards and forwards.

As I soothed my shaking child, Robin tiptoed into the hall, and I heard the front door's latch click open then closed. I knew I was right sending him away, but the knowledge I'd terrified the life out of my daughter made my heart ache. I had no husband, no friends, no job to go to and no idea who the hell I was anymore.

Chapter Thirty-Six

Elle

'Remember what I said.' I stopped outside the glass doors leading to reception and looked into Harry's face to make sure he listened. 'You don't have to talk. You don't have to do anything you don't want.'

'I don't want to go to school,' he said. 'You're making me do that.'

'You break up in a couple of days. Come on.'

Guilt wove itself around my heart. I agreed with Claire and Mrs Wheeler that Harry shouldn't get used to working on his own at home, because that was avoidance, but it didn't make this any easier. Mrs Wheeler wasn't going to ask him any direct questions. Everyone was briefed: this wasn't a speaking issue. It was an anxiety issue. Until Harry felt safe, he couldn't talk.

This first step was to get Harry talking to me inside the school building. I couldn't believe how nervous I was approaching a place I'd been in a hundred times before. 'What dinosaurs have you brought today?' I said, as I rang the bell.

'My stegosaurus and triceratops,' he said. 'What if I lose them?'

'Don't worry about that,' I said. 'Try not to, but if you do, we can get some more.' I pressed the buzzer and tried to think of more questions. 'Which is your favourite dinosaur?'

I glanced down. He was staring at the receptionist who was scurrying towards the door.

'I think you like the T-Rex the best,' I goaded. I knew Harry preferred the velociraptor ever since Cora had given the remote-controlled one to him.

His lips remained in a straight line. The receptionist opened the door. 'Good morning. Hello Harry,' she said, 'How are you today?' She stopped and I saw panic on her face. 'I mean, it's a lovely day out there.'

Harry turned and looked at the grey December weather through the glass doors, then back at her. 'Shall we get you to your classroom?' She flushed and gave me an apologetic look. I felt for her. She'd spent her whole career trying to engage people in polite conversation and now she was being asked not to do what came naturally. 'On you go then,' she said, putting her head down and heading back to the office.

* * *

Harry spoke to me in the classroom but clammed up as soon as Mrs Wheeler put her hand on the door handle. Claire had told me to expect that. We'd follow the same routine tomorrow, but for now, I'd left Harry in class, and I felt like the most awful mother on earth. Ever since Claire had said it was like leaving him with a room full of spiders, I couldn't stop my mind from creating images of Harry sobbing, as spiders crawled all over him. I'd even had a dream last night where Harry's mouth was open in a scream as a tarantula crawled inside.

The day loomed in front of me. I would have liked to go home to brood over a cup of coffee on my own sofa, but Michael would be there, and I couldn't bear to spend the morning avoiding being in the same room as him.

When I'd given him the email list of specialists Claire sent to me, he said, 'How am I meant to pay for this?'

'Ask Rob,' I said. He'd looked at me for a few seconds then ambled away. I didn't know what else I could do. I couldn't afford to pay for his sessions; I could barely cover Harry's. I told myself that it would all be over by Christmas. I wouldn't go back on my word about letting him stay until then. But not a day longer.

I drew into the gym car park and exhaled. I didn't want to work out. I looked at myself in the rear-view mirror and almost laughed at my make-up free, exhausted-looking eyes. Was it only a couple of months since I'd trained most days with Nicky? I used to work hard on my barely there make-up and on trend gym kit, hoping to impress her. I'd worked hard on my body, trying to please my husband. And where had it got me?

I forced myself through the first set of doors, the warm fan ruffling my hair before the second set swooshed open. I kept my eyes down, tapped my membership card on the reader and pushed my thighs against the barrier until it gave way to let me in.

When I got into a rhythm on the running machine, I was glad I'd come. My heart started to pound and the thump, thump, thump of my trainers on the treadmill hypnotised me until all I thought about was my next step, my next breath. The tension in my shoulders released and soon I was nowhere, with nothing and nobody to think about other than the pounding of my feet on the belt.

'Hello stranger.'

My heart jumped. My feet faltered, making me stumble. I staggered to regain my pace, nerves jangled and breathing disordered. I pressed the arrow to slow the machine and turned to Nicky, who was standing by the side of the treadmill looking as polished and shiny as ever. 'Sorry, I didn't mean to surprise you.'

'No, no. It's fine,' I gasped out, wiping the sweat from my face with my towel. Why did I still feel the need to smooth everything over? She had shocked me. She had ruined the only moment of calm I'd felt in weeks. 'How are you?'

'Good,' she said. 'You?'

The question came with a practised nonchalance. She knew what had happened, but she didn't want to appear to pry.

'Fine, thanks.' I pressed the arrow to increase my pace. I remembered her and the other women's faces turning into fanged monsters, greedy to tear people apart the night I went for a curry with them. 'Good to be back here. I can't believe how much I'm enjoying running.'

My heart sank when she lay her towel on the handle of the treadmill next to mine and placed her water bottle in the holder. She climbed on and started up the machine. 'You haven't been here in a while. I missed you.'

There was a time when I would have been flattered by that. 'Busy, busy,' I said, pressing up my speed.

After a quiet moment, she said, 'Oh, I nearly forgot, Grace is having a birthday party at St Nick's church hall at the weekend. You and Harry will have to come.' She lifted her water bottle and held it above her lips, squirting a perfect arc of water into her mouth. 'It's a nightmare, her birthday being on Christmas day. She's always complaining she doesn't get two special days like everyone else.'

'I bet it's annoying, everyone getting presents on your birthday.'

'Yeah. I'm going all out this year to keep her happy. We're having karaoke. It's going to be deafening, but it's what she wanted, so . . .' I felt her eyes on me. 'There'll be a bar for the mums and dads to take the edge off the screeching eight-year-olds.' She paused. 'Will Rob come with you?'

'No.' I took a drink from my bottle.

She waited to see if I was going to say more. After a moment she said, 'But you will bring Harry, won't you?'

'Thanks, but karaoke's not really his thing.'

'Don't worry about that. He doesn't have to join in if he doesn't want to.'

I tried to imagine Harry standing in front of a group of his classmates and their parents belting out '*I am what I am*' at the top of his lungs. It seemed about as likely as travelling back through time and hitching a ride on a stegosaurus. Which I knew he'd prefer. 'I just don't think—'

'It would be good for him,' said Nicky. I heard her sigh. 'Grace has told me he hasn't been . . . I know you've had a hard time . . . but I think it would do Harry the world of good if he tried to integrate a bit more. Even if he doesn't do karaoke, surely it would be good for him to hang out with the other kids doing normal stuff, you know?'

Normal stuff. Normal for who? I ran through the things that were normal for Harry, like learning about how far planets were from earth, researching how long a brachiosaurus would live, reading quietly in his room. Who got to say that Grace and her friends screeching out pop songs was the *normal* way for a child to behave? Who made the rules? Why was their normal right and Harry's wrong?

But it didn't matter who made the rules, did it? The fact

was, there was a way of behaving that would make other people think you were normal, and Harry's life would be a lot easier if he could conform.

'Okay,' I said, slowing my treadmill. 'Text me the details. We'd love to come.'

'Great,' said Nicky. 'I actually sent an invitation. It should be in Harry's school bag.'

'Ah, the black hole that is Harry's school bag.' I kept my voice light, hiding the fact I meant it. Whatever went into that bag could multiply or disappear without a trace. I was as likely to find a half-eaten sandwich as six dinosaurs. The only things I never found in Harry's school bag were the things that were meant to be in there.

She nodded and smiled as I stepped down and collected my towel and water bottle. 'I'll text you.'

When I sat in the gym car park, trying to gather the energy to drive home, a text alert pinged on my phone. It was a message from Nicky, telling me the time and place for Grace's party. I cursed myself for agreeing. I visualised the school, imagining Harry sitting silently in his classroom, doing his work as poisonous spiders crept into his ears.

I remembered what Claire said: the aim was to desensitise him, to introduce him to situations which made him anxious and show him he could feel safe. Maybe a children's party could be part of the process. We didn't have to stay for the whole time, just long enough for him to see there was nothing to be afraid of. I texted back.

Looking forward to it. Xx

Surely it was worth a try?

Chapter Thirty-Seven

Jen

'Thanks for coming in,' said Claire, shaking my hand, then gesturing for me to sit. 'I've had the screening questionnaires back from you and from Cora's teachers. And Cora's been very helpful when I've met with her.'

'By helpful, you mean talkative.'

Claire smiled. 'She's very open.'

'Hm.' I wondered how much this woman now knew about my life. I was half tempted to tell her that I was trying harder to listen to Cora now I wasn't working, that I was trying to be a better mum, because I was all she'd got. And she was all I had too. The thought made tears sting in the corners of my eyes.

'She's very funny too,' said Claire. 'She has a unique way with words.'

I couldn't help smiling. 'She does.'

Claire tapped on an iPad. 'I don't have my own office here, so I have to keep things on my tablet.' She peered at the screen and used her fingers to enlarge a document. 'If

I show you these, you can see she scores highly for the inattentive subtype of ADHD.'

I tried to keep my face neutral. I knew this was coming. I reminded myself it didn't change anything, then hated myself when I still felt like it did. She pointed at the numbers at the base of the questionnaire I'd filled out. 'You've scored her most highly, but—'

Heat ran up my neck. Was I the reason she was being diagnosed? Maybe I was overreacting. 'Are my scores very different?'

Claire shook her head. 'This happens in almost every case. You spend more time with your child, so you see things her teachers don't. For example, look, this question about finding it hard to motivate Cora.' She pointed at the question. 'You've answered that it's *frequently* difficult to motivate her to complete a task.'

I cast my mind about for why I would have said that and came up with a myriad of reasons. 'I can't get her to tidy her room, read a book, do her times tables, but maybe that's normal. She's my only child, so I could be wrong. The reason I put that is because she often can't find the motivation to do the things she wants to do. It takes her forever to get ready for a party, for example, and she loves parties. It's like she doesn't understand how time works, I've got to drag her . . .'

Claire put her hand out to stop me. 'It's fine. Like I said, it's completely understandable you've scored her higher. Look . . .' She switched to another form. 'Her teachers put *often* for that question and from what I can see, Cora likes to please people.'

'Oh, yeah, she's a people pleaser.'

'So, the fact her teachers often can't motivate her, when we know she wants to please them and doesn't like being told off, suggests there's something going on that Cora needs help with.'

'Okay,' I said, when Claire finished going through the forms. I tried to find a word for the dark feeling spreading over me. The only one that felt right was grief. It felt like I'd lost part of my little girl. I'd lost so much recently, and now Cora was not exactly who I thought she was either.

Darkness wrapped itself around me and I didn't have the strength to shrug it off. If things had been different I could have called Elle and said, *I feel like this, do you feel it too?* Instead, I sat straighter in the chair and said, 'What now?'

Claire placed the iPad carefully on the desk. 'That's up to you, your husband and Cora. It will take some time to make the official diagnosis. The reason I've been able to do the screening is because I'm a qualified psychologist masquerading as a school counsellor. It would usually take months to get this far. There are a few options available to you now, but your GP will need to be involved, and if you want Cora to try stimulant medication, then we will need to get her on a waiting list to see—'

'Stimulants?'

'It's an option, that's all. Cora told me she has a hundred unfinished sentences in her head all the time.'

I smiled. That sounded like my girl. She wasn't different. She was still Cora. If I told myself enough times, would I believe it?

'And, from what I know from people who take the stimulants, it allows them to think one thought at a time, or, to put it in Cora's language, finish one of the hundred sentences. It's a focus thing. It might help her to be less open to distraction.' She tapped on her screen. 'I'll email the information to you so you can read it in your own time.

There's no pressure, take your time to think about what's best for Cora.'

My head swam. 'But stimulants? That makes me think of amphetamines, like speed or something?'

'Yes. They're carefully monitored, but you're right, the ADHD medication that's proven to work well is synthetic amphetamine.'

'Shit.'

She nodded. 'It's a lot to take in.'

It was a lot to take in. I would be deciding whether to give my little girl drugs that would alter the way her mind worked.

'Shit,' I said again. However much I hated Robin right now, I didn't feel strong enough to make that decision on my own. I wondered what Elle would do in my situation. I wished I could ask.

* * *

When I made dinner that evening, my head was still swimming. 'I saw Claire, the counsellor, today,' I said, putting a plate of fish fingers and chips in front of Cora, with beans in a small ramekin on the side so they didn't make the rest of her food soggy. I watched her poke at her chips, sorting them into order of crispiness. 'She said you're doing really well.'

'Really well at what?' Cora squirted a puddle of ketchup onto her plate. 'We just talk, and she asks me questions but they're not like a test or anything because she said it didn't matter what the answers were because I couldn't get them wrong.' She looked up, her brow furrowed. 'Was that a lie?'

My heart broke for her. Before her father betrayed us, she would never have asked that question; she would have presumed grown-ups always told the truth.

'It was absolutely true,' I said. 'She asked the same questions to me and Mrs Daniels and we had to answer according to how we see you.'

'Why? How could you answer them because you don't live inside my head? I'm a very thinky person, so I don't know how you and Mrs Daniels could answer the same questions about how I feel and things like that.' She picked up a chip and dipped it in the ketchup.

'Knife and fork,' I said, as I did every mealtime. She lifted the fork and slotted the chip onto the prongs with her fingers. 'Maybe the questions were a little bit different, but they were for the same thing.'

'What thing?' She chewed and watched me. I knew she was trying to gauge my reaction, so I smiled. She carried on chewing.

'Well, you know how everybody is different?'

'Yes, and it doesn't matter if somebody is different to what me and you are like because you still have to be kind to everybody because kindness is the most important *ness*, isn't it?'

'That's right. The thing Claire is asking us all about is called ADHD.'

'What's that?'

Good question. What was that? From what I'd read it was so many things it seemed ridiculous that they all came under the same banner. 'It's different for everybody, but if you have it . . .'

She stopped chewing. 'Have it? Do I *have* something? Am I poorly?' I could see her brain adding things up. Panic sparked in her eyes. 'Have I caught ADHD? Is it bad for me? Am I going to die of it?'

I strode forwards and kneeled in front of her chair. 'No, no, not at all. Listen to me.' I took her face in my hands and looked into her eyes. 'Listening ears, okay?' Her head bobbed in my palms. 'It's not something you get sick with. It's just the way some people's bodies and brains are made. It's completely normal and it doesn't hurt.' I didn't know if I was telling her a lie now. What was *normal*? And even if it didn't hurt physically, from what I understood, there could be mental health issues. Look at Harry.

'It might explain why you find some things hard, like remembering your pencil case and stopping your brain from being too busy to go to sleep.'

She nodded again. 'So, there is something wrong with me,' she said, her eyes filling with tears. 'I've got something bad inside me?'

'No, darling, no. Not at all.' I pulled her into my body. 'No,' I said again and all the darkness from earlier disappeared. Cora was no different. She was gorgeous and perfect and brilliant. 'No,' I said again, and I meant it with every molecule of my being. If having ADHD meant my lovely girl felt everything deeply, that she said every thought that came into her head, that she viewed the world in technicolour, then I was glad for that gene mutation because she was the brightest, most loving girl on this earth. 'There isn't a single bad thing inside you. If anything, it makes you more creative and more brilliant.'

She drew back her head. 'I don't know if I want to have it, though, if it makes me forget things and get told off by Mrs Daniels. I think I just want to be normal.'

I smiled and kissed her forehead. 'If you do have it, then everyone will have to understand that you might forget things now and again. And we'll help you. That's why Claire has been asking you those questions, so that me and Mrs Daniels can find the best way to support you.'

Her bottom lip twitched. 'I still think I'd like to be normal, please.'

I'd never hated a word more. 'You are normal. Perfectly normal. You're normal for Cora. I'm normal for me. Because everybody is different, everybody's normal is going to be different too, isn't it?' When I said it, it suddenly made perfect sense. 'Don't you think?'

She nodded slowly.

'You okay? Do you have any questions? You can ask me anything you like.'

She shook her head.

'You going to eat up then?'

She picked up a chip with her fingers and I didn't have the heart to remind her to use her fork. I wished I could see inside her head. What were those hundred unfinished sentences telling her now? I wished I knew.

Chapter Thirty-Eight

Elle

'I'm excited about Grace's party,' I said to Harry, who looked as miserable about having to go as I felt. I dabbed blood from the gash next to his eye with a tissue, then turned back to my dressing table mirror. 'Please stop picking that. It's going to scar.'

'I want Daddy,' he said.

'I know sweetheart. I know.' In my reflection I saw I'd aged ten years in the last few days. I sprayed salt solution on the ends of my hair in an attempt to make it look tousled and trendy.

'Why can't I see him?'

He stood behind me, shoulders drooped. His sad eyes made my heart contract 'I tell you what.' I turned away from the mirror and took his hands in mine. 'If you come to the party, I'll see if Daddy can take you out for a treat afterwards. Okay?'

He nodded and I felt a rush of panic. What a stupid thing to promise. I didn't know if Rob would be able to take Harry out. We'd only exchanged text messages since I'd asked him to leave, and I purposefully hadn't asked where he was staying; partly because I don't think I could bear it if he was living full-time with Jen and Cora.

It wasn't, I'd realised, that I wanted Rob. When I looked back, it was a long, long time since I'd wanted him for myself, and that felt like a tragedy on its own. I'd behaved exactly like my mum, tried to hold on to a man to make my own life work. I was pathetic. Our relationship had been dead for years and it had taken this for me to see that. Deep down, I knew he'd betrayed Harry more than me.

And if Rob was living with Jen, I was certain Harry would feel like Rob had chosen Cora over him. And that would break both our hearts.

'Go and put on the clothes I've laid on your bed,' I said. 'I'll message Daddy.'

He scampered off. I closed my bedroom door and picked up my phone. My pulse raced as I pressed the button and listened to the dial tone.

'Elle,' said the painfully familiar voice on the other end of the line. 'Hi.'

'Hi,' I said.

'How's Harry?'

I closed my eyes against all the things I wanted to say about Harry's selective mutism and how I was going into school every morning to try to make Harry less terrified of using his lovely voice. 'He wants to see you.'

I heard his breath catch. 'Yeah, great, I mean, of course. I could come around now?'

Relief flooded me. 'Erm, we've got Grace's birthday party, so, could you pick him up at five?'

'Pick him up?'

Did he really think he was stepping foot in this house?

My relief turned to indignance. 'Maybe you could take him for a burger or something?'

There was a pause then a sigh. 'Okay,' he said tersely. 'I've been trying to call Dad. He's not picking up. Is he alright?'

That surprised me. I'd imagined they'd been talking every day, Michael acting as Rob's secret agent. I'd expected Michael to take Rob's side, despite needing to keep me sweet so he had somewhere to sleep. 'I don't see much of him. He's out all evening and he's started to sleep in late.'

'He's still drinking then?'

I thought of the rank smell of alcohol and sweat when I'd last pushed open the door of the spare room. I'd immediately pulled it closed again. 'More than ever. I got a list of addiction specialists, but he doesn't seem to have done anything about it. Has he asked you to help?'

'No. I told you, he's not picking up.'

'I think—'

'Sorry, I've got to get off,' Rob said, cutting me off. 'I'll pick Harry up at five. Bye.'

The phone went dead. My imagination conjured up a vision of him lying in bed and Jen coming into the room wearing a silky negligee, putting a tray with breakfast on at the end of a huge bed with satin sheets, and leaning down to kiss him.

I threw the phone on my unmade bed and opened the wardrobe, wondering what to wear to a party in a church hall that was half for children and half for adults. The rail where Rob's shirts used to hang looked naked. I took a handful of hangers from my rail and hooked them over the bare one. They looked as lonely and out of kilter as I felt. I put them back where they belonged and closed the cupboard door.

* * *

I could hear the noise of the party from the road. Harry glanced up at me, frowning, and I gave him a bright smile. 'Sounds like fun!'

His grip on my hand tightened and when we got to the door, it took all of my strength not to turn around and go back to the safety of the car.

I nodded hello to a couple of the dads I recognised who were standing outside in the corridor wearing Santa hats, with bottles of lager in their hands. A gaggle of girls in sparkly dresses appeared from the ladies' toilet and brushed past us, each yelling 'Hi Harry,' as they scampered towards the door to the main hall. He didn't reply. When they pushed the door open, the noise of a girl singing 'Look What you Made me Do', by Taylor Swift assaulted us. I felt Harry tug my hand, but I pulled him along with me. I repeated *desensitise, desensitise* in my head.

Inside the hall I tried to let go of Harry's hand. I needed to put the present I was clutching to my chest on a table already heaving with brightly wrapped parcels. He grabbed my fingers, and I felt a rush of irritation. 'Just let me put this down,' I whispered in his ear.

He watched my hands place the sickly-sweet smelling bath bombs on the table. I was glad to get rid of them. The smell was so strong it escaped the wrapping paper and had filled the car on the way here with cloying perfume. As soon as I put it on the pile, Harry reached for my hand again.

'Hello! So glad you came.' Nicky appeared from the crowd. Green, sparkly baubles hung from her ears and she looked completely relaxed in a short, shimmery red dress. How did she do it? I felt like I was on a safari in an open topped jeep with a meat necklace around my throat. 'Drink, Elle?'

'Thanks. Something soft, I'm driving.' I would have loved a glass of wine, but my nerves were so jangled I didn't trust myself to drive after even a sip.

Nicky leaned towards Harry. 'Why don't you go over there.' She pointed to where a man in a baseball cap was standing next to a speaker with a crowd of children jostling in front. 'Choose a song to sing. Go on. I think we could do with a break from all these girls' voices, don't you?'

I was about to jump in and tell her Harry wasn't fond of performing when I remembered the desensitising. Maybe if I gave him time to reply instead of always leaping in so he didn't get uncomfortable, he would get used to it.

Harry looked at Nicky, then up at me with fear in his eyes.

'Go on,' she tried again. 'You're a big brave boy. I bet you'll love it when you get going.'

I smelled wine on her breath and her relaxed state made more sense. I was about to speak for Harry when she gave his shoulder a nudge. 'Go on.'

She must have pushed him hard because he stumbled forwards into two women holding plastic glasses full of wine. They turned and glowered at him. One of them dabbed at her blouse where a wet stain made her look like she was lactating. 'Careful,' she said brusquely. Harry righted himself and turned, his face a mask of horror and confusion.

I knew that coming here had been a terrible idea. I gave Nicky an apologetic smile, hating myself because it should have been her apologising to Harry. 'I think we'd better go.'

'Suit yourself.' When she blinked, her eyelids closed slowly, and I realised how drunk she must be. I took Harry's hand and turned to leave.

In the corridor, he gripped my arm and pulled me

downwards until he could whisper into my ear. 'I need a wee.'

My head was thumping. I wanted to get home. The boys' toilet was the second one along. I pointed at it. 'Okay. Hurry up.'

He shook his head.

'Go on. Quick.'

He pulled my arm again. 'You come with me.'

I sighed. 'We'll have to go in the ladies then.' I opened the door and pointed to a free cubicle.

'You come in,' he whispered. I followed him into the cubicle and locked the door. When he'd finished, I decided to have a quick wee myself before the drive home. When I sat down, I saw a red stain in my pants. With everything that was going on, I'd forgotten my period was due. I pulled my knickers above my knees, so Harry didn't see the blood. I didn't have the energy for that conversation now.

I carefully wiped myself, throwing the tissue into the bowl then pinning my thighs together. Harry reached for the door lock.

'Don't open that yet,' I said, scrabbling to pull my underwear and jeans up without him seeing the stain.

He looked at me in panic when we heard the door to the ladies open.

'I bet this won't come out,' said a woman. I heard the sound of the tap being turned on and water running. 'It's pure silk.'

'He didn't even apologise, did he?'

'No. Neither did his mother. If my kid pushed into an adult and made them spill a drink down themselves, I'd have forced them to say sorry. Any right-minded parent would.'

I froze. It was the women who were standing in front of us when Nicky pushed Harry.

'I've heard he doesn't speak at all. Like he's a mute or something.'

'Mute, or just rude? If his mother's anything to go by, he certainly hasn't got any manners. Maybe he's just an ill-mannered little shit.'

'More than likely.' There was a pause. Harry and I stood perfectly still. 'You can see why her husband ran off with another woman, can't you?' Another pause where I imagined them nodding, tight-lipped.

'Is that better?'

'I think so. Dry it under the dryer.'

The sound of the hand dryer roared. Harry put his hands over his ears, and I put my hands over his. I wished he'd done it earlier, then at least he wouldn't have heard what that pair of monsters had to say. But he had. And so had I.

We sat in silence in the car on the way home. At least if Harry didn't speak, he couldn't spear someone with his words and cause the pain we were feeling now.

But it meant he couldn't let the pain out, either. If he didn't talk, then all the trauma he felt was locked inside his small body, with nowhere to go. I wanted to shriek and rail against the world, but I wanted my poor, poor boy to do it more.

Chapter Thirty-Nine

Elle

Harry went straight to his room when we got back. After I'd changed my pants and sorted myself out in the toilet, I sat on the end of his bed and watched him gather up his dinosaurs from where they were scattered among towels and discarded clothes. The cut by his eye was bleeding again. He didn't seem able to leave it alone.

'You know none of that was your fault, don't you?' I said.

'I'm tired.' He swooped the pterodactyl in the air between us.

'Daddy will be here in an hour and a half.' He nodded, not looking at me. 'Shall I stay here and play with you?'

He shook his head. I was torn. I knew I should stay, keep my voice bright and distracting, help enact a T-Rex stalking whatever bloody dinosaur lived on the right continent at the right time, but I was tired too. 'Okay.' I stood, ducked out of the way of the flying dinosaur, and gave him a squeeze. 'Love you, gorgeous boy.'

Downstairs, I took the folders Claire had given me into

the sitting room and started to read through the information on selective mutism. I tried to read the first page of four stapled together, but the words swam around the paper. I began again at the top, but it still wasn't going in. It was like my brain was rejecting the words.

Perhaps now wasn't the right time to be trying to get a handle on what was going on inside Harry's head. Everything was raw. I pulled a cushion onto my lap and hugged it. It was the closest I'd got to a real hug recently and that made my insides ache. Harry hugged me all the time, but his embraces were greedy and scared. They needed the comfort to flow from me to him.

I tried to remember when I'd last been held by someone who didn't want anything from me. It wasn't Rob. His cuddles were a service, fast and perfunctory, as though he knew he had to keep me topped up. Even sex had been a job to get out of the way while I was ovulating.

I realised with a thump to the solar plexus that my last real hug was from Jen. The image came to me fully formed. It was when we met at Rooted for the last time, the afternoon Harry was hurt. She'd wrapped me in her arms and squeezed me tightly. It had felt like she was passing some of her energy to me. I remembered the feeling of warmth I had afterwards. Jen was the last person who held me. That made me sad beyond words.

When I heard a key in the lock, I looked at my watch. It must be Michael because Rob wasn't due for another half an hour.

'Hello.'

It was Rob's voice. Of course it was. That man had no more concept of time than Harry. I stood, adrenaline shooting through me. 'You're early,' I said. I had to lean on the door frame when I saw him. The man standing in the hallway was the one I'd thought was my husband. I tried to think of him differently, as a man who'd betrayed me and Harry, but it was hard after all those years of him slotting into a box labelled, *husband, father, provider . . . man in charge*.

He'd obviously gone to a lot of effort. His white linen shirt was crisp under his vintage leather jacket. He was cleanly shaven, and his eyes were bright. He looked like he'd enjoyed several nights of unbroken sleep and that, more than anything else right now, made me want to kill him.

'Key please,' I said, holding out my hand.

He rolled his neck as though letting go of tension 'Let's not do this now.'

'I would like your key.'

He ambled towards the kitchen. I followed, fury rising from deep in my core. 'I still pay the mortgage,' he said. 'So be careful what you wish for.'

'Be careful?' I snarled, glad to see surprise on his face. He must wonder where his compliant little wifey had gone. 'I've been careful around you for long enough. You might pay the mortgage, but it's tiny, and it's solely in my name, isn't it?'

He opened the fridge and glanced inside. I slammed it closed, incensed by his entitlement. 'Stop paying the mortgage, if you like. I'll put the house on the market. There's enough equity in it for me to get a nice little flat up north by the coast. Maybe it would do us both good. Harry can start again at a new school; I'll get a job. We'll be fine.'

'You can't take Harry anywhere without my permission. We had that drawn into the divorce agreement, remember?' He put his shoulders back, looking pleased with himself.

The divorce! Stupidly, I'd forgotten about how we'd had everything made legal. I hadn't thought much about it since it was eight years ago and hadn't been mentioned again until the last few days. 'Ha! Of course. We had a financial arrangement, didn't we?' His face dropped as I saw the realisation dawn. 'From what I remember, you were trying to keep me sweet, so I'd agree to a divorce.'

He had the decency to look ashamed.

'And I won't have to sell the house, will I? Because the agreement says you have to pay the mortgage and keep both me and Harry in the style we're accustomed to. Until Harry is eighteen, from what I remember.' I crossed my arms, enjoying the frustrated look on his face. 'Which is eleven years away.'

'Well, things have changed,' he said. 'I need somewhere to live.'

I breathed evenly, trying not to let him see my relief he wasn't living happily ever after with his other family. 'Do you think the family courts would see it that way, when they discover what you've been up to for the last eight years? I wouldn't be surprised if they awarded me a bigger settlement.'

He threw his hands up. 'Don't be greedy, Elle.'

'Greedy?' I laughed. 'This, from the man with two wives, two families!' I took a step forwards and pointed. 'And don't forget, you were the one who didn't want me to go back to work. You belittled me. You made me think I should be grateful for the crumbs from your table.'

His forehead creased. 'You're making it sound like I was some kind of monster. I thought you wanted to stay at home with Harry.'

'Not after he started school. I told you enough times, especially since you were always going on about the pressure of making all the money. You wanted me to stay at home, so I had to rely on you. And you wanted me around so I'd always pick up the slack with Harry and your dad, so you could come and go whenever you liked. You needed me to be dependent and available.'

He rested his hands on his hips and shook his head. 'We remember things differently, then.'

I gave him a sarcastic smile. 'That may be the case, but only one of us is a proven liar, so, I know whose version is most likely to be true. Good luck trying to convince anyone else otherwise.' It felt good being able to talk to him like this. In all the years we'd been together, I couldn't think of a time when I hadn't watched my words in case he turned things around until I was in the wrong, or sulked because I'd had the audacity to criticise him.

Jen appeared in my mind's eye again. I bet she was never compliant. I bet she had the strength to stand up for herself. 'So, you're not living with Jen?'

His eyes flitted from left to right. I knew he was working out what would be the best answer. 'I'm giving everyone some space,' he said.

'Giving?' I laughed. 'How generous.'

His cheeks pinked. I was enjoying this and it was clear he didn't have a clue what to do with this version of me. 'Where's Harry? It's time we got going.'

'I'll call him . . . after you've given me your key.' I held out my hand and kept it there, palm flat, while he wrangled the door key from the keyring.

'There,' he said, slapping it into my hand.

'Thank you.' I snapped my fingers closed. I took a step towards the hall, but he put a hand on my forearm to stop me.

'Before Harry comes down, can we arrange what's going to happen on Christmas day?'

I stilled. Thoughts of Christmas plagued me when I lay

awake in the middle of the night. We'd always had fairly small Christmases, just the three of us with Michael and his girlfriend at the time. I wanted Harry to have a good Christmas, especially after this horrendous term at school, but I didn't want to spend it with Rob.

It briefly occurred to me that Rob had always been with us at Christmas. What had Jen made of his absence? What lies had he told her? 'What were you thinking?'

'I want Harry to be with me.'

'What?' The concept was so preposterous I couldn't process it. I'd expected Rob to ask if he could join us so Harry would feel safe and loved. I should have known better. Rob only did what was best for himself. 'No. No way.'

'Come on, Elle. You get him all the time. I'm asking for one night, Christmas day to the end of Boxing day. Thirty-six hours.'

'No. Absolutely not.' I imagined sitting alone at the table with a Christmas dinner for one. I didn't deserve that. None of this was my fault. Then I remembered Michael. He had stopped going to AA altogether and was drinking more than ever. 'And what about your dad?'

Rob screwed up his nose. 'What about him?'

'What were you planning to do with him while you whisked Harry off? Have you even spoken to him about where he's moving to after Christmas? He doesn't seem like he's in a fit state to organise himself and there's no way he's staying here longer than I agreed.'

'I've told you, he's not answering my calls. I'll try him again, alright? Look, Elle—'

I'd had enough. The fact he'd only considered what he wanted, not what was best for Harry, or how his dad might feature was too much of a reminder why I didn't want him anywhere near me. 'No,' I interrupted. 'I'm sorry, but no. There is no way on god's green earth I'm letting you take my boy away from me at Christmas.'

He deflated. He looked bewildered that I wasn't complying.

'You can have him on Boxing day. Then you can help your dad move out,' I said and went to call my lovely boy downstairs.

Chapter Forty

Jen

I said Robin could come around for an hour on Christmas morning for Cora's sake. The thought of seeing him again made my stomach churn. How did you stop loving someone? Even though I hated him for what he'd done to us, something instinctive and out of my control still craved him.

He knocked, which was bittersweet. I was glad he respected the boundaries, but my heart ached that the man I'd thought would share my bed for life, now waited on the doorstep to be allowed in.

The woody smell of him hit my nose when he stepped in from the pavement. It was almost too much to resist. He'd clearly made an effort. He was dressed in a white linen shirt and the battered old brown leather jacket he knew I loved. His chin and cheeks had a few days of stubble, and I knew this was for my benefit too. I loved his rugged, handsome look. I shifted my eyes away before my body reacted without consulting my brain. 'We're leaving in an hour,' I said, closing the door behind him.

'Merry Christmas to you too.' He handed me a small box, elaborately wrapped in gold paper with a fancy bow on top. I took it and threw it on the sofa in the front room.

He raised his eyebrows but didn't comment. 'Where are you going today?'

'None of your business.' I stood at the bottom of the stairs. I thought back to when Femi had called to invite Cora and me for Christmas. It was like the events outside the studio that day had never happened. She was clearly the forgive and forget type and I made the decision then to go against my instincts and take any offer of friendship she made. We'd chatted about how rehearsals were going, and I'd tried to hide how much it was killing me to stay away. When I'd said it was just going to be Cora and me on the twenty-fifth of December she'd shrieked and insisted we went to hers.

'You've got to come,' she said. 'It's a bit of a free for all. All the family pile in, everybody makes something to eat, there's plenty of food and booze. There's always a bit of singing.' She laughed. 'Might be your idea of a nightmare, though. It's a lot. I mean *a lot*. Not everybody's cup of tea, twenty or thirty people in a house, all coming and going.'

I tried to imagine what that would be like. I'd never had the kind of family who held parties and Cora had never complained about it being just her and me on Christmas day. Things had changed, though. Now we wouldn't be looking forward to Robin coming back and showering us with love and gifts. The only thing I had to look forward to was the appointment to see the specialist about my breast in the first week of January, and any distraction from that would be welcome.

'I'm not sure you'd want us. Cora's a very fussy eater.'

I imagined sitting down to a dinner with a load of strangers and having to watch Cora turn down everything except meat and potatoes, and even then, only eating the crispy ones. I'd be so stressed about her appearing to be spoiled or rude.

'Oh, don't worry about that, it's not formal,' said Femi. 'There's too many of us to do a sit-down thing. It's all paper plates and grab what you fancy from a table heaving with fat, sugar and salt. I think my kids only eat roast potatoes, crisps and chocolate all day long.'

'Cora would love that!' I said. I swallowed a gulp of air. 'You know what, we would love to come. Thank you.'

'Cool,' she said. 'See you any time after twelve.'

I returned my mind to the present and shouted, 'Cora, your dad's here.'

There was an instant patter on the landing carpet, then Cora's feet tumbled down the stairs.

'Slow down,' said Robin, rushing forwards to scoop her up. He planted kisses all over her face. 'Merry Christmas, beautiful,' he said. 'Oh, it's so good to see you.'

'Merry Christmas, Daddy,' said Cora, pretending to wipe her face clean of his saliva. 'I miss you all the time. Are you coming to Femi's with us? She's got lots of people coming to her house and so she won't mind if you come as well because it's like a big party and nobody has to sit down and eat Brussels sprouts, which is good for me because I think they are disgusting.' She made gagging noises and seeing them both laughing together made me want to cry.

'Daddy has plans,' I said, ignoring the hopeful look Robin gave me over Cora's head.

Thankfully he didn't try to argue. I had no intention of asking what he was doing for the rest of the day. I hoped Elle wasn't allowing him to spend it with her, but I wasn't about to torture myself by finding out. He bounced Cora in his arms and said, 'Did Santa come?'

I'd told Robin if he did that typical divorced dad act of turning up with massive presents for Cora, I'd slam the door in his face. I wasn't going to let him undermine me or buy her love. I'd set a budget and asked him to transfer half to my account, then I put the gifts under the tree like I'd always done. The only difference this year was that Cora actually got to see him because he wasn't pretending to be in fucking Scotland.

'I'm going to get ready,' I said.

Robin looked disappointed. Did he expect us to play happy families? 'You already look great,' he said.

I scowled at him and forced myself to leave my daughter and the man I couldn't help yearning for and went upstairs to the bedroom we used to share.

* * *

Femi's house thronged with people and good cheer radiated all around. When everyone was hugging me and pushing food and drink into my hands, I was almost able to ignore the weight of sadness that had settled in my abdomen since I'd hurried Robin out onto the pavement and seen the pain and regret in his eyes as I closed the door.

I was glad nobody else from the company was there. The shame of being too unstable to go into work still prickled under my skin. I was also keenly aware the others would all be with their family and friends. I was here because, other than Cora, I had neither.

Initially, Cora stuck close to my side, nervous of the loud strangers and unfamiliar smell I recognised as warm rum punch. I watched her quick eyes take in the white artificial Christmas tree with multi-coloured baubles hanging on every branch and the bright paper chains that criss-crossed the ceiling. Soon, she was eyeing a gaggle of children who looked to be around her age, devouring Celebrations from a bowl in the conservatory. 'Go on,' I said, 'Go and play.' She shook her head.

'In a minute I will,' she whispered, 'when I get more brave.'

I tucked her into my side, overwhelmed with love and pride for my perfect little girl. 'Okay,' I said. 'But I think you're already brave. You're the bravest little girl in the world.'

I chatted to Femi's sister about the school productions where her sister's talents had first been noticed, thankful that she didn't seem to know about my fall from grace, or at least she was kind enough not to mention it if she did. I felt Cora shift under my arm. She moved away and took a few tentative steps towards the conservatory, picking up a chocolate brownie from the table on the way. She shoved it into her mouth and then walked towards the group, stopping on the periphery, chewing and watching, as if trying to work out the dynamics.

A little girl with a round face and neat cornrows looked up and seemed to notice Cora hovering. She shifted on her seat, making a space and tapping it. When Cora didn't move the girl flapped her hand, gesturing Cora to sit. Within a minute, she and Cora were chattering and giggling together as if they'd known each other all their lives.

Suddenly I thought of Harry. I imagined him in the same situation, mute and terrified of the same children that Cora had effortlessly infiltrated. That poor boy. I wondered how Elle was coping today if Robin wasn't with them. It must be additionally hard for her and Harry, since Robin had always been at their home at Christmas, because I'd been the gullible fool believing his lies. I thought I knew Elle well enough to know she couldn't accept an invitation like this. Harry would find it too hard. They might be alone right now. I missed them, I realised. I really missed having them in my life.

I glanced around the room at the people of all ages, some seated, others perching on chair arms, or standing in animated groups. I took in the hands resting warmly on shoulders, the heads thrown back in laughter, and I felt lonelier than I ever had in my life. I caught Femi's eye across the room and raised my glass in her direction. She blew me a kiss and I felt like it landed directly on my breaking heart.

It occurred to me that, even though I'd been happy with Robin, or at least I'd thought I was, losing him had forced me to open my eyes and look at my life, and I didn't like what I saw. I'd isolated myself and now I was practically alone. I remembered the letter with the date of my hospital appointment on, hidden in my bedside drawer. I needed more people in my life. Life was richer and better with friends. But maybe I'd made that discovery too late.

Chapter Forty-One

Elle

I was astonished Rob was thoughtful enough to suggest we bought joint presents for Harry. I would have expected him to want to eclipse anything I could afford. Since he'd stopped putting money in the joint account, I had to get by on the small amount transferred to my bank every month. That used to be for my expenses and household things. Anything extra, like the new trainers Harry wanted, or the massive cost of Christmas, I used to buy from our joint money.

Now we didn't have joint money. We didn't have joint anything apart from Harry and he seemed more depleted than my account.

Despite waking up full of cold and miserable to my core on Christmas morning, I did my very best to put on a show of festive enthusiasm for Harry. As I tiptoed past his room at 7am, I imagined I was the only parent in Britain who was awake before their child that day. I poked my head in, but he was still and breathing steadily, so I went downstairs.

I heard the television on a low volume. My heart plummeted.

Not today. The smell of whiskey hit me as soon as I entered the room. Michael was slouched on the sofa, legs splayed in front of him. His head rose slowly when he heard me, lips lifting on one side in a grotesque smile. 'Merry Christmas.'

A glass half full of brown liquid sat in his hand on the sofa arm. A whiskey bottle was on the coffee table with a dribble left in the bottom. On the television, brightly dressed breakfast show hosts wore Santa hats and grinned from the screen.

'Have you even been to bed?' I took the glass from his hand. He moaned but was too drunk to grab for it. 'Go upstairs. I don't want this to be Harry's first sight on Christmas morning.'

I pulled his arm, hoisting him to his feet. He rose and leaned on me. 'Yes, don't want to upset little Harry, do we?'

His tone sounded sarcastic, but his words were too slurred for me to be sure. I wondered if he thought I wrapped Harry up in cotton wool too. Maybe everyone thought that. Maybe they were right. But either way, I did not want his first Christmas without his dad to begin with seeing his grandfather smashed out of his head in the front room.

Michael was on all fours making his way up the stairs when Harry came out of his bedroom. I could see the bright red of blood next to his eye from downstairs.

'What's Grandad doing?'

'Merry Christmas,' I sing-songed. 'Santa's been. Grandad's a bit tired so he's going for a lie down while we have breakfast and open your presents.'

Michael was halfway up the stairs, grunting with the exertion. I prayed Harry couldn't smell the whiskey or see the drool hanging from Michael's mouth to the stair carpet.

I knew only too well how memories from this age could stick. I'd had plenty Christmas mornings as a child I'd rather forget: men I'd never met coming out of Mum's bedroom, leaving her to sleep off her hangover.

'Just let your grandad get past you and then come down and I'll make you a hot chocolate. I've got marshmallows.'

Harry's face clouded and I bit the inside of my cheek hard. I could tell he was thinking about Cora. I wondered if he missed her, or whether thinking of her was just a bitter reminder.

Michael lay his head down on a step, then his body relaxed until he was prostrate on the stairs.

'No,' I said. 'Don't you dare go to sleep there.' I jabbed at his foot with my fingernail. 'Get up now.' Harry looked at me with wide, worried eyes and I raged at the fact Michael was a massive, useless obstacle between us. One more day and he'd be out of my house. I couldn't wait. 'Move.' I slapped at his leg.

'Alright,' he slurred, pushing the stairs away with his hands and continuing the climb. Eventually he made it to the top. He didn't try to stand. He crawled on his hands and knees towards the spare room, offering Harry a mumbled 'Merry Christmas,' on the way past.

* * *

The day didn't improve. I was determined to do my best to be enthusiastic about Harry's presents but when he said, 'Where are your presents, Mummy?' I had to pretend I needed a tissue to blow my nose so I could hide my face. How had I allowed my life to get so small that I didn't have a single present to open on Christmas day? It wasn't about the gifts; what I missed were people who might see something in a shop and think, '*Elle would love that.*' That would mean I existed outside this house. Outside the lie Rob had woven us into.

I heard Michael moving around upstairs at 3pm. I'd laid a place for him at the table and the food was almost ready to be served when he shouted 'Bye' from the hall. The front door slammed.

I hurried through the front room where Harry was watching *Jurassic Park World*, his new blanket with dinosaurs over his legs, his soft brontosaurus tucked under his chin. I walked past him to the window and looked out in time to see Michael's back disappearing down the avenue. Unbelievable. 'Did Grandad say anything to you?'

'No,' said Harry, not raising his eyes from the TV. 'Is he up?'

Typical Harry. He'd been so engrossed in the film he hadn't heard the door slam. 'Looks like it's just us for dinner,' I said, furious with myself that I'd gone to the effort of cooking even though I felt like death. If I'd known it was just going to be me and Harry, I could have heated up pizza and garlic bread from the freezer. I'd have saved money and energy. And I didn't have enough of either to spare.

'Can I have mine in here?' asked Harry. He was picking at the sore skin near his eye.

I didn't answer. I took his hand and pressed it into his lap then went back into the kitchen and blew my nose. My head pounded and my bones ached. I was so blocked up I could hardly smell the potatoes roasting in goose fat or the chicken I'd put in the oven instead of a turkey. A turkey would have been too big for three.

A chicken was too big for two.

I opened the fridge and took out the bottle of Champagne I'd chilled. Rob and I always had Champagne with our

Christmas dinner. It usually felt like a decadent treat. Last night, when I'd put it in the fridge, it felt more like a risk. After this morning's performance, I'd decided not to open the bottle over dinner with Michael. But Michael had gone, and I deserved a treat. I popped the cork and poured myself a glass, watching the bubbles rush up the flute and explode. I couldn't really taste the first sip, but the fizz on my tongue felt good. I drank down half the glass and topped up the rest. *If you can't beat 'em, join 'em*, I thought, bitterly.

Chapter Forty-Two

Elle

Michael still wasn't home when I put Harry to bed. Harry cuddled his new brontosaurus tightly and interrupted his bedtime stories to ask, 'Is Daddy really coming tomorrow?' and 'What time will he get here?'

'Of course he's coming,' I said. 'He'll be here at about ten.' I hoped Rob would turn up on time. Harry might have no more idea about time than Rob did, but it wouldn't stop him asking every five minutes.

By the time I'd turned off his bedside lamp and pushed his bedroom door half closed, I was shattered. I went back downstairs and poured another glass of Champagne to drink while I emptied the dishwasher. I'd drunk three quarters of the bottle but couldn't tell whether I was drunk or just stuffed with cold. I imagined what Nicky would be doing now. She was probably laying on a chaise longue, dripping in new diamonds, being fed chocolate truffles by her adoring husband, while their children took turns playing carols on the piano.

I lifted a plate from the dishwasher, but it was too hot. I tried to carry it to the cupboard, but the heat seared my fingertips. Letting it drop onto the tiles, I watched as it burst into a thousand pieces. I fell into a chair. How could this be my Christmas day? Why wasn't I surrounded by friends and family, curled up watching a film with a full stomach and a full heart?

Slowly, I gathered the energy to sweep up the shards of porcelain, tipping the broken pieces from the dustpan into the bin. I emptied the rest of the dishwasher, then turned off the downstairs lights and made my way to bed.

On the way, I paused by the front door, momentarily considering putting on the deadlock. That would teach the old soak to walk out without letting me know when he'd be back. But it was Christmas, and frost was already shimmering on the road, and I couldn't face finding him frozen stiff on the doorstep in the morning. He'd be gone tomorrow. That was some comfort.

In the bathroom I hunted through the cupboard for a bottle of Night Nurse I'd bought for Rob when he last had man flu. I found it and tried to unscrew the top. It clicked around in my fingers until I eventually managed the push and turn conundrum to open the damned thing. The plastic measuring cup was missing, so I took a slug of the thick, menthol liquid from the bottle and swallowed.

Twenty minutes later I lay in bed cursing my blocked-up nose. Every time I turned over, the mucus flowed into the other nostril so I couldn't breathe. My head pounded. I just wanted to get to sleep. In exasperation, I threw back the duvet and marched into the bathroom, wrestled open the Night Nurse and took another drink. Then one more. Surely that had to be enough to clear my nose and ease my headache?

Pulling the duvet tight around me, I eventually drifted into sleep.

* * *

Someone's hands were on me. I opened my eyes, but it was dark and something foul in the air stung my eyeballs and pushed up my nose and into my mouth. I tried to scream, but when I opened my mouth, I choked on filthy air. I found the hand that was grabbing my waist and clawed at it, trying to escape. The hand didn't feel like flesh, it was huge and rough. Fear clutched my throat.

There was a screaming sound, like a wailing alarm. The air was swirling and shifting. The hands wouldn't let me go. I punched and kicked. I couldn't breathe. I was coughing, and the effort of fighting off whoever was trying to pull me out of bed made my body convulse, then choke.

'Please calm down,' said a muffled voice. 'We have to get out.'

I squinted through slitted eyes at whoever was pulling at me, and a terrifying mask swirled in and out of view. I screamed, but only a hoarse, strangled sound came out.

'We need to get out. Now,' said the voice again, and I saw a yellow helmet. I swallowed and tasted smoke. Smoke. Yellow helmet. Gloved hands.

'Harry!' I tried to lunge forwards but the figure in the mask caught me and held me.

'I'm going to help you out, okay?'

'Harry!'

'Your son is out. He's outside, okay?'

I choked again, falling to my knees. He put his arms under my armpits and lifted me upright. 'Can you walk?'

I pushed my feet into the carpet and nodded. He put his arm around me and guided me through the smoke to the doorway. Outside the room, the wailing of the smoke detector was deafening. How had I slept through that? I instinctively moved towards Harry's room, but the firefighter gripped my shoulders and pushed me firmly towards the stairs. 'He's out,' he said, 'I promise.'

The smoke was black now. The firefighter put something over my mouth. I could feel his arm around me and the wall on my left shoulder. It was hot. I pulled my arm away.

'Nearly there,' he said. 'You're doing great.'

I put my foot out, feeling for the next step. It was getting hotter, like I was descending into hell. My eyes stung, I couldn't see and I didn't know where the steps were. I missed my footing and tripped, making us both stumble. I put my arm out to the wall and this time it burned my hand.

'Steady.' His voice was faint now, swallowed up by a roaring behind us. I tried to see what was happening, but he pulled me forwards. My bare toes searched for step after step, my body screamed for oxygen. 'Nearly there.'

A new figure appeared through the murk and grabbed me. I was lifted off my feet as I was rushed outside and onto the drive. I collapsed onto the gravel, gasping air into my lungs. I blinked the smoke from my eyes and staggered to my feet. 'Harry!' I croaked, 'Harry!'

'He's here,' said a voice. It sounded far away. I looked around, ignoring the stones stabbing into my soles. Lights blazed, shining on the house. The red of two fire engines, the yellow helmets of firefighters running and shouting. I searched the drive with my eyes but couldn't see Harry anywhere. I screamed so loudly it felt like my throat was tearing, 'Harry!'

A woman in a green paramedic uniform seemed to appear

from nowhere. She put her hand on my arm. 'I'll take you to your little boy. Then we'll have a look at you.'

She led me towards the road. The screaming of the smoke alarm faded with every step. I saw the white of an ambulance. Then I saw a gurney with a small figure strapped onto it. Vomit rose into my throat, and I bent over, retching it up onto the gravel. I tried to breathe. The fireman had said Harry was outside. He'd repeated he was out. He hadn't said he was alive.

I ran to the gurney, sobs pulsing from my throat. I leaned over my poor boy and saw his beautiful pale skin smeared with black. His eyes were closed. An oxygen mask covered his nose and mouth.

'Is he . . .?' I couldn't finish the question.

'He's breathed in a lot of smoke,' said the paramedic. 'He was found on the stairs—'

'The stairs?' Why had Harry been on the stairs in the middle of the night?

'His oxygen level was low, so we're giving him some now.' She lay her hand on my arm. 'Can we take a look at you?'

I shook her off. 'Harry,' I said, 'Harry, it's Mummy. I'm here, Harry.' His face was agonisingly still. 'Oh, my lovely boy. I'm here Harry.'

I heard shouts behind me and turned to see a flurry of people in uniforms all rushing towards the doorway of my house. The paramedic looked at her colleague who was attaching a blood pressure monitor to my arm. He nodded and she ran back towards the house.

The shouting continued. I strained my ears but couldn't distinguish any words. Snot poured from my nose. My eyes stung and all I could smell was smoke. I stroked Harry's hand, desperate for him to open his eyes and show me he was alright.

I sensed a figure behind me. I turned to see a policewoman carrying her hat in her hands. 'Mrs Clarke?' she said.

I nodded, wiping the wet mess from my top lip with my forearm.

'Was your husband downstairs when the fire started?'

I shook my head, confused. 'Rob's not here. We, erm . . .' I didn't have the focus to explain the hellish situation right now.

'We found someone downstairs. We suspect that's where the fire started.'

Fresh tears splashed down my cheeks. 'Michael. Rob's dad, he . . .'

The policewoman dropped her eyes to the ground. 'I'm sorry Mrs Clarke.'

'Sorry?' I looked from her to the paramedic who was now viewing me with sorrowful eyes. 'You mean . . .?'

'The person who was downstairs has died of his injuries. I'm sorry.'

I turned towards the drive and took a step. The policewoman barred my way. 'I wouldn't advise you to—' she stopped. 'They've suffered extensive burns,' she said. 'I think it might be better if you stay here for now.'

I stepped back and took Harry's limp hand in mine. He had been found on the stairs. I looked towards the house and saw smoke billowing out of the door. In front, four people kneeled over a figure lying still on the ground.

Michael. Michael was dead.

And what had my poor boy seen?

Chapter Forty-Three

Elle

The curtain around Harry's hospital bed opened and I turned to see Rob's stricken face. He looked at me and I became aware I was still wearing my torn, smoke blackened pyjamas. We both turned our heads to Harry. He was swamped by the huge bed. The covers lay over him undisturbed. He hadn't moved since he woke up. His rasping breath sounded painful under the oxygen mask the doctors insisted he still needed. And he hadn't said a word.

'Harry,' Rob fell on him, sobbing openly. 'My lovely boy. Thank god you're alright.'

I wanted to ask what his version of alright was. Harry was struggling to breathe, and he might have just watched his grandfather be burned alive. I bit down on my tongue as the image of Harry, wide-eyed on the stairs, frozen to the spot as flames engulfed Michael, played in my mind.

Rob dug an arm under Harry's small body and lifted him into a hug. I saw tears collect in Harry's eyes and make their way down the side of his face, around the mask and into his ears. He didn't try to wipe them away.

When Rob stood back, I leaned forwards with a tissue and dabbed Harry's cheeks and ears dry. Rob turned his bloodshot eyes to me. 'You okay?'

I nodded, pinching my lips together to stop the tears coming. I was very far from okay. I'd stood by as the charred body of my father-in-law was loaded into an ambulance, then climbed into another with my son, not knowing if he was going to live or die. My house had all but burned down. My eyes stung and my lungs hurt, I was filthy, exhausted and my child was lying in a hospital bed. I suspected he had gone downstairs to investigate the fire because I was dosed up on booze and Night Nurse. I didn't know what horrific scenes he'd witnessed and couldn't get him to tell me, so, no, I was not okay. But it wasn't my father who'd died, so I nodded again.

'They think it was a cigarette,' said Rob, his voice cracking.

I glanced at Harry. I hadn't talked to him about what had happened to Michael yet, although he might know more than we did. If only he'd tell us.

'Let's talk outside,' I said. 'We'll be back in a minute, alright?' I waited a second, desperate for Harry to reply, but he just stared at the ceiling. I squeezed his hand and followed Rob into the corridor.

'Is there a cafe?' asked Rob.

'I'm not leaving Harry,' I said. 'We can talk here.' I leaned on the wall next to the door to the children's ward, wishing I could smell something other than smoke. Incongruously, cheerful gold tinsel framed the doorway, stuck down with peeling sellotape. 'You said it was a cigarette, did the police tell you that?' I didn't say I'd been wracking my brains to try to remember if I'd left the oven on, or left something on charge. The Champagne and Night Nurse must have sedated me enough to not hear the smoke detector going off. The fact it had woken Harry but not me loaded me with guilt.

Rob ran his hand through his hair. 'Yeah. That's what they seem to think, anyway. They'll do an investigation. But you know Dad liked a smoke when he was drinking.'

'I asked him not to smoke in the house.' My voice was small. I knew it was a stupid thing to say.

'Yeah, well, blaming him isn't going to bring him back, is it?'

'I'm sorry, I just meant . . . oh, I don't know.' What kind of person was I that I was relieved someone else had burned themselves to death, rather than shouldering all the blame myself? I looked down at my feet in the thin hospital slippers the ward sister had given me.

'I can't believe he's gone.' Rob tugged at the hair at his temples. I wondered if I should hug him. I could do with the warmth of another human body close to mine, but the man in front of me now felt like a stranger.

'Harry won't tell me what he saw,' I said. 'I don't know if . . .' I stopped. I didn't need to transfer that harrowing image from my head to his. Not now. I wound my mind back to the state Michael had been in the last few days. 'Your dad stayed up all night on Christmas Eve.' The image of Michael lying on the stairs, me poking at his foot, crossed my vision. I shook my head. 'I can't believe he got that pissed again, so drunk he . . .'

'Why the hell didn't you stop him?' Rob said, rubbing at the back of his head. 'You were there. You should have stopped him.'

'What?' I searched his face to see if he meant what he

had just said. I thought I'd been reprieved of that, at least. I hadn't caused the fire. Michael had. Was Rob really going to blame me for his father's death?

'And if you'd let Harry be with me like I asked, he wouldn't be in there now.' He stabbed his finger towards the ward. 'What was he doing on the stairs? God knows what the smoke's done to his lungs.'

That much was true. If I hadn't insisted that Harry stayed with me on Christmas day, he would have been safe with Rob. 'I didn't—'

'You never do mean to, do you?' he said. His pink eyes glared into mine. 'Go home and get cleaned up. I'll stay with Harry.'

I didn't move.

'Go on. I think it's best I take care of Harry for now.'

'I can't,' I said, tears clogging my throat.

He drew back his shoulders. 'What? You don't trust me to look after my own son?'

I didn't, but that wasn't it. 'I can't go home,' I stuttered, 'because I haven't got one.'

His eyes grew wide when he realised I was right.

I didn't have a home.

Chapter Forty-Four

Elle

Rob and I sat either side of Harry's bed in silence. Tinny Christmas music played from a television next to a bed further down the ward. The child watching laughed at something on the screen and the strangeness of the sound made us both turn. I looked back at the pale faces of my son and my ex-husband and tried to find some words, but soon gave up. I was too exhausted to speak to Rob. He wouldn't hear me if I did. I tried to recalibrate my brain to get a handle on this situation. I'd convinced myself he was a cheat and a liar who had ruined our lives. But now he'd lost his father and I didn't know how to respond to him. I couldn't work out how I felt. I was numb.

Rob cleared his throat. 'Harry, mate,' he said. He flicked a glance at me, and I knew he was going to tell Harry about his grandad. He might already know. Rob hadn't given any indication he'd thought of that, and I hadn't spoken my fear out loud. I took Harry's hand and held it gently in mine. It was soft and light, and the feel of his small fingers made my heart flounder inside me.

'I need to tell you something.' Rob coughed and I felt the tarry mucus at the back of my throat and wanted to cough too. I swallowed it down, so I didn't draw Harry's attention away from his dad.

'I'm so sorry, pal,' Rob's voice cracked. 'Grandad, he . . .' Tears chased each other down his face.

Harry's eyes grew wide. I hated myself for the hope I felt then. Did his growing anguish now mean he hadn't witnessed the worst of it? He looked from Rob to me and back again, as if he wanted one of us to deny what he knew was coming. I opened my mouth to speak but didn't have the words. Selfishly, I didn't want to be the one to shatter my son's childhood, to confirm the world is exactly as awful as he feared, that terrible, terrible things do happen and people you love can burn to death while your mummy lies sleeping in her bed.

'I'm sorry, Harry,' Rob tried again. 'Grandad died in the fire.' The words curdled in his throat. He covered his mouth with his hand and sobbed into his palm.

Harry turned to me. His face crumpled. He held out his arms and I bent to cradle him as he shook. I stayed there, trying to block out the sound of Rob's crying, absorbing the tremors of grief rolling silently through my little boy.

It was selfish of me to hold him so tightly that there was no space for Rob between us. I knew he needed comfort too, but I was the one Harry turned to. It was me he held out his arms to when his world tipped. Why should I make Rob's life more bearable when he'd made me feel useless and worthless for so many years?

I was sorry Rob had lost his dad, of course I was. But my son had lost the family he thought he had, he'd lost his grandfather and his home. I still wasn't sure of what he'd seen that night and before all of that, he'd lost his ability to speak. I felt sobs ripple through his small body and listened for sounds which should join them, but they never came.

Fear gripped me by the throat. This was too much for one small boy to bear. The trauma of that night might be the thing that locked his voice away for good. I heard Rob's crying, and I hated him even more for being able to make the sound that told the world about his grief.

Shut up, I thought, as my tears fell onto Harry's shuddering back. *How dare you make so much noise when our boy can't make a sound? Shut up, shut up, shut up.*

Chapter Forty-Five

Jen

When Robin called to ask if he could come around, he was sobbing so hard I could hardly hear what he was saying. I agreed, and when I opened the door, his eyes were puffy slits. I gestured for him to go upstairs. I'd put *Encanto* on the TV for Cora and gave her my phone to play with, to make sure we weren't disturbed. The door to the sitting room was closed but we could still hear Cora singing along to 'We Don't Talk About Bruno'. Robin glanced towards the room and half smiled. Cora was spreading her magic again.

'Thanks for letting me come. I thought you might have been working,' he said.

The muscles in my shoulders tightened. It was his fault I wasn't in rehearsal right now. It was his fault my world had fallen apart. But he'd just lost his father in a fire, so I said, 'Nah, not today,' and followed him upstairs.

We tiptoed to my bedroom, and he sat on the end of the bed, dropping his head into his hands. Grief heaved out of him. I sat next to him and lay my hand across his back, feeling his ribs rise then shudder as they fell. He leaned into me. I held him until his sobbing slowed.

'Do you want to talk about what happened?' I said.

He stood and took a tissue from the bedside table, blowing his nose. He took another and wiped his face. He looked at me through bloodshot eyes and started to cry again.

'Come here.' I lay on the bed, and he lay next to me, resting his head on my shoulder. He moved in close, putting his arm across my middle. I pulled him in, making soothing shushing noises. 'I'm sorry,' I said. 'I'm so sorry.'

The situation was bizarre. I hadn't known this version of Robin's father existed until a couple of weeks ago, and here I was, consoling the man who'd lied to me, cheated on me. But cradling him now seemed like the only humane thing to do. He might be a bastard, but he was a bastard who'd experienced a major trauma. And lying on this bed with him felt right. He smelled like the old Bill. He felt like Bill and we slotted together like we always had.

'He'd been drinking heavily, apparently,' said Robin. 'He smoked when he was drinking.' His voice was thick with emotion. I pulled him in a little tighter.

'So, a cigarette started the fire?' I tried not to imagine what it must have been like to die like that. I hoped the smoke got him before the flames.

'They think so.'

Our breathing fell into rhythm. We lay in silence. His body was warm and familiar. I could smell his scalp. I shifted my head to kiss the top of his but stopped myself just in time. We weren't together. I should not kiss this man, however much I wanted to. And despite everything, I really wanted to.

He must've felt the movement because he took in a deep breath and let it out in a long sigh. 'This is the only place I wanted to be,' he said. 'When Elle called to tell me Dad was dead, I could only think of how much I wanted to be with you.'

The skin on my scalp tightened. 'Elle called? How did Elle know before you?'

I felt him stiffen. 'Dad was still staying with her.'

I tried to make sense of what he was saying. 'So, the fire was at Elle's house?' I moved away from him and sat up, staring down at his confused face.

'Yeah. I thought you knew that.'

'How would I know that? It's not as if she's ringing me every five minutes since she thinks I'm the fucking husband snatcher.'

He sniffled. 'I hope he didn't suffer. I can't bear thinking about what his last moments were like.'

My mind swirled. 'Were Elle and Harry in the house?'

Rob lay flat, staring at the ceiling, as though imagining the scene. 'Yeah. Elle's okay, but Harry's in a bad way. He was on the stairs when they found him. We think he might have heard Dad or smelled the fire and gone down to . . . Anyway, he breathed in a lot of smoke. He's not talking to anyone at the hospital. You should see him. He looks so tiny—'

'He's in hospital?' My heart rate doubled, imagining that poor little boy, dragged from a burning building. 'And you didn't think to mention that?'

He sat up, his face full of consternation. 'I didn't think you'd want to know about Elle and Harry.'

I stood. 'Unbelievable.'

He threw his arms out. 'What? What have I done wrong now?'

'You came here to be consoled when your little boy is lying in hospital.'

'There's nothing I can do there. I've just lost my dad.' His voice came out sulky and I wanted to slap his face.

'You are a dad,' I said. 'You're Harry's dad, and he needs you.'

'Elle's there,' he said. 'She won't leave his side. And I needed to see you.'

Did he expect me to feel flattered by that? I closed my eyes and counted to five. All of the things I wanted to say right now were too cruel to say to a man who'd just lost someone he loved. I wanted to point out to him that of course Elle wouldn't leave Harry's side, because she was a good mother. I wanted to say it was fortunate that at least Harry had one parent who put his interests above their own. I wanted to say I admired Elle, that she had been the only friend I had and he'd destroyed that; right now, I'd rather be caring for her than him.

But I didn't. I said, as calmly and kindly as I could muster, 'I think you should be with your son.'

'But—'

'Robin,' I said, firmly. 'For once in your fucking life, do the right thing. Go and take care of your son.'

Chapter Forty-Six

Elle

I'd tried everything I could think of, but I still couldn't make Harry speak. Despite my desperation to find out how much he'd seen on the night of the fire, I tried to keep my chatter light. He looked at me with his huge blue eyes, and I could tell he was trying to respond to me. That was worse than anything. Worse than the red marks around his nose and mouth left by the oxygen mask, worse than the rasping of his breath. The desolation in his eyes, when he looked at me, and I knew he wanted to speak but couldn't, gouged out a pit in my heart. It was like he was locked inside his body and I was terrified about what horrors were trapped in there with him.

When I called Claire, she said she'd come straight away. When I saw her standing at the entrance to the ward, I jumped up and rushed to her. 'Thank you for coming.' I was surprised when she hugged me. I caught a whiff of Pomegranate Noir and was relieved to be able to detect something other than the smoke that still haunted my nostrils.

'How's he doing?'

Her brow furrowed as I told her about the potential damage to his lungs. 'He still won't . . . can't speak.' I corrected myself. 'So, we don't know for sure what he's gone through. The doctors say he's responding well physically. They test his oxygen and listen to his breathing, so we know he's improving physically, but we're all just desperate for him to say something.'

Claire's eyes flitted around the busy ward. 'You don't know what he saw that night?'

I shook my head.

'And he's not speaking to you at all?'

'No. Or Rob. He hasn't made a sound.'

'This must be very stressful for all of you.' She smiled. 'That's a bit of an understatement, isn't it?'

When she sat in the chair next to Harry's bed, he turned to look at her and I willed him to open those rosebud lips and talk. Claire spoke in a quiet, gentle voice, telling him a story about bumping into a little boy from his class in the supermarket. 'His name's Bandon, I think,' she said, scrunching her face as if deep in thought. 'Or is it Brandon?' She looked at Harry. 'Which is it, I can't remember?'

I knew the boy's name was Brandon. I suspected Claire did too. We both looked at Harry. He blinked then looked up at me, his eyes asking for me to answer for him. I could see he wanted to speak. But he couldn't, not even to me, or Claire, or anyone.

'It's Brandon, isn't it?' I said after a long moment, forcing the corners of my mouth to rise into a smile. 'You sit next to him in class, don't you, Harry?' His face relaxed a little, and Claire brought a book about dinosaurs out of her bag and showed the cover to Harry. She continued to chat to him, without asking for anything in return.

Twenty minutes later, she said goodbye to Harry and I went with her to the corridor.

'What can I do?' I said, resisting the urge to grab her hands and demand she stayed until Harry spoke.

'It will take time,' she said. 'I think after everything he's experienced, it might take longer than we hoped when he was diagnosed. I can't imagine how hard this is for all of you.' A nurse smiled at us on her way into the ward. We both smiled back, as though all was well with the world. Claire looked at me and frowned thoughtfully. 'How did he respond to Cora?'

I blinked. 'What do you mean?'

'He used to talk to Cora, didn't he?'

I felt suddenly unsteady. I flattened my back against the corridor wall. 'He hasn't seen Cora. After what happened, well . . .'

Claire pressed her fingers to the top of her nose. 'Sorry, of course. That was deeply insensitive of me.' She grimaced. 'Sorry.'

'It's alright,' I said. 'You deal with a lot of families. I can't expect you to remember the ins and outs of our mess.' She still looked mortified. I rubbed the top of her arm. 'Thanks so much for coming in. It means a lot to me. It really does.'

'If there's anything I can do, please let me know.'

'I will. Thanks again.'

As I watched her walk away, it felt like my last fragment of hope was leaving with her. My poor, poor boy. Would he ever be able to talk again? Would every thought and feeling be forever trapped inside his troubled, terrified head?

Suddenly, Claire's words replayed in my head, '*He used to talk to Cora, didn't he?*'

A jolt of energy ran through me. He did. He always spoke to Cora.

Rob picked up on the second ring. 'Did she know?' I said. 'Tell me truthfully, Rob, when you got together with Jen, did she know anything about me and Harry?' I scrunched my eyes tight and waited for his reply.

Chapter Forty-Seven

Jen

My mouth went dry when I saw Elle's name flash up on my phone screen. I didn't feel strong enough to cope with another tirade. In the early, wakeful hours of each morning, when I wasn't obsessing about losing my job, having cancer or Cora needing help for the rest of her life, I tried out speeches in my head, telling Elle the truth about me and Robin, sometimes screaming at her for the injustice of her accusations, other times begging her to believe me.

As the phone trilled in my hand, I couldn't stop my mind from spinning back to that night Robin and I met. In my mind's eye I saw Robin standing at the bar of a pub in town with another man, his head turning as I walked in. An immediate attraction fizzed between us. I suppose some people would call it love at first sight, but that's bollocks. We are animals, after all. What I felt was physical, instinctive; it was lust, plain and simple. I offered to buy him a drink. He seemed astonished, as though no woman had ever offered him a drink before.

I admit, I didn't ask if he was married, not that night or any time after. The fact he accepted my invitation to come back to mine suggested he was single. We had the most mind-blowing sex I'd ever experienced, and he stayed until morning, so I naturally presumed he didn't have someone waiting for him to come home.

After that first night, I was hooked. Truly hooked. It wasn't just sexual, I felt a connection, like he was *my person*, the man I was meant to be with. All my determination to never again let a man become the centre of my universe came tumbling down and when I got pregnant so soon after meeting him, it didn't seem like the end of the world. I wasn't thrilled, but Robin seemed so sure it was meant to be, that I got caught up in his enthusiasm and dared to hope for the happy ever after I'd given up on twenty years before.

My mind returned to the present when the ringing stopped abruptly. A second later the voicemail icon popped up. I let my finger hover over the little red bin in the corner of the screen. I could just delete the voicemail. I didn't need to listen to anyone else tell me what a shit person I was. My own brain had that covered.

Instead, I sighed and played the message. I hadn't even asked Robin if he was in a relationship that night. I should have. I deserved whatever Elle needed to throw at me. I gritted my teeth and waited for her voice.

'I'm sorry, Jen. God, I'm so sorry that I accused you of knowing about me and Harry and all that stuff I said. I've spoken to Rob and he's admitted that you were just as much in the dark as I was. He told me all about inventing the London flat and conning me into a divorce . . . and, well, everything, really.'

My hand covered my mouth as I stifled a sob. Elle's voice

continued through the phone's speaker. 'I know you probably never want to speak to me again, and I understand that. But I need your help. Not for me, but for Harry. He can't talk.' Her voice was interrupted by hiccupping sobs. 'I don't know how much he saw on the night of the fire and now he can't even talk to me and . . . well, Cora's a magician, isn't she? Do you think . . . I was hoping . . . Could you bring Cora in, just to see if . . .? If you don't want to see me, I could go out of the ward or something.'

I pressed stop. My hands shook as I touched the button to return the call. 'Elle,' I said, when she answered with a tremulous voice. 'Of course we'll come. Of course we'll try to help Harry.'

* * *

My pulse quickened when I walked through the main doors of the hospital. I let go of Cora's hand to press the lift button to the children's unit on the fourth floor, tapping my foot as I watched the red arrow point down until it reached the ground. I turned to Cora. 'Remember Harry's not very well,' I said, hoisting the heavy bag further onto my shoulder. 'He might be a bit tired when you see him. But he's getting better, so don't worry, alright?'

'Will Daddy be there?'

She'd been unusually quiet in the car. Now it made sense. 'Is that what you've been worrying about?'

'It wasn't nice last time Daddy was at Harry's house and me and Harry were there, and Elle cried.' Cora's chin puckered. 'It's too sad when grown-ups cry. It's like double the cries, because they don't want to and so they feel sad about that as well as the thing they were sad about in the first place.'

'Oh, love.' I looked into her concerned face. 'Don't worry

about that. It's not your job to worry about adults. Anyway, Daddy won't be there today,' I said. Elle had confirmed Robin wouldn't be around this afternoon. I hadn't seen him since he came to my house directly after the fire, but we'd spoken on the phone. I couldn't help but feel sorry for him, he was in bits. But then I wasn't living my best life, either. And that was down to him. The complexity of my feelings exhausted me.

I held Cora's hand when we stepped into the lift. 'Press number four,' I said. She still got great pleasure from pressing the buttons at road crossings and in lifts. When do we stop getting small joys from everyday things, I wondered, smiling at my lovely girl as the lift doors closed and it gave a jolt and set off.

A nurse pointed us to a bed surrounded by a blue curtain at the end of the children's ward. I wished I'd reminded Cora not to stare before we passed beds with sick children in. I kept my eyes on the curtain at the end but could sense Cora's head twisting from side to side and braced myself for the barrage of questions which she'd inevitably shoot at me in the car on the way home.

'Knock, knock.' I tapped my hand nervously on the curtain, not wanting to stick my head in, but feeling foolish about pretending to knock.

Elle pushed the curtain aside. Her face was clean of make-up, her hair greasy and lank. I'd never seen her without a sheen before and it made her look vulnerable. She wore a floral dress that didn't look like her style. She stood still for a moment, eyes wide. 'Hi . . .' I started but couldn't finish the sentence because she fell on me, hugging the breath from my lungs.

When she released me, we were both crying. I hoped Cora could tell that my tears, at least, were of relief. I took

Elle's hands in mine. 'Are you alright? How's Harry? I've been so worried about you.'

'Thank you for coming,' she said. 'I'm so sorry about what . . .'

'Let's not think about that now,' I said, letting her go and wafting my hand dismissively. 'There're more important things to worry about. Cora and I . . .' I looked down to where Cora had been standing but she wasn't there. Elle moved the curtain aside to reveal Cora sitting on the bed at Harry's feet. 'Make yourself at home, why don't you?' I said.

'I asked Harry if I could sit here and he nodded, didn't you Harry?'

I looked at the small, blonde boy in the bed and had to stop myself from gathering him into my arms. He looked even tinier than before. There were sore-looking red patches around his nose and mouth, but he was nodding in agreement with Cora.

'I've told him he doesn't have to talk because I'll do all the talking for us. Won't I, Harry?'

Harry nodded again.

'And I told him I've brought him some dinosaurs and, he can tell me about them if he wants because he's all experty about dinosaurs, but if he doesn't want to, he can just play with them with me.'

I dropped the bag on the floor and rolled my shoulder. 'Yep, we've brought in some things to play with and some things you might find useful.'

'You didn't have to,' said Elle, peering into the bag.

I pulled out a red hoodie and a pair of black joggers. 'Thought you'd want something comfortable to wear. I've got a couple of warm tops and comfy bottoms for you and some for Harry.'

Elle pressed her hand to her mouth. 'Thank you,' she said through her fingers. 'Thank you so much.' She pointed down at the floral dress. 'I asked Rob to get me some clothes because all mine are smoke damaged, and he brought this in three colours.'

'You're joking?'

Her lips twitched, then grinned, then a laugh burst out of her mouth. 'He saw this as an opportunity to put me in what he thought suited me,' she guffawed. There was something hysterical in the way she laughed, as though sobs were waiting in her throat, bringing up the rear. 'Of course he doesn't see it like that.'

'Of course not. He was doing you a favour,' I said, laughing as hard as Elle. 'Doing his best.'

She nodded. 'Doing his best.' She was crying now. She turned and thrashed at the liquid spilling from her eyes. I wondered whether I should put my arm around her, but the way she breathed deep into her ribs suggested she wanted to move on.

I dug further into the bag. 'Here's some toiletries, a hairbrush, phone charger and . . .' I delved deep for the bars of chocolate at the bottom of the hold all, then held them aloft. 'Sustenance!'

'You are amazing,' said Elle, giving her wet eyes a rub. 'Thank you.'

When our eyes met, we smiled at each other and I imagined she was thinking the same as me – that for a few moments, we'd almost forgotten we'd been married to the same man.

We turned to the children. Cora was bouncing a plastic dinosaur across Harry's knees. We watched them for a moment. When I looked at Elle, I saw more tears welling. 'Can I drag you away for a coffee in the canteen?'

She bit the inside of her cheek, walked to the head of the bed and stroked Harry's hair. 'If I tell the nurse to call me straight away if you need me, do you think you'll be okay staying here with Cora if I go for a coffee with Jen?'

He didn't look up from where the dinosaur was leaping from one of his knees to the other, but he nodded.

'You sure?' She searched his impassive face with her eyes.

I could tell she was reluctant to go. 'It's okay, I can go and get us one from the machine.'

'Me and Harry will be alright, won't we Harry?' said Cora. She clambered down and lifted a dinosaur jigsaw from the bag. 'Want to do this with me?'

Harry nodded.

'Move your legs then,' she said. 'We need it to be flat.'

Harry did as he was told, sitting up cross-legged, watching as Cora picked away the sellotape from the box's lid.

Elle took a breath. 'They'll be fine, won't they?' she said.

'I think so.'

On the way out of the ward, Elle made sure the nurse knew where we'd be and had her number. She promised to call straight away if Harry was upset.

In the cafe, she sat with her hands around the mug, lips screwed to the side, biting the inside of her cheek. 'This is the first hot drink I've had that's not in a cardboard cup,' she said. 'Tastes good.'

We both sipped our drinks. Now we were here, I had no idea what to say.

'Harry hasn't said a word since he woke up,' she said, eventually. 'Not even to me. Rob told him about Michael. It was awful. Even when he was sobbing, he didn't make a sound.' She looked at me through watery eyes. 'He must be so scared to completely clam up. What's going on in his head?'

I lay my hand over hers and gave it a squeeze.

'Did you tell Cora about Michael?' she asked.

I shrugged. 'I did, but she didn't know him, did she? It's different for her. Of course, she cried because someone had died, but she was more bothered about how her dad and Harry felt.'

'She's a sweetheart.' Elle's bottom lip trembled. 'You know Harry was passed out on the stairs when they broke down the door?' She put a shaking hand over her mouth. 'What kind of mother sleeps through when . . .?'

'It's not your fault. None of this is your fault.'

She sat back. 'That's not what Rob thinks.'

'What?'

'He thinks I should have stopped Michael from drinking. If he wasn't so pissed, none of this would've happened.'

'That's bollocks,' I said. 'Absolute bollocks. You could no more stop an alcoholic from drinking than you could make Harry give a speech in assembly. We all have bits of ourselves we wish were different, but if we can't control them, how can anybody else? I'd be surprised if Robin's dad wanted to destroy himself with booze, I bet he wanted to stop. I bet Harry wants to talk. They just can't. Not without a lot of understanding and support, anyway. It's the way they're wired.'

I took a breath. 'Cora wants to be able to stop her thoughts at bedtime. She wants to be able to remember the right books for the right lessons and stop herself from crying at the slightest thing. She just can't. Claire's taught me that, and it's a relief not to feel like Cora's being obtuse or stupid or weak. It's a lack of dopamine, apparently, not a lack of will. Willpower isn't really a thing. It's just a stick for judgy, self-righteous twats to beat people with. You have to get a squirt of dopamine to motivate you or give you a feeling of accomplishment. Science, brain chemistry and biology innit?' I shrugged. 'Lecture over . . . well, almost.'

I looked deep into Elle's eyes to make her understand what I was saying. 'It's not down to you to fix everyone, Elle. It's not even possible. It's so unfair he's put that on you.'

'But I still feel like such a failure. I can't help my own son, my father-in-law died under my roof and now I don't have a home. God. It's all so, so awful.' Elle rubbed at her temples. 'I don't know what I'm going to do.'

I wished I had a solution for her, but everything was as messy as she said.

She picked up her coffee and took a gulp. 'I'd better get back,' she sniffled.

I swigged mine and nodded. I could see she was starting to panic. 'Come on then. Let's see what trouble Cora's got him into.'

* * *

Back on the ward, the children had put all of the edges of the jigsaw together and were trying to find the next layer in. As we approached Cora picked up a piece and tried to slot it into a space it didn't fit. She pulled a ridiculous face. 'Come on you naughty brontosaurus, I need to stick you in right here. Stick in, you dippy dinosaur.' She danced the piece across the sheet. Backwards and forwards, laughing as she tapped it up and down.

Elle smiled at her silliness. Then Harry's laughter joined Cora's and Elle gripped my arm and froze. His tinkling giggle mingled with Cora's and it was the sweetest sound I had ever heard.

We didn't announce our presence, just sat a little way away, letting the children carry on playing, one ear cocked in the hope Harry might make more sound. He didn't speak, but he nodded when Cora spoke to him, and I could tell from Elle's face that the sound of his laughter was enough for now.

'When are they letting him out?' I said, quietly.

Elle's face dropped. 'They plan to discharge him this afternoon. He's done well, physically, at least. And Claire's getting together a plan to work on . . . if there's any trauma from . . . you know. The trouble is, we can't go back to the house. It's been gutted. The upstairs is alright apart from smoke damage and, apparently, structurally, it's sound, thank god, but it will be months until we can live in it again. To be honest, I don't know if I want to.'

I nodded, trying to imagine how I would feel if I couldn't go back to my little house. It was my sanctuary. I'd be devastated to lose it. 'Will you go to where Robin's staying?' It was still strange we were both talking about the same person when we mentioned the man in our lives. I let the thought go. That wasn't what was important now.

'The Premier Inn off the ring road? It's not tempting.' Elle glanced down. 'I had thought he might be living with you.'

I raised an eyebrow. 'I'd rather live with you than him, quite frankly.' An idea came to me. 'In fact, why don't you and Harry come and stay with us while your house is renovated?' Even as I said it, I knew it was a peculiar thing to suggest, but the more the idea settled, the more right it seemed.

Elle shook her head, 'You don't want—'

'I do,' I interrupted. 'Think about it, the kids could share Cora's room, I could clear out the box room at the back for you. It could be the perfect solution. Admit it, you're dying to spend New Year's Eve with me.' I opened my arms wide as if what I said was obvious.

We both looked over at the children. Their heads were bowed close together over the jigsaw. Cora was giving a quiet commentary and Harry looked completely at peace.

Elle glanced back at me, her face serious. 'Do you mean it?'

'One hundred percent.' And I did.

Elle stood and went to the head of the bed. 'Harry,' she said. 'Would you like to have a sleepover at Cora's house for a bit, while our house is mended?'

Cora's head shot up, her face a light bulb of excited anticipation, her little fists bunched.

Harry tugged at Elle's arm, and she lowered her ear towards his mouth. She listened for a second, then said, 'Harry says yes please.' And I'd never seen anyone smile wider.

Chapter Forty-Eight

Elle

Smoke and lack of use made Harry's voice gruff. I had a brief vision of the teenager he would become, his voice breaking and him growing incrementally further away from me. I pushed the thought away because now, sitting on his hospital bed with my arms around him, I couldn't imagine ever letting him go.

I kissed the top of his head, trying not to concentrate on the intermittent crackle in his throat as he breathed. 'We'd better get you dressed. Can't turn up to Cora's in your pyjamas,' I said. But I didn't move. I watched a nurse take the blood pressure of a wan child in the bed opposite, my breathing keeping time with my boy's.

I closed my eyes. I was so tired. I couldn't sleep for hideous images of what Harry might have seen erupting behind my eyelids. I needed the full picture, not just to stop my nightmares, but so Claire knew what level of trauma Harry had experienced when she planned his therapy.

'Harry,' I said, trying to steady my shaking voice. 'The night of the fire . . .'

His body seemed to shrink away from me. I stroked his hair, keeping my eyes on the nurse who was chatting to the pale-faced girl. 'When you were on the stairs . . .'

Harry turned so his face was buried in my neck. 'It's alright, lovely.' I rubbed his back, berating myself for quizzing him too soon. 'It's okay, Harry. It's alright.'

His small body shuddered under my hand. 'It's not alright,' he whispered into my neck. 'I didn't help Grandad. I should have helped Grandad.'

'No, darling.' I held him closer. 'You couldn't have helped him, sweetheart. None of this is your fault.'

'I think I fell asleep,' he said. 'I don't remember because I went out of my room and it was all dark and it smelled bad. I went to the stairs and I heard Grandad coughing but I couldn't see anything because it was too dark.' I felt wet tears on my neck. 'And then I must have fallen asleep. If I hadn't gone to sleep he might . . .'

'No, Harry, no.' I gently pulled him up until I we were face to face. 'You didn't fall asleep. The smoke got into your lungs and made you pass out. It made you fall unconscious. There was nothing you could have done to stop any of it.' I stared into his wet eyes. 'There was absolutely nothing you could have done.'

'I didn't fall asleep?' His quiet voice fought its way past his sobs.

'No, Harry. You were very brave to try to help, but the nasty smoke stopped you.' *Thank god,* I said to myself, silently rocking my crying child, *thank god, thank god, thank god.*

* * *

Jen's house was smaller than I'd imagined. Inside, it was so distinctively her, it couldn't belong to anybody else. Standing in the hall, I looked around. The wall below the dado rail was painted in terracotta and mustard yellow stripes and above it, the mustard colour was rag-rolled so it looked antiqued.

'I like this,' I said, running my hand over the wall.

'Thanks. Bit hectic, but you get used to it,' said Jen.

Cora had led Harry off to a room on the left that was painted in a deep green. He hadn't spoken since we arrived, but he had smiled, and I felt a new lightness in both of us since our conversation at the hospital. I'd made quick calls to Rob, Jen and Claire while the nurses said goodbye to Harry, to let them know about Harry falling unconscious, and a weight dropped from me with each of their relieved sighs.

I followed the children into the sitting room, noting that Jen's Christmas tree was exactly as I'd predicted: a real fir, dressed in lustrous reds and golds. Turning my head, I looked at the framed theatre posters one by one. I saw her name on the bottom of a couple. 'Did you direct all these?' I thought about my front room at home painted cream with prints I'd bought in Ikea. It couldn't be more different to this. I could see why Jen was always so confident. She was surrounded by beautiful images of what she'd achieved.

'Most of them,' she said. 'There's a couple of plays I saw that inspired me to become a director when I was a kid, like this one.' She pointed at a poster for *Antony and Cleopatra* directed by Peter Hall. 'I saw that production with Dench and Hopkins on a school trip to the National, and that was it; I was hooked.'

I felt suddenly small. This was a room filled with inspiration and achievement. Of course Rob preferred to be here in this bohemian terrace than in our beige new-build. Of course he preferred Jen; she was a woman who was inspired and she'd achieved things in her life. What had I achieved? 'I bet Rob loves it here.'

'Ha,' Jen coughed, leaving the room and heading upstairs. She chatted as I followed. 'He suggested a few changes. Wanted things a bit more matchy, matchy. You know what he's like, all arty-farty. We'd see something in a gallery, and he'd suggest painting something similar for in here.'

I was glad I was behind her. I'm sure the look on my face would tell her I had no idea what she was talking about. Other than the drawings he did for Harry, Rob showed no signs of being arty-farty when he was with me. We hadn't been to an art gallery in the ten years we'd been together.

She pushed open the door to a box room with a small teal-coloured sofa under the window and a glass desk and chair against the wall. 'It's a sofa bed. I hope that's okay. It's quite comfy and I'll stick a topper on the mattress to pad it out a bit.'

I burst into tears.

Jen looked panicked. 'If you'd prefer to stay in a hotel, I expect your insurance would cover it . . .'

'It's not that,' I said. 'The room is lovely. The whole house is lovely. That's the problem.'

'You've lost me.' Jen sat on the office chair and pointed me to the sofa.

I flung my arms wide. 'All this. All this . . . I don't know . . . life.' I sniffed, noticing a framed pencil drawing on the wall above the desk. It was of the three of them, Rob, Jen and Cora, and it was so obviously Rob's style it couldn't have been drawn by anyone else.

Jen followed my eyes and jumped up. She unhooked the picture and put it face down on the desk. 'Is this a bad idea? Is it too much?'

I shook my head. 'It's just that I've realised he lived here. You know, actually lived. With me, he existed. We didn't go to galleries. We watched TV. The only time he drew a picture was with Harry. I didn't inspire him, and he didn't inspire me.' My voice cracked. 'It's all been such a waste.'

Jen came to sit beside me. 'What's been a waste?'

'Me and Rob, the last ten years. I suppose I knew we'd been in a holding pattern; I didn't realise how little we had keeping us together. It was all so functional. When I look at this, you and your home, I see a life. You know? You're really living. You're a director, you do stuff.'

Her gaze dropped to her hands. 'I'm sure you do stuff.'

I laughed. 'I go to the gym. I have coffee with people I want to fit in with, but I don't really like.'

'You're bringing up a child. Don't underestimate that.'

'You're bringing up a child too.'

Jen smiled sadly, 'Honestly? I think I'm making a pretty poor job of it. Robin's always been a far better parent than I have. He's patient, he listens, he's always got time for her. I get irritated with the endless chattering. I get annoyed because I have to leave rehearsals to pick her up. I'm an awful mother.'

'Where are you now?' I said.

She looked confused. 'What do you mean?'

'I mean, who's here with Cora now?'

'Well, yeah, but I chucked Robin out, so—'

'Which of you went to the support group? Who was it that arranged the appointments with Claire, and the ADHD screening? Who is here every single night, night after night after night?'

'Me,' she said. 'I'm here for Cora.'

'All the time,' I said. 'Not just for the fun bits, the drawing and playing. You're making sure she gets the help she needs.

I've seen the adoring way she looks at you. And you're a brilliant role model. You're a strong and capable woman and you're showing her how to live a full life. You're her one constant and, most importantly, you're the one who puts her first.'

The smile which had been building on her face dropped. 'I'm not a strong and capable woman. I just pretend to be.'

'Rubbish—'

'Seriously,' she said. 'I've been off work.' She looked at me sheepishly. 'I was asked to take some time off to sort out my personal life. Apparently, what I thought was my professional persona was actually a bit of an aloof and uncaring knob.'

I was momentarily lost for words. I'd built Jen up in my head to be a giant of a woman, someone who had everything sorted out, but looking at her now, arms wrapped around her body, hugging herself, she was as mortal as I was. 'Would Harry and I be here if you were aloof and uncaring?'

She shrugged. 'That's kind, but I can see where they were coming from. I've been standoffish when I should have been approachable.'

'Well, if you recognise that, it's the first step to changing, right? And you've had a lot to deal with.'

'You and me both, sister.'

'And have you? Dealt with it, I mean, as far as you can, at least?'

She let her arms drop to her sides. 'I don't know, to be honest. Cora's got her diagnosis, so that's one thing off the list.' She grinned at me. 'And I'm not having to cope on my own anymore because I've got a couple of new roomies.' Her voice became quiet. 'I don't want to be a lone wolf anymore. I thought it was how I was, naturally, but I think it was just a mask, to stop myself from being vulnerable.

I've realised I need people around me. I need friends.' She kept her eyes on mine and I hoped she knew that I was wholeheartedly up for the role.

After a moment I said, 'Do you want to go back to work?'

'Hell, yeah!' She didn't hesitate. There was a new energy in her voice when she said, 'In fact, I think I'll pop in straight after the break and show them that I'm ready to come back.' Her face turned serious. 'And what about you?'

'What about me?'

'It's obvious you're a good mum to Harry, but what about you, what do you want?'

I closed my eyes against the shame of what I was about to say. 'I've never given much thought to what I want.'

Jen gasped. 'Elle!'

'I know, I know. It's just that, well . . . I was brought up to put men on pedestals. When I met Rob my mum insisted I'd won the golden ticket. She told me I had to do everything I could to make him happy. So I did.' I laughed through my tears. 'And look how that's worked out. I'm even shit at that.'

'You're not alone there.' Jen rubbed my back.

'Oh, I don't know. I think if I hadn't got pregnant with Harry, Rob would have left me and you two would have had a chance.'

'If a frog had wings it wouldn't bump its ass a-hopping,' said Jen in a Texan drawl, shaking her head when I looked at her quizzically. 'Seriously, though, Robin and Harry aside, what is it that you want? What makes you happy?'

I looked into her eyes and scrambled through my thoughts to find an answer. 'I genuinely don't know. All I can think of at the moment is making sure Harry is okay.'

'Right,' said Jen. 'That's at the top of the list. Let's get

Harry the help he needs, get your house sorted out. But after that . . .' She pointed a finger at me and narrowed her eyes. 'We are going to work out what it is that makes you zing.'

'Not tick?' I asked.

'No,' she said firmly. 'Why tick when you can zing?'

'I think I'd like to zing,' I said, and for the first time since Rob left, I felt the fluttering wings of hope.

Chapter Forty-Nine

Elle

We left Cora reading with Harry in the bedroom. I'd given him the option of sleeping on the sofa bed with me, but he wanted to sleep on the blow-up mattress on Cora's floor. He knew he could come in with me at any point in the night, but looking at him now, following Cora's finger across the page of *On a Tall, Tall Cliff* with his eyes, I saw he was the most relaxed he'd been in weeks.

'I like you being here,' Jen said to Harry. 'And not just because it means Cora has to tidy up her floordrobe.'

'That's what Mummy calls my carpet,' Cora said to Harry, shaking her head. 'She thinks she's funny.'

Harry giggled and my shoulders loosened another notch. I hesitated on the landing after Jen went downstairs, listening to see if Harry spoke. I heard Cora say, 'Do you want a turn at reading?'

I held my breath, then let it out slowly as I heard Harry's quiet voice carry on where Cora had left off. That girl was a miracle worker.

Lamps were on downstairs, making the sitting room look like something from a film. One arm of the sofa was bathed in orange light. Jen sat in shadow at the other side. She leaned forwards and picked up a bottle of wine from the colourful mosaic table by her side. 'Malbec?'

'Please.'

She poured two glasses and held one out for me. I took it and sat in a deep armchair upholstered in different coloured velvet squares. 'Thanks.' I tasted the wine. 'That's nice.'

'We first had it in Venice,' she said, then stopped. 'How do we play this? Do we talk about the Robin-shaped elephant in the room, or do we pretend we met some other way?'

I sipped the wine again and contemplated. 'I think we should talk. I don't know about you, but I want to know how the bastard pulled it off for almost eight years.'

Jen sat up. 'I know, right? I mean, we're intelligent women. How the fuck did he manage to keep it all spinning and not mess up?'

'I've been thinking about that,' I said. 'I think it's part of his superpower.'

'Superpower?' said Jen. 'Are we talking about the same man?'

'You know, when he gets like Harry. Not the silence, but the focus? I've never known anyone be as focused or be able to learn such enormous amounts of information. Much as I hate to say it, he is a bit of a genius, isn't he?'

'Huh,' Jen settled back in the chair. 'That might be a bit rich, but he definitely can compartmentalise things. He's a systematic problem-solver, I'll give him that. I suppose that's how he did it, keeping us in separate boxes in his head.' She sighed. 'He truly believes he did it for all of us.'

'You what?'

'Seriously. He insists it was his attempt to give us all the best chance of family life. He didn't want either of us to be single-parent families and he didn't want the kids growing up without a dad.'

'Like me,' I said, considering whether I believed him.

'And him, to a large degree. Right?'

'Doesn't make being lied to for the best part of a decade okay. Typical Rob, too,' I pulled a face and mimicked Rob's voice, 'Poor me, I was just doing my best. Nobody knows how hard I worked for everybody else.' I glanced across at Jen, expecting her to laugh, but she looked thoughtful. I remembered something I'd been wanting to ask since the first day we found out. 'Why did you always call him Bill?'

Jen laughed. 'Billious Fog. It was his nickname. He used to call me Frank Walters after a band we danced to once, and I called him Billious Fog because he was so farty. I shortened it to Bill, and it just stuck.'

'He never farted in front of me,' I said quietly. 'We were the kind of family who always locked the bathroom door.'

'Intestinal gas is overrated,' said Jen. 'You can have too much flatulence in a relationship.'

We sniggered and sipped our wine. I looked back over the waxwork life I'd led with a man who, when he was real, liked to go to art galleries and broke wind in front of his wife. 'Did you ever go to the London flat?'

Jen's wine glass stopped half-way to her mouth. 'Come on, Elle. There never was a London flat, was there? There isn't even a London office.'

I could feel my cheeks burning. Jen must think I was a complete idiot. 'I'm such a moron. Of course. He wasn't in London, he was here. Sorry.' I bit the inside of my cheek as his lies flooded back to me. 'God, I can't believe I actually just asked that.'

'Don't apologise. If you've been lied to as much as we

have, it's going to take a while to work out what the truth looks like.'

I glanced over at her. Shadows made her face more angular. Her eyes were bright and watchful. I could see why Rob was attracted to her; they were a good fit. 'Did he always get an alert on his phone to call you at seven? He told me it was a debrief with freelancers in London, but it was you, wasn't it?'

'Yep. And when he was here, an alarm used to go off on his phone at seven o'clock every night to remind him to call his pretend dad. Can you believe I thought it was sweet that he set an alarm to make sure he didn't forget? There was no way he'd have remembered on his own. Time doesn't exist for him, does it?'

'Nope.'

After a minute, Jen asked, 'What was his real dad like?'

'Michael?' A chill ran across my shoulders as I wrestled away the image of the figure lying still in front of my house. 'He was a character.' I smiled at Jen. 'A nightmare, most of the time, to be honest, but it was never dull. He had a drink problem when I met Rob. I was a bit scared of him at first. He was larger than life, you know?'

Jen nodded.

'He was always jumping from one business idea to another, sure this one was going to make him millions.'

'Why do you think he started drinking again?'

'I'm not sure. I suppose he got overwhelmed by life. Another business had gone pop, his girlfriend threw him out. He was sixty-two and had no money, no home, no partner. I suppose that's pretty scary.'

Jen nodded slowly. 'I wonder . . .'

'What?'

'Well, I've been doing a lot of reading about ADHD. I

mean, if I'd known how it really presents, I'd probably have been able to diagnose Cora when she was a toddler.' She sat forwards, resting her elbows on her knees. 'It's a gene mutation, not just a brain thing, so it affects the whole body.' She tipped her head to one side. 'Is Harry hyper-mobile?'

It seemed like a random question. 'Yeah, why?'

'So is Cora. Robin is, isn't he?'

'Yes. I think Michael was too. I remember him, Rob and Harry, all showing me how they could still bite their toenails once. Gross. But what's that got to do with ADHD?'

'Because there's a strong link between being hyper-mobile and ADHD. Then there's addiction.'

'Eh?'

'Yep, addiction as self-medication. Impulse control issues, executive function, so things like poor organisation, time blindness.'

'Ah, that's Harry and Rob, the time thing, I mean.'

Jen tapped her fingers on her chin. 'I think we need to get Rob tested.'

'What?'

'I think Rob's got ADHD. I think he's passed it down to our kids and I bet Michael passed it down to him.'

'But he's not hyperactive.'

Jen shook her head. 'Now, Elle.' She wagged a finger at me. 'You're falling into the trap of thinking that's all that ADHD is, and we both know better, now, don't we?'

'Shit, sorry. What would Claire say?' I thought about Claire with her kind eyes and professional, can do attitude.

'You know Claire has ADHD, don't you?' said Jen.

'No? Really?'

Jen nodded. 'Yeah, she has it and so do both her kids. She told me a while after Cora's diagnosis. That's partly why she's so invested in getting kids the help they need early on, that way they can make the most of the elements we might see as superpowers, like the hyper-focus and creative-thinking-outside-the-box stuff, and find strategies to help manage the tricky things like executive function.'

I sipped my wine. 'Wow.'

'Yep.'

'Claire has a private practice for adults in the evenings.' Jen picked up her phone from the arm of the sofa. 'I'm going to make an appointment to get Rob screened.'

I felt a rush of fear. 'You can't do it for him. He'll go mad.'

Jen glanced up from the phone. 'What's the worst he can do? Leave us?'

I thought of all the things I had or hadn't done over the years because Rob would sulk or leave early for the London office. Jen was right. The worst had already happened and the least worst part for me was losing Rob. Now it was time to do everything I could to help Harry regardless of what Rob thought. If Rob was diagnosed with ADHD, then it might be easier to get to the bottom of why Harry was so anxious he could barely speak.

'Will you ask him to go? It would come better from you,' I asked, embarrassed at my weakness.

'I'll tell him,' said Jen. 'And I won't be taking no for an answer. That man's been running this shit show for long enough.'

Chapter Fifty

Elle

At midday on New Year's Eve, I turned the key in the door and held my breath. From the outside the house didn't look too bad, just some bubbling of the paint on the door frame and black stains on the windows. The man from the fire investigation team had told me to expect worse inside.

He'd confirmed the fire began with a lit cigarette falling onto the carpet in the front room. I suspected Michael was asleep when the fire first smouldered and the smoke would have got to him before the flames. At least, that's what I told myself when the images of that night came back to me when I was trying to fall asleep.

The smell of smoke hit the back of my throat as soon as I opened the door. It took me straight back to being woken by those rough, gloved hands and the realisation my house was on fire with Harry inside.

I turned to Jen, who stood behind me on the doorstep, and she gave me an encouraging smile. She'd been doing that a lot since I moved in with her. I honestly didn't think

I could do this without her by my side. I stepped into the blackened hallway, pulling my coat in tight so it didn't touch the blackened sooty walls.

I knew the front room would be the worst. Thankfully, it was the only room which was completely gutted. If the people across the street hadn't stayed up late on Christmas night and seen the flames climbing the curtains, I didn't know what would have happened.

Well, I did. But I chose not to think about it.

The filthy sitting-room carpet squelched under our boots as we stood in the doorway and took in the full horror of it. The brickwork on the far wall was exposed where the lining paper had peeled away and burned. All that was left of the sofa and armchairs were dirty metal carcasses. There was a pathetic stem where the Christmas tree had been. My brain conjured a picture of Michael slouched on the sofa, half-smoked cigarette dropping from his fingers. I shook it away.

I'd expected to see charred photo frames on the mantelpiece, but the mantelpiece wasn't there. There was nothing recognisable at all, just a heap of soggy grey jumble covering the floor. Maybe that was for the best. I didn't want to come across framed photos of Harry where his face had half melted in the fire.

Jen rested a warm hand on my back. Only then did I notice how cold the house was. I shivered. 'It's freezing.'

'We don't have to do this now,' Jen said. 'You're shaking. Perhaps we should come back in a couple of weeks, when you've had chance to put a bit of distance—'

'No, I'm fine.' I walked towards the kitchen. The white units were filthy grey.

Jen wiped a finger across a high cupboard, leaving a white stripe. 'Might come clean?'

'Might have to. Rob says the insurers are trying to avoid paying out because Michael was staying here, and he was a smoker. Rob's told them he was just staying for Christmas, so that might be okay. I'm glad he's dealing with it, not me.'

Jen looked out of the patio doors to the garden. 'Robin will just have to stump up the cash otherwise. He can afford it.'

I laughed. It came out bitter. 'So I've discovered. Can you believe I actually agreed to divorce him to save this house?' I spun around, remembering the kitchen as it was before the fire. It didn't bring back many happy memories at all. 'I don't even like it.'

'What?' said Jen, turning from the window to look at me.

I walked towards her and opened the patio doors to try to smell something other than smoke. 'When we bought this place, I was full of hope. I'd married a handsome, successful man, we had a big house on a nice road. We were trying for a baby. It was everything I'd ever wanted.'

I stood on the grass and breathed in through my nose, but the smoke had lodged itself in my nostrils again. 'But it didn't turn out like that, did it? And now, I feel like what I thought I wanted, well, even when I had it, it wasn't the dream I imagined it would be.'

I turned to Jen, who was nodding thoughtfully. 'Honestly, from what I know of you, I think you're capable of more than just being a man's support system. It's not enough, is it?'

Jen thought I was capable. That made me smile. 'Never thought I'd say it, but perhaps it was a good thing we couldn't have another baby.'

'Well, that wasn't going to happen, was it? With Robin shooting blanks?'

I stopped, the smile falling from my face. 'What do you mean?'

Jen looked horrified. 'Shit. Sorry. God, I really shouldn't have said that.'

'What do you mean?'

'Forget I said anything.' She rubbed her hands together against the cold.

'Please, Jen. Don't do this. We both know what damage secrets can do.'

She closed her eyes. 'Okay. I take it he hasn't told you about the vasectomy yet?'

I blinked, aware of the icy air making clouds of our breath. I spoke slowly, 'What vasectomy?'

She put her flat palms towards me. 'Sorry, Elle. It's not—'

'What?'

'Let's go inside.' She marched back into the kitchen.

'Tell me,' I said, striding after her. 'When the fuck did he have a vasectomy?'

She turned, teeth gritted. 'It shouldn't be me telling you this. I'm sorry.'

'Please, just tell me.'

'Okay, but don't shoot the messenger. It was soon after Cora was born. I hadn't meant to get pregnant. We never planned to have children and I didn't want any more so . . .'

I closed my eyes. All that waiting. All that longing. All the sadness I felt every time I saw blood on the tissue when I wiped, turned to rage. 'The fucking bastard.'

'I'm so sorry. Elle.'

I gripped the back of a dining chair, lifted it and smashed it into a cupboard. The wood splintered. Jen jumped back, covering her mouth with her hand. I picked up another and slammed it down on the table where I'd served that prick his meals. I picked up a third chair and paused. I held it out to Jen. 'Want a go?'

She grabbed the chair and hoisted it over her head before slamming it into the units behind her.

When all the chairs were in splinters and the cupboards smashed to pieces, we laughed, bent double, breathing heavily with the exertion.

'I hope the insurance doesn't pay out and he's got to stump up the cash,' I said, when I could breathe without falling into hysterics again. I surveyed the broken scene in front of us, not really able to believe it was my doing.

'I'll help you design a new kitchen if you like,' said Jen, kicking at the broken cupboard door at her feet.

'No need,' I said. 'But you can help me choose a new house.'

She looked at me in surprise. 'You're going to sell this one?'

The idea had come to me with absolute clarity as I was bringing the chair down on the table. 'Yep. New Year, new everything. I'm going to sell this house and buy somewhere smaller. I'll make Rob give me a better settlement and I'm going to use the money to pay for a course.'

Sunlight appeared from behind the clouds and shone brightly through the patio doors. Jen's eyes glimmered. 'You're going to retrain?'

'Yep,' I said, 'I've been thinking about the question you asked me the other night and I've worked out what it is I want to do with my life.'

'You go, girl,' said Jen.

And in that moment, I felt stronger than I had in my entire life.

Chapter Fifty-One

Jen

The following week, I put my shoulders back before walking into the studio, then checked myself. I wasn't putting on an act anymore. I let my muscles relax and pushed open the door. Inside, Mel, Femi and Ed were standing in the centre of the performance area. Mel saw me first. She broke from the group and came over.

'Welcome back,' she said.

'Do you mean it?' I said, grimacing. 'Weren't you hoping I'd stay away?'

'Mate,' she said, 'No way. I've had to stop myself from ringing you every day to beg you to come in.' She glanced over her shoulder then lowered her voice, 'I've realised I'm happy being a producer, not a director. Give me rehearsals to schedule, props to source, licences to apply for, and I'm all over it. But actors? No thanks. They've had *ideas* since you've been away,' she said, her eyebrows raising comically high on her forehead. 'These people need managing.'

I looked past her at the other members of the cast sauntering into the room, then back at her, panic rising. 'But I need to be less aloof and uncaring. You said that yourself. Now you tell me they need managing?'

She laughed. 'If anyone can find a happy medium, it's you, my friend.' She clapped me on the back, turned and let out an ear-splitting whistle. 'Gather round, people. The boss is back.'

A minute later, the company were all in the studio. Some sat on chairs, the others stood or lounged on the sprung floor. I rolled my shoulders and took a breath deep into my lungs. 'Before we get back to rehearsals, I have something I want to say. I owe you all an apology,' I said. I let my eyes rest on one face at a time. 'It seems like I've been a bit of a tyrant, and for that, I'm truly sorry.' My eyes stayed on Femi's face. Her smile made my next words catch in my throat. 'In the spirit of the openness I want to encourage going forwards, I need to tell you that my personal life turned to shit before Christmas, and I found it hard to keep my emotions in check. My husband turned out to be a lying prick.' I gave a short laugh and looked at Ed. He wore a supportive half-smile. 'And my daughter, the lovely Cora, has needed more of my time and attention.

'So, things have been a bit up in the air with me, and I can't pretend anything has been completely resolved. But . . .' I held my finger in the air. 'This production is a constant and brilliant thing in my life. The way you're all bringing it together is nothing short of incredible.' They were all smiling back at me, and it felt like a wall of positivity and, god, how I needed that.

'Please, please feel like you can talk to me. I'm sorry I haven't been open to that before. I suspect that's impacted negatively on me as well as you, my gorgeous, talented friends. I'm going to change. From this moment on, I'm not an ice queen, I'm just a regular queen.' I dropped a low bow and stayed down for a second to compose myself as the cast whistled and clapped.

'Nice one,' whispered Mel as she passed me. 'Nice one.' She squeezed my shoulder then raised her voice, 'Right, you lot, that's today's love-in over. Let's get back to work.'

There was bustle, and chatter as they shifted around the studio. I stood in the middle of the room and watched the wonderful people I had kept at arm's length get into position for the start of Act Three, wondering, once again, how I'd got it all so wrong.

Chapter Fifty-Two

Jen

The next morning was my appointment and I felt sick with fear. Elle took both children to school. Harry's school had agreed to let his sister – I still wasn't used to that terminology – help with the sliding in programme. Apparently, it was going okay. Every day, Elle and Harry went to his classroom early and set up for the day, with her engaging him in as much conversation as she could. At first, when his teacher appeared at the classroom door, Harry would spot her through the window and clam up straight away.

Elle had been giddy when she got home yesterday because he'd carried on talking after the teacher came into the classroom. He still only spoke to Elle, not the teacher, but that was a step in the right direction. At home, I've been trying to get Cora to pause between sentences, in case Harry wanted to speak, but I probably needn't have worried, because Cora always asked questions as she went along, just to make sure people were paying attention to her. She was a girl who refused to be ignored and that made my heart sing.

I first heard Harry speaking about three days after he and Elle moved in. I was flattered beyond belief that he felt safe enough in my home.

I was checking my watch for the hundredth time when Elle burst in through the front door at 10am. 'I've said it before, and I'll say it again. Cora is a bloody miracle worker.'

'What's she done now?' I couldn't keep the smile from my face. Seeing Cora through Elle's eyes had given me a new appreciation of my little girl's strengths. I was ashamed I hadn't fully appreciated them before.

'She kept Harry chatting until the other children came in. It was amazing. Mrs Wheeler kept glancing up from her desk where she was marking books and smiling at me. Honestly, he only went quiet when the others came in and started asking who Cora was.'

'What did she say?'

Elle grinned. 'She said she was Harry's sister. There were some confused faces, but we didn't stick around because I didn't want Cora to be too late to school.'

'Don't worry about that. I don't think they're studying particle physics until Year Five. Mrs Daniels is happy for Cora to help Harry out. She gets it.'

Elle narrowed her eyes. 'How are you feeling today?'

'Bricking it.' It was strange how quickly Elle and I had fallen into being completely honest with each other. I think I'd told her more of what went on in my head than I'd told Robin in eight years. It wasn't that I hadn't been open with him, it's just that there was still a part of me I kept back, maybe I was scared he would find those elements unattractive. It had been liberating, having a friend. A real friend.

'Come on,' she said, 'Let's get this over with.'

* * *

At the hospital we sat in the waiting room scrolling through our phones, looking up every time a medic appeared from behind a door, then down again as someone else's name was called.

'Do you want me to come in with you?' asked Elle.

'God, no. Thanks but no. I'm not getting my tits out in front of you.'

'You're no fun.'

I knew it was stupid, but I couldn't help being aware of my middle-aged body around Elle. When she moved in I'd started to put my bra on under my pyjamas before I came downstairs. I never used to be body-conscious, but she was so young and so toned. And she'd had sex with my husband.

I hated him for that. Not just for having sex with another woman behind my back, but for choosing a woman who was naturally beautiful and who went to the gym out of choice rather than necessity. I hated him for making me look at my perfectly adequate body and comparing it to Elle's perfect one.

I'd told him this and he'd sworn mine was the body he wanted. I believed him, especially when Elle had told me about their perfunctory, unsatisfying sex life. I hadn't elaborated on the brilliant sex Robin and I had. It didn't seem fair, and I didn't want to dwell on what I'd lost. But I still felt less comfortable with myself than I was before. And I couldn't forgive him for that.

'Ms Glasson?'

Elle and I raised our heads. I said, 'Here.' and put my hand up like a schoolgirl answering the register. I shoved my phone in my bag and rushed to follow the woman in blue scrubs through a door on the right.

'Good luck,' Elle whispered, and I was so, so grateful she was there.

A woman with black hair lacquered in a rigid wave from her forehead looked up from behind a desk. The lines on her face suggested her hair was not its natural colour.

'Ms Glasson?' she asked in a cut-glass English accent. 'I'm Dr Hume. Thank you for coming in. Could you confirm your date of birth please?'

I did, and she scribbled on a note pad printed with boxes and words too small for me to read. I was aware of the woman in scrubs hovering near the door. Maybe they needed chaperones during this kind of investigation.

'You're nearly forty-eight? Any peri-menopausal symptoms?'

I answered all her questions, explaining why I'd started on HRT and how I thought it helped. I told her my symptoms, about the pain, the ridge I thought I could feel and the puckered skin. I poked at the soft flesh. 'Although it's not particularly sore today,' I said.

'Always the way when you eventually get to see a doctor,' she said kindly. 'Please go behind the curtain and take off the clothes on your top half,' she said, pointing to her right. 'Let's have a look at you and see if we can get to the bottom of all this.'

I folded my shirt neatly, tucked my bra underneath, and placed them on the chair beside the narrow bed covered in blue paper. It was chilly and when Dr Hume drew back the curtain, I had to resist the urge to wrap my arms across my chest. The woman in scrubs came in and stood near my head, smiling at me. I forced myself to smile back.

'Could you put your arms in the air for me?' Dr Hume said.

I did.

'Now out to the side.'

I held my arms out.

'Alright if I examine you?'

I nodded, raising my eyes to a point above her head.

She moved flat fingers over my breasts, firmly and carefully. 'Now if you could lie on your back.'

I lay down, still fixing my eyes on the strip-light on the ceiling. I counted the number of dead flies in the casing, too worried to look at Dr Hume's face in case I saw concern.

'Thank you. Please get dressed and come out when you're ready.'

She was writing on the pad again when I sat back down in front of her. I wondered if this was the moment my life would change forever.

Dr Hume looked up and smiled. 'We'll do an ultrasound and a mammogram to make certain, but I'm pretty sure this is hormonal breast tissue change.'

I kept my eyes on her still smiling face. 'So, it's not . . .?'

'Not cancer, no. Obviously we'll all be happier to have it confirmed by the scans, but I've been doing this job for over thirty years, and I'm fairly sure this is a normal change in breast tissue which can occur during menopause and with the HRT medication. Nothing to worry about.' She went back to writing in her pad while I absorbed the news.

Dr Hume ripped off the top sheet of her pad and offered it to the woman in scrubs. 'We're very lucky in this new breast screening unit,' she said to me. 'Amy here,' she pointed to the woman, 'will take you straight from here to the ultrasound suite, then on for your mammogram. After that we'll meet again and discuss how we can make your symptoms easier.'

* * *

'That's what she said,' I told Elle in the car on the way home. 'Take a shit ton of evening primrose oil and I'll be right as rain. No chemo, no radiation, no operations.'

'No cancer!' said Elle.

'No fucking cancer!'

I'd cried with relief when the ultrasound and the mammogram came back clear. Now, sitting next to Elle, heading home on the dual carriageway, I felt elated. The only thing clouding my good mood was the craving I had to share my good news with Robin. He'd been the one I saved snippets of my day up for so long it felt odd not to watch the joy grow on his face when he heard I was fit and well.

Not that I'd told him I was worried in the first place. God, why was it all so complicated?

'How do you feel about seeing Rob at the weekend?' I asked Elle. It was the opening night of *Antony and Cleopatra* and both Robin and Elle had insisted on coming to support me. They'd agreed to call a truce and sit together, but I was nervous about having to be backstage while they sat on the front row.

I tried to put my finger on what I was worried about. I knew it would kill me if they got back together, but that seemed about as likely as Johnny Depp and Amber Heard having make-up sex. I suspected my concerns were more about my feelings for Robin. Try as I might, I couldn't get him out of my head, even after all he'd put us through.

'I won't make a scene, if that's what you're worried about.'

'I wasn't, but I am now.'

Elle laughed. 'I want to support you and if he has to be there as well, then I'll do my best to be civil.' She wrinkled her nose. 'You know what, whenever he's picked the kids up, I haven't felt much at all. Obviously, I hated him when we first found out, but then I felt sorry for him when Michael died, then I wanted to kill him when I found out about the vasectomy, but now . . .'

'Now what?'

'Now, it's kind of like, I don't know . . . like he's lost his power over me and it's liberating. I feel free.'

I thought about what she was saying, and it made sense. But Robin had never had any power over me that I hadn't given him. I didn't feel a release. I was bereft.

'And now I have my future to think about and a new home to find and Harry's getting a little bit more confident every day.' She turned to look at me in the passenger seat. 'And I've got you.'

I grinned back at her. I would get over Robin, in time. I couldn't imagine ever getting to a place where I was relieved the life we had was over. But I had Elle, lovely Harry and my gorgeous Cora, and tonight was the opening night of what I was certain would be the best production I had ever brought to the stage.

Chapter Fifty-Three

Elle

Jen had arranged for the three of us to meet early in a bar close to the theatre. She could only spare half an hour and I was nervous about being with Rob on my own after she'd gone back to do whatever directors did on opening night.

Thankfully, she arrived before Rob. I gripped her hand. 'Why did I agree to this?' I said as she plonked herself down on the banquette beside me.

'Because you are a wonderful friend.'

'I don't mean coming to the play, I mean meeting Rob.'

Jen grinned. 'I know what you meant and the answer's the same. I need you here and Robin wants to see the play. If I'm honest with myself, I want Robin to see the play.'

I huffed. 'It's weird, you still being able to tolerate him.'

She shrugged. 'The heart wants what the heart wants.'

I opened my mouth wide. 'Heart? Are you trying to tell me you still have feelings for him, like positive feelings, not the *die slowly but still pay the maintenance* ones?'

She closed her eyes and shook her head. 'I've told you,

it's complicated. I had a different relationship with him to you, which, obviously, doesn't excuse the lying or the way he treated you and all the shit stuff he did, but . . . we've seen each other a lot since it all kicked off. We've talked. I'm not saying I've forgiven him, but . . . I don't know. I can't just switch off how I felt.'

'It sucks being the practice wife,' I said, and we both laughed. It's a phrase we'd used a lot when we talked about how different Jen's experience of being married to Rob had been to mine. I told her she was benefiting from all the things he'd learned from getting it wrong with me, and I was only half joking. Looking back, Rob and I should never have married. In Jen, he'd met his match. I got it. 'It's the sex, isn't it?' I pretended to shudder. 'You clearly have low expectations on that front.'

She punched me in the arm and laughed. 'I know you don't want to see him, but Harry does, so you haven't got much choice, have you? May as well make it as easy as possible.'

I had to admit, she had a point. 'I'm here, aren't I? I'm going to be civil and I won't pour my drink over his head. That's the most I can offer.'

'Yeah, don't waste the wine. He's not worth what it costs in here.'

We both looked around the trendy bar's shabby chic interior. The door opened and Rob stepped through wearing a black shirt and the battered brown leather jacket. My stomach flipped, but only in a nervous way. I realised I didn't fancy him anymore. Had I ever? It suddenly occurred to me I had taught myself to see he was traditionally handsome and so presumed I fancied him. I couldn't locate a memory where I ever lusted after him.

To the left of Rob, sitting on a bar stool, was a tall,

dark-haired man of about my age. He wore a biker jacket, and his hair reached his collar. He turned towards us and his bright blue eyes made my stomach flip quite differently. He smiled as our eyes met, making heat rise up my neck.

I forced my gaze back to Rob. When he reached the table, he kissed both of our cheeks. The smell of him did nothing for me. How had I ever shared a bed with this man?

'How are the kids?' he asked, as though it wasn't bizarre he could throw that question at two women at once.

'Harry's doing well, thanks.' I was proud of myself for answering maturely and not adding *no thanks to you.* It was Jen's big night, and I was determined not to spoil it for her.

I could see Rob was on his best behaviour too. He spoke to us both equally, eyes flitting nervously between us. I found that, with Jen there, my anxiety seeped away, and I could be polite and indifferent with the man I used to revere. Watching him now, I could see he was just an ordinary person. He wasn't a god, or a golden ticket. He was flesh and blood and he was deeply flawed. I made a vow to myself never to put another man on a pedestal for as long as I lived.

When he spoke to Jen, there was a lightness I hadn't seen in him before. His eyes brightened with admiration when he looked at her. I wondered if I would have been envious a few short months ago. I wasn't now. That was a huge relief.

Jen looked at her watch and started. 'Shit, I've got to go.' She stood, squinted and pointed at us. 'You two, behave yourselves. Play nicely, okay?'

'Okay,' we replied, in unison, both pretending to look sheepish. It was astonishing the three of us could share a joke already.

'See you in half an hour. Don't be late because you're in the front row.' She shimmied out of the banquette and rushed towards the door. I followed her with my eyes to see if the guy in the biker jacket was watching her. He glanced up, but his eyes didn't linger. I wasn't proud of myself for being glad. He looked over at me again and I smiled.

Rob saw us. A look of confusion passed over his face before he set it back to neutral. He nodded towards the man. 'Am I cramping your style?'

'Yes,' I said.

He paused, then shifted in his seat. 'I'm glad I've got chance to talk to you,' he said. 'There's a few things I need to say.'

I looked him directly in the eye. 'Do they start with an apology?' My voice was clipped.

He looked down at the table. 'How did you guess?'

I crossed my arms and waited.

'Firstly, I'm sorry about all the deception. It was cowardly and cruel. I thought—'

'Let's stop at cowardly and cruel. I don't need your justifications.'

He nodded. 'Right. Yes. Understandable.' He glanced into my eyes and quickly away. 'You know Jen made me an appointment to see that psychologist?'

'Claire. Yes.'

'Well, I'm going to go.'

I nodded, wondering whether he expected a round of applause. 'Good.'

'I need to work out . . .' He looked suddenly vulnerable. 'I don't want to end up messed up and alone, like Dad. I don't want to carry on hurting the people I care about. I thought we were so different, but maybe . . .' His voice cracked and he held his hands together in front of him tightly. I had the urge to comfort him, but didn't. I wasn't sure where our new boundaries were. 'And, more importantly, I want to be better for the kids.'

The *more importantly* felt significant. I wasn't convinced he was capable of putting anyone else before himself, but at least he acknowledged he should.

He carried on, 'I don't want my behaviour to impact them any more than it already has. I'm sorry for so many things,' he said, 'For the way I've treated you, for not supporting you with Harry. For not being a good dad when he needed me.'

I couldn't disagree with anything he said. I used to think he was a brilliant father, but he hadn't been there when Harry needed him. I had.

'And I should have been there for my dad, not left it all up to you.' He rubbed a hand over his anguished face.

'I've been thinking about your dad a lot,' I said.

He reached out and squeezed my hand. 'I've been reading up on addiction,' he said. 'I wish I'd done that before. If I'd understood . . .' Tears filled his eyes. 'If I'd known he couldn't help it, that it's likely his addiction was probably some form of self-medication, maybe I could have helped him. I could have helped him stop, or supported him, or at least sympathised instead of judging and condemning him.'

'You loved him, and he knew that.'

Rob nodded. 'I've fucked up in so many ways, but I'm going to try to do better, and seeing Claire is the start. I will be there for Harry. I'll support you and I'll do whatever it takes to help him . . . if you'll let me?'

'I've been thinking about that,' I said, 'I've got an idea about how I can help Harry and do something for myself at the same time.'

I told him my plans and I was delighted to see the enthusiasm on his face. We discussed how we could make it work, and he agreed to help with childcare. He even agreed to the new financial arrangement I suggested.

We shook on it, then his face turned serious. 'I've got something to ask you and I'm not sure how you're going to feel about it,' he said.

'What?'

'It's about Jen,' he said, suddenly looking nervous. 'I've got a plan.'

Chapter Fifty-Four

Jen

Femi, Ed and the whole cast richly deserved the standing ovation. As I stood in the wings, my hands stinging from clapping, pride almost lifted me off my feet. I felt like I could fly.

After the third set of bows, Mel yelled, 'Enough tits and teeth, leave them wanting more!' and let the main curtain fall. She gave me a high-five as she passed me in the flats. 'That rocked,' she said, which was high praise from Mel.

Femi rushed at me from the stage, flinging her arms around my neck and holding me tight. Adrenaline pulsed out of her. I breathed in her scent and her energy. It was my life blood and I adored it. I adored her.

'You were incredible out there,' I said.

She leaned back and looked into my face with glossy eyes. Her smile said it all. 'Thank you for taking a chance on me,' she said. 'I'd forgotten how it feels, looking out into the dark, knowing all those eyes are on you, then just losing yourself in the character.' She closed her eyes as if conjuring up the feeling and relishing it.

'Thank *you*,' I said. 'You *were* Cleopatra tonight. I can't imagine anyone else up there in that role. It was you from the minute you strode into the studio.'

'I did stride, didn't I?' she laughed. 'You have no idea how long I cowered outside trying to get up the courage to come in.'

My mouth dropped open. 'You're kidding?'

She shook her head. 'After such a long break, I didn't think I had a chance, but I thought, *fake it 'til you make it*.'

'Well, you've made it, my friend. I'm already planning the next play with you in mind.'

She covered her mouth with her hand, eyes wide. I put my arm around her shoulder and led her in the direction of the dressing room. When we went inside, a cheer went up and we were engulfed by the cast, hugging, and kissing us both.

'Get off,' I said, laughing and pulling myself clear. 'Save some energy for tomorrow. We've got ten more performances to get through, you know. Don't peak too early.'

A chorus of jovial, 'yes boss,' went up and the cast dispersed to jostle for space in front of mirrors to take off their make-up.

Robin's head appeared around the door. He gestured for me to follow him out of the dressing room. 'That was amazing,' he said, when the door was closed, and we were in the quiet corridor on our own. 'It's the best thing you've done yet.'

'Thanks,' I said. The space between us seemed to pulsate. I resisted the urge to step closer. 'Did Elle enjoy it? Where is she?'

He glanced behind him, as if he expected her to appear.

'Yeah, she loved it. She's waiting for us in the bar.' He looked at his feet, then up into my eyes and I wanted to kiss him. 'We had a good talk, actually.'

'Oh yeah?'

'About everything and . . . whether I should give you this.' He dipped his hand into his inside pocket and pulled out an envelope.

'What's that?' My heart beat faster.

'Tickets,' he said, 'to Venice. To stay at Ca Maria Adele.'

I swallowed. Where we got married. Where we made plans for our future. The future he had lied about. I told my heart to slow down.

'I asked Elle if she was okay with me giving them to you tonight.'

'What did she say?' Lovely, lovely Elle. I hoped she hadn't been hurt.

Robin laughed. 'She made me give some random bloke she fancied her number when we were leaving the bar because she was too squeamish, so I'm pretty sure she was being honest when she said she was alright with it.'

I smiled. 'Ca Maria Adele, eh?'

'Yeah.' He took a step towards me. 'The Oriental Suite, like last time.'

I put a hand on his chest to keep him back. I wanted to respond with my head, not my body. I looked past him at the door which led to the bar. To Elle. 'That's only got one bed,' I said. 'Where will Cora sleep?' I turned back to him and watched his face. His eyebrows knitted, his mouth made an O. That told me what I needed to know.

The dressing room door opened, and we stood back to let two actors pass. They pushed open the stage door onto the street and a gust of wind chilled my hot cheeks. The door banged shut behind them.

'I thought it could just be the two of us. Like before,' he said.

I looked down at my feet, trying to decipher the conflicting messages from my brain and my tingling skin. When I looked back up, I knew exactly what I wanted to say. 'Thanks, Robin, but that's not what I want.' He looked crestfallen. 'Hold on, let me finish. Before all this happened, I was convinced you were a brilliant dad and I was a rubbish mum. I thought I didn't need anyone but you and Cora in my life.' He opened his mouth to speak. I held up my hand to stop him. 'I know now, that, actually, I'm a fucking brilliant mother. I know that, because, even when my life exploded, I put Cora first.'

'I know. You did, I'm so sorry . . . That's why I'm trying to make up for it now.' He waved the envelope. 'Starting with this.'

'You're missing the point,' I said. 'I've had to rethink my entire life. Before, I always prioritised you, our relationship and our little family. I built a wall around us. I thought we were impenetrable. When you smashed that wall down, I discovered there were people on the other side. And I've grown to love those people. They were there for me when I needed them. Not just Elle and Harry, but Femi, Ed and even Mel.'

'That's good,' he said, 'I'm glad you've got supportive people in your life, but I can't take all of them on holiday, can I?' He smiled coquettishly, but it didn't have the effect on me either of us expected. I didn't melt.

'I'm not the only one you need to make it up to. Our daughter has been through a lot. She needs her dad.'

His mouth turned down. 'I suppose I could change the hotel?'

I had an idea. 'Don't do that.'

He lifted his hands. 'What then? Tell me what you want, and I'll do it.'

I put my hand on his arm and smiled. 'I need you to think about what you can do to make things better for Cora and Harry. It shouldn't be about me and you. Sorry, Robin, but I don't know if there will ever be a me and you again.'

He closed his eyes briefly then dipped his head to the side and looked up at me. 'But there is a chance . . .?'

I ignored his fluttering eyelashes. 'You agree you need to make it up to Cora and Harry?'

He nodded. 'I want to be a better dad.'

'Then, give me those tickets.' I plucked the envelope from his fingers. 'And I'll change the room to a twin.'

He nodded, 'Okay. I hear you. I don't want to rush you into—'

'And Elle and I can go to Venice, and you can stay at home with the kids and practise being a better dad.'

'What?' I saw the idea settle on his face and waited for his reaction. I willed him not to fuck it up. A smile lifted the corners of his mouth. He shook his head. 'You're good, Jen Glasson. You're good.'

'Do we have a deal?' I held out my hand and after a brief hesitation, he shook it.

'Deal.'

I hooked my arm through his. 'Excellent. Let's go and find Elle. We've got a holiday to plan.'

Epilogue

Elle

Two Years Later

I looked at the nervous faces, all staring at me, and tried hard to regulate my breathing. I was pleased to see a couple of men among the fifteen or so people sitting on the plastic chairs set out in a wide circle. I recognised the fear in all their eyes. I wondered if any felt like bolting, like I did at the first support group I went to.

I glanced at Jen on my left, then at Claire who was sitting to my right. I wove the fingers of my shaking hands together in my lap, took one more huge breath and stood. The room stilled.

'Hello everyone and thank you for coming.' I saw tentative smiles. That gave me the courage to go on. 'My name is Elle Clarke and I'm the group organiser. I'm studying a degree in counselling, but what really qualifies me to stand in front of you today, is that my son, Harry, has selective mutism. He was diagnosed two years ago by my brilliant mentor, Claire Dixon, who is here with us this evening.'

I gestured to Claire, who grinned and gave a brief wave. I turned back to the circle. 'Harry's been getting help since his diagnosis and he's coming on well, but it's a long process and it takes consistent work. I'm not going to lie to you and pretend the last two years have been easy, but what made them harder than, perhaps, they needed to be, was the fact that, at the start of this process, I'd never heard of selective mutism. And if you've never heard of a condition, how can you look out for the signs or know how to access help and support?

'Even when I realised Harry wasn't just shy, or rude, or defiant, it was difficult to discover what would help him to speak, because there is so little information out there. The reason I've started this support group is so more people are aware of how the condition manifests and more children get the right support for the anxiety disorder that is suppressing their voices.'

I took another breath. 'Because having a voice, and being able to use it, is everything, isn't it?' I caught the eye of one woman whose bottom lip was trembling. My voice cracked. 'I've never experienced selective mutism, but I do know what it feels like not to be heard. I know what it feels like to be ignored and overlooked. I know what it feels like to be scared.'

I sensed Jen leaning forwards in her chair and I imagined her hand gripping mine, giving me the strength to carry on. 'And it's not easy knowing my little boy feels all of those things acutely. Selective mutism is the way his body reacts to fear, and it doesn't matter whether we consider the perceived threat to be real or not. He does. At a primal level, he does.

And I've made it my mission, my purpose, if you like, to help him, and any other child who needs it. And I want to support you, because having a child who's suffering is hard. Really hard. In this group, my hope is that you'll find a tribe who understand you, who can sympathise and empathise and who truly have your best interest at heart.'

I smiled at Jen and laughed when I saw tears in her eyes. 'I met this woman at one of Claire's support groups.' I pointed at Jen. 'And, despite some of the things we've been through that should have divided us, she's had my back from day one.' Jen flapped her hand to move me on, but I had more to say.

'When I was at my very lowest, Jen asked me what it was I wanted to do with my life. It seems like the simplest question, doesn't it? But it's one I'd never asked myself. I'd never really been active in my own life, but realising Harry needed me to act for him, to be his advocate when he couldn't speak for himself, gave me a reason to take charge of my own life, and Jen helped me to see that. And here we are.' I spread my arms and smiled a wobbly smile.

'One of my aims in starting this group, is to stop the secretive way we all behave around mental health issues. We need to talk more about how things really are, instead of curating our lives to make everyone think life's perfect. I used to do that. All it did was put a barrier up between my real life and the one people thought I was living. It's time to break down the barriers.'

I saw heads nodding and paused before I said what I thought was the most important part of my introduction. I filled my lungs, then slowly and firmly said, 'There is no shame in being anxious. Our children are brilliant, unique and brave. They are braver than lots of other supposedly *normal* children, because they step out every day into a world that frightens them.'

I saw a man take his partner's hand and grip it in his own. 'I want the world to know how brave and brilliant these kids are. We know it, don't we? The first, crucial step we need to take is to make sure our children truly understand how courageous and special they are.'

I stopped because everyone in the room was clapping. I clutched my hands together, absorbing the hope on the faces of the people whose eyes were trained on me. They were clapping for me, for Harry, for Jen and Claire, and because, at last, they felt their silent children had a chance of being heard.

I joined in the clapping and turned my hands to Jen, who had, miraculously, always believed in me. She had done what only a true friend would do: she listened to me, and then she helped me find my voice.

Acknowledgements

Huge thanks to my editors, Thorne Ryan and Elisha Lundin, for the early discussions that woke this idea up, got it out of bed and set it on its feet. My additional gratitude to Elisha, whose insightful and sensitive edits improved the manuscript beyond measure. The whole Avon team are a joy to work with and I appreciate their efforts enormously.

Thanks to my agent, Laura Williams, for her enthusiasm for the tatty first draft, and every draft that followed. She also deserves a special mention for talking me down when I'm having a wobble. I am incredibly fortunate to have her.

My early readers, Alex King, Carol Debono and Alison James, have given their time, advice, and friendship throughout the writing of this book. I couldn't have done it without them.

My Writing Group, Suzy and Nichola, thank you for always being there. You are superstars. To my other writer friends, you know what you mean to me since I'm always banging on about it. I'm so very lucky to have you all in my life.

Jodi, Emma, Heather, Julie and Katherine, your unfailing love and support makes my heart swell.

If you want to learn more about ADHD, a condition which is generally misunderstood and often goes undiagnosed (especially in women), additudemag.com is a brilliant resource.

To learn more about Selective Mutism (another little-understood anxiety disorder), go to selectivemutism.org.uk (SMiRA).

I'm sure you'll understand, after reading this book, that I'm passionate about changing the way we view neurodiversity. Until more people understand neurodiverse conditions, society will continue to be misinformed and judgemental. If this book has taught you anything new about ADHD and associated conditions, or Selective Mutism, I would very much appreciate it if you could share that information with others.

Too many people are suffering in silence. Too many people live with shame for things that are entirely out of their control. Let's do what we can to help.

Thanks to my gorgeous family for cutting down the number of times they come into my writing cave when I'm mid-flow, to ask what there is to eat. They make me laugh every day and I am very lucky to share my life with them.

The writing community is bolstered by the invaluable work of book bloggers, online book clubs and reviewers. My gratitude goes to those who have shared reviews of my first two books. I read each and every one. I'm blown away that people are generous enough to take the time to share my books.

I truly love this job and it is readers like you who make it possible for me to write every day, so thank you from the bottom of my heart.

If you have enjoyed *His Secret Wife*, I'd be very grateful if you could write a brief review and spread the word.

If you enjoyed *His Secret Wife*, you'll love Lisa's other gripping and emotional family dramas!

Will her daughter's secret tear her family apart?

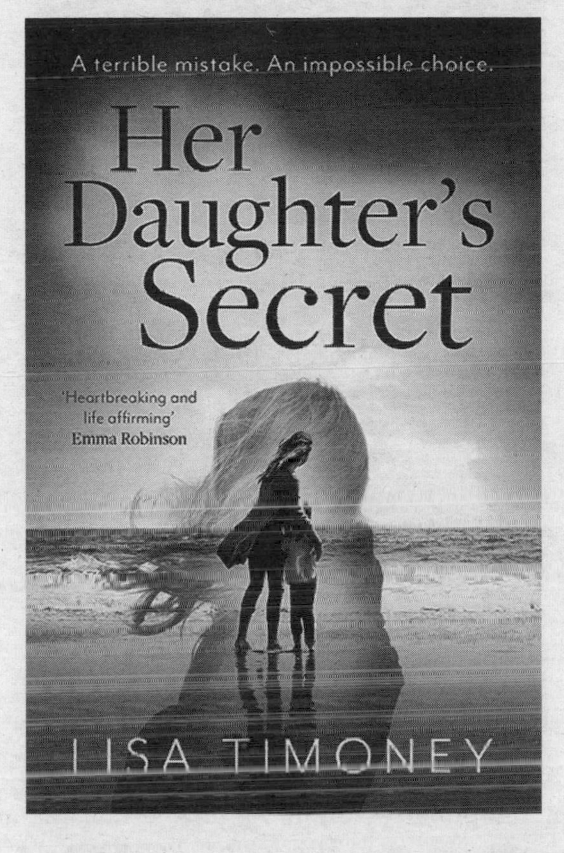

A gripping, heart-wrenching novel about family secrets and the price of love.

Out now!

You can run from a lie,
but you can't hide from the truth . . .

An emotional yet uplifting page-turner about
buried pasts and the price we pay for those we love.

Out now!